*D*everill halted barely a step from her, watching her with searing eyes. Tension throbbed in the air as he asked softly, "So, you don't think I could compare to your betrothed, hmm?"

Perhaps she should never have made that wild claim, Antonia belatedly realized. It was no doubt unwise to challenge a man's sexual prowess. "Well, perhaps I exaggerated a little. . . ."

"Perhaps the problem is that you don't know any better." Deverill stepped even closer, until their bodies almost touched. "I very much doubt that you know what true pleasure is."

He slowly ran the back of his hand down her throat to the square neckline of her gown. Antonia drew a sharp breath, wondering how his barest touch could make her burn like this, want like this. When he trailed his fingers deliberately over her breast in a caress that was calculatedly erotic, her senses skittered wildly.

Deverill smiled, satisfied.

By Nicole Jordan

Paradise Series:
MASTER OF TEMPTATION
LORD OF SEDUCTION
WICKED FANTASY

Notorious Series:
THE SEDUCTION
THE PASSION
DESIRE
ECSTACY
THE PRINCE OF PLEASURE

Other Novels:
THE LOVER
THE WARRIOR

WICKED
FANTASY

A Novel

NICOLE
JORDAN

BALLANTINE BOOKS • NEW YORK

Wicked Fantasy is a work of fiction. Names, characters, places, and incidents are the products of the author's imagination or are used fictitiously. Any resemblance to actual events, locales, or persons, living or dead, is entirely coincidental.

A Ballantine Books Mass Market Original

Copyright © 2005 by Anne Bushyhead
Excerpt from *Fever Dreams* by Nicole Jordan copyright © 2005 by Anne Bushyhead

Published in the United States by Ballantine Books, an imprint of The Random House Publishing Group, a division of Random House, Inc., New York.

Ballantine and colophon are registered trademarks of Random House, Inc.

ISBN 0-345-46786-8

This book contains an excerpt from the forthcoming paperback edition of *Fever Dreams* by Nicole Jordan. This excerpt has been set for this edition only and may not reflect the final content of the forthcoming edition.

Stepback illustration by Jon Paul Ferrara

Printed in the United States of America

www.ballantinebooks.com

OPM   9   8   7   6   5   4   3   2   1

To Linda Francis Lee, who understands.
With love and thanks.

Her first sight of the wicked, dashing adventurer Trey Deverill startled Antonia Maitland immensely, for he was unmistakably, breathtakingly nude.

Seeing his unclothed body was purely accidental, of course.

Glad to be home from her select boarding academy for a spring holiday, Antonia handed her bonnet and gloves over to the waiting butler and turned toward the Map Room, where her father oversaw his vast shipping empire. She was eager to see him for the first time in over a month.

"I believe you will find Mr. Maitland upstairs, Miss Maitland," the butler intoned. "Possibly in the gallery."

"Thank you," she replied with a brief smile, knowing her father must be communing with the portrait of his beloved late wife.

Antonia ran up the wide, sweeping staircase and hurried along the elegant east wing of the mansion. Eight years ago, shortly before her mother's unexpected death of a lung fever, Samuel Maitland had spared no expense to build the grand residence in a newly fashionable district of London just south of Mayfair. But his favorite room was the portrait gallery, where he kept his wife's memory alive.

Antonia's current favorite room was the luxurious, newfangled bathing chamber, located at the far end of the corridor.

When she saw a footman exit the chamber and disappear around the corner, Antonia almost sighed in anticipation. Ever interested in novel inventions, her father had added a boiler in the kitchens last year that carried heated water directly above to the large, uniquely designed copper tub. The thought of a hot bath pleased Antonia to no end, since the elite Baldwin Academy for Young Ladies offered superior education and instruction in genteel social skills, but never such delightful extravagances as hours spent soaking in a steaming hot bath.

Upon reaching the corridor's end, Antonia saw that the door had been left partway open. But when absently she glanced inside, she stopped short.

A man had just stepped from the oval tub.

A sleekly muscular, powerfully built man.

A shockingly nude man.

She could see the side of his tall form—his bronzed back and taut buttocks, his lean hips and long sinewed legs, all streaming with water. Suddenly breathless, she stood riveted at the sight of his body: hard-muscled, vital, beautiful, except for the disfiguring scars on his torso. . . .

As if sensing her presence, he lifted his head alertly and swung toward her, giving her a fuller view of his loins.

"Oh, my . . ." Antonia murmured, startled and fascinated at the same time.

Swiftly, she jerked her eyes away from that forbidden masculine territory, only to have her gaze roam helplessly back up his body. In all of her nearly seventeen years she had never seen anything so stunning as this man. Or magnificent. Nor had she experienced such a purely primal, feminine reaction.

Heat flooded over her skin, and she felt a sudden, shocking warmth between her thighs.

When she managed to drag her gaze higher, from his broad, hair-sprinkled chest and wide shoulders, up the strong column of his throat, she realized that his face was as sinfully handsome as the rest of him. Slicked back, his wet hair was a sun-streaked brown, while his strong features boasted a square jaw and slightly clefted chin, roughened now with a hint of stubble. But it was more his striking, sea green eyes beneath slashing brows that gave him such a bold and wicked appeal.

When those clear green eyes locked with hers, Antonia felt fresh heat sear along all her nerve-endings.

He reached for a towel to cover himself and draped the linen around his lean hips. "I beg your pardon." His voice was low and deep and unmistakably sensual, but fortunately, hearing it served to jolt Antonia from her captive state.

Realizing she had been staring witlessly, she blushed to the roots of her dark red hair and stammered a reply. "No—it was entirely my fault—I should not be here. . . ."

"Miss Maitland, I presume?"

"Yes . . . Who are you?"

At her bluntness, a crooked smile flashed across his mouth.

Appalled by her uncustomary lack of manners, Antonia raised her hands to her fiery red cheeks.

"Trey Deverill," he replied to her question, watching her expression for a reaction.

She gave him one; her eyebrows shot up as she recognized the name. *Of course,* Antonia thought distractedly, with the satisfaction of a puzzle piece fitting into place.

She'd heard tales of the notorious Trey Deverill over the years—from various shipping merchants and sea captains, and from her father as well, since they'd been partners in a minor shipping venture for some time now. Deverill was an adventurer and explorer, renowned in particular for battling pirates on the high seas.

She had often imagined what he was like, but given his celebrated reputation, he was younger than she'd expected, closer to twenty-five than thirty, she calculated. And in the flesh, he was far more . . . *vital* than her wildest fantasies.

Deploring the direction her mind was taking, Antonia cleared her throat to compose herself and spoke, hoping to sound more mature than the green schoolgirl she was. "Forgive me for barging in on you, Mr. Deverill. And for my rudeness. It was merely a shock to find you . . . like this. I am not normally so easily flustered."

"Understandable under the circumstances," he observed, amusement glinting in his remarkable eyes.

He, on the other hand, seemed not the least embarrassed, she noted. Or inhibited. No doubt he was fully aware of the effect he had on females. On *her*. He stood at his ease, his head cocked to one side, contemplating her.

Or perhaps he was merely waiting politely for her to cease gawking and leave.

"Would you oblige me by shutting the door?" he finally said.

"Yes . . . certainly." Coming to her senses at last, Antonia reached forward to grasp the door handle.

"Oh, and Miss Maitland?"

She tensed, wondering what he meant to say. "Yes?"

"I don't think we should mention this unfortunate encounter to your father. He would skin me alive for compromising you."

Her blush only heightened, if that was possible. "Believe me, sir, I have no intention of mentioning this to *anyone*, most especially my father."

Firmly shutting the door, Antonia hurried away to resume her interrupted search for her father, determined to forget her decidedly scandalous encounter with the exciting adventurer.

Yet as she fled, Antonia knew without a doubt that the wicked, breathtaking image of Trey Deverill's body would be indelibly etched in her memory forever.

Dinner that evening was a discomfiting affair for Antonia, since she could scarcely meet Deverill's eyes over the expanse of gleaming china and crystal.

Thankfully, at least, he acted the gentleman. Not by a flicker of his long, dark eyelashes did he let on that they had already met under highly inappropriate circumstances. Yet Antonia had never been so tonguetied in her life.

Her father regularly invited various sea captains and business partners to dine at Maitland House, and sometimes, as in Deverill's case, to stay the night.

Usually she peppered visitors with questions about their ships and their adventures at sea. But in this instance, Antonia remained so rarely quiet that even her father noticed and commented.

When she claimed fatigue after the long carriage ride from school, Samuel Maitland frowned skeptically at her absurd prevarication before resuming his conversation with Deverill.

During three more courses, Antonia determinedly kept her attention focused on her plate, although she couldn't stop herself from casting surreptitious glances at Deverill from time to time.

He looked the part of a gentleman now as well. His fashionably tailored coat of blue superfine molded his powerful shoulders, while the pristine white linen of his cravat enhanced his rugged, rakish good looks. His thick, wavy hair had dried to a lighter shade of brown that glinted with streaks of gold—likely from being bleached by the sun, she surmised. His bold, smooth-shaven features were also sun-bronzed, doubtless because he spent a great deal of time on the deck of a ship.

Then Antonia recalled that much of the rest of him was just as bronzed and caught herself blushing. She might never be able to look at him again without picturing his magnificent, virile body.

It was even more lowering to acknowledge that she was unlikely to have the same fascinating impact on him. An extraordinary man like Deverill would pay her little notice. She was still essentially a schoolgirl— tall and gangly, with unconventional red hair, although *that* fortunately showed promise of darkening into an attractive auburn someday. In truth, her biggest claim to appeal was that as her father's only child she would eventually inherit the vast Maitland wealth and shipping empire.

Samuel Maitland was a self-made magnate, whose firm built the swiftest ships in the world. Although a shrewd businessman with a hand in numerous enterprises, he had chiefly made his enormous fortune with his brilliant designs for sailing vessels.

His genius, however, was considered an anathema to respectable society. He was not only a mere commoner, but worse, he was *In Trade*. A Cit, looked down upon by the snobbish ton. And in truth, he had little polish or refinement—which was why, in an attempt to increase his daughter's respectability, he had sent Antonia to the most exclusive young ladies' academy in England.

Where you had exquisite manners drummed into your head, Antonia sternly reminded herself. So why was she sitting here as mute as the potted palm gracing the rear corner of the dining room?

In an effort to conquer her deplorable bashfulness, she forced herself to speak during a lull in the conversation. "I suppose you have had a good many adventures, Mr. Deverill?"

He turned those brilliant green eyes on her, and she thought she saw a gleam of amusement shimmering in the clear depths.

"A good many, yes."

"I should like to hear about some of them."

Giving a chuckle, her father shook his head. "Oh, no, my girl. Any of Deverill's tales would be unfit for a young lady's tender ears."

Feeling her face warming again, she gave her father an affectionate but exasperated glance as she replied to Deverill. "I love Papa dearly, but he tends to wrap me in cotton wool."

Deverill's sensual mouth curved with definite amusement this time. "But he is right to warn you away from me, Miss Maitland."

"Are you so wicked, then?"

"To you, I am. I'm the black sheep of my family, I fear."

"What did you do that was so shameful?"

Her father snorted in disgust and answered for him. "Deverill dared to join the merchant marine when he was a lad and then had the audacity to make money in the shipping trade."

It was an extreme sore point with her father, being condemned for daring to make his fortune through his own labors.

"I defied my father," Deverill agreed, "and ran off to sea. I and my American cousin set off together to see the world and make our marks on it."

Antonia eyed him with curiosity. "Your father is a knight, I believe."

"Yes, but as the youngest of three sons, I will never inherit the title."

Yet he still had a measure of blue blood running in his veins, Antonia reflected. His Christian name was aristocratic as well, since *Trey* was a shortened version of Treylayne, from his mother's side of the family.

He was also reportedly very wealthy. Deverill owned a small fleet of armed vessels that hired out to shipping companies and provided protection for the huge, lumbering merchantmen carrying valuable cargo, both from the French navy and from marauding corsairs. Rumor was, however, that he had grown rich from confiscating fabulous pirate treasure.

"I should have liked to run away to sea," she remarked lightly, "but it would have disappointed Papa terribly."

"Aye, daughter, you would have broken my heart. But you've made me proud. Antonia," he boasted to their guest, "will make a brilliant match one day."

When she felt Deverill regarding her, she returned her attention to her blancmange pudding, not wishing to discuss such personal matters as her father's dreams for her.

His fondest wish was that she marry a British nobleman to elevate her position in society and diminish the stigma of her breeding. Her mother had been of noble birth, and Samuel Maitland couldn't bear the thought of his daughter languishing on the fringes of society due to his lack of respectability.

Antonia adored her father and would do nearly anything to please him, even it if meant quelling her own secret yearnings for something more exciting and adventurous than the proper, stifling, grandiose life that most society ladies led.

She glanced at her tall, brawny father, noting that he seemed to have grown older in the month since she'd last seen him. His bright red hair was now speckled with gray and his face more lined, while his once jovial personality had dimmed, burdened by the sadness that had stricken him at his beloved wife's death many years ago. The fact that he now lived for Antonia—his only child—was not lost on her.

She didn't realize she had fallen silent again, however, until her father addressed her.

"It's time you leave the men to their port, my girl. Deverill and I have a great deal of business to discuss, and he will only be here this one night."

"Very well, Papa," she said, hiding her disappointment and forcing a smile as she rose and came around the table to kiss her father's ruddy cheek. "I will be in the drawing room if you need me."

Both men politely stood for her, and as she left, she heard her father say, "Let us retire to the Map Room, Deverill. I have an intriguing new design to show you."

The Map Room was what Samuel Maitland called the large study where he sketched out plans for his new ships. Lately, in a further effort to become more respectable, he had begun ruling his empire from home rather than traveling daily to his offices near the London docks.

He enjoyed having an appreciative audience, however, someone who recognized his brilliance as a designer, which only a fellow nautical man like Deverill could truly do. When Antonia heard their shared laughter, she winced at her own selfishness. She might be jealous of Deverill for claiming her father's attention away from her, but she was very glad to hear her father laugh.

She was still alone in the drawing room an hour later when the Maitland housekeeper, Mrs. Peeke, brought her tea.

Antonia would have liked for the kind, elderly woman to stay and keep her company, but Mrs. Peeke was a stickler about servants knowing their proper place. So they merely chatted a moment, with the housekeeper asking her about school before bustling away with a smile and a muttered comment about making certain the master received proper sustenance, since he became forgetful when he locked himself away in his Map Room.

Antonia tried to ignore her loneliness as she finished her tea. Then, feeling restless, she put down the book she was reading and went upstairs to change out of her fashionable white muslin dinner gown into the warmer, green velvet riding habit she usually wore for target practice.

The April night was cool and damp when she made her way out-of-doors. On the grounds at the far rear of the mansion, her father had built her an archery range that ran the entire width of the estate. The target distance was only sixty yards rather than the standard one hundred, which most archery societies used for competitions, but for training it served Antonia well. Archery was one of the few sports that permitted female participation, and she hoped one day to be granted membership to the Royal British Bowmen.

She was severely out of practice now, for the Baldwin Academy considered even that tame sport too indelicate for their young ladies to indulge in. But shooting tended to calm her restlessness, since it required skill and concentration.

There was enough moonlight to see by as Antonia descended the terrace steps and followed the path through the landscaped gardens. She passed a gazebo with its delicate lace woodwork and clinging rose vines, her late mother's favorite spot to enjoy a summer morning, and arrived at a small outbuilding where her equipment was stored. There, she lit two lanterns—one that she placed at the far end of the range to illuminate the circular straw boss, the other on the marble table beside the shooter's line.

Then she retrieved her bow and a quiver of arrows and took up the archer's stance. She was glad to feel the smooth, polished yew of the bow in her hands. And from the moment she nocked a wooden arrow and drew back the bowstring, a sense of pleasurable calm descended over her.

Her skills were indeed rusty. In the first two rounds of twelve arrows each, a majority struck the target but only three hit the golden bull's-eye in the center.

Antonia was in the middle of her third round when she suddenly sensed she wasn't alone. Whirling with a start, she spied Trey Deverill standing in the shadows a short distance away.

She brought her hand to her throat, where her heart had lodged, and let out a breath of relief.

"Forgive me for startling you," he said in his deep, velvety voice as he moved toward her. "From my rooms I heard curious sounds and decided to investigate."

When he halted near her, the lantern light illuminated his striking features. Deplorably, Antonia's heart leapt again, this time with renewed awareness of his undeniable masculinity.

She managed a nod at his apology, yet she was annoyed at herself for always becoming so flustered in this particular man's presence.

"I thought you were with my father," Antonia said coolly, turning back to face the target.

"He suddenly was struck with an idea for a new staysail design, so he wanted to make a sketch and calculate some measurements."

Her mouth curved with wry understanding. "Then he will undoubtedly be up till all hours of the night. When Papa becomes obsessed with a new design, he never sleeps until he has all the details completely worked out." She sighed and nocked another arrow. "I will be fortunate if he emerges from the Map Room before my holiday is over."

"Can't you simply join him there?"

"Oh, he allows me in, but I am not truly welcome. His work is not appropriate for a lady, you see."

She let the arrow fly and watched the whooshing arc. When the tip lodged very near the gold center, Deverill murmured in approval. "Impressive."

"Thank you, but this is a shorter distance than customary for competition."

"Archery is an unusual accomplishment for a lady, isn't it?"

Antonia smiled with wry humor. "Indeed. It is also one of my *few* accomplishments. I am not musical, nor can I draw very well. And I detest sewing. This and riding—and perhaps languages—are my only claims to talent, I'm afraid."

"A virtual Amazon."

She winced at the painful image and pressed her lips together.

"I say that with admiration," Deverill remarked, evidently realizing he had struck a nerve.

"When a lady is as tall as I, Mr. Deverill, she doesn't appreciate comparisons such as that."

She felt his measuring gaze skimming her body. "Your height seems unexceptional to me."

Antonia glanced up at Deverill, who was a full head taller than she. "I suppose compared to you, I am not excessively tall, but for a girl, height is a decided drawback. I tower over a quarter of the gentleman I meet." Picking up the next arrow, she couldn't repress another sigh. "It would have been so much better if I had been born male."

"Better for whom?"

"For my father. Myself. I could have taken over his company, for one thing." She loosed the arrow, watching with satisfaction as it hit the bull's-eye. "Papa wanted a son—I suppose all men do. But my mother died before she could give him one, and he never considered remarrying."

"And for yourself?"

Realizing he sounded truly interested in her answer, Antonia shot Deverill an arch glance. "Why, I could sail around the world, having adventures as you do. I have never had a single adventure. The closest I've come is christening several of my father's new ships. I admit I envy you. You fight pirates; I sew samplers."

He looked slightly amused. "Fighting pirates is not all it's cracked up to be, Miss Maitland. It's hardly glamorous and often dangerous."

Studying him, Antonia suddenly frowned, recalling the scars she'd seen on Deverill's bare chest. She had glimpsed even worse ones on his back. "Is that how you acquired your scars? Battling pirates?"

In the gleam of lamplight, she could see his expression darken. "Some of them," he answered finally.

Regretting that she'd evidently struck a nerve of *his,* she shook herself from her self-pity and contrived a light reply. "Well, it is still more exciting than any pursuits allowed a lady." Her gaze turned speculative. "I don't suppose you would consider taking me with you on your next voyage?"

His eyebrow shot up, as if not quite believing her question.

"Surely you don't hold superstitious objections about permitting females on board your ships, Mr. Deverill?" Antonia asked, her tone teasing.

Deverill answered in kind, humor lacing his voice. "I might not object, but your father would be devastated to lose you."

"Alas, that is true."

"He has very definite plans for your future."

Reminded of her father's dreams, Antonia nodded. "Papa wants what he thinks is best for me. He won't be content until I marry into the nobility."

"The nobility is not all it's purported to be, either," Deverill said, his tone dry.

"Yet for someone of my social station, a noble marriage would be a high achievement. And most young ladies in my situation marry for convenience. Few heiresses ever make a love match or experience a grand passion. And it will make my father extremely happy."

When Deverill's mouth curled slightly at the corner, Antonia regarded him curiously. "I gather filial obedience is not a virtue with you?"

He flashed her a grin. "In your case, I'm sure it's admirable, but my soul shrivels at the prospect of wedding to please my father."

Her lips pursed in speculation. "No, somehow I cannot imagine you tamely making a marriage of convenience at your father's behest."

His chuckle was rich. "That is beyond the realm of imagination. In any event, I am quite satisfied with my life and have no plans to settle down. My lifestyle doesn't lend itself to marriage."

"Because you are always wandering the globe."

"In part."

Turning back, Antonia fitted another arrow to the bowstring. "I still wish I could accompany you. It would be gratifying to have just one small adventure before I settle down to a tame existence." She released the arrow, grimacing when it went wide of the target. "Just once I would like to do something a bit wild and daring. I have never done anything wicked or scandalous or shocking in my entire life."

"And just what would you consider wicked or shocking, Miss Maitland?"

"Oh, I don't know. . . ." She paused, then stilled,

suddenly feeling reckless. "Yes, I do know." She slanted Deverill a glance. "A kiss would be satisfactorily wicked."

"A kiss?"

Antonia turned fully to face him. "Would you show me what it is like to be kissed? I have never been kissed before, Mr. Deverill, and my best friend, Emily, teases me unmercifully about it. Emily is not fast, but she had a kiss a full year ago from a gentleman who was a friend of her brother's. And I admit, I've always wondered what it would be like to be kissed by a dashing adventurer. This could be my only chance. The Baldwin Academy is very strict, never allowing us to associate with anyone the least bit disreputable. And I am not likely to encounter many men like you once I put up my hair and enter society."

She had surprised him, Antonia could tell. He was regarding her with wariness, amusement, perhaps even a glint of admiration for her boldness.

"Besides," she continued her argument, "I might as well hang for a sheep as a lamb, as the saying goes. This afternoon I violated the rules of propriety with a vengeance by seeing you unclothed. A kiss won't be nearly as scandalous. Please, won't you satisfy my curiosity?"

"You are actually serious," he said finally.

"Quite serious. And truly, there is no risk that you will compromise me. And even if you did, there would be no dire consequences. Papa wouldn't force you to make amends by marrying me, since you have no title. Are you afraid, Mr. Deverill?" she asked when he still hesitated.

She could tell her dare had sparked an answering fire in him; his dark eyelashes lowered to hood his

eyes as he appraised her. "You like to live dangerously, don't you, Miss Maitland?"

Antonia laughed. "I probably would, if I ever allowed myself. But I would never go beyond the
bounds of true propriety."

Deverill's gaze dropped to her bow and arrow. "I
make it a point never to kiss an armed female. Put
down your bow and come here."

Her heartbeat quickened when she realized he intended to comply with her request, even against his
better judgment.

Doing as he bid, she stepped closer.

With one finger, he tilted her chin up. Antonia held
her breath as Deverill bent his head to place a gentle
kiss on her lips, the lightest brushing of flesh against
flesh.

His lips were warm and soft and created a delicious
tingle on hers. . . . But the chaste caress was over all
too soon.

Drawing back, Antonia frowned. As kisses went, it
had been far too delicate for so bold a man. "That
was . . . disappointing. Can you not do better?"

Laughter lit his eyes at her deliberate challenge. "If
you insist."

This time he drew her into his arms, flush against
his tall, sinewed body. She barely had time to register
the delightful shock of it before he lowered his head
to bring his mouth fully into slanting contact with
hers.

The pressure this time was hard and scaldingly hot,
and she felt the sensation like a burning brand. Then
he slid his tongue deep into her mouth, making her
heart leap and her senses explode.

His tongue slowly swept and plunged while his lips

plundered. Antonia whimpered as a riot of fiery sensations thrummed through her body. Every part of her flared with heat.

His stunning kiss went on for some time, heightening the fierce, trembling ache burgeoning inside her. Helplessly, she reached up to clutch Deverill's powerful shoulders for support. When he finally drew his mouth away, her limbs were so weak, she could barely stand.

Still clinging to him, Antonia opened her eyes to stare at him, dazed by the hungry yearning he had aroused in her so effortlessly.

When at last she spoke, her voice was as unsteady as her limbs felt. "That was . . . magnificent."

His beautiful mouth curved in a very male smile as he gently released her and stepped back. "I am flattered you think so."

Shakily, she brought her fingers to her burning lips. "Thank you, Mr. Deverill. I will never forget that."

"It was my pleasure. Now I had best leave you to your shooting before your father finds us together and puts those arrows to better use."

Antonia stood motionless as she watched his tall, powerful form fade into the shadows. Her head still swam, her body still burned.

She had never felt such intense sensations in her life. Worse, Deverill's kiss had sparked a yearning deep inside her that made her long for even more of the exciting passion he had barely let her glimpse.

Her fingertips brushed over her swollen lips. She would never tell anyone about his kiss, not even her dearest friend, Emily. She didn't want to share the experience. She wanted to hold it to herself, to treasure it.

Antonia shut her eyes, suddenly filled with regret. Perhaps it had been a mistake to ask him to kiss her, for now that she knew what she was missing, she would find it even harder to remain satisfied with her tame existence.

Yet one thing was certain. She would never, ever forget Trey Deverill as long as she lived.

One

She didn't look much like a damsel in distress, Deverill decided, watching Antonia Maitland across the crowded ballroom. Nothing like a young lady who needed his protection, her life endangered by a murderer. The potential victim of the very man she was privately engaged to wed.

Instead, she seemed in her element at the glittering ball, gowned in an exquisite confection—pearl gray gauze shot with silver—that must have cost a fortune. Of course, as one of England's greatest heiresses, Miss Antonia Maitland could well afford to patronize the most fashionable modistes.

Yet the gown, while splendid, deserved only partial credit for her enchanting looks. Antonia positively glowed in the light of myriad candles burning in the crystal chandeliers overhead.

Deverill's eyes narrowed at the unexpected lust that shot though him. Physically she little resembled the gangly, self-conscious girl he had met four years ago. She was as tall as he remembered, but her figure had ripened to slender, womanly curves, and she carried herself now with an elegance, a graceful self-assurance, that had only been hinted at then.

He would never forget their first meeting—her endearing embarrassment at catching him in the nude— and then later that evening, her bold, completely unexpected request for a kiss.

At the time he'd thought Antonia utterly unique. Despite the advantages of wealth and luxury, she had fretted at the strictures society placed on young ladies, wishing she'd been born male so that she could control her father's shipping empire and sail the world in search of adventure.

Her ambition was the *only* masculine thing about her, Deverill reflected, riveted by her brilliant smile. Certainly her appearance was purely feminine. Her coppery mane was darker now, a glorious deep auburn. That and her creamy white skin gave her a vibrancy that roused all his primal male instincts.

She was a beauty, no doubt about it. And reportedly her hand was sought by numerous gentlemen, despite her late father's low birth and breeding.

This morning, Mrs. Peeke, the Maitland housekeeper and a longtime friend of Deverill's, had proudly summed up her mistress's success: Antonia was genuinely popular with London's fashionable set, accepted in society by virtue of her own lively charm and her claim to genteel blood on her mother's side. And naturally, her vast inheritance.

At present, she was surrounded by a flock of her ardent admirers, including her betrothed, the refined, aristocratic Baron Heward.

Her betrothal was the prime reason Deverill was here in England. He'd returned to London after more than a year's absence, summoned by the housekeeper's fearful letter, imputing that Antonia was in danger. Samuel Maitland had died last year, supposedly of heart failure, yet Mrs. Peeke suspected differently—that he'd actually been poisoned by Lord Heward after a violent argument when Maitland had withdrawn his permission for the baron to wed his daughter.

Deverill's promise to investigate had brought him to this ball this evening in search of Antonia. He planned to renew the acquaintance and question her about her betrothal before deciding how to proceed.

It was not much of a secret that she and Lord Heward had a private understanding. They'd been betrothed only days before her father's death, but at Antonia's insistence had put off any formal declaration for a proper year of mourning. According to the housekeeper, the official announcement of their betrothal would be made public next month at a betrothal ball, with the wedding to take place three weeks later, after the banns were called. Once they were wed, Mrs. Peeke feared, Heward would control Antonia's fortune, so what was to stop him from murdering her as he might have murdered her father?

This was Antonia's first social function since coming out of mourning. Deverill watched as the baron led her out onto the ballroom floor for a cotillion.

She seemed happy enough, laughing at something Lord Heward said. But then, the tall, flaxen-haired nobleman allegedly had the suave charm and patrician allure to win the heart of any susceptible young heiress.

Deverill felt his jaw tighten. He had only a nodding acquaintance with Heward from their few encounters at gentlemen's clubs, except for one occasion that had left an indelibly repellent impression—when he'd seen the baron viciously wield his cane on a beggar boy for the mere sin of daring to touch his elegant coat. That incident alone had roused an instinctive dislike of the man.

Directly after meeting with Mrs. Peeke this morning, Deverill had visited his own shipping offices to discover what his people knew about Heward. What he'd ascertained was mainly hearsay but unsavory enough to warrant further investigation, and he planned to call on his director tonight after the ball to see which if any of the rumors could be substantiated.

However, just because Heward was rumored to be avaricious and ruthless in his business dealings didn't make him guilty of murder.

He wouldn't presume the nobleman guilty without proof, Deverill resolved, but he meant to discover if the housekeeper's suspicions had merit. If so—if Samuel Maitland had indeed been poisoned by Heward—then he would bring his friend's killer to justice. And he would make absolutely certain that his friend's daughter didn't become the baron's next unwitting victim.

Given the warmth of the ballroom, Antonia was glad when at the conclusion of the dance Lord Heward left her with her friend Emily and went off in search of refreshment for them both.

"Isn't it famous—my first ball is a perfect crush," Emily declared, surveying the crowd with delight.

Mustering proper enthusiasm, Antonia agreed. "A decided triumph, just as I predicted."

"I am so glad that you could be here to enjoy it."

Emily, now the Countess of Sudbury after her estimable marriage last fall, had been planning her ball for months but had waited so that Antonia could attend after she put off full mourning.

Additionally, her success had been aided by world events. London ordinarily would be thin of company this time of year, for once Parliament adjourned, a significant portion of the Quality normally retired to their country estates for the summer. But the news last week of the Duke of Wellington's miraculous and bloody victory at Waterloo, which had finally defeated Napoleon Bonaparte once and for all, had brought the ton flocking back to town for the jubilant celebrations.

"Now if only Prinny would make an appearance," Emily said hopefully, "my success would be assured. But I suppose that is asking too much. . . ."

Her voice trailed off as a sudden buzz of excited whispers rippled through the throng of guests during a lull in the orchestra music. Like Emily, Antonia glanced toward the entrance doors, wondering if the Prince Regent had arrived after all.

Then the crowd parted slightly, and she caught sight of the tall, powerful figure of a man moving toward them. Antonia's pulse gave an unmistakable leap as she recognized the daring adventurer who had featured so prominently in her dreams more often than she cared to count during the past four years. Blood suddenly began pounding in her ears, making her light-headed.

"Oh, my word," Emily breathed, dismay and excitement lacing her tone. "Is that . . ."

Trey Deverill, Antonia finished silently for her friend. "I believe," she answered rather unsteadily, "it is Mr. Deverill."

"What is he doing here at my ball? I sent him no card of invitation."

He was heading directly toward them, Antonia realized, her stomach rioting with butterflies. But then, miraculously, he paused to speak to a gentleman who had waylaid him.

"He looks a bit like a pirate," Emily observed breathlessly.

He did indeed, Antonia thought, relieved to have more time to prepare herself before coming face-to-face with Deverill.

Even dressed in a tailored black coat and white satin knee breeches, he was the picture of raw masculinity. His gleaming brown hair, thick and wavy and sun-streaked, was an unfashionable length, almost reaching his shoulders, while his striking features were still deeply tanned. With his height and sleek, powerful build, he commanded the attention of every eye in the room.

Hers in particular. Every inch of him was as vital and bold as Antonia remembered.

Then Deverill turned toward her again, and her gaze locked with his. She couldn't look away. Absurdly, all her nerves began thrumming in anticipation, as if her entire being had suddenly come alive after a long sleep.

Emily, too, seemed unaccountably flustered. "He is moving this way. What should I do, Antonia? Should I refuse him admittance? Mr. Deverill is not considered respectable, even if he comes from a highly genteel family and is exceedingly rich."

"No, you don't want to make a scene," Antonia replied in a rallying tone. "Try to act naturally, as if you expected to receive him."

But when Deverill came to a halt before her, it was Antonia who had difficulty managing the pretense of composure.

He was breathtakingly handsome at close range, captivating with his sea green eyes gazing down into hers so intently. It aroused her just to look at him—although surely the flush infusing her body could be attributed to the warmth of the ballroom.

"Miss Maitland," he murmured briefly in greeting, in that deep, rich voice she still remembered.

To her surprise, though, he barely acknowledged her before bowing politely over Emily's hand. "Pray accept my apologizes, Lady Sudbury, for appearing uninvited. I have been away in India this past year and just heard the terrible news about Miss Maitland's father. I was a close friend of Samuel Maitland's and wished to offer her my condolences."

Emily was not proof against Deverill's easy charm. "That is most kind of you, Mr. Deverill. And you are welcome to join us if you wish."

Returning his attention to Antonia, he took her gloved hand. "I am keenly sorry for your loss. Your father was a remarkable man."

Antonia winced, feeling the familiar sharp stab of grief that had diminished little in the year since her father's passing. "Thank you," she murmured, discomfited by the touch of Deverill's fingers as they pressed hers.

"No doubt you miss him."

"Very much." She missed her father dreadfully. Yet she was determined to throw off her gloom and look to the future; it was what Papa would have wanted, she was certain.

Deverill was regarding her sympathetically. "Since you are out of black gloves now, Miss Maitland, perhaps you will honor me with a dance for old times' sake."

She eyed him in surprise, wondering what his purpose was, knowing it would not be quite the thing to dance with a man of Deverill's notoriety. She was glad to have an excuse to refuse him. "I am afraid my dance card is full, Mr. Deverill."

He flashed a slow grin. "I expected nothing less. But surely your intended partner will understand that we wish to renew our acquaintance. If you will excuse us, Lady Sudbury?"

Not giving either lady a chance to respond, he took Antonia's elbow to guide her through the crowd.

Caught off guard, she lacked the presence of mind to protest Deverill's presumption before he steered her onto the ballroom floor. She might even have admired his boldness if she hadn't been the target of it. Over her shoulder, Antonia saw her next partner approaching, saw the gentleman's jaw drop in puzzlement at being abandoned. And her betrothed was moving toward her as well, bearing two cups of punch. Lord Heward directed a dark frown at Deverill as the orchestra struck up the music.

The dance was a waltz, Antonia realized with a sinking heart as Deverill took her in his arms. She was required to tilt her head back to look up at him, which made her feel uncharacteristically small and feminine. Worse, she felt an undeniable heat at his closeness. Trying to pretend nonchalance, however, she braced herself and followed his lead as he swept her into the dance.

He whirled her around the ballroom with fluid grace, matching his steps to hers in perfect rhythm. At least he held her at a proper distance, yet the solid feel of his shoulder beneath her gloved fingertips was highly disturbing. She knew from experience how hard and lean his body was, but touching him only brought to mind the image of his magnificent nude form. . . .

When her cheeks warmed again, Antonia raised her eyes to the ceiling and muttered an imprecation to herself. She was an utter nitwit for dwelling on such forbidden memories. She was no longer that tongue-tied green girl who had been struck spellbound by a dashing adventurer so long ago. She was four years older now—and determined to hold her own with Deverill.

"I confess surprise," she made herself comment airily, "that you dance so well, Mr. Deverill. I would not have guessed that dancing would number among your unusual accomplishments."

He raised a dark eyebrow. "Why would that surprise you?"

"Because I thought you held an aversion for polite society."

"I do occasionally consort with civilized company in other countries, Miss Maitland," he answered her dryly. "It's primarily London society that has never appealed to me."

She wanted greatly to ask him why, but instead she essayed a polite smile. "Where did you say you have been this time? India? It must be delightful to travel to such exotic quarters of the globe. But I should tell you that Lord Byron is proving to be something of your rival. Have you read *The Corsair* from his 'Turkish Tales'?"

"No, I haven't had the pleasure."

"All the ton is talking about his poetry. I admit I thought of you when I was reading it—although I suspect your real-life adventures are more exciting than Byron's fictional accounts."

A lazy smile curved Deverill's lips, as if he agreed. But he made no reply as he expertly negotiated her around a knot of dancers. After a moment's silence,

Antonia continued the conversation, since talking helped distract her from the unruly sensations that were still flooding her at being in his arms.

"I actually had one small adventure since I last saw you, Mr. Deverill. In truth, I should thank you for inspiring it. Two years ago, I persuaded my father to take me to Cyrene when he had business there."

Cyrene was a small island in the western Mediterranean, not too far from the southern coast of Spain. Antonia had relished every moment of her visit there, and every moment of the voyage to and from the island as well.

That topic had caught his attention. "And what did you think of Cyrene?" Deverill asked with evident interest in her answer.

"I found it remarkably beautiful. I can understand why you make it your home when you are not at sea. You have an estate there, I understand. My father told me," she said at Deverill's quizzical look, not wanting him to know how avidly curious she was about how he lived his life or where he chose to live it.

Deverill was measuring her again with that striking green gaze, which deplorably only made her heart beat faster. "I was told that you remained in London after your father's passing."

"Yes. London has always been my home. But for propriety's sake, I hired an acquaintance of my late mother's as a companion, to come live with me and act as chaperone. And my trustee is a barrister who was a close friend of Papa's, so I am well cared for."

Deverill's eyes narrowed a degree. "I also believe felicitations are in order. You are soon to announce your betrothal, isn't that so?"

It was Antonia's turn to be surprised. "How did you learn of my betrothal?"

"Your housekeeper told me when I called at your home this morning."

"You know Mrs. Peeke?"

His broad shoulders lifted in a slight shrug. "I performed a service for her husband once, so she tends to think of me as her prodigal son whenever I'm in London."

Antonia studied Deverill's enigmatic expression, dearly wanting to know what he had done to win such loyalty from her housekeeper. But he forestalled her with another remark about her betrothal.

"Mrs. Peeke says you are happy with your choice of Baron Heward."

Even if she had no desire to discuss her future marriage with Deverill, the skepticism in his tone made her want to defend herself. "I am indeed quite happy."

"Do you think your father would have been pleased?"

Antonia's brow furrowed. "Yes, of course. Papa was delighted when we became engaged, since it was the brilliant match he always wished for. Lord Heward holds an illustrious title that goes back to Richard Lionheart, and he is considered the height of good ton, accepted everywhere. What is more, Papa approved of his business acumen. Heward has extensive interests in shipping—he owns his own firm, in fact. So our marriage will be a merger of fortunes and business interests as well."

"But what of your own feelings? Are you in love with him?"

Antonia blinked at the frank question. "That is scarcely your concern, Mr. Deverill."

"Your father was a friend of mine, Miss Maitland.

I feel obliged to make certain his daughter is protected from unscrupulous fortune hunters."

Her eyes narrowed. "Lord Heward is hardly a fortune hunter! He has a significant fortune of his own. And he certainly is not unscrupulous."

"Are you so confident of that?"

Antonia could only stare back at Deverill, frankly startled by his intense interest in her impending marriage and by his probing questions.

Suddenly, though, Deverill shook his head, as if becoming aware he had gone far beyond the bounds of polite discourse. "Forgive me, sweeting. I didn't mean to distress you." He flashed her a charming smile. "I know you believe you are doing exactly what your father wanted."

Momentarily speechless at how he had turned his apology into an indictment of her judgment, Antonia mentally reviewed all the arguments she could make in retort. The crucial one being that by marrying Lord Heward, she would be fulfilling her father's most ardent wish. As a baroness, she would be assured of a place in the elite ranks of the Beau Monde.

It would be a marriage of convenience, true, not a love match. Yet her handsome, charming betrothed was the sort of husband every young lady dreamed of. And she was very fond of Lord Heward and enjoyed his company—although he could be a bit stuffy and proper at times. Not that she would ever admit it to Deverill.

Finally finding her tongue, Antonia gave him a frigid smile. "This marriage is *precisely* what my father wanted. But tragically, he died before he could see it come to fruition."

"I'm surprised Heward didn't press to declare your betrothal before now."

He *had* wished to announce it, she reflected, but she had insisted otherwise. "Lord Heward was quite understanding when I put off our official betrothal so I could properly mourn. And in the interim, he has been wonderfully supportive. He stepped in to help oversee Maitland Shipping's extensive concerns, which naturally, as a female, I could not do."

"Naturally. But I don't wish to discuss Heward any longer. I merely want to enjoy dancing with the most beautiful woman in the room."

Antonia's eyebrows snapped together at Deverill's sudden about-face and dubious flattery. But she could think of no appropriate retort and so fell silent as he spun her around the ballroom.

She still had not entirely lost her annoyance with him by the time the waltz came to an end. When they drew to a halt, however, she found herself distracted, since Deverill didn't immediately release her.

She stared up at him, aware that the heat shimmering between them had suddenly returned full force to assault her senses. His embrace was unnervingly intimate, his face disquietingly close to hers. Her gaze dropped to his mouth. His beautiful, sensual mouth that could give such intense pleasure . . .

Abruptly Antonia shook herself from the memory of his kiss. Most decidedly she ought not feel this fierce attraction for Deverill, particularly not when she was betrothed to another man.

She glanced about her, realizing that his provocative attentions had attracted undue notice from the highbrowed ball guests. And Lord Heward was casting a jealous scowl from the sidelines, she saw.

Abashed, she extricated herself from Deverill's embrace and stepped safely back.

Seeming to ignore that he was the focus of such keen attention, Deverill sketched her a polite bow, although his mouth held a sardonic twist when he spoke. "I will pay my respects to your betrothed some other time. I would very much like to speak to him, although I doubt the feeling is mutual, considering the way Heward is looking daggers at me just now. He'll be pleased that I must take my leave, since I have another engagement. Your devoted servant, Miss Maitland."

With another bow, he turned away, leaving her to stare after him.

As Antonia stood there trying to gather her scattered wits, her friend Emily suddenly appeared at her side.

"Oh, my," Emily exclaimed, "what did he say to you?"

"Nothing much," Antonia managed to reply. "We discussed my father. And he asked me about my betrothal." She offered her friend an apologetic smile. "I regret that Deverill showed up uninvited to create a stir, Emily."

"Goodness, I don't blame you in the least. He reportedly delights in flouting the rules of polite society. In fact, I believe I am quite pleased after all, Antonia. His notoriety is sure to make my ball a success, for it gives my guests something to prate about. Indeed, I heard all manner of juicy gossip about Deverill while you were dancing. So tell me, is he as fascinating as everyone says?"

Antonia was not about to answer that question honestly, or admit that Deverill's powerful, breathtaking presence still affected her as much as it had when she was a mere schoolgirl. "He was a friend of my father's, simply that."

"Well, Heward looked quite put out because Deverill danced with you. And any number of ladies are jealous as cats that he spoke only to you. I hear Lady Follows has been hopelessly in love with him for years, but no one has ever succeeded in rousing the slightest longing in his heart—if he has one, which they consider debatable. There is no question, however, that women find him irresistible, with that combination of raw virility and elusiveness. Not to mention his celebrated sexual expertise—"

"Emily!" Antonia chastised, feigning shock. "You know you shouldn't say such disgraceful things in my tender hearing. Miss Baldwin would box your ears if she knew."

"Well, I don't see why I must hold my tongue around you any longer. You will be wed to Heward soon enough, and then you will understand the delights of the marriage bed."

But until then, Antonia reminded herself, she ought not be discussing a man's sexual expertise. *Particularly* not Deverill's. It was difficult enough to forget the magnificent image of his nude body and the scandalous fantasies he still roused in her dreams.

She let out a long breath. To her dismay, her attraction for the bold, exciting adventurer was stronger than ever, but she needed to remember that she was engaged to wed Lord Heward. Deverill needed to remember it as well.

It was none of his concern whom she married, although clearly he had not approved of her intentions. Inexplicably, Antonia shivered, recalling how his green eyes had darkened with searching intensity when he spoke to her of unscrupulous fortune hunters.

She suspected that she hadn't heard the last word

from him on the subject of her betrothal. For now, however, she intended to dismiss all thought of Deverill from her mind, since her fair-haired nobleman was approaching her, bearing two long-forgotten cups of punch.

Excusing herself from Emily, Antonia pasted a welcoming smile on her lips and went to meet him.

Deverill had a distinct frown on his face as he left the overheated ballroom. Dancing with Antonia had been a mistake, he'd realized the instant he took her in his arms. Holding her, touching her, had been dangerously, unexpectedly arousing.

Roughly he locked his jaw to counteract the still-painful swelling in his loins.

Of course, his lust had a likely explanation. It had been months since he'd enjoyed a woman's charms, with no female companionship during the long voyage from India to Cyrene. And once he'd discovered the housekeeper's urgent letter waiting for him on the island, he'd been too impatient to reach London to give any thought to dalliance.

Moreover, Deverill admitted with grudging honesty, he'd always been partial to red-haired temptresses. And Antonia's auburn hair glowed with a molten flame that made a man eager to singe his hands.

He wondered if her lovemaking would possess the same fire that shone in the depths of her hair. He suspected it would, even though on the surface she appeared every inch the polished, proper, gracious lady. The flash of temper he'd seen tonight in her vivid blue eyes suggested she had merely banked the fire in order to present the genteel facade expected of her.

It was that hint of fire that called to him.

He'd had a glimpse of it four years ago, during his first intriguing encounter with Antonia, but he had managed to ignore his male urges then, sternly quelling his inappropriate desire for her. Even though he'd satisfied her curiosity by giving her her first kiss, he knew full well she was innocent and untried and completely off limits, with a protective father who intended for her to make a brilliant marriage. A rakish adventurer was assuredly not proper husband material, no matter how much Samuel Maitland had professed to admire him.

Not to mention that Deverill was too dedicated to his life's calling to ever consider settling down in wedlock, particularly in a proper society marriage dictated by the ton.

Antonia's appeal, however, had taken him by surprise. And now that the enchanting girl had turned into a beautiful, spirited woman, he found himself in a quandary: his fierce attraction was still bloody inappropriate.

Honorably, he couldn't touch Antonia. Not only was she essentially betrothed to another man, but out of respect for her late father, Deverill knew he had to shield her from a slightly disreputable—and untitled—adventurer like himself.

At the end of their waltz, it had taken iron-willed control to force his desire to remain in check, even knowing they were in the middle of a crowded ballroom, the focus of all eyes. He certainly didn't want to tarnish Antonia's hard-won reputation.

And if Heward was *not* a murderer, Deverill reminded himself as he stepped into the warm June evening, he had no reason to ruin her chances for an exceptional marriage. If she truly wanted the baron for her husband, then he had no right to stand in her way.

At least in that respect, he'd accomplished tonight what he had come here to do—to discover just how enamored Antonia was of her betrothed. The answer apparently was: *extremely.* Whether or not she truly loved Heward, she had rallied to his defense so ardently that Deverill knew she was unlikely to believe her housekeeper's suspicions without definitive proof.

Deverill himself wasn't even certain he believed the accusations, even after he had relentlessly questioned Mrs. Peeke this morning within hours of his arrival in London. But the woman's fear couldn't simply be dismissed. She was still dreadfully worried for Antonia.

The day before Samuel Maitland had died, Mrs. Peeke claimed, she'd overheard him fiercely arguing with Lord Heward about the baron's ships illegally transporting slaves. A staunch opponent of slavery, Mr. Maitland had declared that no man who promoted it could marry his daughter. Mrs. Peeke had expected him immediately to call off Antonia's two-day-old engagement when she returned to town from visiting Brighton. But then Maitland had suddenly died of heart failure the following day, shortly after another, less contentious meeting with Lord Heward.

"Just think of it, Mr. Deverill," the housekeeper had implored him. "The master was as hale and hearty as they come, rarely suffered so much as a sniffle. Why would he collapse after drinking barely half a glass of brandy? I feel certain it was poison. Lord Heward had brought him that bottle of fine French brandy—trying to worm his way back into the master's good graces, I'd say. After dinner Mr. Maitland took the bottle to his Map Room to drink it. I found him there lying facedown on the carpet when I brought his tea."

"But the physician determined his heart had failed?" Deverill asked.

"Yes, but it was not *Mr. Maitland's* physician who pronounced the cause of death. It was Lord Heward's. His lordship insisted, when he happened to return to Maitland House that evening. That alone was exceedingly queer. And then the bottle of brandy disappeared as well. I did not even think of it at the time—I was too struck with grief and too concerned for poor Miss Maitland to consider what his lordship might have done. But afterward, I began to wonder . . . had nightmares about it, to tell the truth. And once they began, I could not get the suspicions out of my mind. If Lord Heward killed the master to stop him from forbidding the marriage, what is to keep his lordship from murdering Miss Maitland after they are wed to claim her fortune solely for his own?"

Deverill's hesitation had elicited an earnest plea from Mrs. Peeke. "Please, Mr. Deverill . . . You were the master's friend. For his daughter's sake, won't you help me discover the truth? If I were to accuse Lord Heward, no one would heed me. He is a nobleman and I am a mere servant, an old one at that. But if you could somehow prove his lordship's guilt or innocence either way . . . I know I won't rest until I am certain that dear girl is safe."

Deverill had agreed to investigate the housekeeper's claims. Her conviction that Antonia was in grave danger was still merely a gut feeling, yet he'd learned to trust his instincts over the years, since they'd saved his life and the lives of countless others numerous times. And of course the housekeeper was right: His friendship with Antonia's father alone obliged him to make certain she was safe.

More crucially, however, protecting innocents was his sworn duty. He was a Guardian, a member of a secret society that operated as a small, select arm of the British Foreign Office, performing missions far too difficult and dangerous for the Foreign Office to undertake.

The Guardians of the Sword functioned something like a modern force of mercenaries but with a higher calling: protecting the weak, the vulnerable, the deserving. Fighting tyranny. Working for the good of mankind.

Deverill had joined the centuries-old order nearly a decade ago. While battling pirates in the Mediterranean, he'd gained their leader's attention—because of his courage and inventiveness, he was told—and so was invited into their elite ranks. Deverill had leapt at the chance offered him, not only in order to serve a noble cause, but perhaps more importantly, to avenge his own personal ghosts.

Since then, in addition to harassing Napoleon's navy, ridding the seas of the scourge of pirates had been his prime responsibility, and in fact what had taken him to India this past year—to aid the huge and politically powerful British merchant enterprise, the East India Company.

Deverill believed fiercely in the Guardians' ideals and considered serving the order his life's calling. Samuel Maitland, although not actually a member, had also been a strong supporter of their cause, and had supplied all the Guardians' ships for decades. Ergo, if his daughter was in danger, she deserved their protection as well.

It was through the Guardians that Deverill had initially come to know Maitland—by defending the company's commercial vessels from Barbary corsairs. Shortly, however, Deverill had begun buying his own private ships from Maitland's firm, for their remarkable speed and maneuverability, as had his American cousin and fellow Guardian, Brandon Deverill.

Brandon had spent the past two years during America's war with Britain defending his country from the powerful British navy and protecting his shipping empire from their ruinous blockade.

But his cousin's business issues would prove useful, Deverill reflected, for they would give him a legitimate pretext to associate with Antonia, and more notably, with Lord Heward, who was now a chief adviser of her shipping firm. Under the guise of untangling his cousin's dealings with Maitland Shipping, he could pursue his much more crucial goal of investigating the housekeeper's charge of murder.

Yet even if he disliked admitting it, one constant motive continued to drive him, Deverill knew. One deeper even than friendship or duty. His own personal vow to save those under his protection.

Absently he touched his chest above his left breast, feeling the savage, unsightly scar made by a Turkish blade. The scars still burned, doubtless because they were a physical reminder of his worst failure.

Not that he could ever forget. His dreams were still haunted by the agonized screams of his men. Men he had been powerless to save. His first crew, during his first captaincy. As their commander, he'd been responsible for keeping them safe, but he'd failed disastrously.

He wouldn't fail this time. He would die first before he allowed any harm to come to Antonia.

Whether she knew it or not, she was now under his protection.

He might be required to put an end to her brilliant

match, which would surely disappoint her and likely earn her wrath. But that was far better than seeing her fall victim to an unscrupulous fortune hunter who might eventually murder her to claim her inheritance.

Two

His naked body was magnificent. Heat and vitality throbbed from him with a dangerous beauty that made her breath falter.

Her heart hammering, Antonia watched as Trey Deverill moved closer, his jeweled gaze riveted on her. The next moment she was in his arms, his hungry mouth hot as it claimed hers.

His kiss was scorching and sweetly ravaging. Flooded by yearning, she opened to him, molding herself against his powerful body, clutching the hard muscles of his shoulders.

He drank of her mouth as his hands roamed over her skin, gentle and ruthless at once. His touch was dangerously, wildly sensual, shooting arrows of pleasure downward to her moist, feminine center.

Then his lips followed his hands, kissing the arch of her throat, her collarbone, her breasts, the blistering heat searing her flesh. Her head fell back, and she moaned in surrender, overwhelmed by blind desire. . . .

With a start, Antonia awakened from her dream, her skin burning, her body shivering with longing. In the dim light of early morning, she lay in bed, tangled in her sheets, aching for the elusive fulfillment that had drifted just out of reach.

Giving a sigh of frustration, Antonia rolled onto her back to stare up at the canopy overhead. The dream always ended the same way—with a disappointing emptiness that left her restless and unfulfilled.

She was hot and moist between her legs, her body feverish with the desire her vivid fantasy had aroused. Regrettably, that was all it was—sheer fantasy. As a girl she'd had lovely dreams of a dashing pirate who carried her off on a glorious adventure. Then she'd met Deverill and tasted his stunning kiss. From that point on, he had become the sole focus of her dreams. For four years now she'd imagined him making love to her, kissing her, caressing her, sweeping her away to a world of dark desire and searing pleasure.

Not that she had much experience to base her fantasies upon, Antonia thought sardonically. She knew in principle what it was like to make love, for Emily had told her. But she'd never felt the ecstasy of a man's flesh filling her, burning deep inside her. Deverill's flesh.

Her eyes closed on the memory of her dream. She was achingly aware of her own flesh beneath the fine lawn of her nightdress. Her tingling breasts, her peaked nipples, the throbbing need between her thighs . . .

Trailing her fingertips over the budded crests, she imagined Deverill's masterful hands stroking her. The mere thought kindled a wild, sweet fire in her blood. He had large, strong hands, ruthlessly gentle and demanding at the same time. Much like his mouth. His incredibly arousing mouth . . .

Hearing the strangled moan she made, Antonia suddenly drew her hands away from her body and forced her eyes open. She was only tormenting herself by dwelling on him this way.

She might have no control over her dreams, but now that Deverill had returned to London in the flesh, it was imperative that she quell her wanton imaginings, or she would never be able to again look him in the eye.

With another sigh, this one of self-disgust, Antonia threw off the covers and rose to dress for her usual morning ride.

She was still feeling restless and out of sorts by the time she left the house, although the bright, sunny summer morning raised her spirits somewhat as she descended the front steps of the elegant mansion.

Her horse and groom awaited her in the drive, but her thoughts were so distracted, she noticed nothing else until she came face-to-face with the very object of her wicked fantasies.

Antonia halted abruptly, her eyes widening. With complete nonchalance, Trey Deverill leaned against the stone-and-ironwork livery post, watching her, his arms folded over his broad chest, one highly polished boot crossed over the other. He was dressed for riding in a tailored, bottle green coat that reflected the green in his eyes, and he wore a tall beaver hat over his thick, unruly hair, which seemed to tame his rakish good looks the slightest degree.

For a moment, Antonia simply stared at his strong, rugged features. It was disconcerting to find Deverill on her doorstep, and even more disconcerting to re-member how thoroughly he had occupied her thoughts only a short time ago—

Heat rose in her as unwillingly she met his gaze. Could he tell that she'd been entertaining erotic visions of him all morning long? That vivid dreams of him had haunted her sleep last night and so many other nights?

Closing the final distance between them, she forced herself to offer him a calm greeting. "Were you waiting for me, Mr. Deverill?"

"No, I thought I would call on the milkmaid," he replied, a lazy, amused charm in his sea green eyes. "Of course I was waiting for you, sweetheart."

Beyond him, Antonia saw, her groom stood holding the bridles of her skittish bay mare along with his own hack, while a big strapping chestnut stood patiently nearby, chewing the bit—evidently Deverill's mount, she deduced.

"How did you know to expect me? I suppose Mrs. Peeke told you I usually enjoy a daily ride in the park?"

Deverill shrugged. "It wasn't difficult to determine your routine, since the stables have a standing order to deliver your mount at this time every morning." He glanced at her solitary groom. "Heward isn't accompanying you, I see."

"He doesn't care to rise so early," Antonia answered truthfully. "Nor is he as fond of riding as I am."

"Good. I prefer to enjoy your company uninterrupted."

Antonia arched an eyebrow. "I don't recall inviting you, Mr. Deverill."

His smile was innocent and devilish at the same time. "You didn't. But I have a business matter to discuss with you that wasn't appropriate to introduce at the ball last night."

Antonia didn't know whether to believe him, but

she made no further protest. A morning ride in Hyde Park with Deverill, chaperoned by her groom, was unexceptional, and since he wasn't the kind of man to give up, she suspected she would do better to concede gracefully now and get any conversation over with.

She hadn't counted on Deverill touching her, though. When she went to mount, he ignored her groom and took hold of her waist. Antonia drew a sharp breath, her spine tensing as her body eagerly responded to the memory his touch evoked. For a moment their eyes locked, and she felt certain Deverill understood exactly how he affected her. Then, with an ease that betrayed immense physical strength, he lifted her onto her side-saddle.

Trying to remain cool, Antonia busied herself adjusting the skirts of her riding habit and gathering the reins while Deverill swung up on his chestnut. The spirited bay mare danced a little in anticipation, but Antonia easily brought her under control, and they set off at a sedate pace toward the nearby park, her groom following several discreet lengths behind to give them privacy.

It was a glorious morning for London—cool but bright with sunshine, the traffic mild enough that they negotiated the streets with ease.

"I had forgotten how pleasant an English morning could be," Deverill remarked after a moment.

"India is extremely hot, is it not?" she asked politely.

"Intensely. Even at sea, the air was hot. I much prefer a more temperate climate."

"Will you be remaining in England long?"

He shot her an enigmatic glance. "That remains to be seen."

"So what business matter could you possibly need to discuss with me?" Antonia said. "Since Napoleon abdicated his throne last year, Maitland ships have no longer needed your protection from the French navy. And the Barbary corsairs have generally been tamed. The only business connection I can think of is the steam venture you engaged in with my father."

Years ago Deverill had invested in her father's attempt to design and build a sailing vessel that could additionally be powered by steam, although that enterprise had yet to bear any fruit—and most likely would not, now that Papa was no longer here to lend his designer's brilliance to the scheme.

"I'm not here to talk about the steam venture," Deverill answered. "I'm more interested in discussing how Baron Heward is running your father's shipping empire. It seems odd that he would assume control of such a vast enterprise when most peers wouldn't stoop to dirty their hands with trade."

Antonia lifted a questioning brow. "I think it rather magnanimous of Lord Heward. He stepped in to act as adviser because neither I nor my trustee have experience running a shipping firm. I am indeed grateful to him."

"And your new director. How much do you know about him?"

"Barnaby Trant? Why . . . not much. I have little to do with the company's inner workings. I do know that Lord Heward hired Mr. Trant last year to manage the shipyards and the merchant trade."

"I visited my own offices yesterday and learned some troubling news about how Trant is operating."

"What news?" Antonia asked warily, giving him her full attention.

"It regards my American cousin, Brandon Deverill. When Brand inherited his family's Boston shipping concerns some years ago, he began purchasing an occasional vessel from your father. Before America's war with England broke out, he commissioned four ships from Maitland Shipping and paid seventy percent of the purchase price. All four were completed but never delivered. Yesterday I learned they were confiscated nearly a year ago by your Director Trant, shortly after he was hired. And he never returned the commission. Obviously he took advantage of Britain's hostilities with America to default on the contract, but I'm inclined to consider his actions theft."

Antonia felt her mouth pull in a puzzled frown. "Surely Mr. Trant means to refund your cousin's money."

"He's had plenty of opportunity before this. The war has been over for six months now. Besides, Brand wants his ships. But Trant has refused his repeated requests for delivery. It's unlikely Trant made such a significant decision on his own. More probably, Heward authorized it."

A furrow formed between Antonia's eyes. She had difficulty believing Heward would have supported such an unethical action. "I will ask Lord Heward to untangle the problem with your cousin's ships, although I doubt he is responsible for their confiscation."

Deverill smiled faintly. "You might also mention that if necessary, Brandon will apply to the British courts and bring suit against Maitland Shipping to insure his vessels are delivered as promised. But that would be tedious and expensive. And I expect a nobleman like Heward would prefer to keep our dispute quiet. I myself would prefer to avoid an altercation, since I want Maitland Shipping to continue building our ships."

"Very well, I will tell him," Antonia replied.

"The missing ships aren't my only concern, either," Deverill said as they crossed the street to enter the park. "I don't believe that Heward is the best man to advise you. Or that Trant is the kind of director your father would want in charge of his legacy."

Antonia gave Deverill a cool glance. "You wouldn't be basing your opinion on personal dislike, would you?"

His mouth curved briefly. "I admit I don't much like Heward, but in this case, my qualms are based on his business practices. Since he took over as your adviser, Maitland Shipping has developed a reputation for being ruthless, some might even say unprincipled."

"Pray what are you talking about?" she demanded, not liking Deverill's suggestion that the company's reputation had diminished. "What practices have they engaged in?"

"For one thing, they've crushed several smaller competitors by hiring away their captains and spreading unfounded rumors about their ships being unseaworthy."

The accusation concerned her greatly, yet even if it was true, that didn't mean Lord Heward was behind it; Director Trant was the more likely culprit.

Antonia found herself rallying to her betrothed's defense. "I expect there must be a mistake. Lord Heward would never do anything dishonorable."

"I'm not so certain about that. There are other rumors about Heward's business dealings also, some even more unsavory."

She gave Deverill a sharp glance. "What rumors?"

His unexpected hesitation surprised her. "I'm not certain I should tell you. I don't want you running back to Heward and sharing my suspicions."

Antonia felt herself stiffen. Deverill was treating her like a child—or worse, a helpless woman without a brain in her head. "I am not one to bear tales, Mr. Deverill."

He shook his head slowly. "On second thought, I might do better to discuss it with your trustee and leave you out of it altogether. I don't want to put you in any danger with Heward."

"*Tell* me, Deverill! Before I ride off and leave you right here."

He scrutinized her for another moment, as if debating whether he could trust her. "Very well. I've heard two different reports about Maitland Shipping running slaves."

"Slaves?" Antonia repeated blankly. "But slavery was abolished in Britain nearly a decade ago."

"True, but the profit is immense enough to make the risk worthwhile for unscrupulous merchants."

The allegation startled her into silence. *Unscrupulous;* there was that word again, Antonia thought, disquieted. It was the second time Deverill had used it in conjunction with Lord Heward. She wanted to hurl the accusation back in Deverill's face, but when she examined his expression, she knew he was deadly serious. Another sudden reflection also made her hesitate: Her father might have trusted Heward, but then Papa had also trusted Deverill, for many more years.

"You are saying you think Heward is unscrupulous?" she asked carefully, keeping her tone noncommittal.

"I am saying," Deverill replied, "that I suspect Heward of colluding with your new director in illegal activities, specifically transporting slaves."

Antonia eyed him with a troubled frown. "Those are grave accusations, Mr. Deverill. Do you have any proof of your suspicions?"

"No, but rumors have a way of being true, and you ought to have them investigated. Your father would have adamantly opposed using his vessels to transport slaves."

Dismayed, Antonia nodded. Her father had despised the very idea of slavery. It alarmed her to think Deverill's charges might have even an ounce of merit.

"But you will need to step carefully," he added. "You can't mention a word of this to either Heward or Trant. Alerting them will only give them the opportunity to hide the evidence."

"I assure you, I won't breathe a whisper to Lord Heward," Antonia responded. "I don't want him thinking for one moment that I don't trust him—because I do. Besides . . . have you considered that he may be entirely innocent? He could very well have been duped by Trant."

"If so, then he isn't properly supervising his hireling and shouldn't be in charge of your father's legacy."

Antonia's frown darkened. It was indeed possible she had made a grave mistake by letting Heward appoint Trant as director. "Very well, presuming Trant is guilty . . . then how do I investigate?"

"The barrister who oversees your fortune in trust is considered highly reputable. Can you vouch that he has your best interests at heart?"

"Phineas Cochrane? Why, he is one of the most honest men I have ever met," Antonia declared. "Papa trusted him implicitly, and so do I."

"Then you can begin by having him carefully examine the account books. As your trustee, Cochrane is obliged to periodically review your holdings to see how they are being managed, so his scrutiny shouldn't raise any undue suspicions."

"But what would that prove?"

"It could expose any irregularities . . . any vast sums unaccounted for. The tonnage for each merchantman is fixed, and a captain must record cargo. Since slaves fetch ten times the price of tea, it shouldn't be hard to determine if your captains are falsifying ladings. Unless they are pocketing the extra profit, in which case, you need to know."

Antonia's frown deepened. "And if they are?"

"Then you will have a harder time rooting out the problem. You'll need to put agents on each of your vessels to report directly to you."

When her mare suddenly shied at a passing curricle, Antonia had to direct her attention to maintaining her seat. And when she had the horse under control once more, she shook herself. Deverill's suspicions were purely speculation as yet. She would not leap to any conclusions. Lord Heward and Director Trant should be considered innocent until proven otherwise.

"Very well, I will have Phineas look into the matter," she told Deverill.

"If you need help in any way, I am staying at Grillon's Hotel," Deverill offered, naming a fashionable hostelry on Albemarle Street.

"Thank you, but I believe I can manage." She didn't

want Deverill interfering with her concerns; if there was a problem with Maitland Shipping, then she would have her trustee deal with it. "Now, if you don't mind, Mr. Deverill, I came here to ride."

She urged her horse into a canter, leaving him to follow if he wished.

Deverill did wish. Yet he was satisfied that he'd given Antonia a warning to ponder. He'd seen the understanding in her keen eyes; the concerns he'd raised about Heward and her director had troubled her. She wanted to protect her father's legacy even more than Deverill did.

And even if, as a woman, she was at a disadvantage in the exclusively masculine world of the merchant marine, she was intelligent and shrewd enough to find a way to scrutinize the operations of the company she'd inherited.

He did not, however, intend to tell Antonia of his suspicions regarding the much more emotional subject of her father's death. In the first place, she was unlikely to believe him, Deverill reasoned. She didn't know him well enough to trust him over and above the nobleman she planned to marry. And if she did credit the possibility of murder, then she might be disturbed enough to confront Heward directly about the accusations. And that would not only warn the baron he was being investigated, but conceivably put the housekeeper, as his accuser, in danger as well.

In any case, Deverill knew he would have to proceed cautiously, since he couldn't come right out and accuse an English baron of murder without solid proof. In the British justice system, a nobleman was nearly inviolate. The privilege of peerage dictated that a lord must be tried by a jury of his peers. Thus, to be convicted required irrefutable evidence.

Still, he wished there were some means of persuading Antonia to postpone her betrothal announcement until he could be certain her life wasn't in danger. He would have to think of a way, Deverill told himself as he watched her cantering up ahead.

Admiring her straight back and elegant figure in her tailored riding habit of chocolate brown broadcloth, he held back until they reached the end of Rotten Row and then caught up with her as she drew her horse to a halt. From her bright eyes, he could tell her mood had lightened after all their talk of scruples and slavery, and he resolved to lighten it even further.

With a nod, Deverill indicated the grass field to their left. "Let's give our horses their heads. Your mare is itching for a run, and so are you."

Antonia glanced around them, probably to see who might be observing. The park was sparsely populated just now, with a few dozen riders and pedestrians and governesses supervising young children.

When she hesitated, Deverill pressed her. "Come, I dare you. A race to that stand of trees."

Antonia wrinkled her nose. "A lady does *not* race through the park like a hoyden," she intoned primly, as if quoting the mistresses of the elite academy she had attended, although Deverill heard a hint of wry amusement in her voice. "But I do admit you tempt me sorely."

"I will give you a head start if you are worried about being defeated."

A flash of defiance sparked in her blue eyes, and she replied to his insulting offer with disdain. "You are riding a hired hack, Mr. Deverill. My mare will leave you in the dust."

"You are welcome to prove it."

He saw the struggle on her face as she debated the wisdom of accepting his challenge, so to tip the scales, he tossed out another provoking remark. "Ah, I see. You fear what your betrothed will say if he hears of you acting like a hoyden."

Antonia's brows narrowed at that. "Lord Heward has nothing to say about how I conduct myself."

"You mean to claim that you are your own woman?"

"Precisely."

"Good. And if he objects to your immodest behavior, you can blame your corruption on me."

Glancing back at her groom, she asked him to wait there for her before nodding at Deverill. "Whenever you are ready, sir."

"Now," he said, spurring his horse forward.

Beside him, Antonia urged her eager mare into a gallop.

For a moment, the pounding hooves remained in rhythm, but then she bent low over her horse's neck and easily moved ahead of Deverill on his slower chestnut.

He heard the reckless joy in her laughter as the wind snatched it away, saw the exhilaration in every line of her body as she won by six lengths.

"That was glorious!" Antonia exclaimed with another exuberant laugh as she pulled up.

When he drew his own horse to a halt beside her, Deverill found his attention riveted on her. Her smile was dazzling, her ivory complexion flushed with exertion, as if she'd just indulged in a passionate bout of lovemaking. Her auburn hair, which was pinned in a sleek chignon beneath a plumed shako hat, had suffered from the gallop, so that flaming tendrils now spilled around her lovely face. But it was the excitement in her eyes that affected him most. The blue depths were filled with a brilliant vitality and warmth that called to the adventurer in him.

Deverill drew a sharp breath as a jolt of pure desire shot through him; he couldn't remember being this hard this swiftly.

Yet Antonia didn't seem in the least aware of her allure as she turned her mare to ride more sedately back the way they had come.

"Quitting so soon?" Deverill queried, wishing he could preserve the moment.

"Indeed, I am. I've indulged in more than enough immodest conduct for one morning."

"Not because you fear a rematch?"

Her eyes still bright with laughter, Antonia sent him an accusatory glance. "Oh, no, Mr. Deverill. I have your measure. And I refuse to let you provoke me into any further displays of wildness."

"I hardly provoked you," Deverill prevaricated.

"You did so. You lured me into behaving like a hoyden."

He returned a wicked grin. "Yes, but you enjoyed every moment of it, admit it."

She dimpled. "Perhaps. But I won't let it happen again. I intend to make a valiant effort to recoup a modicum of decorum."

"A pity," he said truthfully, his fingers tensing with the urge to drag Antonia off her horse and pull her beneath him.

Watching her glowing eyes and ripe mouth, he was hard-pressed not to act on his primal male urges. She was vibrant and intoxicatingly alive—he'd recognized that about Antonia from the first. She relished life, possibly as much as he did. He could no longer deny he wanted her in his bed.

He knew what her lovemaking would be like: eager and hot, passionate and wild. She would meet his every challenge with spirit and fire, retaliating with challenges of her own.

It was damned difficult to picture her wed to the suave, aristocratic, undoubtedly cold-blooded Baron Heward. Just the image made Deverill shudder.

In truth, he was growing more and more certain that Antonia, with her vitality and love of life, would not be happy in such a mismatched union, no matter that she'd convinced herself otherwise.

"You are making a damnable mistake, you know," he said into the silence.

"I beg your pardon?"

"By marrying Heward. He's entirely the wrong husband for you."

For a moment she just stared at Deverill speechlessly. Then her eyebrow arched coolly. "And what leads you to that opinion?"

"He's a cold fish, and you're a warm, vibrant gypsy at heart."

Her eyes widening at his audacity, she pressed her lips together briefly before she carefully formed a reply. "Lord Heward is handsome, witty, intelligent, wealthy, titled . . . as well as being my father's choice for me. What more could a lady wish for in a husband?"

Deverill's voice was dry when he replied. "Integrity, honor, honesty, perhaps?"

He could see the annoyance flash in Antonia's eyes. "I'll thank you to refrain from making unfounded accusations out of pique. Just because you dislike Heward is no reason to impugn his honor."

Deverill drew a long breath, striving for patience. "I don't blame you for wanting a title, a place in society—especially when it's what your father wished for you. But surely there are other noblemen eager to win your hand."

"Oh, dozens," Antonia said, her tone a touch sardonic. "All more interested in my fortune than in me."

He resisted pointing out that Heward was after the same thing. "I'm sure Heward is the very paragon of desirable manhood, but I think you should find another candidate for your husband," Deverill said instead.

"But I don't *want* any other husband."

"Then at least postpone your nuptials until you have a chance to determine Heward's complicity in the slavery scheme."

Antonia shook her head adamantly. "Since I don't believe there *is* any complicity on his part, I have no intention of postponing our nuptials. We have deferred more than a year, as is. My father was eager for me to wed Lord Heward, and I intend to honor his wishes without further delay. Now, pray be kind enough to spare me any more displays of your appalling manners, Mr. Deverill, and mind your own affairs."

Deverill felt his jaw clench at her icy dismissal, but with great effort, he bit his tongue. There was no point in antagonizing Antonia even more. He would simply have to find another way to persuade her to break off her betrothal to Heward. From now on, he would seek out opportunities to show her how insufferably boring and dull the very proper baron would prove to a woman of her spirited nature.

In any event, the opportunity for further intimate conversation was thwarted when they encountered her waiting groom, for Antonia brought her mount alongside the servant's and remained close as they rode toward the park gates.

"You needn't escort me home," she told Deverill once they had left the premises.

"But I must," he replied evenly. "It is impolite for a gentleman to abandon a lady before their outing is properly ended."

Now he professed to be a gentleman? Antonia thought, torn between vexation and exasperation.

She maintained a stiff silence all the way back to her house, much of that time reproving herself for losing her composure. She had resolved to treat Deverill with cool aplomb, but she hadn't accounted for his deliberate provocations or his uncanny talent for getting under her skin.

Or her own deplorable inability to resist him.

It was shameful, how strongly she was drawn to him. The boldness in his glance, his tantalizing smile, combined with his blatant sexual magnetism managed to scatter her wits and weaken her limbs, while his provocative challenges only brought out the reckless, daring side of her nature, the one she usually strove to keep hidden.

She was glad when at last they reached Maitland House and halted in the drive. Ignoring her groom, however, Deverill swung down from his horse and came around to her side. Antonia tensed, realizing he intended to help her dismount.

"Are you afraid of me, princess?" he asked when she hesitated, his tone amused.

It was another obvious challenge, yet she couldn't

stop herself from taking the bait. Her chin rose. "Hardly. I simply don't trust that your manners have undergone any miraculous transformation in the past ten minutes."

"I can be civilized when the need suits me," Deverill drawled. "Now, come here."

Still wary, she reached out to place her hands on his broad shoulders. Catching her waist in his hands then, he lifted her down.

She had been right to distrust him, Antonia realized as he set her on her feet. For the span of several heartbeats, he stood holding her much too close for comfort. Their bodies brushed in the barest contact, but the effect was searing.

Antonia froze, the thrill of excitement skimming her nerves. He was all honed muscle and lithe strength, she could feel him through all their layers of clothing. Yet the intensity of her body's reaction dismayed her more. The coiling sensation she felt in her breasts and stomach and loins was the same sweet, aching frustration that tormented her in her dreams.

And even knowing his action was deliberate, she could not have moved if her life depended on it.

Then Deverill reached up and tucked a strand of hair behind her ear, his touch oddly intimate. "Until next time," he said, the shallow grooves in his cheeks deepening with his soft smile.

A warm weakness broke loose in her chest, but Antonia fought it, knowing he delighted in keeping her off guard. "There won't be any next time," she said firmly.

His smile was wicked and utterly confident. "I assure you there will be."

Lord, was he dangerous, she thought, finally finding the willpower to step back.

Quickly turning, Antonia ran up the steps, seeking refuge in the safety of her house. But she knew with utter certainty that she wouldn't be truly safe from Deverill as long as he was anywhere within a hundred leagues of her.

Three

After her discomfiting ride with Deverill, Antonia was especially nice to Lord Heward when he called that afternoon to escort her to the lending library—possibly because she felt the need to atone for her disloyal fascination for a provoking adventurer. Yet as she strolled beside the handsome baron, she couldn't help comparing the two men and her reaction to each.

Unlike Deverill, James Heward went out of his way to charm her. Certainly Heward was the more polished and refined, with his pale blond hair and aristocratic features and unmistakable air of elegance. But she had never pictured his lordship naked as she regularly did Deverill, never imagined him touching her or making passionate love to her.

It was curious that she'd never felt anything remotely resembling a fierce attraction for her intended husband. Nor did Heward rouse in her even a hint of the forbidden longing she experienced in all her wicked dreams of Deverill.

But real life had nothing to do with dreams, Antonia reminded herself. And attraction and passion were not necessary to a good marriage.

Furthermore, Heward had one major advantage over all her other suitors: He could keep her father's legacy alive. For three decades, Maitland Shipping had built the swiftest, most reliable ships in the world, and would continue to do so under Heward's guidance. She was grateful to have him.

She rarely intruded in the operation of the company, since she had no experience, and since mariners in particular were adamantly averse to having females give them orders. But she intended to resolve Deverill's charge that his American cousin's ships had been illegally confiscated, which meant bringing up Deverill's claim to Lord Heward.

She waited until they had returned to Maitland House and were taking tea in the parlor before asking her betrothed what he knew about the matter.

Heward's blue eyes narrowed as he surveyed her. "When did you speak to Deverill about this? Last night at the ball?"

"I encountered him on my ride in the park this morning," Antonia fudged.

His frown deepened. "You should not be associating with men of his ilk, my love. His character is not at all seemly. It is bad enough that he approached you last night."

Antonia stiffened a little, not caring for Heward's disapproving tone or his presumption that he could dictate whom she should or should not associate with. With effort, she kept her own tone even when she replied, "Deverill was a friend of my father's, and I am certain Papa would not want me snubbing him."

Seeing her displeasure, the baron instantly softened and offered a charming smile. "Forgive me, my dear. I confess I am a trifle jealous of Deverill's interest in you. He has a devilish reputation with the ladies."

"Last night he was merely paying his respects to me," Antonia said, mollified by her betrothed's graciousness. "And this morning he wished to discuss his cousin's business. Is it true that Mr. Trant ordered those ships confiscated?"

Heward's grimace held a measure of distaste. "It is true the vessels were confiscated, but the act was entirely justified."

"How so?"

"It was war, my dear," he said firmly. "Deverill's American cousin was a violent privateer, destroying British merchant ships and harassing our naval vessels. He was an enemy of our country. But I suppose Mr. Deverill neglected to mention that minor detail."

He had indeed failed to disclose that his cousin was a privateer, Antonia reflected. But she wasn't certain it mattered now that the war was over.

At her hesitation, Heward smiled a bit smugly. "So you see, Mr. Deverill has no right to demand his cousin's ships be returned."

"His cousin paid for them, did he not? Seventy percent upon commissioning?"

"I believe those were the terms."

"Then he is the rightful owner. I would like those ships delivered to Mr. Brandon Deverill. Either that, or he should be reimbursed for the sums he expended."

"But my dear, you really should leave this to me—"

Antonia looked at Heward with a cool eye. "I am not empty-headed or slow-witted, my lord. Just inexperienced. But fairness was always a prime tenet of my father's, and I mean to see that it continues. Of course, I can always have Phineas settle the issue, if you aren't willing to act for me."

Heward's smile was pained. "That won't be necessary. I will look into the matter."

"Good, since Deverill says his cousin will seek restitution in the courts if we cannot come to an amicable agreement."

She could see the flash of ire in Heward's eyes as he struggled to restrain a sardonic comment. But then the expression on his face smoothed out. "Whatever you wish, my dear." Reaching across the tea table for her hand, he raised her fingers to his lips in a tender gesture. "I don't want you angry with me."

Relenting, Antonia promised that she wasn't angry with him, that she was only concerned about acting as her father would have wanted. As she poured the baron another cup of tea, she couldn't help but note another difference between him and Deverill: She knew how to manage Lord Heward, while she could barely hold her own with Deverill.

Of course, her betrothed was desirous of keeping on her good side because of her fortune, she knew very well. But she couldn't imagine Deverill bowing to her wishes simply because she commanded enormous wealth. In fact, just the opposite was doubtless true. Deverill was unlikely to toady to her or to anyone else.

It was another ten minutes before Heward took his leave, saying he would call for her at eight that evening to escort her to the Ranworth soiree.

As soon as he had gone, Antonia went to her writing desk and penned a note to her trustee, Phineas Cochrane, asking him to call on her tomorrow morning if possible. She could go to his offices in the City, but she would rather not let Lord Heward know she was making a formal visit to her barrister.

That same niggling uneasiness had kept her from

confronting Heward about the charge of transporting slaves, for fear he would deny it or possibly even alert Director Trant. But she had every intention of having her trustee review the account books of Maitland Shipping and quietly investigate Deverill's allegation.

When she had sent a footman to deliver her message, Antonia rang for Mrs. Peeke, determined to satisfy her burning curiosity about another subject.

"I did not realize you were well acquainted with Mr. Deverill," she said when the housekeeper arrived.

At the remark, the elderly ruddy-cheeked woman looked a bit flustered. "Truth tell, it was my late husband who was closer."

"Deverill mentioned that he once did a service for Mr. Peeke."

"Yes. 'Twas a long time ago, but he saved my Rob from a press gang. Rob had left a tavern by the docks when he was set upon. It would have been the death of him, to be forced to serve on a navy warship at his age."

"It seems Deverill is quite the hero," Antonia prodded casually, hoping for a more detailed reply.

Mrs. Peeke nodded with enthusiasm. "Indeed. My Rob owed his life to him—as do any number of people."

"No doubt Deverill's recollections make for some exciting tales."

"Exciting, yes, but Mr. Deverill never talks about himself. However, I heard plenty of tales from my Rob before he passed away. Now Mr. Deverill calls on me whenever he comes to London, to make certain I'm faring well and to bring me a present from whatever country he's last visited." Her eyes twinkled. "Of course, he's right fond of my ginger biscuits, so that possibly has something to do with his interest—" The housekeeper suddenly looked worried. "I hope you don't mind that he visits here, Miss Antonia."

"No, of course I don't mind," Antonia said, although the thought of Deverill being in her house without her knowledge was a little unsettling. But Mrs. Peeke had her own rooms near the kitchens and could entertain anyone she liked. "I am curious, though. Do you know how Deverill came by his scars?"

"Scars?" the housekeeper repeated in obvious puzzlement.

Antonia mentally berated herself for the slip, realizing she was never supposed to have seen Deverill's naked body. "Never mind."

But Mrs. Peeke's perplexity cleared. "If he has scars, no doubt they're from when he was tortured by those heathen Turks. Rob heard about it from one of Mr. Deverill's crew who survived."

"Survived?" Antonia asked, wildly curious now.

"Supposedly they were held captive and tortured by a band of vicious pirates. Mr. Deverill eventually managed to lead an escape, but not before nearly half his men had died."

Antonia's brows drew together in a frown as she recalled what Deverill had once said to her, his tone dry yet inflected with a serious note: *Fighting pirates is not all it's cracked up to be, Miss Maitland.* Antonia winced at the memory. How naive could she have been, thinking it would be exciting to battle corsairs as Deverill did, when doubtless his profession was often treacherous and sometimes deadly? She was ashamed now that she had ever entertained such absurd notions.

"Thank you, Mrs. Peeke," she said finally. "The next time Mr. Deverill calls, you should bake him an entire ovenful of ginger biscuits. I'm certain he deserves it."

"That he does," the housekeeper said fervently, before clearing the tea tray away and leaving Antonia to her dark musings about the horrors Deverill might have suffered during his career as an adventurer.

Not liking her thoughts, Antonia rose from the settee and went to stand at the parlor window. Yet the bright sunshine outside only temporarily lifted her spirits. The mansion that Samuel Maitland had built for his highborn wife in Chesham Place seemed oppressively quiet, Antonia thought sadly, without her father's booming voice and larger-than-life personality to fill it. His death had left the huge house empty except for herself and a legion of servants.

Miss Mildred Tottle, Antonia's companion and nominal chaperone, was out for the afternoon, visiting an ill friend in Chelsea. Mildred was rather flighty and scatterbrained, and spent much of the day napping and reading gothic novels and eating sweetmeats, but the two of them genuinely enjoyed each other's company. Mildred had been a godsend for Antonia after losing her father so tragically and unexpectedly.

Feeling suddenly restless, Antonia made her way upstairs to the gallery where her parents' portraits hung. She finally understood why her father had regularly communed with her mother's image, for she felt closer to him when she gazed upon his beloved face.

"How I miss you, Papa," she murmured, staring up at his portrait.

She would have given anything to have him back.

But the remembrance of her grief didn't wholly explain the vague discontent she felt now. Perhaps it was her dissension with Lord Heward that had her blue-deviled. Or perhaps it was Deverill's earlier, unwanted observation: *Heward is entirely the wrong husband for you.*

Antonia muttered a mild imprecation, vexed with Deverill for his presumptuous interference. More likely, though, her dissatisfaction was merely the last vestiges of a foolish rebellion against the lack of choices in her life. Ladies did not become adventurers who sailed the seas performing daring deeds to save the world, as Deverill did. Ladies did not realize great achievements that impacted the future of mankind, as her father had done.

True ladies did not dream of finding heart-stirring, breath-stealing passion, the kind that touched the soul.

Even heiresses with the means to live independent lives had little real freedom. Unless she wished to remain a spinster or become a byword for scandal, marriage was the only path open to her. And marriage to a cultured nobleman like Baron Heward would greatly diminish the taint of her common, merchant-class origins.

Before his death, her father had been fully supportive of her betrothal to Heward, indeed proud of her, for he loved her dearly and wanted to see her respected and admired instead of shunned by society as her mother had been after their marriage.

If Antonia ever considered truly rebelling and embarking on a fate of her own choosing, she had only to summon one bitterly poignant memory of her father, here in the gallery when she could not have been more than ten years old.

She had come upon him sitting alone, sobbing. The devastation she'd seen upon his face had wrenched her heart. When she'd fearfully asked him what was the matter—if he was going to die like Mama had—Samuel tried to smile as he wiped tears from his eyes and drew her down onto his lap.

"No, I am not going to die, puss. The truth is, it near kills me to think how I hurt your mama." He glanced up at the portrait of Mary Maitland. "She swore she never blamed me, but I know the sacrifices she made to wed me, spurned by all her hoity-toity friends. I can't forgive myself for that."

Only when Antonia was older, however, did she truly comprehend the depth of his guilt. As a Cit, Samuel had attempted to buy respectability by wedding an impoverished nobleman's daughter, but although they came to love each other deeply, his greatest regret was that his wife was repudiated socially for marrying him. He wanted much better for his daughter.

"But you'll make a grand marriage," he'd told her that day. "Promise me, 'Tonia. I can't bear to think of you suffering because of me."

Antonia had solemnly promised.

If in later years she'd secretly dreamed of loving a husband who loved her in return, of finding the remarkable love and devotion her parents had found, she had willingly relinquished such ideal notions for her father's sake. It was a small price to pay after all his devotion to her, the sacrifices he himself had made for her—giving up all his former friends, his own joy in life—to gain respectability for her. His fierce effort to ensure she had the education and refinement to land an aristocratic husband had driven him until the day he died.

And in truth, she'd never met any man who had remotely tempted her to forsake her sworn promise to marry for duty instead of love. If she had ever met such a man . . . But it was pointless to speculate. Even though her father was no longer here, Antonia reflected, she wouldn't destroy his dream for her. The remorse of knowing how she'd disappointed him would be too much to bear.

In any event, she was quite happy to wed Lord Heward. And she refused to allow the uninvited, uninformed comments of a rogue like Trey Deverill to raise doubts in her mind.

Her blue mood carried over to the soiree that evening—a very proper affair hosted by the Earl and Countess of Ranworth. Yet a half hour later, Antonia was taken aback to see Deverill stroll into the stately drawing room.

With his height and powerful build, he managed to dominate the sea of people and to make every female head turn. It frankly amazed her, however, to see not only Lord Ranworth greeting Deverill with warmth, but the cold, formidable Lady Ranworth unbending her reserve enough to bestow a smile on the interloper. The countess was a stickler for propriety, and welcoming a notorious pirate-fighter into their elite midst was wholly unexpected.

Also unexpected, Antonia realized, was how suddenly her spirits had lightened. She promptly scolded herself. She had wanted something to enliven a dull evening, yet she suspected Deverill's presence would be proof of the adage "Take care what you wish for," for he was moving directly her way.

Beside her, Lord Heward had stiffened. Antonia

held her breath as, with a bland smile, Deverill bowed politely before them.

It surprised her that during an exchange of pleasantries, his gaze was cool and impersonal. And when their eyes met, not by a flicker did he betray the heat that had arced between them this morning. Antonia felt almost . . . disappointed.

Her betrothed did not seem particularly happy, either, especially when Deverill brought up a more personal subject.

"Lord Heward," he remarked, "what a surprise to discover you playing such a prominent role in Maitland Shipping. Miss Maitland informs me that you have been of invaluable help to her."

"I do what I can," Heward replied, his chill reserve obvious—in part, Antonia knew, because he preferred not to have his involvement in trade broadcast to the world.

The baron practically gnashed his teeth when Deverill asked to be introduced to the other guests who were standing in their group, since short of cutting him directly, Heward was forced to acquiesce.

No doubt Deverill was making a deliberate effort to provoke him, Antonia surmised, and his drawled observation a moment later confirmed it. The conversation oddly had turned to a discussion of gentleman's attire, comparing the best tailors and bootmakers in London.

"I commend *your* tailor, your lordship," Deverill said, a lazy, mocking gleam in his eyes as he pointedly studied Heward's evening coat made by Weston. "You put us to shame with your sartorial elegance. And you tie your cravat with such devilish skill . . . I confess I am envious."

For Heward's sake, she was glad when Deverill finally excused himself to mingle with the other guests at the assemblage.

He proved remarkably popular. During the next hour, Antonia couldn't help but notice how the ladies fluttered their eyelashes at the tall, ruggedly handsome newcomer. And the gentlemen, rather than turn away, actually seemed to hang on Deverill's every word.

Yet it was absurd that when he eventually took his leave, the sparkle seemed to fade from Antonia's evening.

To her further dismay, that same pattern was repeated often in the succeeding week. Deverill appeared at many of the same social functions she attended—first at Drury Lane Theatre, then a musicale, then a rout party, and finally another ball.

His behavior toward her was everything that was proper, but the frequency of their meetings began to seem more than mere coincidence; they were downright suspicious.

Even her friend Emily noticed. "I wonder if Mr. Deverill is making an effort to turn respectable," Emily said as they stood watching him a short distance across the ballroom.

Antonia gave an unladylike scoff of amusement. "Deverill? I hardly think so. A black sheep doesn't readily change his hue."

Emily turned curious brown eyes on Antonia. "Then perhaps *you* are what draws him. He seems very interested in you, dearest. If I didn't know better, I would say he might even be courting you."

"He knows I am betrothed to Heward."

"Not officially. Not until next month. So until then, you are fair game."

Antonia shook her head. If Deverill *was* pursuing her, she was certain it was only because he was trying to come between her and Lord Heward.

And at the moment Deverill wasn't showing her any interest at all. Instead he was being fawned over by a half-dozen young ladies who were gazing up at him adoringly, obviously hoping to be chosen for his dance partner. But then, Antonia was well aware, the dangerous edge of his appeal was enough to make most women go weak in the knees. It simply annoyed her that *she* could be counted among their number.

It disturbed her more that Deverill might deliberately try to ruin her brilliant match. And as she stood watching him, she silently vowed to withstand any efforts he made to break up her betrothal, and almost as importantly, to resist being bowled over by his powerful personality.

Her resolve was tested within the hour, for he approached her just as she finished a set of country dances with Lord Heward.

Heward had rarely left her side all evening, as if he was keeping guard on her. And when Deverill asked his permission to waltz with her, the baron firmly refused.

"I hardly think it good for Miss Maitland's reputation to be seen standing up with you, Deverill," his lordship observed. "Particularly the waltz."

Antonia felt herself stiffen. Given the chance, she would have refused Deverill's offer on her own, but her betrothed's proprietary air was beginning to fray her nerves.

She smiled sweetly at Heward, even as she placed

her hand on Deverill's arm. "I believe my reputation can withstand a simple waltz," she said, before allowing Deverill to lead her onto the floor.

He evidently noticed the tightness of her jaw, for the corner of his mouth crooked with satisfaction. "I didn't think you would take kindly to Heward ordering you about."

Antonia kept her glance cool as she looked up at Deverill. "I don't take kindly to your effrontery, either. You are deliberately attempting to provoke him."

"How did I provoke him?" he asked, all innocence. "My request to dance with you was perfectly unexceptional. Any number of ladies have stood up with me this evening."

"Perhaps because they mistake you for a gentleman."

Deverill's eyes glinted with amusement. "Not everyone has your discernment, love."

Trying not to respond to that appealing gleam, she glanced around them to see that, once again, they were the focus of intense curiosity. Wincing inwardly, she returned her attention to Deverill. "You seem to be developing the annoying habit of appearing uninvited everywhere I turn."

"But I *have* been invited. Believe it or not, I've been inundated with invitations since my return to London."

"I suppose hostesses do enjoy having you for the novel value," Antonia remarked. "That, and to partner the wallflowers at their balls."

"Not only the wallflowers." The mocking deviltry was back in his eyes. "I am considered fairly eligible, you know."

She did know. Deverill came from an excellent family, despite his long-term quarrel with them, and the size of his fortune would make him a matrimonial prize, no matter his lack of title or his questionable reputation.

The music began then, so Antonia was required to wait until they were settled into the rhythm of the waltz before speaking again. "I see why you would be invited everywhere. What I don't understand is why you accept. You told me you don't care for London society."

"I don't. The shallowness grates on me. My family gave me an aversion to superficiality and pretentiousness at an early age. Actually, I much prefer the American perspective, where a man's worth is not measured by his origins or his rank in the peerage." He paused, then said pointedly, "Your father was a prime example of that."

Antonia wrinkled her nose at him, knowing it was a jab at her determination to wed a nobleman. "Yet you seem to be on excellent terms with Lord Ranworth."

"Ranworth is a man of substance, despite his title."

"How do you know the earl?"

"I performed a service for him once."

She raised an eyebrow, remembering Deverill saying the same thing about her housekeeper. "Did you save his life, perhaps?"

"Nothing so exciting. Ranworth is a heavy investor in the East India Company. He petitioned the Company to commission my services this past year, to protect their valuable convoys of merchant ships from a resurgence of piracy."

"Mrs. Peeke told me how you saved her husband from a press gang."

Deverill leveled a disapproving look at her. "I never would have credited Mrs. Peeke with having a loose tongue."

"I persuaded her to tell me. She also said that you are a hero, that you have saved countless more lives from corsairs over the years. I wondered if that is how you came by your—" Antonia broke off abruptly, realizing how insensitive her curiosity was.

"Wondered what?" Deverill pressed.

"Never mind. I should not have mentioned it."

"Come now, Miss Maitland, are you turning missish on me?"

"Very well, then, I wondered about your scars. Mrs. Peeke said you were captured by vicious Turkish corsairs and they . . . hurt you."

Antonia felt the abrupt tightening of Deverill's grip around her hand, while a sudden darkening of his eyes further betrayed him. For an instant, she glimpsed the unmistakable flash of devastation in the green depths.

Then just as swiftly, Deverill's expression turned impassive. "You are damned inquisitive about something that is none of your affair, Miss Maitland."

Antonia remained silent. She had finally found the means to get the upper hand with Deverill, yet she didn't like to use it. Not when it was so obvious that the subject caused him great anguish.

"You are right," she finally said. "Your past is none of my affair. Just as whom I marry is none of *your* affair."

That made his eyes kindle. "On the contrary, it *is* my affair. I am making it so. I respected your father too much to let you throw your life away on a man of Heward's ilk."

"But then," Antonia retorted archly, "you are

hardly an expert on happiness in marriage. If I recall, you intend to remain a confirmed bachelor."

He smiled back at her with lazy, mocking eyes. "True."

"I knew it!" she exclaimed. "Emily thinks you are courting me, but I was certain you intended nothing of the kind."

The slash of dark eyebrows lifted. "No, I am not courting you, sweeting. Until recently I never even thought of you as a woman."

"Thank you very much," she said wryly.

Deverill's grin was very male. "What I meant was, four years ago you were far too young for me. And now . . . your father would turn over in his grave if he thought I was making a bid for your hand."

"Then why do you appear to be following me? You mean to break up my betrothal, don't you?"

"I admit I want to sway your opinion of Heward. To make you comprehend that you're making a grave mistake. You're an intelligent woman, Antonia. You should be able to see how badly you are deluding yourself. Heward isn't worthy of you. And he isn't being honest if he claims he doesn't want you for your inheritance."

She pressed her lips together, striving for control. "Speaking of honesty, I believe you failed to mention that your cousin was a privateer in the recent war."

Deverill's gaze narrowed. "How does that matter? Brand spent the war running the British blockade—which, I might add, practically bankrupted the American shipping industry—protecting his own and other American ships. His actions were fully sanctioned by the American government. And his privateering doesn't change the fact that his ships were illegally confiscated by your director."

"I agree, which is why I asked Heward to see that they are turned over to your cousin."

"And your account books?" Deverill asked probingly.

"I've spoken to Phineas Cochrane, and he has agreed to review them."

"You didn't mention your concern about running slaves to Heward?"

Inwardly Antonia squirmed uncomfortably, knowing she was being disloyal to Heward by not trusting him. "No, I didn't mention it. I am certain he will be vindicated, but you will only believe his innocence if it's proven by an impartial observer."

When Deverill didn't reply, she realized he was unlikely to ever believe in her betrothed's innocence.

They both fell silent. And when the waltz ended, both left unsatisfied with the conversation—Deverill more so.

He had made little progress, he was aware, in raising doubts in Antonia's mind about her betrothed. With her advantages of beauty and fortune, she could have any man she wanted. It didn't have to be Heward. There were far better candidates, Deverill was convinced.

He himself certainly didn't fit the bill, with his lack of title and his notoriety. And marriage of any kind was not in his plans.

He had a seaman's need for freedom, an explorer's sense of wanderlust, a Guardian's claim to duty. And his own, deeply personal mission that required his complete devotion; a sworn vow that could not be fulfilled by half measures.

There was simply no place in his life for entanglements. He couldn't afford to be shackled by the demands of a wife. In truth, the last thing he wanted was to settle down tamely with a proper, genteel lady who would need to be handled like fine porcelain and who would reluctantly perform her duties in a passionless marriage bed.

Antonia would be different, he expected, but that hardly mattered. He had dedicated his life to the Guardians, and his responsibilities would keep him far from England. And she, of course, must marry a nobleman.

That didn't prevent him from craving her, though, nor did it ease the fierce stab of desire he felt every time he saw her. He wanted her, in spite of everything. When she turned that cool, disdainful expression on him, he longed to give in to his primal urges, to turn her pretense of ice to fire.

Acting on his urges was out of the question, Deverill sternly reminded himself. He couldn't have Antonia. But he damned sure wouldn't let Heward have her, either.

This past week he'd had his own people investigating the baron, asking questions of servants and employees and business acquaintances. And he'd solicited the help of three other Guardians in London, all peers of Heward's, to subtly interrogate his lordship's friends.

What he'd discovered thus far was highly disturbing. On the surface, Heward appeared the picture of refined elegance and suave charm, but that charm was apparently deceptive, for it concealed a vicious temperament and a proclivity for brutality.

Deverill had already personally seen one instance of it several years ago, against a beggar lad, but now he'd begun hearing tales of Heward's cruelty to his servants, as well as several even more unsavory allegations about his dealings with the lightskirts he patronized.

Where once Deverill had wanted to make Antonia see how boring and stuffy and pretentious a husband Heward would make her, he was now determined to show her the baron's dark side. If Heward could be provoked into losing his temper in front of her, his display of rage would at least raise suspicions in her mind about his true nature.

Eventually, Deverill swore, he would succeed in his goal. He was more resolved than ever to pry her away from Heward.

He had to be clever how he went about it, though. Antonia would have to decide on her own to break their betrothal. He couldn't push her. She was just stubborn enough to dig in her heels and do the opposite of what she was being pressed to do. But he had no intention of giving up.

If necessary, he would find her another noble husband, Deverill thought without enthusiasm, even with distaste.

His next opportunity would come the day after tomorrow at a Venetian breakfast. Mrs. Peeke kept him informed of Antonia's social plans. The only difficulty was securing his own invitations from the hosts after so many years of shunning London's Beau Monde.

For this particular event, Deverill easily managed to secure an invitation, since it was hosted by the Duke of Redcliffe. The duke's only son, Viscount Thorne, was a close friend of Deverill's, as well as a fellow Guardian. At the moment, Thorne was still on the Isle of Cyrene with his brand-new bride, Diana, no doubt enjoying the start of their blissful union.

A Venetian breakfast was misnamed, since it was actually an afternoon feast in the open air, and Deverill was only one of nearly four hundred guests in attendance. The duke had somehow arranged a perfect summer afternoon at his palatial estate in Wandsworth on the Thames River, and even Deverill was impressed by the spectacle that boasted myriad sounds and colors and scents.

Three huge marquees, erected on the rear lawn in view of the river, bustled with an army of servants preparing a banquet fit for royalty. An orchestra played to one side, while ladies dressed in pastel muslin and sarcenet, gentlemen in tailored coats and pantaloons, strolled though the gardens and wandered out under the trees, listening to the music, sipping refreshing fruit punches, and nibbling on ices.

And after the guests had feasted, the company turned to various games provided for their entertainment—bowling and cricket and Pall Mall, and for the more experienced competitors, an archery competition.

It didn't surprise Deverill in the least to find Antonia participating in the contest, and he eagerly took up a position beneath an alder tree to watch.

She made a fetching sight. She wore a high-waisted, short-sleeved lavender gown of Swiss muslin that showed her tall, elegant figure to advantage, while her dark-flame hair had been tamed in a chignon beneath a low-crowned bonnet.

A half-dozen gentlemen and several ladies were competing with her, and a score of spectators had congregated beside the range to observe, Lord Heward included. Deverill also recognized a small, bespectacled, silver-haired lady as Antonia's companion, Miss Mildred Tottle. Antonia's close friend, Emily, Lady Sudbury, was there as well to cheer her on.

Deverill remembered Antonia saying that archery was her chief talent and one of the few sports allowed women, and her incredible skill was apparent from her first shot. Arrow after arrow found the bull's-eye a hundred yards away.

Deverill thought her performance amazing. What struck him most, however, was her fierce concentration and her quiet delight each time her aim struck true.

This, he knew, was the genuine Antonia Maitland displaying her true colors—her obvious joy in life, her enthusiasm, her competitive spirit. Deverill felt his jaw tighten. The devious, savage-tempered Lord Heward bloody well didn't deserve her.

The competition really was no contest. Antonia won handily, to fond applause from the audience. As she accepted her prize of a silver cup, Deverill stepped forward, determined to make his point.

Seeing him approach, Antonia felt her stomach leap. She had been keenly aware of Deverill all afternoon, first because he was the center of female attention, which absurdly roused pangs of jealousy in her breast. Then because for the past half hour, he'd lounged a shoulder carelessly against a tree trunk as he watched her win the competition.

He wore a faint smile on his face now as he congratulated her on her impressive victory.

"I had plenty of time to practice during the year I was in mourning," Antonia answered honestly, "since I could not go out in society."

"Of course," Deverill commented, "a straw target is not much sport. In former eras, the aim of archery was to defeat enemies in battle or to bring down live game. It would prove more challenging if you had to deal with an animate target."

Antonia eyed him with puzzlement. "What are you suggesting?"

"I'm proposing a further test of your skill."

"A test?"

Many of the guests had begun to stroll back to the tents, Antonia saw, but Lord Heward, Mildred Tottle, and Emily remained. All three of them turned to look at Deverill, Heward's expression the least amicable.

"I'll wager that you couldn't hit the hat off a man's head," Deverill asserted. "Say, Lord Heward's head?"

The baron's countenance immediately darkened to a frown, but Antonia kept her tone light when she replied. "I expect I could, but I would never risk ruining his lordship's expensive hat."

Deverill's amused glance skimmed over the baron's stiff form. "In any case, I doubt his lordship would agree to be your target. He would think it too dangerous."

Was he trying to make Heward appear a coward, Antonia wondered, or simply to get under the baron's skin?

Either way, Heward went rigid. "Don't be absurd, Deverill. I am not afraid. I simply don't choose to make a spectacle of myself or Miss Maitland."

"Or is it because you have so little faith in her abilities?"

Stiffening herself, Antonia came to her betrothed's defense. "If you care to volunteer as the target, Mr. Deverill, I might consider shooting at you."

A lazy smile touched Deverill's lips. "I would be happy to oblige."

Realizing it had been his goal all along to provoke her into accepting his dare, Antonia hesitated.

"Come now, Miss Maitland, where is your sense of adventure?" His smile was charming, his gaze wicked. "It should be easy for an Amazon princess to shoot a hat."

That did it! Antonia rose to his bait; she couldn't help herself. "Very well, I accept your challenge," she declared, flashing him a taunting half smile of her own.

She heard the gasps and titters from the audience that still lingered. Beside her, Emily clapped a hand over her mouth to stop a chortle of shocked mirth.

Ignoring the reactions, Antonia handed her silver cup to her friend, then returned to the shooters' table, where her bow rested.

Miss Tottle's slender hands fluttered nervously in the air. "Should you, my dear? You might k-kill him."

Perhaps she shouldn't, Antonia reflected. It was foolish, mad even, but if Deverill was daring enough to risk his life at her hands, she wasn't going to gainsay him.

"My dear," Heward interjected, his tone sharp, "this is not wise." Moving to stand beside her, Heward leaned close and lowered his voice. "I forbid you to make a spectacle of yourself in this demeaning manner."

At his tone, Antonia sent him a chill smile, but Deverill drawled before she could reply. "Perhaps you *should* reconsider, Miss Maitland, since his lordship obviously doesn't approve."

He was prodding Heward even more than he was

testing her mettle, Antonia knew, but her temper had been inflamed by Heward's command. It was not his place to forbid her to do anything.

Pressing her own lips together, she began untying the ribbons of her bonnet. "You are not wearing a hat, Mr. Deverill, but I am willing to sacrifice mine this once. Come here, if you please."

When he obliged, albeit warily, she reached up to perch her bonnet on top of his head.

The frilly confection looked absurd on him, and the appreciative gleam in Deverill's eye told her he knew it. She had managed to get a little of her own back at him, Antonia was pleased to note.

Beside her, Heward stood stiffly, anger in every line of his body, but she ignored him and instead pointed at one of the alders that lined the bank of the Thames. "Pray, go stand in front of that tree. I don't want my bonnet to go flying into the river. The trim can probably be saved if I hit the crown."

She waited while Deverill did as she bid. Walking over to the tree some thirty yards away, he turned and casually leaned back against the trunk, crossing his arms over his broad chest, his stance one of supreme confidence. "Whenever you are ready, Miss Maitland."

Antonia picked up her bow and nocked an arrow.

"Antonia?" Miss Tottle repeated weakly.

"Don't worry. I won't miss at this distance."

She wouldn't miss; she couldn't. She couldn't imagine hurting the beautiful, rugged, provoking devil who stood gazing steadily back at her with amusement and challenge and—she had to admit—complete trust.

Antonia inhaled a slow breath and raised the bow.

It was not her own weapon, but the feel was similar, and the draw was nearly the same strength.

Deverill was right, though. Shooting at a live mark was far different from shooting a straw target. Her palms were damp, her nerves a little shaky. But she knew her fortitude would only lessen the longer she waited.

Her heart pounding, she took aim and let the arrow fly.

Four

The arrow struck true, spitting the crown precisely in the center.

"A pity," Antonia mused, hiding her fervent relief. "I was rather partial to that bonnet."

Deverill laughed outright. Stepping away, he pulled the arrow from the tree trunk and disentangled the disfigured bonnet, then returned both to her with a gallant bow. When he flashed her a hot, easy smile, Antonia caught the deadly glance Heward sent him. If looks were arrows, Deverill would have been instantly skewered.

Heward was still furious at her as well, she realized as she tied the ribbons around her throat and let the ruined bonnet hang down her back.

When she was done, his lordship took her elbow and turned her toward the manor house. "I will escort you home now, my dear."

His grip was actually painful. Flinching, Antonia pulled her arm away. "I think not, my lord. If you wish to leave just now, I will have Lord and Lady Sudbury take me home."

Lowering his voice, he said through gritted teeth, "I insist you oblige me in this, Antonia."

She shook her head. It was wiser to let the baron's temper cool, not to mention she had no desire to suffer a scolding from him, which he was clearly set on delivering just as soon as he could speak privately. "I'm certain Miss Tottle is not ready to abandon the festivities just yet."

Heward stared at Antonia, a muscle working in his jaw as he struggled for self-control. "Very well," he ground out finally, before spinning on his heel and stalking away.

She watched him go, fury seething from him. Then she noticed the shocked and disapproving glances from her audience.

Their censure, Antonia suspected, was not so much because she had accepted a bold dare and shot a hat off a man's head, or even because she'd engaged in a lover's quarrel in public, but because she had defied Lord Heward in a very unladylike manner and made him appear impotent.

Embarrassment singed Antonia's cheeks. She regretted her behavior already. Heward was a proud man and would hate to seem weak—which probably had been Deverill's purpose all along.

She glanced up at Deverill, who was watching her intently. Meeting his unsettling gaze, Antonia grimaced, vexed at both him and at herself. He had managed to goad her into a dispute with her betrothed, but she had allowed it. She had to admire Deverill's methods, though, for they were quite effective.

"I must congratulate you," she said sardonically. "It seems you won that round."

From the wicked gleam in his eyes, he knew exactly what she meant. "But not the battle."

"No, and you won't, either."

"We shall see."

Attempting to shrug off his confident retort, Antonia returned to the tents with Emily and Mildred Tottle, but the afternoon was spoiled for her. And her remorse only grew as the day wore on. Even though the guests seemed mostly to have forgotten about the contretemps, Antonia could not. By the time the breakfast ended at six o'clock, she was more than eager to leave.

She and Mildred were driven home by Emily and her genial, handsome husband, Lord Sudbury. When Mildred professed a desire to retire upstairs and take a nap before dinner, Antonia had no objections. "Please go ahead. I would be poor company just now."

Instead of settling in the drawing room as usual, Antonia found herself wandering out to the gardens at the rear of the estate. She had thought about shooting off her frustration at the archery range, but she didn't want to be so pointedly reminded of the disagreeable incident this afternoon.

When she came to the secluded little gazebo that her father had built for her mother, Antonia climbed the two steps and settled on a wooden bench to her right. The gazebo was the perfect place to be alone with her thoughts. The elegant, white latticework and domed roof were overgrown with ivy and climbing roses, hiding her from view of the gardens and offering welcome tranquillity. Golden rays from the setting sun filtered through the greenery, warming the interior and scenting the air with the sweet perfume of summer blossoms.

Wrapping her arms around her updrawn legs, Antonia rested her forehead on her knees and gave free rein to her disturbing reflections.

She would have to apologize to Lord Heward, of course, for she'd behaved badly toward him. He didn't deserve such thoughtless treatment from her. Heward had been nothing but kind and helpful to her in the year since her father's untimely death.

And he was appropriately concerned for her reputation. Like Caesar's wife, she had to be above reproach if she hoped to rise above her common origins, as her father had wished. It wasn't only a title her father had sought for her; it was the full acceptance of the ton into their hallowed ranks. If she failed to achieve their sanction through her own reckless behavior, then everything her father had striven for would be for naught.

Yet that wasn't the true source of her emotional turmoil; it was her feelings for her betrothed that troubled Antonia most. Or rather her *lack* of feelings.

She should be perfectly content with Lord Heward for her husband. They had much in common. They enjoyed the same literature, the same plays and art. He was not as inordinately passionate about riding as she, but they both relished long drives in the country in his curricle and pleasant strolls in the park.

She was quite fond of him, and yet . . . she only wished she could love him. Wished she could feel the slightest spark of passion for him. Physically Heward was appealing, with his elegant, aristocratic looks. And he was athletically fit as well, for he regularly practiced fisticuffs at Gentleman Jackson's boxing rooms and fenced at Angelo's salle, in addition to shooting pistols at Manton's shooting gallery. He was not as fit as Deverill, however. . . .

Antonia gave a soft groan. *That* was the problem. She kept comparing the two men, and her betrothed came up short every time.

It was not Heward's fault that she found Deverill so dynamic and magnetic, so exhilarating to be near. Or that Deverill had always been her ideal: strong, courageous, bold, exciting. That for years she had admired and envied his adventuresome spirit.

The deplorable truth was, she found Deverill's brazen behavior secretly enticing. He defied society's rigid rules the way she often longed to do. And his provocative charm, no matter how exasperating, was nearly irresistible.

Oh, why did it have to be Deverill who attracted her so fiercely? Who made her blood tingle? Who filled her with forbidden desires to do more and be more and feel more? Deverill made her dream. He made her reckless and daring. He made her feel gloriously alive.

Worst of all, he made her yearn for the kind of passion and adventure she knew she would never have in a marriage of convenience to Lord Heward.

Damn him, damn him, damn him—

A footfall on the wooden steps made Antonia warily raise her head. When she saw who it was, she went rigid.

"I am surprised you aren't at your archery range," Deverill said in his deep voice. "I expected to find you shooting me in effigy about now."

"Oh, it's you," Antonia said irritably, putting her forehead back down on her knees. "Will you please go away? I prefer to lick my wounded sensibilities in private."

"Why are you hiding yourself here?"

"I am not *hiding*. I am determining how best to grovel. I owe Heward an apology."

"I disagree. You did nothing wrong."

"Indeed, I did. I knew taking up your dare would upset him, yet I let you provoke me into it. You deliberately challenged me so I would quarrel with him."

"How wicked of me. How could I have been such a cad?"

Antonia raised her head to glare at him. "It is extremely rag-mannered to gloat, Mr. Deverill. Now, pray go away! You are a dreadful influence on me, and I want nothing more to do with you."

Rather than leave, however, he settled on the bench beside her, stretching out his long legs and lacing his hands over his flat stomach. "I beg to differ. I'm an excellent influence on you. I shake you out of your stifling, decorous pretenses."

"To my immense regret. I was foolish to risk your life today. I could have killed you."

"I don't regret it. Taking risks lets you know you're alive. My guess is that you've only been half alive these past four years, buried under your prim and proper rules of social etiquette."

Raising a plaintive gaze to the ceiling, Antonia gave another low groan. "Whatever did I do to deserve you?"

A chuckle escaped Deverill. "You're only nettled because you've begun to see I am right: You don't want Heward for your husband. He is far too tame and stiff-necked for you."

Even if it was true, the accusation brought Antonia loyally to her betrothed's defense. "He is not too tame!" She leveled an arctic stare at Deverill. "So what if he isn't brave and dashing? Not every man is like *you*. Lord Heward is gentle and caring, and he is always willing to put my interests above his own. He loves me."

"Does he?" Deverill sounded highly skeptical.

"Yes! And I love him."

One slashing eyebrow shot up, as if he knew very well her claim was a lie.

In frustration, Antonia jumped up from her seat and whirled to frown down at him. She didn't love Heward, but even if she was privately having second thoughts about wedding him, she was not about to let Deverill know it. In fact, she would do better to convince him she was entering into a love match, for then he might drop his absurd campaign to end her betrothal.

"I *do* love him," she insisted.

"I take leave to doubt that. You could never be swept away by a cold fish like Heward."

"He is not in the least a cold fish. He is a very passionate man."

That made Deverill smile.

"It's true. Lord Heward is as passionate a lover as any woman could wish. A better lover than you could ever be, I'll warrant."

His green gaze sharpened. "So now you expect me to believe you're not a virgin?"

A blush stained her cheeks, but Antonia was determined to feign nonchalance. "That is precisely what I expect you to believe. After waiting so long for our nuptials, I saw no reason to hold off becoming intimate with Heward. I asked him to indulge my curiosity and consummate our union a trifle prematurely, so you see why I have no intention of ending our betrothal—"

Antonia broke off suddenly, for Deverill had risen

to his feet and wore a scowl on his face that alarmed her.

She took a wary step back, toward the arched entryway. She hadn't expected him to be so angry simply because she professed to have bestowed her innocence on her betrothed.

But Deverill did indeed look angry. A muscle flexed in his jaw, as if he was striving for control. When he advanced toward her, she retreated, yet she never made it to the doorway. Instead, her back came up against the wooden lattice.

Deverill halted barely a step from her, watching her with searing eyes. Tension throbbed in the air as he asked softly, "A better lover, hmm?"

Perhaps she should never have made that wild claim, Antonia belatedly realized. It was no doubt unwise to challenge a man's sexual prowess. "Well, perhaps I exaggerated a little. . . ."

"Perhaps the problem is that you don't know any better. You have no other lovers to compare to."

Her chin lifted. "I don't need any comparisons."

He was regarding her through half-closed lids. "Has Heward brought you to pleasure?"

Caught off guard by the question, she hesitated a moment too long. "Yes, of course."

"I wonder."

Deverill stepped even closer, until their bodies almost touched. He stood unmoving, holding her with nothing more than his glance.

Exhilaration made Antonia's heart pump harder, while the very air crackled between them.

"I very much doubt," he murmured, "that you know what true pleasure is."

Remembering the incredibly pleasurable kiss Deverill had once given her, she found herself staring at his mouth . . . that sensuous, beautifully carved mouth. She couldn't bring herself to look away.

His eyes were focused on *her* mouth as he reached up to touch her. When his knuckles brushed over her parted lips, a frisson of fiery sensation sparked from his fingers to her flesh.

Startled, Antonia clutched at his arm, holding him away. "You can't kiss me, Deverill."

"I won't. It would leave your lips swollen and passion-bruised, and I don't want to give the appearance that we have been making love."

Instead, his thumb stroked her jaw, his touch lingering and provocative. She wanted to move, to flee his disturbing nearness, yet she was held captive by the intensity of his gaze, by the raw, powerful sexuality emanating from him.

And his low, rich voice stroked her senses like velvet, further weakening her defenses. "I don't intend to caress your breasts as I would like, either, since I don't want to dishevel your gown."

A heated tremor eddied deep in the pit of her stomach, even before she felt his glance travel along the line of her face and throat to the swell of her bosom. She couldn't prevent the shameful tingling of her breasts, the brazen warmth that coiled inside her.

Despite her restraining grasp, Deverill slowly ran the back of his hand down the side of her throat to the square neckline of her gown, then lower still to lightly brush the lavender muslin of her bodice. Antonia drew a sharp breath, wondering how his barest touch could make her burn like this, want like this. When he trailed his fingers deliberately over her breast in a caress that was calculatedly erotic, her senses skittered wildly.

Deverill smiled, satisfied.

Antonia clutched more tightly at his arm. "Deverill, stop!"

"Why? I can see how much you want me."

"I *don't* want you."

"Then why are your nipples peaked and throbbing? Why is your pulse racing?" The backs of his fingers stroked her nipple again, making her pulse throb even more wildly. "I doubt your proper, starched nobleman affects you like this."

Antonia took a deep breath, struggling to resist him, even as her body shuddered with longing. Deverill's arrogance galled her, but it infuriated her more that all he had to do was touch her and she melted.

Then he leaned forward, so that his hard, muscular form pressed fully against her softer one.

Antonia's heart leapt when she felt the hard bulge of his manhood through their clothing. She wasn't ignorant about lovemaking, thanks to her friend Emily's divulgences. She understood enough to realize that a man's member grew long and hard and swollen when he was aroused. So she knew that Deverill was most definitely aroused.

She also knew very well that he was trying to intimidate her. The knowledge, thankfully, gave her the willpower to hold her ground against him. Trey Deverill might be her ideal, but he was also vexing and arrogant and entirely too self-confident.

Arching an eyebrow, she managed a cool, superior smile. "I can see that you are not unaffected yourself."

"No, I'm burning for you." His voice was low and husky. "I intend to show you the kind of pleasure I'm certain Heward never has."

That made Antonia give a start and widen her eyes. "You can't. It would be scandalous."

Deverill's hot gaze raked her face, a bold and steady challenge. "What if it is? You like living dangerously."

Her mouth went dry as she stared back at him. She did like living dangerously, Antonia thought, enticed by the sizzling lure of temptation. The shocking truth was, she wanted Deverill to make love to her. She had dreamed of this man as her lover for years.

He bent closer then, his hot breath fanning her ear, his husky voice prodding her. "You don't want me to stop, princess. You want me to make you remember that you're a flesh-and-blood woman, not a prim, sheltered debutante."

Moving slightly, he wedged his knee against her gown, between her thighs.

A hot, biting arc of awareness shot through Antonia. She curled her hands into fists as she struggled to breathe evenly, but she could feel moisture gathering in her most secret feminine places.

"I intend to show you pleasure like you've never felt before." That velvet voice, so rough and hoarse, made her shiver.

Then Deverill moved again, pressing the sinewed flesh of his thigh slowly, rhythmically, against her woman's mound, creating a burning friction from the muslin of her gown.

Antonia's breath fled at the primitive sensations he aroused in her, and a whimper escaped her lips. Involuntarily her hands rose to clutch his shoulders.

Deverill must have considered that an invitation to continue, for his hands slid around her hips to grip beneath her buttocks and raise her up so that she actually rode his thigh.

The pleasure was sharp and riveting in her secret

folds where her sensitive flesh had become so damp and swollen and hot.

She made a final murmur of protest, but Deverill pulled her body totally flush to his, pressing her breasts against the hard wall of his chest. Then he settled his hands at her hips and began to slowly undulate her.

"Move against me," he ordered, showing her how.

Antonia squeezed her eyes shut and obeyed. Instantly wild desire flared though her body, tightening her nipples and kindling a fierce ache between her thighs. Helplessly she wound her arms around his neck and moved her pelvis against him with urgent need. Sheer, sensual instinct swept away her inexperience, guiding her, driving her.

Deverill nurtured her excitement, rocking her, arousing her, rubbing her wet, swollen cleft harder against his muscled thigh, until her skin burned with fever.

The rhythm of her breath turned frantic. Her hips bucked, but he mercilessly held her in place, letting her twist and struggle and strain against him.

The pleasure built unbearably; the heat became excruciating. Her breath coming in ragged gasps now, she dug her fingernails into the fine fabric of his coat and clung to him as intense pulsations began deep in her feminine core.

She was still shocked, however, by the explosion that racked her body. The hot sunburst of sensation made her jolt and arch in his arms, while her low, keening moan became a cry.

"Shh," he murmured, and covered her lips with his own to quiet her.

But she couldn't remain quiet. Her whole body coiled around him, spasming with the wrenching pleasure, her thighs clenching desperately around his, all her senses obliterated as a shimmering, flaming brightness took her.

As the shattering paroxysm faded, Antonia sagged against him, burying her hot face in his shoulder. She felt Deverill's lips press against her hair, calming her violent trembling, soothing her.

When finally he lifted his head, she opened her eyes. His beautiful, ruggedly chiseled face came into soft focus. She stared at him, dazed with sensation, torn between dismay and desire. Never had she had such a primal reaction to anyone or anything.

The glorious, searing pleasure that had swept through her had left her stunned. It was part of what she had yearned for, Antonia knew deep in her heart; part of the unfulfilled longing that had haunted her dreams for so long.

And Deverill knew it as well. She could see triumphant satisfaction in his eyes, and his husky voice held a raw edge when he spoke. "*That* is what it feels like to be a flesh-and-blood woman, sweeting. That is what you've been missing with Heward."

The mention of her betrothed sent a wave of cold reality rushing over Antonia and made her stiffen.

"You need to go," she said in a shaken voice.

Deverill held himself rigid for a protracted moment. Then drawing in a long, ragged breath, he released her and let her slide to her feet.

His hands braced her until her weak limbs could support her, but Antonia hastily pulled away. "Please! Just . . . go."

He inhaled another measured breath and stepped back, his jaw tight. Then he turned on his heel and disappeared down the steps, through the arched doorway into the gardens.

A wave of disappointment crushed Antonia. She hadn't wanted Deverill's embrace to end—nor had he, it seemed.

Moving unsteadily over to the bench, she sank down and buried her face in her hands, aghast at what she'd done. Once again she had allowed Deverill to provoke her into behaving like a wanton.

Yet what had she expected? She lost every shred of willpower when it came to him. She'd never known a man so overwhelming, so damnably tempting. From the first moment they'd met, she had felt the heat between them. Deverill made her heart pound and her senses reel. He tore down her defenses and made her do wicked, scandalous things, as he had just moments ago. She could still feel the delicious moistness that seeped from her swollen flesh-folds.

Antonia groaned. If she didn't stop, she would ruin all her plans for her future. She couldn't afford any hint of scandal to her reputation.

Shivering, she made herself stand up, girding herself with fresh resolve. She had to crush her attraction for Deverill, before she did something irrevocable. He was simply too dangerous. Meanwhile, she had to end all contact with him. Otherwise she couldn't trust herself—or him.

Clenching her jaw, Antonia left the gazebo, heading for the house. She intended to write Lord Heward without delay, to ask him to move up the betrothal announcement.

She would still have three weeks until they said their vows and the marriage became irrevocable. Surely by then her trustee would have resolved the appalling allegation that the company's ships were transporting slaves and disproved Heward's complicity.

A public announcement of their engagement would show Deverill that she was serious. And once she was officially betrothed, she would be in a far stronger position to resist the arrogant, vexing troublemaker who was proving to be far too irresistible.

Seven hours later, Deverill was still cursing himself for allowing his rampaging emotions to get the better of him.

He'd spent the evening at a gaming hell with one of his fellow Guardians—Beau Macklin, who answered to "Macky"—but upon returning to his suite of rooms at Grillon's Hotel, rather than retiring, Deverill had made major inroads into a bottle of the hotel's finest brandy.

Coatless now, he lay on his bed, his hands laced behind his head, staring up at the ceiling, a half-empty snifter of brandy on the table beside him.

During the entire evening, he'd failed to get Antonia off his mind even for an instant. He kept remembering his rage when she'd divulged that she had been intimate with her betrothed.

His first automatic response had been denial. He was unaccountably jealous at the thought of any man making love to Antonia, particularly Heward. And if she had shared the baron's bed, it was too late for her to quietly call off the betrothal.

It was a distinct possibility, however, that she had permitted her deflowering, even requested it, just as she'd asked for *his* kiss four years ago. She was certainly adventurous enough.

Deverill was still reeling from that blow when she'd boasted about Heward being the better lover. All his primitive instincts had been aroused, and he'd been filled with the fierce determination to prove her wrong, to show her that she knew nothing about pleasure.

He had given her her first climax, he was certain. But then, he wouldn't expect a man of Heward's stamp to be concerned about a woman's pleasure.

The trouble was, Deverill admitted, that *he* had been the one caught off guard. He had reacted with pure, jealous male rage. And then controlling his desire for her had become nearly impossible. Hearing the smokey, sultry sound of Antonia's whimpers, seeing her eyes hazed with desire, he'd wanted nothing more than to plunge into her honeyed warmth and devil take the consequences.

Damn Antonia anyway. He should take himself back to Cyrene and leave her to her fate. Except that he couldn't. Not until he knew for certain if her betrothed was guilty of murder.

Remaining in London would require every ounce of patience and adeptness he could muster, though, since dealing with Antonia after this latest storm would prove an even greater challenge. And crushing his own desire for her would be the hardest trial of all. She brought out duel urges to protect and conquer, even as she clouded his senses.

He could envision her now, her burnt-flame hair streaming across her passion-flushed face, her lithe body straining for his touch. She would arch and moan beneath his teasing caresses. . . .

A rap sounded on his door just then, pulling Deverill from his erotic thoughts. He frowned, knowing it was nearly two o'clock in the morning, and barked an invitation to enter. To his amazement, Baron Heward stepped into the room.

The nobleman still wore elegant evening clothes, as if he'd spent a night on the town. And he carried a walking stick that looked curiously like the sword sticks of an earlier era, a prosaic accessory that hid a deadly steel blade.

"Pray, don't rise on my account," Heward said as Deverill sat up. "I don't wish to put you to any inconvenience."

Pushing back against the headboard, Deverill leaned against the pillows and rested an arm on his updrawn knee. "To what do I owe this honor, my lord?"

Heward tendered a faint smile. "I have come to extend the proverbial olive branch, if you will, Mr. Deverill."

Few things managed to surprise Deverill, but this definitely was one. He knew Heward was quietly furious at him, both for his unwanted interference with Antonia and for raising the issue of his American cousin's confiscated ships. But Deverill kept his surprise to himself.

He gestured toward the armchair near the bed, offering his unexpected guest a seat. "Would you care for a brandy?"

"Thank you, no," Heward replied as he settled in the chair and suavely crossed one leg over the other.

"Olive branch?" Deverill repeated curiously.

"I have instructed Maitland Shipping's director to turn over the four vessels your cousin purchased before the war. Director Trant tends to become . . . overly zealous in his management at times. But I want you to know that he acted without authority in this case. I did not approve the confiscation."

With effort, Deverill kept his skepticism from his tone. "And is your approval required for such decisions?"

"Not required, but Trant normally follows my

wishes, since he knows I will own Maitland Shipping one day soon. In fact, within the month." A glint of smugness entered Heward's eyes. "Perhaps you will congratulate me, Mr. Deverill. Antonia and I have made up after our little spat this afternoon, and she has agreed to make me the happiest of men. We are advancing the date of our nuptials and plan to make the formal announcement at week's end and to begin calling the banns this Sunday."

Deverill felt all his stomach muscles clench.

Heward smiled pleasantly, obviously knowing his revelation had struck home. "I comprehend entirely why you have been pursuing her. A woman of Antonia's beauty and spirit is an exceptional prize. But I confess to great relief. For a time there, I thought you might manage to turn her head. Admittedly I was jealous of you."

"I trust you will understand if I don't congratulate you," Deverill said finally.

"I understand. *You* are jealous."

When Deverill felt his jaw tighten, he forced himself to relax and say calmly, "I merely want Antonia to be happy and well cared for."

"I will take excellent care of her, I assure you. As my baroness, she will lack for nothing."

Deverill subjected the nobleman to a hard scrutiny before saying softly, "Good. But let me offer you a warning, Heward. Samuel Maitland was a close friend of mine, and I intend to do everything in my power to see that his daughter is protected. If I discover you have mistreated Antonia in any way whatsoever, you will answer to me."

Heward's forehead furrowed in a puzzled frown, his expression all innocence. "But of course. And I appreciate your concern for her. But you truly have no cause to worry."

The baron smiled again as he fingered the knob of his walking stick. "Now that we have the air cleared, Mr. Deverill, I hope that we can cry friends. Samuel Maitland held you in high esteem, and any friend of his is a friend of mine. And since I won the prize . . . A victor should be gracious in victory, don't you agree?"

Deverill found it difficult to maintain even a pretense of civility when what he wanted to do was wipe that self-satisfied smirk off Heward's face with his fists. "I fail to take your meaning," he said coolly.

"I would like to make amends for us getting off on the wrong foot. A show of goodwill on my part. I would be honored if you would allow me to sponsor you for membership at White's."

For the second time in as many minutes, Heward had surprised him. White's was one of the premier gentleman's clubs in London, a bastion of conservative Tory politics. Perhaps Heward thought he was being generous to throw his support behind a man with questionable claims to gentility.

"Thank you," Deverill replied, "but I have a subscription to Arthur's. A less aristocratic club, to be sure, but I prefer the company there."

Heward did not appear overly disappointed. "Perhaps you would be interested in a different sort of sport, then, Mr. Deverill. You have heard of Madam Bruno's?"

Bruno's was a notorious sin club that catered to the more adventurous clientele, Deverill knew. "I have heard of it, but have never attended."

"I would very much like you to be my guest there. They offer exquisite female companionship . . . which might serve as consolation for the disappointment of failing to win Antonia. Of course"—there was that faintly taunting smile again—"their sensual charms in bed cannot compare to my lovely Antonia's, but I can vouch that several of Madam Bruno's beauties are quite skilled."

Deverill nearly leapt up and reached for his guest's throat. It was infuriating to hear Heward boast about having lured Antonia to his bed. No doubt he'd sought to make her his conquest from the beginning, since seducing her ensured she would eventually have to wed him.

Deverill's first inclination was to refuse the invitation outright. The last thing he wanted was to attend a sin club with Heward. And yet he was curious to know what sort of sexual sport Heward regularly chose to indulge in. More critically, he could observe for himself how Heward dealt with his ladies of the evening, to see if there was any truth to the tales of his brutality.

It would also be an opportunity to become further acquainted with the baron and perhaps discover how he'd initially insinuated himself into Samuel Maitland's good graces.

So Deverill gritted his teeth and accepted the invitation. "You are very gracious, Heward. I would enjoy visiting Madam Bruno's."

Heward flashed a gratified smile. "Oh, I am certain you will. Are you free tomorrow evening?"

"For such a pleasant diversion, I will make myself free."

"Excellent," Heward said, rising to his feet. "Shall we say eight o'clock, then? My carriage will call here for you. We can dine in the company of Madam Bruno's doves and then sample their delights for the remainder of the evening. No, don't get up," he added when Deverill swung his legs over the side of the bed. "I can show myself out." Heward made an elegant bow. "I am gratified that we could clear up this minor misunderstanding between us."

Staring after his departing guest with severe dislike, Deverill waited until the door was closed before reaching for the half-full brandy glass beside the bed and draining the contents in one long, burning swallow.

Five

In the elegant private parlor of Madam Bruno's sin club, lamplight gleamed off the crystal and silver gracing the dining table. In the darker corners of the room, strategically placed daybeds awaited the pleasure of the guests.

Deverill lounged at the table, silently sipping a fine port wine. On his left, a pretty blond Cyprian tried to attract his wandering attention, while across from him, Heward was engaged in a flirtation with a sultry brunette.

Upon arriving, Heward had chosen both beauties from a selection of nearly two dozen on display in the large drawing room of Madam Bruno's house of pleasure. "You will appreciate Felice, I promise you," Heward said of the blonde.

Deverill had shrugged with indifference. As long as his partner didn't have auburn hair to remind him of Antonia, he was satisfied. With Felice clinging to his arm, he'd followed Heward upstairs to the private parlor to partake of an excellent dinner.

While eating, Deverill steered the conversation to the baron's plans for Maitland Shipping, and was both surprised by Heward's candor and rather impressed by his mutual belief that the future of the maritime industry was in steam. After a dessert course of fruit and cheese, footmen unobtrusively cleared the dishes and brought a selection of prime wines.

Just as he'd done with the women, Heward selected his preferences of the various vintages, claiming that the Spanish port was exceptional.

"So you are a connoisseur of wines?" Deverill asked, recalling Mrs. Peeke's assertion that Heward had brought a bottle of French brandy to Samuel Maitland immediately before the magnate's death.

"Indeed, I am. There are few things I appreciate more than a good wine . . . or a skilled woman. But of course, once I am wed, I will have less need to patronize establishments such as this one, since my bride is capable of satisfying my requirements."

It was a deliberate jab, although delivered with a charming smile, and Deverill had difficulty repressing a scowl. With the wedding date moved forward, the urgency of discovering any sort of incriminating evidence against the baron that would make Antonia reconsider had just increased tenfold.

The port was as good as claimed, at least. Deverill had just drained his second glass when Heward rose to his feet.

"I expect you prefer privacy, Deverill, so I will take the lovely Dawn and retire to a different chamber."

Seeing the two demireps exchange a glance, Deverill had the impression that Dawn would have preferred to remain in the parlor rather than leave with Heward. But she made no protest as the baron escorted her from the room and shut the door behind them, leaving Deverill alone with the blond Felice.

At once, she rose and moved to stand beside his chair. Through her diaphanous gown he could see her full, ripe breasts and dusky nipples as she bent to whisper a husky question, "What is your pleasure, sir?"

Deverill hesitated, debating whether he wanted to share her favors. He knew why he found himself curiously unenthusiastic. The only woman he wanted to bed was a flame-haired heiress, and the blond beauty offering herself to him was a poor substitute. But it was possible she could make him forget Antonia. . . .

"Please, sir . . . his lordship will be extremely provoked if I do not satisfy you, and he is not a man to cross."

Her dark eyes were filled with worry, Deverill noted. "What will Heward do if you cross him?" he asked, very interested in the answer.

A shudder swept through Felice's lush body, but her expression became guarded. "I don't like to tell tales about our clients. . . . But I am glad he chose me for you, sir."

Deverill decided not to push her, although he made a mental note to question the club's madam at a later date about the baron's sexual preferences. When Felice reached to untie his cravat, he didn't stop her.

Instead, he let his eyes drift shut. To his dismay, he found his senses assaulted by an entirely different fantasy. One where it was Antonia bending to kiss him seductively, teasing her tongue over his lips. Antonia kneeling before him, running her hands down his chest to the placket of his breeches. Antonia drawing her fingers over the bulge of his erection beneath the satin, stroking him, arousing him.

After what had happened between them yesterday,

the need to make love to her still fiercely stung his body, and he leaned back in his chair, letting himself indulge the heated images that flickered in his mind. Antonia naked in his bed, her blue eyes dark with desire, her creamy ivory skin flushed, her tangle of dark-flame hair spread wildly over his pillow. Antonia lithe and wanton, arching against him as he explored the mysteries of her silken body . . .

The sensual images set him on fire. A throbbing ache began to pulse in his swollen cock as she grasped his hands and guided them to her now bared breasts.

"Tell me what you like, sir. . . ."

The moment she spoke, a sharp stab of disappointment speared through Deverill. The beauty kneeling between his thighs was not Antonia. The hair was pale yellow, not lustrous auburn. The eyes gazing up at him so slumbrously were light brown, not sparkling blue.

Reaching down, he closed his fingers over Felice's naked shoulders and drew her onto his lap.

"There's no rush," Deverill murmured in response to her questioning look. "I want to enjoy this wine first."

Settling her there, he used one hand to pour another glass of port. When he offered a sip to the woman in his arms, she drank a little, then wet her finger in the wine and ran the tip over his mouth.

It was an erotic gesture that did little to rouse Deverill's amorous instincts. Swearing silently at himself for becoming too damned discriminating, he let Felice kiss him again.

She was working his lips with her tongue when he became vaguely aware of the sound of the door opening. Presuming a footman had returned to finish clearing the table, Deverill lifted his head in time to see three hulking figures, all masked and hooded, slip into the room and quietly shut the door behind them.

Their appearance was evidently part of the entertainment offered, but Deverill felt annoyed by the interruption. It flashed through his mind that Heward might have requested this particular diversion for him, since some adventurous patrons enjoyed special stimulation such as bondage and flagellation and sexual games such as abduction and multiple partners.

He was about to decline their services and order them out when one of the ruffians rushed forward and grabbed Felice's arm, roughly yanking her from Deverill's lap. She gasped in startled pain, automatically resisting, while Deverill surged to his feet and reached for her assailant, instinctively determined to protect her.

He caught the glint of a knife in the ruffian's hand an instant before the blade stabbed upward, into Felice's chest, directly between her naked breasts.

Shock speared through Deverill, swiftly followed by raw horror. *This was no game.*

And he was too late to save Felice.

Her lips parting in a cry of agony, she clutched instinctively at the knife handle as blood spurted between her fingers.

Catching her limp form as she sank to her knees, Deverill stared at her white face. The entire incident had taken barely three seconds. Then the ruffian turned to flee. . . .

Shaken out of his paralysis, Deverill eased Felice down on the carpet and lunged for the port wine on the table. Grasping the neck, he threw the bottle at the fleeing villain's head. It landed with a satisfying crack, felling the man.

The other two were brandishing knives, Deverill saw, and were moving toward him menacingly. He glanced quickly around, searching for a way to defend himself. Snatching up his discarded cravat from the table, he wrapped the cambric around his right forearm. . . .

But they didn't come at him directly. Instead, one circled around the table with the obvious strategy of coming up behind him. Deverill grabbed the back of a dining chair and threw it at the opponent in front of him, sending him sprawling backward.

Then trying to catch his assailants by surprise, he leapt up on the table, knocking over decanters and wineglasses haphazardly. The second man stared up in shock and raised his arms as Deverill launched himself into the air. Their bodies collided with a thud, the hooded man giving a whooshing grunt as he landed hard on his back.

Sitting up to straddle the ruffian's bulky chest, Deverill let his fists fly, then yanked off the masking hood. His assailant had black hair and an ugly face marred by a scar that ran from temple to chin, Deverill saw an instant before the back of his neck prickled in warning.

He glanced back just as a chair came crashing down upon him. Blinding pain shot through his head . . . and then his ribs as a booted foot connected with his side.

"Yer to stay here, guv'nor," his attacker declared, bending to rescue his colleague.

They fled the parlor, stopping only to haul their other, half-conscious compatriot with them.

Shaking off his painful daze, Deverill stumbled to his feet and followed. He heard boots clattering down the stairs, but by the time he reached the corridor, it was deserted and all was quiet. A dozen doors along the hall were closed.

Behind him, Felice made a small sound. She was still alive, Deverill realized.

"Fetch a doctor!" he shouted down the hall, hoping someone heard.

Returning to the injured woman, he dropped to his knees. Her hands were still clutched around the knife that protruded from her breast.

"It hurts," she mewled, blood wetting her lips.

"I know, sweetheart," he said hoarsely, his own voice ragged with fury and grief.

As gently as possible, he withdrew the blade, but he had seen too many fatal wounds to mistake this one. When blood gushed from the wicked gash, Deverill grabbed the tablecloth and yanked, sending fine crystal shattering to the floor. He pressed the linen to Felice's chest and gathered her to him, hopelessly trying to offer her comfort.

"Why?" she rasped, bewildered pain in her dark eyes.

He had no answer for her. This whole moment seemed surreal. He might have thought he was experiencing a nightmare, except that the copper scent of blood was all too pungent in his nostrils. And the rattle of her breath was all too recognizable.

He knew Felice was breathing her last.

A hollow anguish knotted in his chest. He'd held dying men in his arms, just this way. Felt this same helpless agony . . .

Then her body went limp against him. Her head fell back and her mouth went slack as she stared unseeing up at the ceiling.

For a moment, Deverill remained unmoving, shock still gripping him. Then slowly, a red fog of rage swamped him at her senseless death, while his mind roiled with questions.

Their attackers could have killed him, or at least severely wounded him. But all three men had suddenly turned and fled before they did him any serious injury. They had murdered this beautiful young woman instead.

Just then he heard a gasp from the doorway. When he glanced over his shoulder, the raven-haired Madam Bruno stood just inside the parlor, a look of horror on her face. The same horror that Deverill knew was reflected on his own face.

"What have you done?" she demanded in a hoarse whisper. She moved closer to stare down at the dead woman. "You killed her."

Deverill stiffened, vaguely wondering why the madam had leapt to that conclusion so readily.

"I did not kill her. Three men burst into the room—" He stopped short, realizing how absurd the tale sounded.

Tossing the tablecloth aside, he lowered Felice to the carpet and drew up her bodice over her bare torso for modesty. Then he closed her eyelids with gentle fingers. "I assure you, I did not kill her."

But Madam Bruno was scrutinizing the blood on his hands, his brocade waistcoat, his white satin breeches. She took a step back and shouted for help.

Barely an instant later, several burly footmen ran into the room, almost as if they had been posted in wait. The club doubtless employed bruisers to control unruly patrons, as well as the usual male servants, but these were definitely the former.

Madam Bruno pointed at Deverill but addressed

her bruisers as she backed toward the door. "He murdered Felice. Watch him. Don't let him leave the room. I intend to summon the Bow Street Runners."

Obediently her brawny underlings came to attention, their stance belligerent, arms crossed over their massive chests as they stood blocking Deverill's path.

Yet he had no intention of leaving. Because he wasn't guilty. Rather than give the appearance of running from the law, he wanted to get to the bottom of this.

Lifting the dead woman in his arms, he carried her to the daybed in the corner and laid her down, draping her arms over her stomach. She looked uncommonly pale but at peace, as if she were merely sleeping.

Another stab of pain sliced through Deverill. She hadn't deserved slaughter. She'd merely been an innocent bystander.

Turning away, he began to pace the room while the bruisers warily watched his every move. When he realized what he was doing, Deverill forced himself to return to the dining table and take a seat.

His mind was racing, though, as he tried to determine just what the hell had occurred. How had the attackers even known where to find him? He couldn't believe *he* had been their target. They had gone straight for Felice, stabbing her with ruthless efficiency and then leaving him virtually unscathed. *Yer to stay here, guv'nor.*

Why? So he could be charged with her murder? Who even knew he was here at the club besides Heward?

Deverill suddenly stiffened, all his instincts screaming. Heward had arranged this trap for him, he felt it in his gut.

He spent the next ten minutes pondering other possibilities, but he kept coming back to the baron. At the end of that time, Madam Bruno returned to the parlor, accompanied by a tall, wiry man with thinning brown hair and shrewd eyes—exactly what one might expect of an officer of London's private police force that had been formed to apprehend thieves and criminals.

Identifying himself as Horace Linch, the Bow Street Runner gravely inspected the scene, asking no questions at first but paying particular attention to the dead female body on the bed, the mortal wound in her chest, and the bloody knife that still lay on the carpet near Deverill's feet.

Linch was just straightening when Baron Heward strode into the room. He wore no coat or waistcoat, and his shirt-tails hung over his evening breeches, as if he had rapidly dressed.

"What the devil is happening here? I heard a woman was murdered—" He broke off as he caught sight of Felice.

If it was a performance, Deverill thought, then it was worthy of Drury Lane Theatre, for Heward's face was the picture of bewildered shock and horror.

Linch identified himself again to the baron and explained the facts as he knew them—that he'd been summoned to the club because one of the madam's employees had been stabbed to death. "Perhaps Mr. Deverill will give us his account of her demise," the Runner suggested.

Deverill calmly explained how three masked intruders had burst into the room and stabbed the girl, with no provocation whatsoever. He had fought them and hurt two of them slightly, but then they had fled.

Linch looked rather skeptical, while Madam Bruno shook her head.

"Do you expect anyone to believe such an outrageous tale?" she demanded. "You murdered that poor girl."

"It does look bad for you, sir," the Runner said more respectfully.

"Why would I want to kill her?"

"Mayhap your play got too rough? I was told you have a propensity for violence."

Deverill lifted an eyebrow. "Told by whom?" When the Runner glanced at the madam, Deverill realized where the spurious information had come from. "I have never met Madam Bruno before this evening, so she can hardly know my propensities, violent or otherwise."

"Your reputation precedes you," she insisted stubbornly.

"If you considered me dangerous," Deverill replied in a silken tone, "I wonder that you not only allowed me entrance but encouraged my patronage."

Her face flushed. "Lord Heward sponsored you."

"Did you witness me killing Felice?"

"No, but there was no one else here."

"Because they fled before you arrived." Deverill returned his attention to Linch. "So your theory is that I stabbed a willing beauty in a fit of excessive sexual violence? What of the state of this room?" He gestured at the overturned chair and broken crystal. "Am I supposed to have caused that as well?"

"An altercation appears to have taken place here, sir, but it could have been staged to make it look as if ruffians had attacked you."

"Or I could be telling the truth." Deverill reached up to touch the painful gash on his temple that was still welling blood. "If you will inspect that chair closely, Linch, I'll warrant you'll find a stain that corresponds to my wound. Moreover, it seems rather apparent that a woman like Felice was too delicate to be capable of throwing a piece of heavy furniture at me."

"True," Linch conceded, "but that does not exonerate you, sir."

"Would you care to hear my theory? Someone—obviously an enemy of mine—sent his minions here in a premeditated attack, to kill her and make it appear as if I was the culprit."

"Why would someone frame you that way?"

Deverill had his suspicions, but absolutely no proof. He glanced at Heward, who had stood silently observing. "Where is Dawn?"

"In bed, where I left her."

Very convenient, Deverill thought, that Heward had arranged such a solid alibi for himself.

For a moment, Linch hesitated before finally appearing to make up his mind. "I am afraid I must place you under arrest, sir, until this is all sorted out."

To Deverill's surprise, Heward stepped in to champion him. "There is obviously some mistake. I can vouch for Mr. Deverill. And I am certain it happened just as he said."

"It *is* possible," Linch said, "but I still must take him in."

Heward looked intently at Deverill. "Perhaps you *should* go with him. I promise I will do everything in my power to see that you are freed at once."

Even if he believed such assurances, Deverill's every instinct was howling at him to resist. He would spend the rest of the night in prison at the very least. . . . Reflexively, his fingers clenched on the wooden arms of his chair. He'd endured a hellish Turkish prison once and that was more than enough. And once he was locked behind bars, it would be difficult to prove his case.

Which no doubt was exactly what Heward intended.

So he would be free to wed Antonia without interference.

What better way to deal with a rival than by framing him for murder?

A cold, hard knot settled in Deverill's stomach as he locked gazes with the baron.

"I will tell Miss Maitland," Heward said sympathetically. "Pray, don't worry. She would never believe you capable of murder. She is too good-natured and innocent to think ill of anyone."

"You are too generous, my lord," Deverill replied with only a hint of sarcasm.

"Think nothing of it."

The nobleman's face was impassive, his expression one of perfect innocence. But for the barest second, a faint smile flitted across his mouth, while a gleam of pure triumph shone in his eyes.

That sly smile disappeared instantly, but Deverill suddenly knew the truth without a doubt: The killing had been orchestrated to frame him and get him out of the way, and Heward was responsible.

It made a perfect, perverted sort of sense. Deverill had been getting too close to Antonia, attempting to raise suspicions in her mind about Heward, trying to turn her against her betrothed. But the baron was extremely clever. He couldn't kill Deverill outright because it would be too obvious, so he'd devised a more cunning plan, to murder a high-class prostitute and see that Deverill was blamed for it.

And if Heward was willing to kill an innocent bystander, then what would become of Antonia when she was his wife, at his mercy, when he was in full control of her fortune?

A simmering rage swept over Deverill. He had allowed himself to be gulled like the veriest green mark. But just now he had to repress his anger and determine how to get himself out of this mess. If he was thrown in prison, even if he could eventually clear his name, by the time he got out, Antonia could likely be Heward's wife. The prospect made his stomach heave with dread.

The Runner spoke then, interrupting his turbulent thoughts. "I have a carriage waiting below, Mr. Deverill, to convey you to Bow Street."

Unresisting, Deverill rose to his feet. Feeling Heward's triumphant gaze digging into his back, he allowed himself to be escorted downstairs by the four brawny footmen and out onto the street, with the Runner following. But when they reached the carriage, Deverill acted.

Sweeping out a leg, he tumbled one guard to the ground and let fly his fists at another. As Linch drew a pistol from his belt, Deverill lunged and rammed a shoulder at the remaining two footmen, shoving them both into the Runner and sending all three men toppling backward.

The pistol discharged harmlessly, allowing Deverill to make his escape.

He sprinted into the shadows of a nearby alley, the sounds of curses and shouts following him. But his unexpected assault had bought him enough time to disappear into the unlit warren of alleys behind the club and elude his pursuers.

As he negotiated the dark London streets, his cold fury returned. Until now, he hadn't been solely convinced of the baron's evil nature. Nor was he willing to accept that Samuel Maitland had been murdered. But this latest inexplicable death left him with little doubt: Heward had killed Antonia's father to keep Maitland from preventing their marriage.

Deverill's basest instincts were urging him to turn around and find Heward; ten minutes alone in a room would be enough time to beat a confession out of him. But he might fail. And his first concern had to be for Antonia. He couldn't leave her in London with Heward. Nor could he stay here as a wanted man, he realized, his mind planning furiously.

They would both be better off away from England. The Isle of Cyrene seemed a good choice, since he had plenty of allies there, including the Guardians' elderly leader, Sir Gawain Olwen. But being such a great distance from London could prove a major disadvantage.

He would have to think of someplace closer, where he could work to clear his name and prove Heward's guilt. More importantly, where Antonia could be protected and be kept safe from her murderous betrothed. Deverill wasn't nearly as concerned about absolving his name as he was about protecting Antonia.

But either way, he had to act now, immediately, so they could sail with the midnight tide, before Bow Street could mount a hunt for him. . . .

He paused to get his bearings. He was in London's Covent Garden district, and he'd instinctively been moving west toward Mayfair. Making a decision, Deverill shifted course slightly, heading for Macky's lodgings on St. James Street.

What he needed most at the moment was trusted allies, and who better than his fellow Guardians to rely on in dangerous times of trouble?

Six

Macky's manservant was not overly distressed to see the blood on Deverill's clothing, since it was not a unique event. And Deverill was not surprised to find Macky away from his lodgings for the evening, reportedly playing cards at a nearby gaming hell.

While the servant summoned a closed hackney carriage to await Deverill on the street, he scribbled a quick note for the captain of his ship, with orders to round up his crew and ready his schooner to sail within the hour. Then he sent the servant to fetch Macky home and carry the note down to the London docks where his ship was located.

After washing the blood from his hands, Deverill sat at the desk to pen a list of instructions, outlining the steps that needed to be undertaken while he was away. Macky was already privy to the current investigation of Heward, but after tonight, there were several more actions that Deverill wanted executed as soon as possible.

As he compiled the list, he crushed his smoldering remnants of anger as emotion he couldn't afford;

anger altered judgment, caused errors. Instead he focused on the threat of danger, welcoming the rush in his adventurer's soul that kept his mind sharp and his senses wary. The gauntlet had been thrown down and he was happy to pick it up, but at this moment, he had one mission only: He would see Antonia safe or die trying.

When he was done, Deverill washed his face and cleaned the gash at his temple, then shed his bloody waistcoat. The rest of his clothing couldn't be helped. He couldn't borrow a coat or trousers from Macky, since he was taller and had wider shoulders than his fellow Guardian. And returning to his hotel room was out of the question, since it might possibly be watched. But he had sufficient clothing on his schooner, which would be more difficult for his pursuers to locate. He needed to be armed, however, in case he encountered his adversaries.

When Macky appeared moments later, Deverill had just begun to load and prime a set of pistols from among his colleague's cache of weapons.

Beau Macklin was a former provincial actor turned Guardian. A few years older than Deverill's age of thirty, Macky boasted curling chestnut hair and a handsome visage that, combined with his roguish charm, made him a great favorite with the female sex. His excellent thespian skills allowed him to play numerous roles, although his most usual guise these days was that of a gentleman about town.

Macky listened intently as Deverill related the grim events of the evening.

"I gravely underestimated that bastard Heward," Deverill said at the conclusion.

"I suppose staying to fight him is not an option?"

"With a warrant out for my arrest, my effectiveness will be limited at best, since I can't show my face. Moreover, I'll be at a disadvantage, opposing a nobleman of Heward's consequence. As a social rebel, I'll be given little benefit of the doubt, as I would if I bore a title and pandered to the nobility." Deverill frowned. If he left London, his flight would make him appear guilty, but that couldn't be helped. "If it were only my skin at risk, I would chance staying, but Antonia Maitland is in Heward's clutches. I'll be damned if I will let him take his sweet time arranging her demise."

"Obviously, drastic action is called for," Macky agreed. "What will you do?"

"Take her to Cornwall. To Lady Isabella's castle near Falmouth. Heward will never find her there."

"Will she go?"

Deverill's mouth curled. "Not willingly, I expect. I'll need to come up with some story to get her on board my ship tonight." He gestured toward the desk. "I'll rely on you to handle matters here. I've written down my instructions. Read that list and tell me if you have any questions."

As Deverill finished loading the pistols, Macky glanced down the list. "I'm to start with Madam Bruno—to discover why she was so insistent that you committed the murder."

"Yes. She had to be part of Heward's plot. Her accusations were too pointed for her to be merely an innocent bystander."

"She was an actress before she took to the demimonde," Macky divulged.

Deverill grimaced. "That doesn't surprise me. Her performance tonight was quite convincing. I'll leave it to you to determine how best to persuade her to confess her role."

Macky pursed his lips as he reviewed the second item. "Find the coves who actually killed the girl."

"That scarred face shouldn't be difficult to trace using your contacts in the underworld. But then we need to prove that Heward hired him and his fellow ruffians."

"I understand. And this doctor?"

"Heward's physician examined Samuel Maitland's body for cause of death, so he might also have supplied the poison that killed Maitland. Find out the doctor's name and where he purchases his medicines. As for the rest, you can enlist the aid of Ryder when he returns from his latest mission, and Thorne, when he arrives from Cyrene," Deverill said, naming two of their fellow Guardians. "I will stay in touch by courier. If my strategy works, I should be able to return to London in a matter of weeks to implement the rest of the plan myself."

Macky nodded. "You can count on us, sir."

"I never doubted it." He trusted Macky and his other friends to set his plans in motion. When he returned, he would ascertain if the Director of Maitland Shipping could be induced to bear witness against Heward. But regardless, he would concentrate on devising a trap to lure the baron into revealing his crimes.

Deverill suddenly paused. "I just recalled, I left out something. Talk to Venus and discover what she knows about Heward's sexual predilections. The dashers at Bruno's seemed somewhat frightened of him, which only supports the rumors you uncovered about him."

As the proprietress of one of London's most exclusive sin clubs, Madam Venus would have made it her business to observe her potential clientele among the gentry and aristocracy. And only last month she had agreed to work for the Guardians in exchange for staying out of prison after committing treason.

"Anything else?" Macky asked.

"You should keep an eye on the Maitland housekeeper, Mrs. Peeke. I doubt she's in any danger, since Heward isn't aware of her accusations, but let her know how to contact you should she require help. We'll need her to testify against Heward if we build a case against him. And when Sir Gawain arrives in London next week, brief him on what happened and relay whatever instructions he has for me."

In his capacity as leader of the Guardians, Sir Gawain Olwen usually traveled to London once or twice a year. This time he was visiting to participate in the ongoing festivities celebrating Napoleon's defeat at Waterloo.

Pocketing one of the pistols, Deverill handed the other to Macky. "Now I'd like you to ride down to the docks and keep watch on my schooner until I can get there with Antonia. Dispatch any of Heward's minions who might come there searching for me. We have barely an hour."

Macky grinned, obviously relishing the challenge of knocking heads with Deverill's enemies.

They both went downstairs, but Macky left for the docks, while Deverill took the waiting hackney to Antonia's mansion barely two miles away.

He left the carriage standing down the street and knocked at the servants' entrance. A sleepy scullery maid admitted him and went to fetch Mrs. Peeke, who invited him to her rooms for privacy.

The housekeeper immediately understood the implications of the Cyprian's killing. "So he likely *did* murder the master," she muttered darkly.

"I'm convinced now that that's the case."

"Thank God you came, Mr. Deverill."

He shook his head. "So far I've accomplished nothing but getting myself arrested and branded a fugitive. I'll deal with that eventually, but first I have to see to Miss Maitland's safety. I want your blessing to take her away from here."

"You have it, dear sir."

"I will be delivering her to Lady Isabella Wilde in southern Cornwall, since I'd like to shield her reputation as much as possible. Lady Isabella should be in residence any day now—at her late husband's castle near Falmouth. She'll provide adequate chaperonage."

He didn't point out that the voyage would take at least two days, and that Antonia would be alone in his company all that time. But at the moment, getting her away from the deadly Heward was more crucial than keeping her reputation spotless.

"I expect Heward will call on her tomorrow," Deverill continued, "so we need to supply a reasonable explanation for her disappearance."

"Have you thought of something, sir?"

"I suggest you put about the tale that Miss Maitland is making an urgent visit to the country to provide solace to a dying friend. And to support the ruse, it would be best if her companion could be induced to follow her to Cornwall. Miss Tottle could travel by coach tomorrow. You could tell her that Antonia wishes her to come, but it would be wiser to mislead her about the destination until after she is on the road, so Heward will have no chance of following her."

Mrs. Peeke nodded in approval. "You leave Miss Tottle to me. She will be eager to see that Miss Maitland's character remains unblemished."

"Good. Now if I might speak to Miss Maitland alone? I have to convince her to come with me tonight, and we have no time to lose."

Mrs. Peeke evidently understood the need for secrecy, for she gave him a candle and showed him upstairs to Antonia's bedchamber door.

Breathing a bit more easily, Deverill silently let himself in and shut the door behind him. Now he had to lure Antonia on board his ship, and quickly. He had little time to spend on accusations or explanations, in case Heward decided to search for him here. He wanted Antonia to accompany him willingly rather than be forced, however, so he resolved to use reason first, and prevarication if necessary.

He planned to tell her he had a letter on his ship that contained evidence of his allegations, which was not wholly a lie. The housekeeper's original letter recounting her fears about Samuel Maitland's death by poison *was* in his schooner's cabin, although Deverill knew that alone would never be enough to convince Antonia of Heward's guilt. But it would be far too complicated and time-consuming just now to call Mrs. Peeke in here to relate her tale. And Antonia still might not believe her suspicions and thus would refuse to accompany him to his ship.

No, even if he had to use underhanded means, he had to act. Antonia would not be happy to discover she'd been tricked, but he would deal with her wrath once they were safely at sea.

Holding the candle aloft, he crossed to the bed, where she lay fast asleep. The sight of her caused an unwelcome jolt to the rhythm of his heart. Deverill halted, desire clenching in his gut.

A cloud of shimmering auburn hair framed her face, drifting about her shoulders and the ripe swell of her breasts. Since the night was warm, she'd drawn the sheet up to cover only the lower half of her body, and through the thin cambric of her nightdress, he could see the sweet globes crowned with dusky-rose nipples.

He swore softly as a hard ache settled in his loins. Yet he knew his reaction was more than carnal. Admittedly he'd always had a fiercely protective streak. And he had a definite weakness for vulnerable beauties. Yet his raw desire to protect and cherish Antonia was not due solely to his sworn duty as a Guardian, or his own personal vows, or even his obligations to his good friend, her father.

Shaking himself, Deverill forcibly returned his focus to his purpose. Depositing the candle on the beside table, he settled one hip on the mattress, then pressed his hand gently over Antonia's mouth to keep her silent when he woke her.

Her eyes fluttered open, while her body tensed.

"Don't be alarmed," he murmured, easing his hand away.

"Deverill . . . ?" Antonia asked in confusion.

Fighting the cobwebs of sleep that befuddled her mind, she blinked at the grave, handsome face hovering over her. Then she suddenly came fully awake, realizing that Deverill's presence was real and no sensual dream. He was actually here, in *bed* with her, while she wore only a nightshift.

Every inch of her body flooding with acute aware-ness, she dragged up the sheet to cover her breasts as she sat up and scooted back against the headboard. "What the devil are you doing in my bedroom?"

"Mrs. Peeke knows I am here." When Antonia eyed him warily, he added with a humorless smile, "I'm not here to ravish you, if that is what worries you."

"Then why *are* you here?"

"Urgent business. I need you to listen to me, Anto-nia."

She searched his rugged face, suddenly noticing the gash on the right side of his forehead . . . and the dark stain on his shirt collar. "Is that *blood*?"

"I'm afraid so. But it isn't mine."

"Whose, then?"

"I was at a club tonight with your betrothed—"

"Oh, my word. Did you fight with Heward?"

"No. I was with a woman. . . . She was attacked and killed. And I believe your Lord Heward was re-sponsible."

Antonia stared at Deverill in blank bewilderment, seeing a slight tension to his jaw, a bleak flatness to his eyes. "What do you mean . . . responsible?" she fi-nally said.

"I suspect Heward ordered her killing and set it up so that it looked as if I had done it. I barely managed to avoid arrest afterward. I'm wanted by Bow Street for murder."

"*Murder?*" Her confusion only increased. It was alarming to see the blood on Deverill's clothing, and for an instant, she wondered if he might even be a danger to *her*. He looked dark and formidable just now. . . .

Trying to gather her scattered wits, Antonia raised

a hand to her forehead. She had no doubt Deverill was capable of violence, but never murder. Yet he seemed to be accusing Heward of the same thing. Perhaps she was dreaming after all.

"There's more," Deverill said grimly before she could think of any response.

"More?" Her voice was a mere rasp.

"A year ago, Heward likely poisoned your father and caused his death."

"*W-what?*" she stammered. "You cannot be serious."

"I would never jest about something like this, Antonia. Two days after you became betrothed, your father discovered some damning information about Heward that caused him to withdraw his support of your marriage. So Heward brought him a bottle of brandy that later was suspected of containing poison. I don't believe your father's death was due to heart failure."

She was too shocked to say a word. For the span of a dozen heartbeats, she simply stared.

"That is preposterous," Antonia finally gritted out in a shaky voice.

"No," Deverill insisted. "It's entirely too credible."

His sincerity gave her pause, but then denial welled up in her. "How could I possibly believe such a wild accusation? The notion is mad—"

"Not at all. I've suspected Heward for some time now."

"Then why are you just now telling me?"

"Because I wasn't convinced he was guilty."

"And you are convinced now?"

"Yes. A woman is dead tonight because of him. I just can't prove it yet."

Antonia shook her head, not wanting to hear such terrible allegations against the man she had promised to marry.

Deverill grasped her chin, forcing her to look at him. "Your father trusted me. You can do the same, Antonia."

A feeling akin to panic churned in her chest as her conflicting instincts battled inside her. Trust Deverill? And believe that Heward was a murderer? The choice was impossible. "You will need to give me some reason to trust you," she exclaimed, her tone stubbornly heated.

"I have evidence. There is a letter on board my schooner I want to show you. I'm leaving London tonight, within the hour, since I can't stay without risking arrest. I want you to accompany me to my ship."

"Now?"

"This minute. You need to get dressed."

"You truly *are* mad!"

Deverill rose from the bed. "I don't intend to debate with you," he said in the voice of a man accustomed to command. "You have two choices, princess. You can dress and come with me, or I can carry you out in your nightshift."

Her mouth dropped open. Watching Deverill's grim, set expression, though, she realized he would do exactly as he threatened if she didn't give in gracefully.

After another mutinous moment, Antonia clenched her jaw and slid out of bed. When his gaze raked over her thin nightshift, she felt the sudden, stomach-tightening awareness of Deverill as a man, but she squared her shoulders and hurried to her dressing room. Fuming, she quickly pulled on a brown muslin, long-sleeved gown, then stockings and sturdy half boots, not bothering with a shift or corset or garters.

When she came out again, Deverill was waiting by the door. He scrutinized her choice of attire and gave a qualified nod. "You need to wear a cloak with a hood. I don't want you to be recognized."

Antonia shot him a darkling glance. "How was I to know what to wear? I am not in the habit of skulking about in the middle of the night as you obviously are."

"Humor me just this once."

She fetched a cloak and put it on. As she was fastening the clasp at her throat, Deverill came up to her. Reaching up, he drew the hood around her face, tucking tendrils of her hair inside the collar. "You'll do." He took her hand. "Now come, we have very little time."

Instinctively resisting his orders, she pulled back. "But I want to write a note to Miss Tottle first and tell her—"

"I've already told Mrs. Peeke where you are going."

Antonia gaped at him. "You are rather sure of yourself, aren't you, Mr. Deverill?"

"I hoped you would be curious enough to want to know about your father's murder."

Antonia stiffened, but she pressed her lips together to stifle a retort. She might be compelled to accompany Deverill to his ship, but she didn't intend to give his outlandish allegations any credence whatsoever until he showed her his so-called evidence.

She determinedly held her tongue, even when he ushered her out the servants' entrance instead of the front door.

He had a hackney carriage waiting down the street. Deverill handed her in and gave the coachman directions to the docks, then joined her inside.

They maintained a taut silence during the entire drive. Antonia's thoughts were a mass of confusion as she contemplated Deverill's incredible charge that Heward had murdered her father. It stunned her that he would even make such an outlandish allegation. Stunned and shocked and upset her. Even the possibility was too dreadful to credit.

She clamped down on the turmoil of emotions warring within her and tried to digest what else he had said. Had a woman really died tonight? Was Deverill actually accused of her murder? And was he truly leaving London? Leaving England?

She knew she should be relieved to see the last of him, but the hollow feeling in the pit of her stomach was nothing at all like relief.

On his part, Deverill expelled an uneven breath, gratified that he'd brought Antonia this far, and hopeful that he might just manage to pull off his scheme. Through the carriage window, he could see that the docks were alive with activity, even though it was nearly midnight, since half a dozen ships were making ready to depart.

He had the hackney stop several berths away from his destination. Handing Antonia down, Deverill drew out his pistol and took her arm to escort her to his schooner. It further gratified him to see seamen scurrying to raise sails, for the tide was already well out. But a swift calculation told him that nearly half his crew was absent, which only increased his sense of urgency. He would have to help them get under way, Deverill decided, before they missed their chance to sail.

Even so, he paused before reaching the gangplank in order to survey the dimly lit quay. When Macky stepped out of the shadows, he felt Antonia tense beside him.

"Is everything in order?" Deverill asked quietly.

"Yes," Macky replied. "Two of his men showed up here, but they are now tied up and slumbering peacefully."

"I owe you a debt, my friend."

Macky grinned. "Think nothing of it." His gaze gliding over Antonia, he tipped his hat to her, but all he said was, "Best of luck, sir."

Deverill felt Antonia watching him and knew she was eager to ask what Macky meant. She maintained a tight-lipped silence, however, as he escorted her on board and then below-deck, along the dark companionway to one of three passenger cabins.

When he lit a lantern, she blinked in the sudden brightness. "Now where is this 'evidence' you wished to show me?" she demanded, her gaze sweeping around the cabin.

He stepped close and startled her by taking her face in his hands. "I need you to trust me this once, Antonia. I swear to you, I will explain everything to you shortly. But I haven't the time just now."

Turning, Deverill let himself out of the cabin.

Caught off guard, Antonia was slow to follow. When she heard the key turn in the lock, she stared at the closed door in frozen disbelief.

"He *wouldn't*," she breathed.

But when she tried the handle and found the door wouldn't budge, her heart sank.

Deverill, she realized with sudden brutal clarity, had made her his prisoner.

Seven

Antonia stood reeling at his audacity, fury welling in her at his deception. Deverill had duped her, and she hadn't put up the slightest resistance. Well, that was about to change!

Pounding on the door and shouting brought no results, however. All she could hear was the muffled sounds of barked commands above and the faint slap of waves against the hull.

When the ship swayed scant minutes later, Antonia realized they were moving. Her hands clenched into fists. It was just as she feared; she was being abducted!

Struggling to remain calm, she glanced around the cramped cabin, searching for a weapon of some kind. The inventory was not promising: A narrow berth with two bunks, one above the other. A large wooden seaman's chest. A tiny desk and single chair. A washstand. And shelves and hooks along the bulkheads for storing belongings, all of which were currently empty. She went straight to the chest, but found it also empty except for some woolen blankets.

Biting her lip, she tried frantically to think, to determine how she could orchestrate an escape. She would have to hurry. If the ship left the docks, she would be in desperate trouble, since she didn't know how to swim.

She wasted precious seconds stewing, dredging her memory for stories she'd heard at her father's dining table from captains and seafarers. Fire! Of course. Fire was one of a sailor's worst fears. She could start a blaze in the small cabin. If any of Deverill's crew noticed, surely they would come running. It would be disastrous if she let the flames burn out of control, for she would only defeat her own purpose if she caused her own demise. But if she could generate enough smoke to gain someone's attention but not so much that it would choke her . . .

Rapidly Antonia reinventoried the cabin, noticing things she had missed before. A pitcher of water on the washstand. Towels. An empty brass chamberpot.

Latching on to an idea, she pushed opened the window of the small porthole so she would be able to breathe, then began creating her diversion, stuffing towels in the chamberpot and lighting them with the tinderbox.

The first time the flame fizzled out, so she tried again. When she had a small blaze going, Antonia added a few drops of water to the chamberpot, then dumped the smoldering mess of linen at the base of the door, onto the polished wooden planks of the deck.

She watched with satisfaction as smoke seeped under the cabin door. Tilting her head back, she screamed at the top of her lungs for help from the fire, then stood behind the door with the chamberpot raised.

She had barely time to repeat her cries when the key jangled in the lock and the door was thrust open. When a wiry, gray-haired old man came rushing into the room, Antonia brought the chamberpot crashing down on his head.

He fell hard, whether unconscious or merely stunned, she couldn't tell. She spared only a moment's regret for the grizzled old fellow before turning and fleeing the cabin.

The corridor was dark as she groped her way along, but she found the ladder at the end and quickly climbed up. After the acrid smoke, the fresh night breeze was like perfume, but it also filled every sail above her head.

Her heart plummeted. She was too late! To her utter dismay, the ship was already well out into the Thames River.

In the moonlight she could see the deck swarming with sailors, who hadn't noticed her yet. Antonia rushed over to the rail to stare down at the swirling black water below. The quay was receding quickly. If she intended to act, she would have to do so immediately.

Gritting her teeth, she threw one leg over the railing . . . but then she froze, knowing she would never find the courage to jump. Even if she survived the fall, she would never make it to shore—

"Antonia." The firm voice behind her made her start. "Come down from there."

She glanced over her shoulder to find Deverill watching her. "And let you abduct me? I think not."

"You could hurt yourself if you jump from this height."

Of course she wouldn't jump, but the threat was

the only leverage she had over Deverill at the moment. He wouldn't want her demise on his conscience.

Antonia scowled at him. "Jumping will likely kill me, since I never learned to swim. But drowning is preferable to letting you carry me off to who knows where. At least I will foil your despicable plan."

"You don't even know what my plan is. You haven't given me a chance to explain."

His infuriating calmness goaded as much as her own impotence. "And I don't intend to after you lied to lure me here. You have wholly misjudged me, Deverill, if you expect me to meekly surrender to your treachery."

Deverill shook his head. "I don't expect you to meekly surrender. I doubt you've ever done anything meekly in your life."

The edge of sardonic amusement in his tone was the last straw. "Turn this ship around," Antonia demanded, "or I *will* jump!"

He was silent for a moment, obviously evaluating her threat, no doubt wondering if she was angry—or idiotic—enough to risk drowning rather than let him win.

Holding her gaze, he took a step toward her. All of Antonia's muscles clenched. "Stay away from me! I mean it, Deverill. I will jump if you don't return me to the docks."

"Antonia, love," he said with maddening patience. "Please come down from there."

"Not until you turn the ship around."

She held her breath, suspecting they were in a stalemate; she refused to surrender and Deverill refused to comply with her demand.

To her surprise then, he shrugged. "Very well. Captain Lloyd," he called out to the man at the ship's wheel. "A hard jibe to port, if you please."

"Aye, sir."

"Antonia, you need to look above your head," Deverill warned calmly. "Beware the spanker boom doesn't hit you."

She glanced up at the billowing sails above her and saw a triangular sail attached to a thick wooden boom shifting her way. It was too high to actually hit her, but the distraction caused her to take her concentration off Deverill. Then the schooner suddenly dipped, making Antonia nearly lose her shaky balance. She grasped frantically at the railing to keep from falling overboard.

An instant later, strong arms pulled her back from her precarious perch, into the curve of a hard, male body.

She thrashed against Deverill furiously. "Damn you, you tricked me!"

"It was for your own good."

She tried to pry herself away from that powerful body, but he trapped her close with both arms around hers.

His relentless embrace only riled Antonia more. When she continued to fight him, he bent her over the rail to keep her still, so that the wood pressed painfully into her stomach and ribs.

"Let me go!" she gasped. "You are squeezing the breath out of me!"

"Not sufficiently, it seems," he retorted dryly.

His taunt only added to her fury. She threw her head back, connecting with his chin at the same time she stomped her foot down hard on his boot. Surprise more than pain made Deverill release her.

Antonia scrambled away from him, glaring and shaking with resentment. "You . . . you . . ." Words failed her.

"Devil?" he supplied helpfully, rubbing his bruised chin.

"Exactly! You're a devil, a fiend, a villain!"

"Perhaps. But I am only trying to save you."

When Deverill moved toward her, Antonia frantically searched the deck for a weapon with which to defend herself. When she spied a length of chain, she picked up the end. Although it was heavy, her frenzied wrath gave her the strength to wield it.

With fire in her eyes, she swung the chain in a wide arc, nearly striking Deverill on the shoulder. He had to jump back to escape a serious blow.

Antonia swung again, although even she wasn't certain whether she meant to do him real injury or was simply acting out of fear and frustration.

Oddly, he held up a hand. "Fletcher . . . I can handle this."

He appeared to be speaking to someone on her left, but she wasn't about to fall for Deverill's tricks again. She hefted the chain, advancing on him. Yet she'd taken barely a step when a warning sound sent a prickle of uneasiness through her. From the corner of her eye, she glimpsed the grizzled old man she'd struck down in the cabin. He had snuck up on her, holding what looked like a large canvas sack or piece of sail.

He had halted at Deverill's command, but when Antonia pivoted in alarm and flung the end of her chain at him, the aged seaman gave a startled yelp and charged her, his canvas raised high as if to throw it over her head and capture her. Somehow, though, he tripped over one corner of the cloth and barreled headfirst into her side.

The effect was like a battering ram. When his forehead hit her rib cage, Antonia gasped as the air rushed from her lungs and she was sent spinning. She felt herself flying to the deck, with the old man splayed on top of her.

Then pain lanced through her head and everything went black.

Ten minutes later, Deverill sat beside an unconscious Antonia, remorse filling him as he bathed her purpling brow with a wet cloth.

When Fletcher had tackled her to the deck, she'd hit her head against a belaying pin with enough force to knock her out cold. A sick feeling of dismay knotting his gut, Deverill had carefully carried her to his own cabin and laid her on the bunk. She hadn't stirred when he removed her cloak or when he'd chaffed her wrists to try to rouse her.

For a time Fletcher hovered behind him, grumbling reluctant apologies and muttering imprecations. The old seaman's pride was severely wounded, since he'd first been hit over the head with a damned chamberpot by a mere girl and then had unintentionally rendered her unconscious with his bumbling effort to apprehend her chain weapon.

Deverill had finally dismissed him, wanting to be alone with Antonia. She was hurt, but at least she was alive. His heart had nearly failed when she'd threatened to drown herself rather than be taken captive.

He understood the sentiment, though. During his two hellish months in a Turkish prison, he'd longed fiercely to rebel against his captors, but his survival instincts had triumphed, and he'd conserved his strength until he contrived the opportunity to escape and rescue what was left of his crew. Briefly Deverill squeezed his eyes shut, his mind sweeping back ten years to that terrible time of agony and guilt.

Crushing the gruesome memory, he dipped the cloth in the basin beside the bunk, then gently drew it over Antonia's ivory skin. He wouldn't lose her like he'd lost nearly half his crew. There was nothing he wouldn't do to protect her.

Hating to see her so helpless, he traced her pale face with his fingers. Searing heat and fierce tenderness pulsed through him, the primal response of a man's need to protect his woman. Yet she wasn't his woman, he reminded himself. Far from it.

Deverill gave a scoffing huff of laughter, remembering Antonia's eyes sparking with outrage just a short while ago.

He hadn't expected her to acquiesce without a fight, but her ingenuity had caught him off guard. She'd been clever to start a fire as a diversion. And if she'd known how to swim, she would have escaped him. Instead, she'd threatened to take his head off with that chain.

Yet he would far rather have her railing at him and menacing him with a chain than lying here so pale and still. She was feisty and brave, qualities he admired in a woman. She was tough and vulnerable all at once, a combination that touched him far more than he wanted to admit—

Just then Antonia stirred. Softly groaning, she arched slightly, inadvertently pressing her breasts against the muslin of her bodice.

Deverill's gut tightened, locking the air in his chest. Then she came awake with a start, looking dazed and puzzled as she gazed up at him. Holding his breath, Deverill watched her beautiful face with its cloud of flaming hair, her trembling mouth. He wanted nothing more in that instant than to kiss her, to taste those ripe lips and reassure her. But he fought the urge, knowing he needed to protect Antonia from himself, in addition to the deadly nobleman she wanted to marry.

Therefore, he merely lifted a hand and gently brushed wild strands of hair away from her face.

At his light caress, Antonia felt a sigh whisper through her. She had been dreaming of Deverill again, yet if this was a dream, why did his touch feel so real? And why did her head hurt so abominably?

Slowly she looked about her. She was lying in a bunk, while Deverill sat beside her, holding a damp cloth to her aching brow.

"Where . . . am I?" she asked in a hoarse whisper.

It surprised her a little that he actually answered her, proving that he was no figment of her imagination. "In my cabin."

She wondered how she had come to be here, yet she couldn't think clearly when Deverill's long, bronzed fingers were stroking her forehead so tenderly. Her pulse fluttered, while all her senses came to vivid life.

"You struck your head when you fell," he murmured.

Reaching up tentatively to feel her forehead, she found a lump the size of a robin's egg.

Then suddenly she remembered.

Antonia flinched as the events of the past hour came rushing back with a vengeance. Deverill's treachery. Her attempted escape. The sudden blackness.

He must have brought her here while she was senseless, she realized. His cabin resembled the one where she'd been held prisoner earlier, only larger and more luxuriously furnished.

With effort Antonia narrowed her eyes at him. "When I was assaulted, you mean," she retorted hoarsely.

Deverill grimaced, but his gaze boldly held hers, never wavering. "I am sorry you were hurt, Antonia."

"So you claim. But it appears you are still abducting me."

"For your own protection. I misled you because I knew you wouldn't listen to reason."

"Reason! Don't speak to me of reason. You are no better than a pirate!"

He gave a long-suffering sigh, shaking his head while eyeing her as if both annoyed and fascinated by her stubbornness. "I am touched by your gratitude, sweeting. The truth is, I'm preventing you from wedding a murderer and becoming a victim yourself."

"I wish you would spare me your concern and your infuriating high-handedness!" Antonia struggled to sit up, cringing at the pain in her head. "Since when did it become your providence to rule my life, Deverill? To make such choices for me?"

"Since I learned of Heward's villainy. With your father gone, I consider you my responsibility."

Knowing it was hopeless to argue that point with him, Antonia merely glared. "You said you had evidence of your allegations. Or was that a lie as well?"

Rising, Deverill carried the damp cloth and the basin of water to the washstand, then went to his desk. Retrieving a well-worn piece of vellum, he returned to Antonia and handed it to her. "This is the letter Mrs. Peeke sent me several months ago. Read it and tell me I don't have justification for suspicion."

She scanned the contents, her heart plummeting as she read. The housekeeper's letter insisted that Mr. Maitland had intended to call off Miss Antonia's betrothal to Lord Heward but was murdered before he could do so, and it pleaded for Deverill's help in uncovering the truth.

"Mrs. Peeke must be mistaken," Antonia murmured faintly to herself.

"Why do you say so?" Deverill interrupted her shaken thoughts.

Because it was too horrifying to contemplate, Antonia responded silently.

"These really are only suspicions, not proof," she finally said aloud, looking up. Then another thought occurred to her. "You had Mrs. Peeke's letter all this time? You should have told me about it from the first."

"Perhaps," Deverill replied. "But consider my perspective. What would you have done if I had shown you this letter a week ago? You would have confronted Heward with the accusations, wouldn't you?"

"Possibly," she answered honestly.

"And as a result, you would have put Mrs. Peeke in grave danger and foiled any chance to draw Heward out."

Antonia raised a hand to her aching forehead, wondering if Deverill could possibly be telling her the truth. She couldn't bear to think that her beloved father might actually have been murdered by her betrothed, yet deep down, she felt doubts creeping in about Heward.

She shuddered involuntarily. Only yesterday she had told Lord Heward she would be agreeable to moving forward the date of their nuptials. Had she truly been that gullible? Or was she overreacting now? She had never seen the slightest hint that he was capable of so horrible an act. And she owed him some measure of loyalty . . . didn't she?

She focused her gaze on Deverill again. "Why did you not let me speak to Mrs. Peeke tonight instead of dragging me off in that barbaric fashion? I could have questioned her directly about her suspicions."

"Because there was no time. You might still have refused to come with me, and I couldn't risk it."

"So you abducted me from London in the middle of the night? You had no right, Deverill!"

Her heated declaration rang in her head, making Antonia flinch as a fresh wave of pain stabbed her skull. She wasn't certain she could deal with this just now. She was still reeling from the shock of her abduction. Deverill had turned her world upside down in an instant. *And Heward could be entirely innocent.*

She clung to the hope. She didn't want to examine why she was resisting Deverill's damning allegations so fiercely, for then she would have to acknowledge her own culpability in her father's death—

Antonia abruptly cut off that too painful line of thought. "What other evidence do you have against Heward?" she forced herself to ask.

"None yet. But I have every intention of proving Mrs. Peeke's beliefs."

She latched on to that as a drowning sailor would a lifeline. Deverill had no proof! If he hadn't deceived her so outrageously, she might be willing to give more credence to his reasoning now. But she would be damned before she gave him the satisfaction of knowing he had raised grave doubts in her mind about Heward. She was too upset at him just now for tricking her. And her head throbbed too acutely for her even to think straight.

When he took the letter from her, she forced herself to say coolly, "This is not enough to convince me that Heward is a villain. And you won't be able to cajole me into believing him guilty."

Deverill's mouth curled. "I would sooner wrestle a tiger than try to cajole you, love."

Antonia felt herself scowl. It had just struck her why Deverill had paid her such close attention during the past week. Because he had feared for her safety. And not because he was attracted to her. Her cheeks colored. There had been moments in the past week when she'd wondered if he might be feeling the same bewitchment she'd felt for him.

It was humiliating to remember her own yearnings for him. What a fool she had been. Deverill didn't want *her*. He didn't find her nearly as fascinating or alluring as she found him. He was acting merely as a guardian, not a lover. He'd set himself up in the role of her deliverer, whether she wished him to or not.

Her frustration returning full force, Antonia swung her legs over the edge of the bunk and stood, the better to face Deverill. When a wave of dizziness hit her, she shrugged it off. "This has gone far enough, Deverill. I demand that you take me back to London."

"No." His handsome features were set in uncompromising lines. "I am not letting you return until I'm certain you are safe from Heward, so you might as well accept it."

"Where are you taking me?" When Deverill hesitated as if he couldn't trust disclosing their destination to her, Antonia wanted to hit him. "If you don't tell me, I swear I will . . ." She couldn't think of a threat impressive enough, so she simply finished, "I will make you sorry."

"I am terrified."

She nearly kicked his shins at his sardonic humor. "I don't believe I am in danger from Heward!"

"Tell that to the innocent young woman who gave her life tonight."

Antonia stiffened at the grisly reminder, but she was determined not to let Deverill distract her. She raised her chin in the air, giving him a haughty look. "For all I know, *you* murdered that woman and are putting the blame on Heward."

She knew the moment the words left her mouth that she had gone too far; Deverill's eyes suddenly blazed at her with unnerving intensity.

Boldly advancing, he brought his body a hairsbreadth from hers. She had to lean her head back just to see his dark expression. She'd thought him intimidating before, but his nearness made his body seem even more powerful and overwhelming, especially compared to her slighter form. His eyes gleamed hot and dangerous as he raised his hand to glide his fingers into the tresses of her hair.

Her heart hammering hard on her ribs, Antonia stared up at him, knowing he was holding his anger tightly leashed. The air about them seemed to crackle with tension and something more . . . a potent sensuality. His eyes were hooded and fixed on her lips.

But then he gave a low curse and let his hand drop abruptly, stepping back as if he didn't trust himself to be near her.

A faint swell of relief washed over Antonia. She wouldn't know how to defend herself against Deverill if he truly became enraged.

His voice, however, was ominously soft when he spoke. "I expected better from you, princess. Do you really think me capable of murder?"

He wasn't feigning the pain in his eyes, the bleakness, she knew. He felt anguish over the death of that woman, she was certain.

Antonia drew a shaky breath. "No. No more than I think Heward capable of murder." Deverill's scowl deepened, but she went on. "There is one more thing I don't understand. If you suspected Heward of being such a villain, what were you doing with him at a club anyway?"

His dark eyebrows lifted in mocking crescents. "What do you think I was doing?"

Antonia flushed. "Well, I mean . . . I know what you were doing. . . . I mean . . . you were obviously with a ladybird. But why were you there with Heward?"

"Because he invited me there. He intended all along to frame me—and I fell for it like the greenest gull."

Her own frown deepening, Antonia gingerly rubbed her aching forehead. Deverill had been at a pleasure brothel tonight, savoring the charms of a highflyer. Strange how it bothered her more to think of him with another woman, when Heward's actions had been just as dissolute . . . and when Heward professed to love her. But she didn't want to cloud the issues at hand.

"So do you mean to answer me?" Antonia asked. "Where are you taking me?"

"To Cornwall, where you'll be safe from Heward."

"Cornwall is a large place, Deverill."

He ran a hand roughly through his hair. "Did you meet Lady Isabella Wilde when you visited Cyrene?"

"Yes." She recalled that Lady Isabella was a lively, elegant noblewoman of half-Spanish, half-English descent who had survived three husbands. Antonia had liked her immensely.

"Isabella," Deverill said, "owns a castle near Falmouth that belonged to her last husband. She plans to be there for the next month at least, to attend the lying-in of her sister by marriage. I'm certain she'll be willing to take you in."

Antonia gave him a disbelieving look. "And you just plan to deposit me on her doorstep without warning? You have the manners of a heathen, Deverill."

"Perhaps, but Bella won't mind."

"*I* mind!"

"You can think of it as an adventure."

Her fingers clenched into fists at his provoking tone. When her father had taken her to the beautiful Isle of Cyrene two years ago, she'd thought it a wonderful adventure—in fact, the only real adventure she'd ever had. And she would have loved to visit Cornwall under different circumstances, but *not* as Deverill's captive.

"I'm not giving you a choice," he added, his tone more curt.

Suddenly exhausted, Antonia sank back down on the bunk. Despair had started to replace her fury, for they likely were nearly out to sea, and she knew Deverill wouldn't change his mind about returning her to London. She didn't have the strength to argue with him any longer, though. She couldn't think clearly with her head splitting open, when she was so dizzy she might faint at any moment.

She needed time to digest his terrible accusations, in any case.

Tomorrow, Antonia promised herself. She would face them tomorrow when she could think more logically, when she was feeling less vulnerable, when her spirits were not so devastated by the unthinkable events of the evening.

"You should be thanking me for taking you to Lady Isabella," Deverill commented. "She has enough consequence to shield your reputation."

Realizing that her situation would soon become public knowledge, Antonia dropped her face in her hands. Regardless of whether or not Heward was guilty, Deverill was going to spoil everything her father had striven for since the day she was born. Papa would have been devastated to see all his efforts for her ruined by scandal.

"I suppose it doesn't much matter where I go," she said dismally. "My reputation is probably already sullied beyond hope—or it will be once I'm discovered missing from London."

"No one will know about your abduction. Mrs. Peeke is to put about the tale that you're making an urgent visit to the country to provide solace to a dying friend. And Miss Tottle should be joining you in a few days in Cornwall."

Antonia raised her head to stare at him. "You arranged that?"

"I asked Mrs. Peeke to see to it."

"But Heward will never believe that spurious falsehood."

"True, it's unlikely. In fact, he'll probably conclude—

rightly—that I took you to prevent you from marrying him. He'll doubtless be enraged that you are gone and that his goal has been thwarted. But he won't want the world to know his enemy has you, for it makes him look impotent and could also ruin you socially—an unwanted stigma for his future bride if he can manage to salvage his marriage scheme. So I expect he'll stick with the story of you visiting the country."

Even with her head swimming, Antonia was able to follow Deverill's logic and realize that it made sense. But there were others who would be concerned by her disappearance as well. "Emily . . . Lady Sudbury, will be worried sick for me."

"I'm sure Mrs. Peeke will reassure her. And it shouldn't be for more than a few weeks, a month or two at most."

"Two months!" Antonia repeated weakly.

Then suddenly she gave a start, realizing that Deverill had removed his coat and was unbuttoning his shirt. "What are you doing?"

"Taking off my blood-soaked clothing. I've had one hell of a night, and I intend to get some sleep."

"You mean to sleep *here*?"

"It *is* my cabin, after all."

Antonia glanced at the single bunk. "Then I should move to another cabin."

"That's impossible, I'm afraid. The one I originally put you in is damaged by smoke and needs to be scrubbed down to make it habitable." He paused pointedly. "You remember whose fault that is, don't you?"

She ignored his sarcasm. "You can't expect me to sleep in the same cabin with you!"

"You can have the berth. I will put up a hammock in the corner."

"That is totally unacceptable."

Turning, Deverill folded his arms across his formidable chest and stood scrutinizing her. His stance was outwardly relaxed, but the look in his eye was all dominant, challenging male.

"You can scream and pout all you wish, vixen. But you'll stay here with me, where I can keep an eye on you and prevent you from burning down my ship. After you knocked Fletcher witless, I don't trust anyone else to guard you but me. You'll find I'm not as easy a mark as poor Fletcher was."

Antonia rose to her feet, silently fuming. Deverill's attempt to protect her reputation had done little to lessen her smoldering resentment of him, and his continued provocation was enough to incite her to mayhem. But she strove to maintain a reasonably calm tone as she voiced her protest. "Surely even you realize the impropriety of such a sleeping arrangement."

He did indeed realize the impropriety, Deverill reflected darkly as he proceeded to string a hammock in one corner of the cabin. He didn't want to sleep here alone with Antonia, either. Not when he was so easily aroused just looking at her. But he couldn't trust that she wouldn't attempt some other damnable stunt, one that would result in a worse injury than she'd already suffered.

Thinking of her injury made Deverill grimace. If he was any kind of gentleman, that nasty bruise on her forehead would be enough to quiet his sexual urges. He sure as hell shouldn't be lusting after Antonia when she was hurt.

Yet seeing her now—her wild-eyed, stormy look, her cheeks flushed with temper—he wanted badly to turn that ire to passion. He wanted to strip her of her gown, stretch her out naked in his bunk, and spend what was left of the night making love to her. Just the thought was enough to drive his throbbing manhood tight against his breeches.

Deverill cursed silently. He didn't want to want her this way. Rather, he should be remembering the accusation she'd thrown at his head only moments ago, when she'd accused him of murder.

But then, he understood why she had lashed out with wounded fury and knew he had to make allowances. She hadn't asked for any of this—her revered father conceivably murdered, her own life in danger, an abduction in the middle of the night, a blow to her head that had rendered her unconscious. . . .

With a jerk, Deverill shed his shirt, then sat in the stuffed leather wing chair to remove his shoes and breeches.

Antonia watched him wide-eyed, tensing when he wadded up his blood-soiled clothing and tossed the bundle in the wastebasket.

"If you want to burn something," he said dryly, "you can burn those."

She scarcely heard his comment, though, for Deverill was now wearing only his drawers. He was apparently unconcerned with the lack of privacy, yet her senses jolted at the sight of that sleek, heavy body half naked.

He was broad and lean and hard, with muscles rippling under the smooth skin of his chest, sinews chording his arms. There were wicked patterns of crisscrossing scars on parts of his torso, but despite the ugly disfigurement, his body was sinfully, beautifully male. It was alarming how badly she wanted to touch him.

When he stood, he glanced her way. "Don't you intend to undress?"

Antonia had to clear her throat before she could speak. "No, of course not. Surely you realize I have no clothing other than the gown I am wearing."

Deverill's green eyes gleamed at her. "I will be happy to loan you a nightshirt."

"I am not about to undress with you in the same room."

"Please yourself. But it will be two and a half days before we arrive. I thought you might want to keep your gown fresh until Lady Isabella can supply you with more."

"I will make do," she said stiffly.

To her surprise, Deverill crossed the cabin to her. With determination, Antonia stood her ground, but his starkly masculine appeal was having a deplorable effect on her weakened senses. The scent of his bare skin, warm and faintly musky, assailed her, making her impossibly aware of his heat and vibrancy, while the span of his naked, hard-muscled chest made her feel small and utterly feminine.

Her body reacted to his nearness as well. Her breasts suddenly became acutely sensitive against her bodice, while a treacherous tremor of desire pulsed between her thighs.

Deverill apparently noticed her growing arousal when his gaze drifted down her body. "You might want to reconsider. That muslin gown is almost as revealing as my nightshirt would be."

Antonia drew a sharp breath, realizing he could clearly see the sharp points of her nipples through the thin fabric.

Her lips parted wordlessly, and she took a step back, but came up against the bunk.

Deverill smiled knowingly before shaking his head. "I told you, sweeting, I don't intend to ravish you. I wouldn't even if you begged me to."

"Beg you . . ." Antonia's eyes widened, and she nearly sputtered. "You arrogant lout. I am not about to beg you. And if you dare touch me—"

Provocatively, he tapped a gentle finger on her nose. "Easy, love. I'm putting out the lantern. Get into bed. You need to rest after that blow to your head."

She obeyed, although mutinously, cursing Deverill beneath her breath all the while. She had never met a man so abominably sure of himself. She took off her half boots and stockings, then slid beneath the covers.

A mistake, she shortly realized. The cabin was warm, even with the porthole window open.

Suddenly darkness enveloped them, and she heard the creak of the hammock ropes as Deverill settled in.

Quietly she pushed off the blankets, leaving only the sheet, and turned her back to Deverill.

But it was awkward, being in the dark with him, in the same small enclosed space. His cabin was not much larger than the gazebo at home. . . .

Antonia shivered at the reminder. Her body tingled as she remembered the way he had touched her, aroused her that day. She was aching just thinking about the pleasure he had given her.

Trying to force away the memory, Antonia buried her face in the pillow.

After a few long moments, she could hear Deverill's deep, even breathing. Yet she still had difficulty falling asleep—and not simply because of the unfamiliar pitch of the ship, or the appalling possibility that her father had actually been murdered by her betrothed, or the dismay she felt at her abduction, or her fury at Deverill for betraying her trust.

But also because Deverill had promised that he had no intention of ravishing her. And somehow that smarted almost as much as all the other indignities he'd subjected her to thus far.

Eight

Waking alone in the cabin, Antonia winced at the bright sunshine streaming through the porthole window, then groaned upon recalling the events that had brought her here.

For a moment she lay unmoving, taking stock of her predicament. She had slept fitfully, and her body felt bruised, but at least her head didn't ache quite so abominably.

Her heart was another matter entirely.

Determined to keep despair from overwhelming her, she rose slowly and made her toilet at the washstand. She had no brush, so she borrowed one that must be Deverill's and tied her hair back with a piece of twine she purloined from his desk. His shaving mirror showed her that the right side of her forehead was sporting a large, purple-black bruise, but her appearance was the least of her concerns.

Wondering if she was his prisoner, Antonia went to the door. To her surprise, she found it unlocked.

And to her startlement, the old man who had milled her senseless last night stood in the corridor, hand raised as if preparing to knock.

His bronzed, weathered face drew up in a scowl when he saw her. "I brought yer breakfast," he muttered.

Last night, Antonia remembered, Deverill had addressed her assaulter as Fletcher. She stepped aside warily, allowing him entrance. "Thank you."

"Don't thank me, missy. 'Tis my punishment for flooring ye. But I didn't ken I could stand by an' watch ye clout his nibs."

"His nibs?"

"Cap'n Deverill. He was right unhappy that I scuttled yer nob, but ye had just done the same to me. I'm right sorry for that."

She supposed he was apologizing for hitting her on the head. "I am sorry I hit you, too, Mr. Fletcher."

"Just Fletcher, if ye don't mind. Name's Fletcher Shortall, but I'm not partial to the short part." He set the tray down on the desk. "I'd say we're even with the mufflers. 'Course, at the time I didn't know who ye were."

"And that would have made a difference?"

"Aye. Ye're Sam Maitland's gel."

"You knew my father?"

"Not him. Know his ships, though. Ye're safer in a Maitland vessel than any craft on the seas. So ye can't be all bad."

Antonia managed a smile. "I normally don't go about, er, scuttling perfect strangers, but I was desperate. I suspect you would have acted similarly if you had just realized you were being abducted."

"Mayhap I would. But his nibs took ye for your own sake. There's a bad man after ye."

Her smile faded. "Deverill told you about that?"

Fletcher shook his head. "Didn't say much. Just that yer both in the suds." He gestured at the tray.

"Eat yer breakfast now, missy. 'Tisn't grand, but it's tasty. I'm standing in as cook this voyage. We're shorthanded, having to leave port so sudden-like. Now, if ye'll give me leave to go, I'm ter clean up the cabin where ye set that blaze."

Feeling a trifle guilty, Antonia sent him a rueful look. "I expect I should be the one to clean it, since I made the mess. Especially if you are shorthanded."

He looked startled by her offer. "But yer a lady. And like I said, 'tis my punishment. I have to fancy up the cabin so ye can sleep there tonight."

It was a small consolation, Antonia reflected, that Deverill evidently hadn't liked their sleeping arrangements last night any more than she had. When the old sailor turned toward the door, she stopped him. "Fletcher, am I a prisoner here? Am I required to remain belowdecks?"

"His nibs said ye could go topside if ye like. Just don't get in the way of the crew. And take care ye don't get too close to the rail, if ye please. If ye're hurt again, he'll have my nob on a platter."

The breakfast *was* tasty, Antonia discovered. Oat porridge, smoked ham, wheat-flour cakes instead of the usual sailor's hardtack, and a mug of ale. And she was unaccountably hungry. She felt better after the nourishment as well.

Afterward, she took the tray above decks. She knew enough about a ship's design to locate the small galley, where she left the tin breakfast dishes.

Then she made her way to the starboard bow, where she would have a good view of the ocean and the distant coast of England. She spied several seamen scurrying about the decks. And standing at the wheel was the man she'd last night heard addressed as Captain Lloyd. There was no sign of Deverill, however.

Seeing the gray-blue waves rushing past the sleek ship's hull, Antonia couldn't help feeling an unexpected surge of elation. It was a glorious morning, with sunlight sparkling on the vast expanse of white-capped sea and a brisk wind billowing the tall sails overhead, even though it was chilly enough to make her realize she should have worn her cloak.

The truth was that she loved being on a ship. She had always longed to sail the open seas, always envied men like Deverill their freedom. She'd hungered for adventure her entire life.

An abduction was *not* what she'd had in mind, but in any other circumstances, she would have thoroughly enjoyed herself here—although she would cut out her tongue before she admitted it to Deverill. Being the pragmatic sort, however, she was resigned to going to Cornwall.

She was also being craven, she knew—for avoiding the terrifying reason she was even on board the schooner.

Antonia bit her lower lip to keep it from trembling. She wanted desperately to deny that she'd been witless enough to be duped all this time by her betrothed. And more crucially, to deny that her father had been murdered for attempting to prevent her marriage. For if it was true, she would feel to blame for his death, and she couldn't bear to face that possibility. Her union with Lord Heward had once been her father's greatest desire, but even so, if she had never agreed to the marriage then her father might be alive today—

Oh, God, she couldn't bear to think of it.

She *wouldn't* think of it, Antonia promised herself furiously, or such tormenting thoughts would drive her mad.

Crushing her ruminations, she spun around and focused her gaze upward—and then promptly caught her breath. She recognized Deverill's powerful form high overhead. Coatless, he was moving along the rigging of the foremast, hauling in and letting out sheets. With less than a full crew, he must be pitching in to help . . . and perhaps working off some of his restless masculine energy at the same time, she suspected.

Despite her vexation with him, Antonia couldn't help but admire his efforts. In genteel British circles, no gentleman would deign to stoop to real physical labor. That was doubtless how Deverill had come by the hard muscles in his body. And his years of command had induced the innate authority in his stance—

Cutting off her deplorable thoughts about his commendable qualities, Antonia turned back to the railing to stare out at the sea.

It was perhaps a quarter hour later when she sensed Deverill's nearness, even before he came to stand beside her at the rail.

"You might as well go away," Antonia advised, still feeling uncharitable toward him. "I am not speaking to you."

"Should I be glad for small favors?" he responded. "Muteness on your part might allow me time to recover from the wounds your tongue inflicted on me last night."

Glancing sideways up at him, she gave Deverill a peeved look. She had been awkwardly tongue-tied around him as a girl, but if her retorts now sometimes stung him, she was only acting in self-defense, attempting to stand up to his forceful personality. She refused to be bullied by him, even if she *was* at his mercy for the moment.

Regrettably, he took the opportunity to inspect her

injury. Laying his fingers alongside her jaw, he tipped her chin up, his gaze examining her bruised forehead.

Antonia tensed, her senses assailed by his potent male presence. He made her feel as if she couldn't take a deep breath.

"You'll live," he pronounced, finally releasing her.

"No thanks to you."

His smile was bland. "It is only reasonable that you don't feel kindly toward me—"

"How clever of you to comprehend the source of my aggravation."

"—but I consider your fortitude admirable. You are taking this better than I hoped."

"What did you hope?" Antonia asked, arching an eyebrow. "That I would fall into strong hysterics? A tantrum would achieve little beyond my own exhaustion and your disdain. And I don't intend to give you cause to think me a weakling."

"I could not imagine ever thinking you a weakling, sweetheart."

She swept a hand out, gesturing at the ship. "Well, my fortitude is quickly failing me. Just what am I supposed to do for the next two days until we reach Cornwall?"

"There are some books in my cabin that you can read. And you can have the freedom of the deck, as long as you don't decide to jump overboard."

"I am overwhelmed by your generosity."

At her dry quip, his green, reproachful gaze ensnared hers. Antonia had difficulty looking away. Pursing her lips, she glanced back over her shoulder. "I should like to meet Captain Lloyd."

"Why?" His question held a touch of suspicion.

"Because it is only polite. Will you perform the introductions, or shall I do it myself?"

Deverill appeared reluctant, but he took her elbow and steered her across the deck to the ship's wheel to meet his captain.

A robust, muscular man with a touch of gray at his temples, Captain Lloyd seemed genuinely pleased to meet her as he bowed over her hand. "I knew your father, Miss Maitland. He was a remarkable man."

She felt a decided lump in her throat. "Thank you, sir." She paused. "I was wondering, Captain, I have only been on one other voyage. Perhaps you might enlighten me about your ship. This is a schooner-rigged vessel, is it not?"

The captain glanced questioningly at Deverill, as if asking permission to reply.

Deverill took her arm again to lead her away. "I'll tell you anything you wish to know about the ship. Captain Lloyd has his hands full just now."

Normally she would have loved to hear what fascinating things Deverill had to say about his ship, but not daring to subject herself to any extended time in his company, Antonia tugged her arm from his grasp. "Never mind. I believe I prefer to remain in ignorance."

She turned away, feeling the force of his gaze burning into her back as she paced over to the railing.

Deverill refrained from following her, knowing it was wiser to keep as much distance as possible between them.

He'd dreamed about Antonia last night, sweet erotic dreams that had left him feverish and aching. He'd woken at first light, his body alive with desire, keenly aware that she lay sleeping only a short space away.

For a time, he couldn't prevent himself from watching her, couldn't stop imagining how she would look if he had shared the berth with her all night long . . . her hair tangled by the wildness of their passion, her mouth red and swollen, her body warm and sweetly flushed. Their lovemaking would be raw and hot and elemental, he knew—

Cursing, Deverill had risen and dressed quickly. Upon leaving the cabin, he'd thrown himself into physical activity, determined to work off his sexual frustration as much as to aid his overtaxed crew.

But he swore that tonight he would return Antonia to her own cabin. It was far too dangerous keeping her in his. If he had to spend one more night with her, he wouldn't be able to keep from taking her. And then he would never want to stop.

The notion was incredibly appealing—spending weeks satiating himself with Antonia in his bed. Watching her now as she stood at the rail, her long, slender back held rigidly, sunlight glinting off her shining hair and turning it to flame, Deverill fully understood the lust that drove him. Her combination of defiance and vulnerability and vibrant beauty was impossibly arousing. And the hint of fiery, untamed sensuality that lay beneath her elegant demeanor was irresistibly tantalizing.

He wouldn't take up the challenge of uncovering her sensuality, though, Deverill promised himself. She was under his protection now, and he couldn't take advantage of her defenselessness.

The impropriety of her being the sole female on board his ship was bad enough. If their subterfuge about Antonia being chaperoned during her abrupt visit to the country didn't work, her reputation would wind up in shreds, and he would have an entirely different dilemma on his hands.

Even so, he couldn't stop fantasizing about transforming his erotic dreams into reality . . . Antonia arching beneath him in passionate surrender as he drowned himself in the sweetness of her taste, the silken heat of her body. Just thinking about it made him so hungry, a deep ache settled in his loins.

"Have a care, man," Deverill muttered under his breath.

He blew out a long breath and turned back to work, knowing it was going to be a long, tormenting voyage.

When Fletcher informed her that lunch had been served in the captain's stateroom, Antonia discovered Deverill already there before her. Not wanting to be alone with him, she turned to leave, but his curt command stopped her.

"Sit down, Antonia. Fletcher went to some trouble to prepare a meal for you, and you will eat it, even if you don't fancy sharing my company."

She sent Deverill an annoyed look, but reluctantly obeyed and joined him at the table, where a surprisingly appetizing repast had been laid out.

"You might remember," Antonia said coolly, "that I am not obliged to do your bidding, Deverill. I am not one of your deckhands."

"Be glad that you aren't, my sweet termagant," he replied, "for I might be tempted to keelhaul you for your childish display of temper."

Antonia could think of no suitable retort. She *was* acting childishly. Her predicament, combined with the excess time on her hands all morning long, had left her feeling frustrated and restless. More to blame, however, was that she was trying desperately not to dwell on Deverill's damning accusations about Heward. She needed something to occupy herself, or she would go mad.

"It would help," she said finally, "if I had something to keep my mind off my captivity. Perhaps I could be of use to your crew."

Deverill's eyebrow rose. "You are volunteering to work alongside my crew?"

Antonia shrugged. "It is galling to be treated as a helpless female. I have no training in sailing a ship, but surely there is some task I could perform."

Deverill eyed her thoughtfully. "There are always sails that need mending."

She made a face. "You probably don't remember that I told you I hate to sew."

"I remember quite clearly."

Which is precisely why he'd suggested that particular onerous task, she discerned. Antonia sent him an exasperated look. "You enjoy watching my hackles rise, don't you?"

"It has its pleasures. But seriously, unskilled seamen start with the lowest form of menial labor. I doubt you would be interested in soiling your hands to that extent."

"Everything about a ship interests me. And I am not afraid of a little hard work. I would even scrub decks. It would be preferable to being idle the entire voyage."

"I suppose you could work under Fletcher's supervision. He has trained enough green recruits to crew a dozen ships."

Antonia brightened. "Would he teach me about sailing?"

"He doesn't like having females on board a vessel—he thinks it brings back luck. But you're already here.

And considering that you are Samuel Maitland's daughter, I expect he will make an allowance."

"Then you will ask him for me?"

"Yes, princess. If you're certain."

"Thank you," Antonia murmured. Smiling for the first time since her abduction, she picked up her fork and applied herself to the luncheon fare, wanting to eat quickly so she could get on with the exciting prospect of learning how a real sailor spent his days.

Fletcher balked at first, not only because of her gender but also because she was a member of the gentry.

Deverill had put the question to him when the old tar came to the stateroom to retrieve the dishes. Fletcher looked startled at first, then suspicious, as though wondering if he might be the butt of a jest.

Finally he shook his head mulishly. " 'Tain't fitting for a genteel lady. Nay, won't do it."

Holding up a hand to forestall Deverill's reply, Antonia jumped to her feet and grabbed one of the trays to follow Fletcher from the stateroom into the narrow corridor, determined to convince him to reconsider.

"Please, Fletcher. Cannot you overlook my station just this once? My father's family was not the least genteel. He came from the lower classes and was not ashamed to work for his living."

The old man stopped in his tracks, his skeptical gaze sliding over Antonia's elegant gown, which seemed to contradict her claim.

"Do you have any notion," she pressed, "how vexing it is to always be proper and sedate and ladylike? How stifling it can be?"

"Don't rightly know," Fletcher acknowledged.

"Well, pretend you always had to wear a coat and

cravat and take tea with the vicar's wife three times a day."

When Fletcher merely looked confused, she could tell that argument wasn't working, so she took another tack. "Pretend you could never go to sea again. That you could never feel the wind on your face or the swell of the waves beneath your feet. It would be worse than prison for you, isn't that so?"

He scowled at that, and Antonia knew she had struck a nerve. "Aye, I suppose it would."

"Well, I have been in a sort of prison all my life. A very pleasant one, to be sure, but I've always longed to escape for a few moments of freedom. This is my one chance, Fletcher."

His hesitation gave her hope, so she kept on. "I know a mariner's life is a hard one, but I have something to prove to Deverill. I want to show him that I am not a worthless fribble. He calls me 'princess,' but I am not like that, truly."

"Princess, eh?"

"Yes. Please, I only want to learn. I promise I will do whatever you tell me, exactly as you tell me. Won't you just give me a chance?"

Hearing a soft chuckle behind her, she realized that Deverill had come to stand at the door of the stateroom and was listening to their conversation. In the dim companionway, she could see the gleam of amusement in his eyes.

"You might as well give in gracefully, Fletcher," he suggested. "She will eventually wear you down anyway."

Antonia ignored Deverill's vexing remark, since he was actually promoting her case, and held her breath, waiting.

Fletcher looked from her to Deverill and back

again, before finally shrugging. "Very well then, come along. Ye can start by helping me clean the galley."

It wasn't precisely what she had hoped for, but resolving not to press her luck, Antonia followed Fletcher meekly, feeling Deverill's amused gaze on her all the while.

It took all afternoon, but Antonia gained a measure of respect from Fletcher that day. After she helped him wash dishes without a word of complaint, he fashioned a makeshift apron to cover her gown and set her to another menial chore, but one crucial to the seaworthiness of a ship: She learned how to smear pitch on hempen rope and barrel staves and deck planks to make them waterproof. Then she graduated to more interesting lessons.

The first was how to correctly tie a sailor's knot. Fletcher showed her six different kinds and made her practice until she could tie them blindfolded.

Finally he nodded with grudging approval. "Not bad for a gel."

Antonia grinned, considering that high praise indeed.

She saw something of her father in the crusty old seaman. Fletcher was blunt-spoken and hardworking, qualities her father would have admired. He was also an exacting taskmaster, but she found herself enjoying every challenge he threw at her.

Having observed her father's designs for years, she knew the names of all the myriad sails on the schooner, but not how to haul on a line or to raise a sheet. Her hands were red and smarting by the time she completed those introductory exercises.

When Fletcher proposed she quit, Antonia declined, reluctant to end an afternoon that had been one of the most intriguing she could ever remember. She was also aware that Deverill had been observing her progress from time to time, and she didn't want him thinking that she was giving up. Moreover, there was yet another task she had always longed to attempt: climbing the rigging.

Fletcher balked at that request, too, at first.

"Please," Antonia pleaded. "I won't try to wrestle with a sheet. I just want to know what it feels like to be up in the sky."

She could see from his hesitation that he understood her longing. "Ye can't go up in skirts," he said at last. "Ye'll break yer pretty neck."

"Do you have a pair of breeches you could loan me? And perhaps a shirt?"

"Breeches?" He nearly squeaked the word. "For yerself?"

"Well, yes. It might be a bit scandalous, but I will be completely clothed."

" 'Tain't right for a female to wear breeches," he muttered, scowling at her.

"Perhaps not." She sighed. "Deverill probably wouldn't approve, either, but I intend to show him that I am up to the challenge."

Fletcher's scowl slowly faded, to be replaced by a sly look of glee. "I reckon ye've earned the right after today."

From his sea chest in his own shared quarters, he fetched her a rough linen shirt and a pair of dark blue seaman's trousers, along with a belt to fasten them. Antonia went below to her new cabin. When she returned, dressed as a young mariner, she felt several pairs of curious male eyes riveted on her.

Fletcher snapped at the crew, ordering them back

to work, then instructed her how to securely grip the ratline—a rope ladder attached to the horizontal shrouds of each mast—and how to hook an arm or even a leg over to brace herself should she become unbalanced. He chose the shorter foremast so she would have a view from the front of the ship, and told her to pause upon reaching each of the five yards to make certain she could handle each height without growing dizzy.

Taking a deep breath, Antonia began to climb, with Fletcher following directly beneath her to prevent her from unexpectedly falling.

Exhilaration filled her with each step, along with relief that she had no trouble with the height. When she reached the top yard of the fore skysail, joy bubbled up inside her. She felt as if she were on top of the world, flying.

The view was incredible. Her spirits soaring, she gave a shout of pure jubilation, which startled Fletcher enough that he demanded to know if she'd gone daft.

It was a long while before he finally persuaded Antonia to come down from the rigging, and she was laughing with elation when she dropped the last few feet to the deck. And when she hugged Fletcher to thank him for the experience of a lifetime, he blushed to the roots of his grizzled hair.

"Now, there, enough of that, missy," he muttered upon catching several crew members grinning at him.

He stalked off toward the galley to begin preparing supper, while Antonia went below again to change back into her gown, flashing a brilliant smile at Deverill as she passed.

He felt the impact like a sensual blow. He'd been keeping an eye on her instruction all afternoon. Even though he'd had reservations about letting Antonia go up so high, he trusted Fletcher to keep her safe. And seeing her spontaneous joy had been a sheer pleasure.

Being the recipient of her smile, however, made tenderness twist in his chest and desire stir in his loins. He did his best to ignore both responses but found it impossible. Just watching Antonia embrace life as she did was damnably arousing. So was seeing her in male trousers, her shapely derriere defined by the wool fabric.

It was remarkable, the hunger she roused in him so effortlessly. Remarkable and annoying—even if it did help him to forget the grim reason she was even on board the schooner with him.

Dinner that evening in the stateroom was just as disturbing to him, although they weren't alone. Antonia peppered Captain Lloyd with questions about navigation, which stirred a distinct spark of jealousy in Deverill. He could have answered all her questions, but she still wasn't speaking to him if she could avoid it, for she hadn't yet forgiven him for snatching her away from the danger that he was convinced threatened her.

He would do it again in an instant, yet living in such close quarters with Antonia had made him continually aroused and short-tempered. His erotic dream last night about her had only increased his cravings, almost to the point of pain.

As soon as politeness allowed, Deverill excused himself and escaped up on deck, leaving her with the captain. He remained there until nearly midnight, at which time he retired to his cabin to sleep alone. But her scent was on his pillow, and his body's primal response was so keen that Deverill resigned himself to passing another restless night fighting his lustful urges.

Antonia, on the other hand, slept better than she had the previous night. And the following morning, she woke eagerly, looking forward to her next lessons with Fletcher. She didn't even mind when he set her to mending sails.

He showed her how to repair rips in the heavy canvas with sheep-gut sinews threaded through a whalebone needle. The task further pained her hands, but she made no complaint for fear Fletcher would put an end to their sessions, which she found far too fascinating to give up.

To her delight, Fletcher became expansive, recounting tales of past adventures that Deverill and his crew had encountered on the high seas.

She was most interested in learning about Deverill. "Have you known him long, Fletcher?"

"Been with him since his first command, and I'm honored to serve under him. Saved me life more than once. A braver man ye'll never find. His nibs is a legend, don't ye know."

"I've heard something of the sort."

At her request, Fletcher told her of some of Deverill's heroic exploits during his career of fighting pirates, primarily the Barbary corsairs in the Mediterranean, and more recently, in the Indian Ocean on behest of the British government. According to Fletcher, the danger Deverill regularly faced would have defeated any ten normal men.

"I know he bears scars," Antonia confided quietly. "How did those come about?"

Fletcher abruptly scowled, while his tone turned grim. " 'Tis not a tale fit for a lady's ears." For a long moment then, he remained mute, while his expression took on a faraway look.

"I heard it was Turks," she murmured, a chill shiver sweeping through her.

"Aye." Fletcher nearly spat the word. "The bloody Turks."

From her smattering of history at school, she knew the rulers of the Turkish Empire had conquered many of the lands of the Mediterranean and remained to rule with iron fists. "So what happened? My house-keeper said Deverill's crew was taken captive and . . . abused. Were you with him then?"

Fletcher nodded, a blaze of anger in his eyes. Yet it was another long moment before he spoke. " 'Twas nigh on ten years ago. Cap'n Deverill—he was our cap'n then—had already made a name for himself thwarting pirates, confiscating their treasure and such. Earned their wrath something fierce. Well, he paid an official call on a local pasha who'd signed a treaty with Britain. Turns out the pasha wanted to make an example of the cap'n. When we put into port, his nibs and officers were invited to a feast, but 'twas a sham. Those bloody devils took 'em all pris-oner, then boarded our ship and took the rest of us, too. Commenced snuffing us, one every few days, and made his nibs watch. 'Twere saving him for last, but they carved him up with one of those scimitars, a mark for each man who died."

Fletcher squeezed his eyes shut, a shudder running through him as if he was remembering the horror. " 'Twas two months of pure hell," he whispered, "but it seemed like two years."

Antonia's heart wrenched. She felt herself shudder as Fletcher had, unable even to imagine what it must have been like to endure such agonizing torture. "But you somehow managed to escape?"

"Aye. The cap'n could barely stand for the pain, but he overpowered his guards and then made the pasha *his* prisoner. He could have escaped with his mate, but he wouldn't leave any of us behind, though some of us were sorely wounded. We fought our way to the port and took back our ship. Sailed away— what was left of us, at any rate—and returned a month later with a man o' war sister ship to raze the port and put a period to those bloody savages for good. I owe Cap'n Deverill me life, and that's a fact."

"It seems so horrible, what you all suffered," she murmured in a raw voice.

"Aye, it was. Wounds of the flesh heal in time, but 'twas worse for Cap'n Deverill, since he was the captain and responsible for the crew."

She understood what Fletcher was implying—the depth of guilt that must have racked Deverill ever since. His body bore vivid scars from the ordeal, and doubtless, so did his mind and heart.

Scrutinizing her, Fletcher spoke again gravely. "I'll wager 'tis why he wouldn't let ye jump ship t'other night. Yer his responsibility and he won't give up. He'll spend his last breath saving ye." The old man let that sink in, then continued in a voice that held an odd note of pleading. "Ye shouldn't be vexed at him, missy. Cap'n Deverill is only taking the course he feels is right. Ye can trust him with yer life, I swear to it."

Looking away, Antonia bit her lip. She had always known Deverill could be trusted, that his honor and integrity were above question. It was just that she'd been furious with him for tricking her and for his high-handedness in thinking he knew what was best for her. Yet she could no longer deny he'd acted on his heartfelt conviction, taking her away from London and Heward for her own protection. And if his belief was true, what did that say about her father's death?

For two days now she had tried desperately to ignore the damning possibility that her father had been murdered by her betrothed, for if she stopped fighting the notion for one moment, the full horror of it would seep into her soul. But she was losing the battle with herself.

It was a struggle for Antonia to force her agitated thoughts back to mending sails. And her mind was still in turmoil a while later, when Fletcher showed her how to tie off a line attached to the jib.

Distracted, she failed to give the task her full attention and thus was caught off guard when a sudden burst of wind caught the sail and nearly ripped the line from her hands.

Both her palms suffered stinging rope burns, while three of her fingers were scraped raw to the point of bleeding. The injuries stung fiercely, but she instinctively hid them from Fletcher, not wanting to appear a weakling. A half hour later, however, the throbbing pain in her hands was so acute, she could barely keep from moaning.

When Deverill came up to speak to Fletcher just then, he caught one glimpse of her face and demanded to know what was wrong.

"N-nothing," Antonia managed, but her reply sounded breathless and shaky even to her own ears.

She tried to elude Deverill, but he caught her elbow and barked out a soft command, "Tell me, Antonia."

Gritting her teeth, she turned her palms faceup to show him the oozing raw welts.

Deverill swore under his breath and threw a savage

glance at Fletcher. "I thought I told you to keep her safe."

"It was not his fault!" Antonia exclaimed, leaping to the old tar's defense. "It was mine."

"I have no doubt of that," Deverill grated. "You were too intent on not showing any weakness to ask for a respite." He grasped her elbow again. "Come with me."

"Come where?" Antonia asked, trying to resist.

He steered her toward the companionway ladder. "Below to my cabin, so I can see to your hands."

Antonia gave in almost meekly, feeling too much pain to argue.

When they reached his cabin, he made her sit at his desk while he gathered supplies, including a basin of water, some cotton gauze, and a jar of ointment.

"Evidently I was wrong when I credited you with a high degree of intelligence," Deverill said, inspecting her hands more closely. "I should have known you would be this hardheaded."

Antonia held herself stiffly, trying not to cry. "I don't begrudge you your amusement at my expense, Deverill, but I would appreciate it very much if you would refrain from crowing just now when I am suffering."

"I'm not crowing."

"You aren't?" Her tone held skepticism.

"No. I'm provoking you to take your mind off the pain. I imagine this hurts like the devil."

"Oh." She didn't know what to say to that. The fact that Deverill sympathized with her plight helped somehow.

His touch was gentle, but she still gasped when he cleansed the savage weals. When he blotted the raw skin dry, unavoidable tears sprang to her eyes, and she clenched her teeth to keep from crying out.

Deverill glanced up at her briefly, his own jaw tensing. "This will take away some of the pain."

He spread ointment over the raw flesh, thankfully bringing her hands a measure of cooling relief, and then carefully wrapped her palms and her three injured fingers with gauze.

Antonia tried to sniff back her tears, but Deverill's kindness only made her feel worse. Here she was whining at her minor injuries when he had endured terrible torment that had left his body forever scarred. She wasn't proud of herself, either, when she remembered how she had questioned his integrity, his very honor.

And then there was the matter of her father's death.

Numbing cold seeped into her as she remembered how delighted her father had been when she became engaged to Lord Heward, a man of noble stature, of impeccable breeding. . . . Her throat tightened on the aching memory.

"You truly believe Heward is guilty, don't you?" she asked in a tremulous voice.

Deverill stilled in his ministrations. "Yes. I no longer have any doubts. Your father intended to break off your betrothal, so Heward poisoned him. If I hadn't believed it, Antonia, I would never have taken so drastic a step as abducting you."

She closed her eyes tightly as the tears threatened.

"I felt I had no choice," Deverill said quietly. "You had no one else to stand champion for you."

Her blurred gaze lifted to his. "Is that what you are, my champion?"

He was silent for a moment as he finished the last

bandage. "Perhaps more accurately, I am filling the role of guardian. I want you safe, Antonia."

It was inexplicably comforting to know Deverill was watching over her, but a sick wretchedness gnawed at her heart: Dismay that she had been so stupid as to believe Heward's lies. And horror that she had contributed to her father's death.

Perhaps it was the accumulation of emotional strain during the past two days, or the acceptance of her father's senseless death, but her defenses gave way and she couldn't stop her tears from spilling over. "If Heward is guilty of murder . . . then my betrothal led directly to it. I caused my father's death."

Deverill gave her a hard look. "Don't be absurd. Of course you didn't cause it. Heward was solely to blame."

But she couldn't absolve herself so readily. A sense of grief swept through her with oppressive force. It was as if she had lost her father all over again. A sob caught in her throat, and she couldn't stop it.

"Antonia, don't. . . ." Deverill's voice was low and pleading.

She felt his strong hands close around her upper arms as he pulled her to her feet. She averted her gaze, not wanting him to see her cry. She hated that he understood her pain so well. Yet at the same time, she felt so vulnerable and raw that she ached with a need to be held. It was all she could do not to bury her face in Deverill's hard chest and ask him to hold her for just a little while.

But she wasn't required to ask. Deverill drew her against him, tucking her head beneath his chin and wrapping his arms around her.

Her tears came furiously then, and she sobbed out her grief. For a long while, Antonia clung to him, letting Deverill console her. Eventually her sobs quieted, but she still stood there in his embrace, feeling the solid strength of him. He made her want to curl into him and never let go.

Thankfully, he seemed in no hurry to release her, although he repeated his earlier plea. "Don't cry, sweetheart. I can't bear it."

The protectiveness in his voice felt strangely wonderful. She had missed having someone be protective of her.

She felt his fingers brush her hair, then her face. Infinitely gentle, they stroked her damp cheek, her jaw, then raised her chin. When she met his brilliant green gaze, something turned over in her chest, sweetly painful.

"I suppose I am a weakling after all," Antonia whispered.

"No. Never." He fished in his coat pocket for a handkerchief, which she used to wipe her eyes and nose, a task that was made more awkward because of her bandaged hands. "But I would much rather see you cursing me than weeping."

She gave a final sniff. "I am sorry. I didn't mean to ruin your coat."

His smile was tender. "It's for a good cause."

The corners of her mouth quivered, and she smiled bleakly in return.

She might as well have grabbed him by the heart. Deverill felt an aching tightness in his chest as a protective tenderness rushed through him. Against his will, he reached up to rest his hand against her tearstained cheek.

He knew he was on dangerous ground, but he could only think of how damned soft and vulnerable Antonia was just now, how beautiful. He wished she weren't so damned lovely, for it filled him with a nearly savage kind of wanting.

Deverill clenched his teeth, deploring the sensation of not being in control. Yet he had a sweet, self-destructive urge not to even fight it.

Unable to help himself, he tilted her face up to his and slowly bent to kiss her. Antonia stilled instantly, but Deverill felt her instinctive response to him, felt the way her mouth softened and shaped itself to his.

He breathed a sound between a curse and a prayer. It was a simple kiss, but the sharp pleasure of it stabbed him in his midsection, in his loins. Worse, when he drew back, he could see her eyes were luminous with heat, and he knew Antonia was fighting her desire as much as he was. He knew, also, that he didn't want her fighting him any longer. . . .

His palm cradling her face tenderly, he bent his head again.

Antonia watched, spellbound as his beautiful mouth moved closer. When his breath fanned warm against her lips, her bandaged hands rose to press lightly against his chest. Yet she had no thought of pushing him away; she only wanted to anchor herself against the stunning sensuality of his kiss.

She held her breath as Deverill's lips caressed hers again, alluring, whisper soft. His mouth was as warm and hard as she remembered from her dreams, his taste as heady. Antonia gave a breathless whimper as his lips twisted and pulled softly, brushing sparks across the surface of hers. Then he deepened the pressure, settling his mouth more fully on hers, and she very nearly moaned.

Why did her heart lurch so wildly at his touch? How could she resist the aching need he aroused in her? Deverill made her feel so many emotions, it was bewildering, frightening. When his tongue penetrated her lips in a sensual invasion, a heated rush of feeling assaulted her.

Her body shuddered at the riveting sensation. His kiss was an intimate knowing of her mouth, one that stole her breath away. She could feel the hardness of his corded muscles beneath her fingertips, the heat of his powerful torso, smell the arousing scent of him, warm and faintly musky.

Then, to her dismay, he broke off his kiss. A sense of loss filled her, but only for a moment. His hands caressing her shoulders, Deverill turned her and urged her backward a few steps, until her back was pressed against the bulkhead. When he pulled her close to his body, she could feel him . . . his power and strength, the sinewed length of his legs, the breadth of his chest, the hardness of him.

His eyes smoldered with heat as he stared down at her. Antonia's mouth went dry at the fierce yearning in his look, while a wild tingle of excitement surged through her blood. "Deverill . . . please . . . kiss me again."

"I intend to, love. I don't think I could stop myself."

He bent his head once more, feathering kisses along her jaw and lower, along the column of her neck. His warm lips sent a sweep of sensation surging over her skin. Then his tongue caressed the jumping pulse in the hollow of her throat, while his fingertips rose to her bodice and skimmed the underside of her breasts.

"So sweet," he murmured, his voice a husky rasp.

His strong hands cupped the swells beneath the muslin, his thumbs coaxing, making the sensitive tips engorge painfully under his light touch. A moment later, his mouth joined in, grazing her breasts with arousing caresses.

Urgent longing gathered in the pit of Antonia's stomach, in her loins. Then his lips closed over one taut bud, flooding her veins with shuddering heat.

Arching against him, she shut her eyes at the sweet spasm that arrowed down to her loins. Desire churned inside her, awakening a wonderful aching weakness that pulsed to life in that secret place between her thighs.

Still suckling her nipple, Deverill reached down to raise the hem of her skirt. He growled softly as he found the naked skin of her thigh. When his hand moved higher to brush her woman's mound, Antonia instantly felt her soft, secret flesh melting with sweet moisture. Then he touched the wet cleft between her legs, his thumb gliding over the folds of her sex, pulling her open, stroking.

Antonia gasped aloud as the melting hunger inside her turned into a relentless, gnawing ache. His touch became both vital and unbearable. Flushed and straining, she pressed against him, wanting more, needing more.

At her eager response, Deverill took her mouth again, his kiss turning suddenly hot and hungry. Antonia responded with frantic ardor, her body trembling violently against his. She couldn't remember how to breathe; her skin burned with a fever too hot for her to bear.

When he slipped a finger into her, her moan of pleasure was hoarse and raw at his probing invasion. The hunger in her was like flame, licking her flesh, consuming her.

Then abruptly Deverill lifted his head, his jaw tight. He pulled in a deep, shuddering breath, as if striving for control. "God, you are dangerous. Just touching you is driving me to the brink."

Almost faint with desire, Antonia raised her mouth to his, pleading against his lips, "Please . . . don't stop."

This was what she had dreamed of. In her dreams, Deverill had kissed her this way, loved her this way. She wanted him, wanted his passion. She felt as though she might die if he didn't give it to her.

Following her instincts, she reached down between their bodies, deliberately brushing the front placket of his breeches. She saw his response in his flared nostrils, the darkening of his eyes, heard the sudden intake of breath.

She didn't have to plead with him again. He drew back only long enough to unfasten his breeches and drawers and free his rigid arousal. Raising her skirts to her waist, Deverill eased her thighs apart and wedged his knee between hers. His eyes seared her as he cupped her bare bottom, pulling her hard into the cradle of his thighs, firmly against his naked erection.

At the delicious pressure, her knees nearly buckled. But then Deverill was bracing her, lifting her up, pulling her legs around his hips as his kiss slanted down fiercely over her mouth again, taking, devouring.

The hard bulge of his sex throbbed against the soft yielding of her loins while his tongue thrust into her mouth, plunging rhythmically, just as she knew his flesh would do. Her heart pounding, Antonia tensed with a woman's fear of the unknown. The hot, throbbing maleness of him pulsing against her felt enormous and alien.

But she needed desperately for him to assuage the terrible, yearning ache inside her, needed to feel him deep inside her. When Deverill gripped his hard shaft and began to ease its silken head into her quivering flesh, Antonia whimpered in surrender.

Her breath coming in ragged pants, she shut her eyes tightly and gave herself up to the bliss his sensual assault promised.

Nine

Frenzied need surged through Deverill; the need to plunge deep inside Antonia, to feel her wet heat close around him.

His mouth still plundering hers, he lowered her onto his engorged length, allowing her own weight to impel her. Instantly she stiffened as his rigid flesh rended and stretched her soft woman's tissues.

As his penetration dredged a startled whimper from deep in her throat, Deverill's eyes flew open, and he froze for a heartbeat, shock flooding him as he realized how much he was hurting her.

"Oh, God . . ." he rasped, "you're a virgin."

Were a virgin, his mind corrected as he saw the pain contorting Antonia's face. She was panting softly, while her body struggled to accept the fullness of him.

Remorse speared through him. He should have realized she'd exaggerated her carnal experience that afternoon in the gazebo. In truth, he'd suspected it. But just now his mind had only been focused on possessing her.

Groaning, Deverill filled his lungs with an uneven breath and pressed his forehead against hers, straining for willpower. "Damnation." The word was not only a curse but a jagged prayer for self-control. The sweetness of her hot, tight body was driving him to madness, but somehow he had to find the strength to master himself before he lost all control and hurt her even more severely.

With herculean effort, he carefully pulled himself free and lowered Antonia to her feet, but he was too late to stop his fierce climax. Gritting his teeth, Deverill closed his hand over the head of his shaft to catch the shooting spurts of his seed as his body shuddered.

For a long moment, he simply remained there leaning into Antonia, his breath coming in harsh pants.

"Did I hurt you badly?" Deverill finally asked.

"Not . . . badly."

Swearing a low oath, he drew back, while Antonia remained braced weakly against the bulkhead, unmoving. His handkerchief was still balled in one of her fists, so he took it from her and wiped his wet hand, then went to the basin to wash away the final remnants of his seed.

"You told me that you and Heward had been lovers," he said tersely. He heard the anger in his voice, but he was angry at himself rather than Antonia. He should be shot for what he'd done. And she should have guarded her innocence more stingily. "Why the devil didn't you stop me?"

"I suppose . . . I got carried away."

He understood her answer at least, remembering his own wildness. Their simple embrace had inflamed him beyond reason. He'd lost his head, his blood surging thick and hot in his need to finally take what he'd been craving since the first time he'd held Antonia in his arms.

Deverill stared at her, trying to come to terms with the passion that had ignited between them. He had never known such hot, wrenching desire. And perhaps he was lying to himself. Despite her innocence, he might still have made love to her just now—but he certainly would have taken much more care if he'd known this was her first time. He hadn't given her any pleasure, only pain.

"You should have warned me," Deverill muttered, raking a hand through his hair. "I would have tried not to hurt you."

Slightly dazed, Antonia stared back at him. She could still taste Deverill on her lips, still feel the imprint of his mouth burning into hers, the hard flesh that had possessed her throbbing inside her. His abrupt withdrawal, however, had left her with the same unfulfilled ache that had haunted her dreams for years.

Her senses were in turmoil as well. One part of her was dismayed by her wantonness, while another part was glad it had been Deverill who had breeched her womanhood.

"You needn't feel remorse," she murmured finally. "It was my fault, not yours. I wanted you to make love to me."

She saw Deverill's hard, virile face tighten at her declaration, but he kept silent as he wrung out a cloth and carried it over to her.

When he started to draw up her skirt, Antonia snapped out of her daze. "What are you doing?"

"Washing away the blood."

"I can do it myself."

"Not with your hands bandaged. You need to keep them dry. Now be still, vixen, and let me take care of you."

Antonia felt a flush of embarrassment sting her cheeks, but Deverill's gentle stroking over her thighs and feminine cleft was perfunctory rather than loverlike.

His next words as he straightened were just as perfunctory. "You realize, don't you, that this leaves us with little choice but to marry."

Antonia sucked in a sharp breath. "*What?*"

"You heard me. We will have to marry. We'll hold the ceremony as soon as we reach Cornwall and can call the banns."

"You can't possibly be serious," she said, staring at him. "You have no desire to wed me. You don't wish to wed anyone."

His mouth twisted wryly. "Perhaps not, but I took your innocence. Marriage is the only honorable course."

"You did not *take* my innocence, Deverill. I gave it to you. There is a difference."

"Not from my standpoint. And not in the eyes of the ton. I won't leave you unprotected, Antonia. If our carnal union becomes public knowledge, you'll be branded a fallen woman."

If her legs had been limp before, they nearly gave out now. Quickly she moved over to the armchair and sank down there before she toppled over.

She had no intention of accepting Deverill's unwilling proposal. In the past, he'd made it very clear he had no interest in settling down in marriage. Certainly not a society marriage, since he had no use for the idle, shallow, pompous pretensions of the ton.

He had no desire to give up his bachelorhood, she knew very well. For mercy's sake, only two nights ago he had been carousing at a brothel with a light-skirt—

No, he didn't want a wife, and even if he did, she doubted he would choose *her*. They were like tinder and flame together, always kindling sparks that threatened to erupt in a conflagration. She didn't want Deverill, either, Antonia told herself firmly . . . an arrogant, overbearing, exasperating rogue who would only provoke her to distraction.

"No," Antonia said firmly. "Fallen woman or not, I won't marry you. I don't require you to fall on your sword to save me."

Deverill walked over to a cabinet and pulled out a decanter of brandy and a glass. "It needn't be a true marriage," he said brusquely, pouring a large measure of the spirits and swallowing half of it in one gulp. "It can be in name only. I'll give you the protection of my name, then leave you to your own devices. We can each go our separate ways. You can continue to reside in London, while I'll live on Cyrene when I'm not at sea."

Admittedly her pride was piqued at his casual dismissal of their entire relationship. She held out her hand for the glass. "May I have some?"

He raised an eyebrow, but crossed to her chair to hand the glass of brandy to her. Antonia took a small swallow, gasping as fire burned down her throat.

The idea of marriage between them was absurd. Deverill might always have been her ideal. A man of passion and daring—strong, courageous, bold, exciting. She might envy everything he represented: adventure, freedom, life on one's own terms. But the very qualities she admired most about him made him exactly the wrong husband for her.

"The whole idea is absurd," she repeated aloud. "I don't want to marry you, Deverill. And in any event, you are nothing like the kind of husband my father wanted for me."

"At least I'm wealthy enough that you needn't fear I am claiming you for your fortune."

"But you have no title."

"True," Deverill agreed, taking the glass from her and pouring himself another brandy.

His tone was dry, but Antonia was only reminded of the prime reason she could never marry Deverill. Even though she no longer intended to have Lord Heward, she would eventually have to wed *some* nobleman to honor her father's fondest wish. She owed it to him, particularly considering that he might have given his life in her defense.

Antonia flinched at the fresh stab of pain that shot through her, wondering what her father would think of how she had betrayed his dream. He might understand her losing her virginity in a blind moment of passion, but he would turn over in his grave if she had foiled her chance for a noble match.

But perhaps his dream could still be salvaged, as long as she handled it discreetly and created no overt scandal. . . .

It was another moment before she realized Deverill was speaking to her again.

". . . you have no choice but to wed me. I've ruined you for any other husband."

"No, you have not," she replied, her tone slightly bitter but pragmatic. "As an heiress, I have the wealth to buy a titled husband, even if I am no longer a virgin. Although I assure you, this time I intend to take more care to choose an amiable, placid gentleman who won't ruthlessly manipulate me as Heward did, or dictate to me as you do."

The cool smile Deverill flashed her held little humor. Before he could retort, though, Antonia took a steadying breath. "I appreciate that you saved me from Heward's clutches, Deverill, and obviously I owe you a debt of gratitude. But forcing you to wed me would put me even further in your debt."

"And that would be too galling."

"Exactly. Moreover, my reputation is hardly my chief concern just now. What I care about most is getting justice for my father. If Heward murdered Papa as you believe, I want him punished."

"You may trust me on that score," Deverill said darkly. "I grieved for your father, Antonia, and I fully intend to see Heward punished."

"What do you mean to do? You cannot return to London as a wanted man, can you?"

His gaze grew hooded. "Before I left London, I put some plans in motion with surrogates acting on my behalf, searching for proof of your father's murder and for evidence to clear my name, so I can bring the real killers to justice. As soon as we reach Cornwall, I mean to take additional steps. And I'll send Captain Lloyd back to London to bring me reports."

"But you eventually mean to return to London so you can expose Heward?"

"Yes," Deverill replied, his jaw tight. "I wouldn't miss it for the world."

Antonia nodded in satisfaction, thankful for the shard of vengeful anger that pierced her pain. In her heart, she was persuaded that Deverill was right: that

Heward had indeed killed her father so he could be certain to wed her and assume control of her fortune. And if she had accepted that, it was even simpler to believe he had framed Deverill for murder to eliminate him as a rival and prevent his interference in her marriage.

If Heward *was* guilty, she wanted him to pay for what he had done—to her father and to Deverill as well. "I intend to return to London with you," she declared, her thoughts racing ahead.

"No, you won't. Heward is far too cunning and dangerous an adversary. Until he is securely in prison, you'll remain in Cornwall where you will be safe."

When she pressed her lips together, refraining from arguing, Deverill shot her a suspicious glance. He was reluctant to share his plans for confronting Heward, or to involve Antonia in any way, for he wanted her well out of the crossfire. And of course he couldn't reveal anything to her about the Guardians, since his oath of service swore him to secrecy.

But his strategy wasn't the issue at hand. Somehow Antonia had managed to change the subject. They had been discussing the necessity of marrying.

She had made several pertinent arguments against it, Deverill acknowledged. It was indeed probable that as an heiress Antonia could find another titled candidate who would be eager to fill the role of her husband. Someone complacent enough to accept a marriage of convenience on her terms.

The corner of Deverill's mouth curled. Antonia would be bored silly within a fortnight with a milksop for her mate. But perhaps a milksop was preferable to the proper, stiff-necked nobleman she had chosen the first time. Having watched her on board his ship these past two days, Deverill was even more convinced that she would be miserable trapped in a society marriage with a husband who would only repress her spirit and stifle her hunger for life.

She deserved far better. She needed a man who could prove her match, one who could challenge her and keep her wits sharp.

He fit the bill in that respect, but he was completely wrong for her in all the ways that counted. He certainly wouldn't be the sort of genteel, malleable husband Antonia thought she wanted. More importantly, he couldn't play the role in the Beau Monde that she needed.

His reluctance for their union was not because he was averse to marriage or because he craved freedom and adventure, as Antonia presumed.

Once, years ago, the thrill of adventure had been enough to satisfy him. But that was before his life had changed so drastically, shattered by the devastating loss of his crew. Since his escape from captivity, he had dedicated himself to one purpose, and he would let nothing interfere.

He wouldn't let himself dream of anything more. Wouldn't even consider a future with a family, a life with love and warmth and laughter . . . perhaps children. He couldn't permit himself to be like every other man. He had forfeited the right.

There was also, Deverill added sardonically to himself, the minor detail that he was suspected of being a criminal and would be arrested for murder the instant he showed his face in London. He had every intention of proving his innocence eventually, but the tarnish to his name would hardly do Antonia's standing any good.

Still, such a rationale couldn't appease his nagging sense of guilt. He had taken her innocence, and he was a gentlemen, Antonia's beliefs to the contrary. As such, he was honor-bound to make amends.

He would simply have to convince her to wed him, Deverill knew. He intended to make Antonia his bride, whether or not she accepted it at the moment.

"You are forgetting one other advantage," he said, returning to the subject. "If you marry me, Heward's main goal of claiming your fortune will be thwarted."

Antonia frowned at that. "Perhaps so, but his goal will be thwarted no matter whom I marry. It needn't be *you*."

Unperturbed, Deverill drained the last of his brandy. "But it will be me."

"Deverill, did you not hear a single word I said?" she exclaimed in exasperation.

"Yes, love, but it hardly matters. You might as well resign yourself. You will wed me as soon as I can make the arrangements."

Antonia rose to her feet. "You can go to the devil. I certainly will *not* marry you!"

Deverill hid his smile of satisfaction; she had grabbed the bait as he'd expected. He liked watching her blue eyes flash when she was riled, yet his purpose in provoking her was more for her own sake. He would far rather see Antonia fighting mad than crying those heart-wrenching tears as she had a short while ago. And he didn't want her languishing here, morosely contemplating her father's loss or her own guilt in the manner of his death.

"It should prove an interesting contest of wills," he said mildly. Setting down his glass, he turned toward the door.

"Where are you going?" Antonia demanded.

"To inform Captain Lloyd of our intentions. It just occurred to me that he can marry us without calling any banns."

"Curse you, Deverill, don't you dare walk away! We are nowhere near finished with this conversation."

He made his escape, leaving Antonia fuming where she stood—but only for a moment. Refusing to allow him the last word, she stalked after him, determined to make him see reason.

She failed.

Their ensuing battle of wills, however, lasted the entire afternoon and into the evening. Deverill strove to avoid being alone with her, and Antonia was too well-bred to confront him and create a spectacle in front of his crew. But her smoldering glances followed Deverill everywhere he went on the schooner. And she was waiting for him at every opportunity to repeat her impassioned arguments against their matrimonial union.

At least it took her mind off her despair, Deverill told himself. Even so, he realized the necessity of plotting a strategy to counter hers.

Unlike Antonia, he had accepted the inevitability of their marriage, for it had always been a possibility. From the moment he'd abducted her, he'd known the consequences might be so damaging to her reputation, he would have to act. He had hoped they could manage to avoid it, for her sake more than his, but now he had no honorable choice. And he was resolved to overcome Antonia's resistance to the notion.

Fighting with her, however, was hardly the best way to compel her surrender. Instead, he realized, he would do better to use her own passionate nature against her. Every time he touched her, Antonia melted, and he intended to employ her weakness to his advantage.

This was a sensual game he would win.

He only hoped he could control his own weakness for her, Deverill reflected, remembering how swiftly passion had slammed into him earlier today in his cabin. He'd never been so hungry for a woman before, so hot. His primal need to possess Antonia might very well prove to be his undoing.

After partaking of dinner in the captain's quarters, Antonia retired to her own cabin, her frustration with Deverill still simmering. It was too early to sleep, since it was still daylight, with the setting sun casting a golden glow through the open porthole window. But she hoped that reading would at least distract her mind from the provoking adventurer who was proving to be the bane of her existence.

She was surprised to find a hip bath taking up a significant portion of her quarters, and more surprised to find the tub already half filled. Then Fletcher knocked a moment later and carried in two steaming pails of hot water.

"His nibs says yer in need of a bath" was Fletcher's curt explanation. "And yer allowed fresh water, since yer a lady."

Antonia would indeed relish a bath, since hot baths were her weakness, but she wasn't quite certain how to manage it with her hands bandaged. However, Fletcher had no sooner left than Deverill knocked and let himself in without an invitation.

When he shut and locked the door behind him, Antonia eyed him with barely controlled vexation. "I trust you mean to tell me what you are doing in my cabin?"

"I am here to play lady's maid." When her eyebrows shot up, he added mildly, "With your hands injured, you're in no position to care for yourself."

"I will manage somehow."

"Perhaps, but there is no reason for you to try. Turn around so I can unfasten your gown."

Her breath caught audibly. "You actually expect to *undress* me?"

"And to help you bathe."

Retreating a step, Antonia shook her head adamantly. "*No*, Deverill. It would be too improper."

"What if it is? I've already seen much of your beautiful body. And assisting your bath can hardly compromise you any further, considering that I was inside you barely a few hours ago."

Her face flooded with color as she regarded him mutely.

"You have already seen *me* nude in my bath," Deverill pointed out.

"That was different. That was purely accidental."

"Our making love this morning was not at all accidental." When she started to protest further, Deverill held up a hand. "The damage is done, Antonia. I can't give you back your innocence. So stop acting so missishly."

Her eyes narrowed. "There is a difference between acting missishly and behaving like a perfect wanton. I won't allow you to bathe me."

"I am capable of undressing you without your cooperation," he warned.

Mutinously, Antonia crossed her arms over her chest. "You are welcome to try."

Their gazes locked and warred, clashing like swords. The lust that surged through Deverill at her defiance was sharp and sudden. No one challenged him the way Antonia did—and no one aroused him more. There was a fire in her eyes that dared him to try taming her. Yet he knew better than to engage blades with her directly.

"Come now, vixen, I don't want to fight with you. Here, I brought you a peace offering." At her suspicious look, he fished in his pocket and brought out two jeweled combs. "Captain Lloyd intended these for his sister but thought you would appreciate them more, since we have a shortage of hairpins on board. You can use them to hold up your hair."

To his gratitude, his bribe actually worked. Antonia hesitated only a moment before reaching out to take the combs. "I appreciate Captain Lloyd's generosity, but I will return them when we reach Cornwall."

Loosening the twine that tied back her auburn hair, Antonia piled the silken mass high on her head and used the combs to secure the tresses. Deverill heard the faint sigh she gave, as if she found pleasure in having the weight off her neck.

"So you will let me help you bathe?" he asked, not planning to allow her refusal.

Her eyelids lowering, Antonia studied him with speculation, obviously debating with herself. "You'll forgive me if I don't trust your benevolence, Deverill. You are up to some scheme, I know it."

"Not at all. I promise to be on my best behavior."

"That is hardly reassuring. Your definition of good

behavior is nothing like the rest of the civilized world's."

He gestured toward the copper tub. "The water is growing cold. Do you want to bathe or not?"

She cast a longing glance at the hip bath.

"I am not leaving until you do," Deverill added. "So you might as well accept my offer graciously."

Evidently she knew him well enough to take him at his word, for she gave a huff of exasperation, then turned and presented her back to him. "Very well, but I am not undressing entirely. I mean to wear my nightshift."

"I wasn't aware you had a nightshift."

"I fashioned one from a pillowcase to sleep in last night. If you insist on bathing me, I will wear that to preserve a modicum of modesty."

"As you wish."

Not giving her a chance to change her mind, Deverill quickly applied himself to unfastening the hooks of her gown. Regrettably, just seeing the smooth, white expanse of Antonia's back affected him painfully, for it made him too vividly recall how her long, slender legs had wound around him as he thrust into her sweet warmth. He'd been half-aroused all afternoon, remembering their explosive passion.

Cursing the restrictions of his trousers now, Deverill renewed his resolve. He wanted Antonia naked and willing in his arms, and he intended to have her there.

When he finished with the hooks, he made her turn around to face him. Then he knelt to unlace her half boots and peel off her stockings.

"See," he said casually, "I am kneeling at your feet. There are few women who can claim to have brought me to my knees."

"I cannot claim it, either, since you are clearly there of your own accord."

Repressing a smile, Deverill stood and watched as Antonia went to the chest and withdrew her improvised nightshift—a straight sacklike contraption made of white muslin with openings for her head and arms. With her back to him, she eased her gown over her shoulders and arms and struggled into the shift, pulling the hem down carefully with her bandaged hands before pushing the gown over her hips and letting it fall in a pool at her feet.

When she turned to face him, his breath faltered at her beauty. The shift covered her breasts and loins, but the nearly diaphanous material clung to every curve and failed to obscure her feminine charms, instead revealing the outline of her rose-hued nipples and the dark thatch of curls crowning her thighs. The sight was perhaps more erotic than total nudity would have been. When Antonia stood proudly, refusing to cower at his bold scrutiny, his loins hardened even further.

"You truly are lovely."

"You needn't flatter me, Deverill."

He wasn't flattering her in the least. She was absolutely perfect, from her ripe breasts to her slender waist, to her gently flaring hips, to her creamy thighs, to her long, shapely calves and feet.

His gaze swept back up her body to her bosom. He could imagine kissing those provocative nipples, could almost taste them taut and hard against his mouth. And from there it was an easy step to imagine her naked body, pale and frenzied, as he took her. Heat exploded in Deverill's groin, nearly searing him with the intensity.

"Get in the tub," he commanded gruffly, forcibly restraining his desire.

He held out his arm, supporting Antonia as she stepped in. Careful to keep her bandaged hands dry, she sank down in the water, her knees drawn up in the confined space. Another sigh escaped her, this one of bliss.

From the desk, Deverill fetched a linen towel, a face-cloth, and a cake of soap, before kneeling beside the tub. Lathering soap into the wet cloth, he washed Antonia's face, then her arms and legs. Next he washed her back through her shift. Then finally he returned to her breasts. Dropping the cloth, he glided his slick palms over her muslin-covered nipples.

Antonia sucked in a sharp breath. Her shift was still better than nothing, but she hadn't counted on the fact that once the muslin was wet, it would be nearly transparent. Nor had she realized how impossible it would be to resist Deverill when he was bent on seduction.

Until then, she had done her best to ignore his ministrations, but when his caresses turned slow and erotic, she felt a hard ache flare between her shivering thighs.

She watched, fascinated, as his dark hands moved against the pale fabric covering her breasts. Deverill was watching, too, his gaze frankly, sharply male.

Striving for control, Antonia pushed his hands away.

"You can't pretend you don't relish my touch," he murmured.

"That is entirely beside the point," she said all too breathlessly. "I realize now what you are doing, Deverill. You are trying to seduce me into agreeing to wed you."

"What if I am? You would enjoy your seduction, we both know it."

The cool conviction in his voice maddened her. "I won't marry you," Antonia repeated for the twentieth time.

His smile was slow and dazzling. "So you say. But I mean to do everything in my power to persuade you to."

She started to argue, determined to withstand his ruthless charm, but then every thought fled when he suddenly stood and began to undress. "Deverill . . . what are you doing?"

"I intend to make use of the bathwater. On a ship, it is a sin to waste fresh water."

If he entered the hip bath with her, Antonia realized, it would be an extremely tight fit. Not wanting to put it to a test, she ducked lower to rinse off the soap, then groped for the towel and stood up, wrapping the dry length of linen around her dripping shift.

Meanwhile Deverill had removed his shirt. She froze, seeing his brutal scars. Her heart ached for him. But then he shed the rest of his clothing, and her mouth went dry. His sleek, muscular body was beautiful, rawly masculine. When her gaze dropped to fix helplessly on the turgid length of his jutting phallus, her breath caught in her throat at the amazing size of him.

Deverill surely noticed her shaken response, for he was watching her with an intensity that was unsettling. "Do you remember the feel of me inside you?" he murmured, his voice low and provocative.

How could I forget? And she knew he understood quite well the piercing arousal he stirred in her.

Still watching her, he returned to the hip bath and gazed challengingly into her eyes as he deliberately slid her down his body. The hot shock of contact made Antonia gasp with pleasure.

Deverill just smiled that wicked smile of his.

Without speaking, he tugged the towel away from her body, pulling it from her nerveless fingers. But he didn't use it. Instead, he reached out and fondled one nipple lightly through her shift. It stiffened anew and seemed to thrust out against his fingers.

Antonia shut her eyes in dismay. How could her body turn traitor again this way?

He plucked at the wet muslin covering her. "You won't dry if you leave this on."

To her dismay, she couldn't bring herself to protest when he pulled the garment over her head and tossed it aside.

Deverill dried her off then, running the linen lightly over her skin, taking particular care with the damp curls that shielded her woman's mound. Antonia nearly whimpered, the throbbing heat between her thighs an insistent drumbeat in her blood.

Finally satisfied, he tossed the towel aside. Surprisingly, though, he went to the bunk and turned down the covers.

Antonia bit her lip. "Deverill, you cannot sleep with me."

"I wasn't planning on sleeping." He slid an unnervingly thorough glance over her. "I failed to give you any pleasure earlier, and I intend to remedy my error."

"Deverill . . ." she began, wanting to protest, but when he crossed back to her, she couldn't move.

He was staring down at her breasts. The nipples

were pebbled and hard, as if begging to be touched. Obligingly, he raised his hands to caress her while bringing his naked lower body fully against hers. She could feel the ridge of his arousal pulsing vitally at her stomach, feel his sinewed thighs pressing into her softness.

Antonia gasped at the exquisite sensations, her heart going wild with excitement. Every brush of his skin against hers spread heat and hunger.

"Shall I make you want me, princess? I can, you know."

Dear God, he was dangerous. His voice was maddeningly sensuous now, his eyes bright with challenge as he cupped her breasts, defining their shape, making them ache under the delicious pressure.

He was deliberately wielding his seductive powers, weaving a spell to make her helpless with desire. A shiver stole through her. She wanted to resist his sensual assault, but her own body assailed and betrayed her.

"Please, Deverill . . ."

"Oh, yes, I intend to please you." Bending, he touched his lips to her ear. "I mean to make you scream with pleasure, love."

The soft words were tauntingly seductive, threatening and promising at the same time, and they made Antonia's entire body clench in anticipation.

His head dipped farther, his mouth skimming the side of her throat, down over her collarbone to her right breast. He nuzzled her softly, his lips roughly tender, his tongue tracing burning caresses around her fullness. "I mean to have you panting and whimpering with need for me," he murmured huskily.

She was already panting and whimpering, Antonia

thought, dazed. Then his mouth closed hot and moist over the taut bud, and fire plummeted to her yielding, throbbing center.

Her knees going weak, she clutched at his shoulders. For a time he went on suckling, stroking each crest with his tongue, till both were hard, aching points.

Then suddenly, Deverill lifted her up in his arms and carried her to the bunk. He joined her there, stretching out on his side in the narrow space, facing her so that their bodies touched. Antonia stared into Deverill's hot, sea green eyes as he slowly began to stroke her stomach. His heat, his rougher skin and stronger hands, felt incredibly different from her own softness, and she quivered with arousal, barely able to breathe.

Then his hand moved lower over her abdomen to her loins, seeking, probing, opening her downy curls to his teasing fingers, until he held the hot center of her in his palm. Antonia's hips jerked as a moan escaped her.

"Be still," he ordered, his voice deep and resonant and sensual. "Lie there and let me pleasure you."

She wanted to obey him, but he was slowly rubbing his finger down one swollen lip of her sex and up over the other. Then his thumb found the slick bud secreted between the folds, moving maddeningly in a light caress, circling the tiny pearl that was already tight and hard and aching. Antonia shuddered at the riveting pleasure.

Deliberately, he increased the pressure. When she moaned again, Deverill caught the sound with his kiss, settling his mouth firmly over hers.

His tongue played in a leisurely, erotic dance while

he continued his tender assault with his fingers. She could feel her dampness grow, seeping and spreading from her woman's core to her inner thighs.

A moment later he pushed her thighs apart and gently slid his finger inside her. She arched wildly against him, her heart racing with echoing thunder.

A second finger joined the first, and in another score of heartbeats, she was writhing. She could feel a mounting fire centered around the imprisoning caress of his hand. Her whimpers turned to near sobs, until finally she was able to bear the torment no longer. She gave herself up to the shattering climax Deverill urged upon her, her body shaking and contracting before falling limply back against the pillows.

With satisfaction, Deverill watched the flush of orgasm heat her face and spread down her throat to the crimson tips of her breasts. Even when her spasms faded, he kept his fingers where they were, lingering along her plump lips, spreading her juices. Yet he was gritting his teeth all the while. He felt his cock surging up toward his belly, felt the fierce ache in his sacs as they swelled nearly to bursting.

He wanted more than anything to spill himself in the welcoming warmth of Antonia's body. But she was undoubtedly too tender for him to enter her again so soon. He also didn't want to run the risk of impregnating her. Yet he could still show her the ecstasy she had missed this morning, could still find a way to take his own pleasure.

He drew back, gazing down at the dusky triangle between her thighs, watching the play of his fingers in and around her glistening sex. Her sweet, musky scent rose to tease him, stirring his arousal even more savagely. He wanted to know what she tasted like there, wanted to savor her.

Shifting his weight, Deverill moved over her, using his knees to spread her legs.

Lying limp and sated, Antonia vaguely realized he was kissing her bare breasts again. His lips moved over the swells, caressing provocatively, then lower, brushing over her still-pounding heart, the skin of her abdomen, his tongue darting out, hot and slick, to trace a sensuous path down her body to the apex of her thighs. . . .

When she realized his intent, she went rigid, her fingers grasping reflexively at his hair.

"No," Deverill commanded, "don't tense your muscles. You'll enjoy this," he promised, his rich, deep voice dark and seductive.

When he bent his head again, the appalling realization struck Antonia that she wanted him to kiss her there between her thighs.

Deverill obliged, his tongue grazing over her folds, making her breath hiss through her teeth. And when he settled his open mouth on her pulsing cleft, her hips nearly came off the mattress.

Holding her still so he could have his fill of her, Deverill drew the sensitive nub into his mouth, forcing her to start another shuddering climb. Antonia wailed softly, her fingers tightening in the thick waves of his hair as the coiling heat inside her burned higher.

"That's right, give in to it . . ." Deverill whispered hoarsely.

She could do nothing else as fire leapt from his mouth to her flesh. The sensation was too intense to bear.

Her head thrashing frantically on the pillow, she shifted her grasp and dug her nails hard into his shoulder blades, hearing her own rasping cries, the sound of a woman in the throes of pure bliss.

When her hips heaved and bucked beneath him, his fingers clamped down hard to keep her still, driving her higher and higher until at last a shriek tore from her throat. As she arched and convulsed in ecstasy, his lips kept on plying her, dredging the final exquisite spasms from her shaking body.

In the hushed aftermath, Antonia lay weak and dazed, panting harshly. She could scarcely believe the intensity of her own incredible response. She'd gone wild in Deverill's arms as he pushed her to discover the depths of her own intense pleasure.

Yet he still was full and swollen. He'd had no release, she realized, remembering how he had spilled his seed into his hand this morning.

She inhaled a slow breath, suddenly feeling bold. She wanted badly to touch him.

Reaching down, Antonia brushed her fingertips over his surging, hard, silky flesh. His body instantly went rigid, as hers had done moments before.

Seeing his reaction, she felt her confidence growing. "Deverill . . . let me pleasure you this time."

He sucked in a breath and grimaced, as if in dire pain. "Antonia, love, there is no need."

"But I want to, truly."

"Your hands are bandaged."

"Then show me how to manage with them."

She watched as his features became taut with passion and the denial of releasing it. Finally, he gave in. Holding her gaze, he grasped her wrist and moved her hand to stroke the thick, pulsing heat of him with just her fingertips. His wide shoulders were rigid with tension, the tendons in his neck drawn taut as he showed her how to caress him.

No longer tentative, Antonia drew her fingers lingeringly over his arousal, closing them over the swollen head with delicate pressure, taking pleasure in the strangled groan he gave.

Deverill shut his eyes at the sublime sensation and tightened his fingers around her wrist, guiding and tutoring her, displaying how to stroke his cock and sacs with the same erotic rhythm he'd used to pleasure her, teaching her the spots where he was most acutely sensitive.

When she caught on easily, his body clenched, his mind imagining that he was taking Antonia, surging into her. The sweet fantasy was his undoing. The explosion that ripped through him was as powerful as any he'd known, rocking his body and sending him hurtling into ecstasy.

The tumult of his furious release left him spent and shuddering. It was a long while before Deverill realized he'd spilled his seed onto Antonia's stomach. Promising himself he would bathe away the evidence later, he rolled onto his back and pulled her to him, resting her head in the hollow of his shoulder.

She gave a soft sigh of contentment. "I still won't marry you," she whispered tiredly.

Deverill had barely enough energy to smile. She was warm and weak from his lovemaking yet still spitting fire. Just the way he wanted her.

Then her lips pressed into one of the puckered scars on his chest, and his entire body tensed. He didn't want her asking questions he had no desire to answer.

A few moments later, though, he caught the sound of her soft, even breathing and realized she had fallen asleep.

Feeling a fresh stirring of desire and a dangerous tenderness, Deverill let his own eyes fall shut. He wanted to sink into sleep with Antonia all soft and warm and curled around him, but he would have to leave her soon. He couldn't spend the night with her and still hope to maintain any pretense of her innocence to the world. And if she refused to wed him . . .

Deverill tightened his arm about her, unsure whether tonight had been his victory or hers. Yet he couldn't deceive himself that he would easily win the war.

Ten

At breakfast the next morning, Antonia could scarcely meet Deverill's eyes. She was still a little shocked by his lovemaking last evening, for it had been more stunning than her wildest dreams. Even more unsettling, their sexual intimacy had only served to heighten the smoldering sensuality between them now.

They were not alone in the schooner's stateroom; Captain Lloyd was providing them adequate chaperonage. And the conversation was hardly erotic; the two men were discussing plans for dropping anchor based on harbor depths. Yet to her chagrin, Deverill's slightest innocent action had a deplorable effect on her senses.

When he took a sip of coffee, it made her remember the taste of his mouth and skin.

When he pointed on a map with a long forefinger, she thought of his magical hands caressing her, bringing her to pleasure.

When he met her gaze across the table, she felt a stark sizzle of heat shiver through her body.

The very air seemed to vibrate between them. Deverill was watching her intently, silently reminding her of all the wanton things they had done last evening, the incredible passion they had shared.

His glance was so spellbinding, she found it impossible to tear her gaze away. And she couldn't begin to quell her memories, not when they were so fresh and powerful, drumming through her like a vivid heartbeat. Even though Deverill had not spent the night in her bed, leaving her well before midnight, she knew their intimacy during those few hours together had marked her forever.

As soon as she finished eating, Antonia politely made her excuses and escaped above decks. Breathing deeply of the fresh sea air, she moved to stand at the port rail to watch the Cornish coast glide by.

Cornwall, the southernmost county of England, was purported to have a remarkably temperate climate, and the reports seemed true, judging by the pleasing mildness of the summer morning. But it was the splendor of the land that held her in awe—the rugged shoreline scored by sandy coves and rock cliffs and picturesque fishing hamlets. The only views she'd seen that were more splendid were on the Isle of Cyrene. The wild beauty here called to her somehow, making her blood race.

Or perhaps her quickened pulse was solely due to the man who had come to stand silently beside her. Trey Deverill, her lover. She was aware of him with every nerve and sinew in her body.

"So when do we arrive?" Antonia asked in an earnest effort to take her mind off Deverill and last evening.

"Two hours at most. We won't sail all the way to

Falmouth Harbor. We'll anchor off Graeb Point and hire a carriage at St. Mawes to take us to Wilde Castle, where Lady Isabella lives. Her estate is close to the village of Gerrans."

She glanced at Deverill with curiosity. "Have you visited her castle before?"

"No, although I've docked at Falmouth a number of times, for refurbishing and to take on supplies. And I'm familiar with this stretch of coast." He gestured toward the shore. "It's riddled with smuggling coves and secret hideaways for French spies."

Antonia's glance turned amused. "It wouldn't surprise me to find you on terms with all the local criminals."

The corner of his mouth lifted in a smile. "At least I'm normally on the correct side of the law. I've been called on several times to help contain the local smuggling rings."

That surprised her. "Why you? I thought your specialty was fighting pirates."

"Because smugglers' luggers are small and fast and difficult to apprehend, and my ships have the swiftness and maneuverability that few Royal British Navy vessels possess. Thanks to your father's designs, of course."

At the mention of her father, Antonia felt another sharp arrow of pain shoot through her.

Deverill must have seen her flinch, for he quickly changed the subject. "I'm certain Isabella will welcome you."

"And I will be glad to arrive," Antonia said, striving for lightness, "if only for the opportunity to borrow a fresh gown. I wonder, however, if Lady Isabella will be as welcoming to *you* once she learns how barbarously you treated me."

He ignored her provoking gibe. "Captain Lloyd tells me the castle has some magnificent grounds and overlooks a spectacular cove that is ideal for swimming."

Her mouth quirked. "I consider that fortuitous. If I must languish there for several weeks or more, then I mean to learn how to swim. If I had known how the other night, I could have jumped ship and escaped from your clutches, foiling your abduction."

Deverill's grin was slow and lazy. "Where is your gratitude, princess? I saved you from a wretched fate with Heward, you must admit."

"So you did." She shuddered to think how close she had come to wedding Heward. "But I don't intend to award you a halo just yet, Deverill. Not until he confesses to his crimes and is locked away in prison for life."

"Trust me, I intend to see to it. Meanwhile . . . come below with me. I will change your bandages."

Antonia hesitated, not wanting to be alone with Deverill. He was clearly an expert at seduction, and she knew very well he would try again to persuade her to accept his marriage proposal. But she could also use the opportunity for her own purposes: chiefly, to quiz him about his plans for proving Heward's guilt in her father's death and the Cyprian's murder. Moreover, although her hands didn't pain her much and seemed to be healing, she suspected it *was* wiser to apply fresh bandages.

Without protest, she accompanied Deverill below to his cabin, where he proceeded to unwrap the gauze on her hands. His merest touch brought a rush of memories of their passion last evening, but despite the pleasure he had given her, Antonia was determined not to give in to him. She was through being a pawn to men who sought to control her. Her main goal now was resolving her father's death and acquiring justice for him. If Heward had committed murder, she would see that he paid for it, whatever the personal cost.

Dragging any information out of Deverill, however, was another matter altogether. When she asked him how he specifically meant to gather evidence against Heward and expose him, Deverill merely repeated that he had surrogates in London who would be investigating.

"Yes, but what will they *do*? I think I have the right to know," Antonia asserted. "After all, it is *my* father's death at issue."

At her passionate declaration, Deverill pursed his mouth as he considered how much he should tell her. There was little risk Antonia could misuse any information he gave her, since for the immediate future she would be isolated in Cornwall, out of touch with anyone in London. And it was indeed her father whose life had been forfeit, Deverill reminded himself, along with the ill-fated young beauty who'd been his companion that night at the pleasure club. He could certainly share enough details to reassure Antonia of his intentions. Even though he had to act through his fellow Guardians, now that she was out of danger he intended to do everything in his power to bring Heward down.

"It's fairly simple," Deverill said finally. "Not only must we show that Baron Heward is a murderer, but the evidence must be solid enough to convict him in the Lords." As a nobleman, Heward could be tried only by the House of Lords, by a jury of his peers.

Her blue eyes gazed up at Deverill solemnly, with

trust and expectation. "How will you manage to find such evidence?"

"To start with, we'll try to locate the ruffians who killed the young woman I was with and confirm they were hired by Heward."

"That will be very difficult, won't it?"

"Possibly not. One of them has a vivid facial scar, which clearly distinguishes him. And the London underworld is not so large that he can hide forever." Deverill concentrated on washing the raw areas on her palms. "As for your father, I admit it will be harder to prove a crime that happened more than a year ago. And I don't want to raise your hopes too high. But it might be feasible to discover how Heward acquired the poison he used to kill your father. It's curious that Heward's own personal physician pronounced the cause of death. And it should be simple to learn from a reputable doctor or apothecary what poisons would cause heart failure."

When Antonia's brow furrowed in contemplation, Deverill could see the wheels turning in her head. He almost smiled, gratified to have given her a new problem to chew on.

"I would never have thought of trying to determine how he was poisoned," she acknowledged. "What else?"

"I want to know what hold, if any, Heward has over the Director of Maitland Shipping. If there is something, then we could perhaps use it to persuade Trant to turn against Heward."

Antonia nodded slowly, observing with a hint of admiration, "Those seem like shrewd steps. I should have trusted that you would devise an able plan."

"I am gratified you approve," Deverill observed

wryly, although not as sanguine as his tone implied. His immediate plan might be a good start, but he was accustomed to taking command, not having others execute for him. He was not about to let fate dictate to him, but being unable to return to London tied his hands and put him at a severe disadvantage. It meant forcibly summoning the patience to oversee events from a distance when he was gnawing at the bit to act.

On her part, Antonia was struggling with both impatience and a new wave of guilt, for it occurred to her that Deverill had left out one very important element while explaining his strategy: He was wanted for murder.

Another painful twinge hit her. *She* was to blame for his predicament, at least in part. Deverill had likely been dragged into her affairs and unjustly accused of a deadly crime because he had dared champion her. He was now a criminal simply for trying to protect her.

Her jaw tightened in determination. She wanted to clear his name as much as she wanted to see Heward in prison. She would have to ponder possible ways she could help Deverill prove Heward's guilt and his own innocence as well.

The difficulty, no doubt, would be in persuading Deverill to accept her help. He had seemed adamant when he said he wouldn't allow her to return to London with him.

But if he thought she would meekly remain behind, Antonia mused silently, he didn't know her well.

The reflection, however, was driven from her mind when Deverill finished with the bandages.

"This should suffice," he said, returning the medical supplies to the cupboard. "And we've had enough solemn contemplation."

Startling Antonia where she sat, he took her face in his hands and bent down to kiss her.

She drew back sharply at the burning contact, glaring, although her pulse was racing and her voice was far too breathless when she exclaimed, "Deverill! I'll thank you to stop assaulting me!"

The rogue merely grinned. "You had best become accustomed to it, love, for I don't intend to let up until you accept my proposal."

She tried to rise from the chair, but he trapped her by bracing his hands on the wooden arms on either side of her. Then he bent lower, brushing his mouth seductively along her jaw to her cheekbone.

Antonia clenched her teeth, struggling for the will-power to resist him.

"You can't fool me by claiming to be unaffected, sweeting," he whispered against her ear. "I know how hot and wet you become the moment I touch you."

It was true, she realized with dismay. Already she felt a damp heat between her thighs at his merest touch. When he lifted one hand and ran his thumb teasingly over her lips, her entire body shivered.

His low murmur stroked her like his fingertips. "I am half inclined to take you back to bed and resume where we left off last night."

"*No*, Deverill." Grasping his hand in desperation, Antonia pushed it away and slipped out from between the chair and his arms, making for the door. "I intend to find Fletcher. *He* will protect me from your lecherous advances, I hope."

"Perhaps for now, but you can't escape me forever."

"We shall see about that," Antonia retorted.

She heard Deverill's low chuckle follow her, even when she shut the cabin door forcefully behind her.

The remainder of the morning was supremely trying for Antonia, what with Deverill's continued attempts to shake her resolve against wedding him. She was hard-pressed not to succumb to his charm when he wielded it so ruthlessly, but she knew she couldn't let him make such a sacrifice merely to protect her honor, especially when she was capable of seeing to her own future.

Concluding that she needed a stronger declaration of refusal, however, Antonia decided to venture another bluff. She just hoped it worked better than the first time when she'd threatened to jump overboard. Regardless, it would at least show Deverill she was serious.

When the crew began lowering sails, she knew they were nearing their destination. She searched the galley for the pistol she'd seen there, then went to her cabin for her cloak and returned to find Deverill on deck.

"Before we disembark," Antonia said calmly, drawing the pistol from her cloak pocket, "we have an issue to settle."

Deverill's eyebrows snapped together as he gave her a piercing look. "Where did you get that?"

"I found it in the galley. It belongs to Fletcher, I believe, but I'm of half a mind to use it on you."

"Is it loaded?"

She sidestepped the question and aimed the muzzle at Deverill. "I want your word that you will cease pestering me about marrying you."

His arms crossed over his chest, the picture of lazy defiance. "You won't shoot me."

Antonia hesitated, her frustration mounting. "Not fatally, but I could certainly wound you. Enough so that you would be bedridden and unable to pursue me." Letting her gaze slide lower, she pointedly considered his loins encased in buff leather breeches. "Or perhaps I might aim for a more . . . strategic area. If your manly attributes were damaged, you would have difficulty acting the lover, I expect."

Deverill stared at her, consternation warring with amusement and admiration. She had surprised him once again, threatening to shoot him if he wouldn't stop pressuring her to accept his marriage proposal—and he suspected she had the skill to back up her threat. The determination in her gaze was challenge incarnate and had a distinctly arousing affect on his loins, but Antonia armed with a weapon was more than he wanted to deal with.

He grinned, appreciating the fearlessness of her manner, but raised his hands in temporary surrender. "Very well, you have the advantage for the moment."

"I want your word that you will leave me alone, Deverill."

"I'm sorry, love, but I can't comply. I suppose that means you will just have to shoot me."

For a heartbeat she looked as if she might take him up on his dare. Then she pinched her lips together in obvious resignation, apparently accepting that they were at a standoff.

"The pistol isn't loaded just now," she muttered. "But I *will* shoot you someday, I swear it."

When she turned and stomped away, Deverill shook his head, unable to quell his grin. Antonia riled was magnificent, but if he wasn't careful, he might wind up with a cherished part of his anatomy in serious distress.

Their standoff held for the time being.

Once the schooner anchored, they rowed to shore and hired a carriage for the three-mile drive to Wilde Castle. The name was somewhat misleading, since Lady Isabella's summer residence was more grand manor house than castle. From the ship, Antonia had glimpsed the magnificent mansion of mellow stone perched on a bluff overlooking the sea, but it was even more impressive at close range—large enough to contain at least sixty rooms, she suspected.

Promisingly, Lady Isabella was at home. And when Antonia and Deverill were shown into the parlor, they were greeted with surprise and delight.

Half Spanish, half English, Isabella was a sultry beauty with jet hair and sparkling black eyes. Although she was well past her fortieth year and thrice widowed, she possessed an allure that stemmed as much from her earthy vivacity and joie de vivre as her striking, aristocratic features and curvaceous figure.

Rising, the countess offered her fingers for Deverill to kiss, then warmly reached for Antonia's hands in welcome. "It is so good to see you again, my dear—" She gave a start upon noting her guest's bandaged palms and then her bruised forehead. "Merciful heavens, whatever happened? No, wait." She held up an imperative hand. "I suspect this will be a long tale. First I will ring for tea and we will be comfortably seated, and then you will tell me all."

After the butler was summoned and asked to fetch the tea tray, Deverill gave the noblewoman a brief account of the past three days, explaining why it had been imperative to spirit Antonia away from London and to protect her from her murderous betrothed.

"That I understand," Isabella said, frowning. "But how could you have allowed her to be hurt so?"

Antonia couldn't refrain from sending Deverill a smug look before she came to his defense. "In all fairness, Deverill thought he had no choice. I wouldn't listen when he tried to convince me of Lord Heward's malevolence, so he felt compelled to use unconventional methods to get me on board his ship. And he is not to blame for my hands. I hurt them myself when I was learning to raise a sail. My palms merely suffered rope burns."

"But to take you away with only the gown on your back! It is shameful."

The countess's indignant tone gave Antonia confidence that she might have a champion in Lady Isabella—one who might be inclined to lend her support on a broader matter. "Truthfully, my lady, none of that concerns me as much as Deverill's insistence that I wed him."

"Indeed? *Deverill* proposed marriage to you?"

When Isabella's eyebrows shot up in astonishment, Deverill supplied a further explanation. "In my zeal to protect Antonia, I fear that I compromised her reputation beyond salvaging."

"That is your embroidered version," Antonia observed.

"It is the same version the ton would support if your circumstances became known."

"I'm certain I will find a suitable husband eventually."

"You don't want a complacent, boring mate. You would be less discontent with me."

Isabella looked curiously from Antonia to Deverill and back again.

"The fact remains," Antonia said firmly, "that I don't want to be forced to wed you simply to safeguard my reputation."

"I do not think well of forced marriages," Isabella interjected lightly. "My first marriage was arranged by my illustrious father. However, my next two were love matches and I was extremely happy. In my experience, it is far better to marry for love."

Antonia would have replied that she and Deverill were certainly not in love, but the tea tray arrived just then, and she was required to wait until the servants had withdrawn before continuing the discussion. "I *do* intend to marry for convenience, Lady Isabella. It was my own father's greatest wish that I wed a nobleman, and I intend to honor his request."

Isabella gave her a shrewd glance. "But what do *you* wish, my dear? You mean to tell me that you do *not* want Deverill for your husband?"

Antonia found the question too complex to answer easily. Undoubtedly it was difficult for the countess to understand why any woman would refuse to wed Deverill, a man of smoldering vitality and irresistible appeal. But Antonia didn't want to chain him to her in marriage, knowing he could very well come to resent her for causing him to lose his cherished freedom. Moreover, the prospect of becoming his wife, in what would undoubtedly be an unsettlingly stormy union, was frankly unnerving. She would be far more comfortable with a gentle, pliable husband than a powerful, charismatic adventurer who would overwhelm her senses and drive her to distraction.

"No, I do not want Deverill for my husband," she said, pleased with the conviction in her voice.

"Very well," Isabella replied as if making a royal pronouncement. "You shan't have to wed him if you don't wish to."

Antonia gave a sigh of relief and forcibly ignored the odd twinge of disappointment she felt at having escaped the prospect of marrying Deverill. "I would also be grateful if you will allow me to take refuge here for a time, my lady."

"Pray address me as Isabella. And of course you must stay. It will be a delight to have you."

"If events go as arranged, my companion, Miss Tottle, should arrive in a few days."

"She is welcome here as well. *You,* Mr. Deverill, are not," Isabella said, turning to him. "Since you are not betrothed, it will be better for appearances if you stay at an inn. There is an adequate one in the village and a better one in St. Mawes."

Deverill's first inclination was one of protest. He was amused that the two ladies had united against him, yet also felt strangely dissatisfied. Noting that Antonia's expression was both hopeful and wary as she awaited his answer, Deverill mentally shook his head in wonder. Any other woman would be elated by a proposal of marriage from him. But of course Antonia was not any other woman. She truly didn't wish to marry him.

And he couldn't force her acceptance. So that was the end of the matter.

He had offered; she had refused. Honor was satisfied.

He should be pleased to have eluded the chains of matrimony. So why did he feel so damned discontented with the outcome?

The realization startled Deverill; a part of him had actually anticipated with pleasure wedding Antonia. But it was the potential bride herself who had incited his conflicting urges.

He met her gaze, remembering the sweet taste of her, the delicious feel of her ripe breasts straining for his touch. . . . Even now the memory affected him.

More dangerous than her allure, however, were the tender emotions Antonia made him feel. Tenderness and affection were complications he didn't want, couldn't afford.

It was fortunate he no longer had any claim on Antonia as her future husband, for he needed to put some distance between them if he wanted to vanquish his lust and avoid any further emotional entanglements. His billeting at a local inn would be advantageous. . . .

Stifling the perverse urge to argue further, Deverill inclined his head in a brief bow. "As you wish, Lady Isabella. I will hire rooms at a nearby inn. And you, Antonia, will be pleased to know that you have won. I hereby officially withdraw my suit."

Antonia's look of relief was almost insulting. Deverill found his thoughts so occupied with her response, it was a moment before he realized that the countess had changed the subject and was asking him about his plans for the next few weeks—when he meant to return to London, and what he intended to do in the interval.

"I'll go as soon as I have evidence linking Heward to either murder," Deverill said. "I want Antonia to remain here until he's incarcerated. His rank will make arresting him extremely difficult, and it will doubtless take time to secure all the proof we need."

He didn't add that the Guardians could employ quicker, more effective methods if necessary to ensure that justice triumphed. Isabella was aware of the order's existence, as well as their noble purpose, since many years ago she and her distinguished father, a Spanish statesman, had been granted asylum on Cyrene from persecution by the Spanish government. And just last year, Isabella had been rescued by the Guardians from captivity in Barbary.

But Antonia knew nothing of the Guardians, and Deverill had sworn a solemn oath to keep their league secret.

As expected, however, Antonia wasn't willing to sit by meekly while the issue was discussed. "Then how will you gather evidence?" she asked.

"Our best hope," Deverill replied, "is to compel Heward to make an admission of guilt. It's likely we will have to devise a trap to lure him into revealing his crimes."

Isabella spoke up, her tone indignant once more. "It is outrageous that you could even be *considered* a suspect for murder. Does Sir Gawain know of this travesty?"

"He should be in London by next week for a special visit, and Beau Macklin will inform him how events stand."

Antonia gave Deverill a curious look. "Sir Gawain Olwen?"

"Yes."

"He was a longtime friend of my father's. But why would he need to be informed of the charges against you?"

"I perform some work for him from time to time," Deverill hedged.

"Sir Gawain," Isabella added, "commands a small, elite department of the British Foreign Office on Cyrene."

Antonia's eyes narrowed at Deverill in speculation. "You never told me you worked for the Foreign Office, but I suppose it doesn't surprise me. Can Sir Gawain help you?"

"I trust so. He has more powerful connections than anyone else of my acquaintance."

From the first, Deverill had intended to secure the assistance of the Guardians' leader. Sir Gawain had numerous confederates in the highest echelons of the British government, including the Foreign Secretary, who owed their allegiance if not their very lives to the order—and who, if asked, would champion any of the Guardians. "But I also plan to write the Foreign Office at once and engage the support of the Foreign Undersecretary."

Lord Wittington was the chief governmental contact for the Guardians. The undersecretary knew Deverill well and would vouch for him when he returned to London. Although perhaps not powerful enough to keep him out of prison, Wittington would at least see that Deverill's case was fairly investigated.

"Meanwhile," he continued, "there are several people in London carrying out my orders. Macky will send me regular reports on their progress, and once we have enough information, I will return to implement the remainder of the plan myself."

"But how do you intend to exonerate yourself?" Isabella asked.

"Yes, how?" Antonia seconded.

"Macky is to concentrate on Madam Bruno, the owner of the club where the murder occurred, and discover why she claimed that I killed her employee when it was a bald lie. She insisted I was guilty, but without her accusation, the evidence against me is circumstantial. I hope to convince her to recant her story."

Isabella looked thoughtful. "What of Venus? Is it possible that she can aid you?"

"I've already thought of that. We will utilize Venus to discover what she can about the baron's personal life."

"Who is Venus?" Antonia asked.

"The madam of another sin club." He didn't add that Venus was in debt to the Guardians for recently sparing her imprisonment for treason, or that she had agreed to work on their behalf in an effort to redeem herself.

"Very well," Isabella said, apparently satisfied for the moment. "You will let me know what I may do to help, Deverill."

"At present, things are well in hand. If you will see to Antonia's comfort . . ."

"But of course." Isabella's sparkling black eyes turned to survey her guest. "You will need a new wardrobe at once, my dear. Our social circles are small, but there are regular assemblies and balls at Falmouth and St. Mawes. You, Deverill, must make yourself available to escort us."

Antonia shook her head. "Entertaining me will not be necessary, Isabella. I am not here to socialize, although I would appreciate finding a dressmaker."

"It is indeed necessary. We must keep up appearances so that no one believes you have run away from London helter-skelter. Then when you return home, you will have numerous witnesses here who can account for your whereabouts, who will observe you with me and in the presence of your chaperone . . . Miss Tottle, did you say her name was?"

"Yes. Miss Mildred Tottle."

"It will also clearly benefit Deverill to be seen in *your* company, for it will show the world that you do not believe him to be a murderer. As for you, Deverill, how do you mean to remain occupied?"

Deverill hesitated. He was already battling frustration at being unable to confront his adversary immediately. There were, however, two Guardians residing in the vicinity, and he planned to offer them his services. And Sir Gawain would perhaps assign him a local mission or two to keep him occupied until he could return to London.

"I have some potential avenues to pursue. You needn't worry about me, Bella."

Isabella eyed him with sudden deliberation. "Truthfully, I am glad you have come, Deverill. There have been several killings here recently. Murders, actually. Some of our local smugglers have had their contraband stolen and their throats cut. It is beyond outrageous, for they are merely fishermen who are trying to supplement their meager incomes by selling goods to those wishing to avoid exorbitant taxation. Smuggling is illegal, of course, but they do not deserve to die for such a minor offense! It seems fortuitous that you arrived just at this moment, for I imagine you can be of great assistance. My brother by marriage, Sir Crispin Kenard, is the local magistrate. It is his wife Clara whom I have come to keep company for her lying-in. I will ask Sir Crispin to call on you to discuss the matter, if you are amenable."

"Yes, of course, I would be happy to oblige."

"Excellent! Now then, you may take yourself off and leave me to see to Antonia."

With a wry grin at his summary dismissal, Deverill rose to his feet and bowed to both ladies. "I am leaving you in good hands, princess. Take care to stay out of trouble."

Antonia didn't respond to his baiting, but looked a bit dissatisfied as she rose also. "Might I have a private word with you, Deverill?"

When he agreed warily, she followed him across the drawing room to the door.

"You must hurry back, Antonia," Isabella called after her. "We should see to your hands without delay. I have a superb lotion for burns. If you wrap your hands in kidskin gloves, they will heal in a trice."

Once in the corridor, Deverill turned to glance down at her. "What is so urgent, love?"

"I want to help you, Deverill," Antonia answered in a low voice. "I *need* to help. I will go mad here with nothing to do but attend assemblies."

The passion in her entreaty struck a chord in him. She was clearly her father's daughter, putting her all into whatever she attempted, and she would not be content to sit idly by, any more than he himself was. But it was her pleading look that brought a strange jolt to his heart. Her bright eyes would be his undoing, Deverill feared.

Before he could reply, Antonia went on hurriedly, as if she had already put some thought into the matter of helping him. "I can write Phineas Cochrane and explain the trouble you are in. As a respected barrister, he has numerous connections in the courts who could be influential on your behalf. And I need to contact him in any case, since he will worry for me. I must reassure him that I am well, so he won't be alarmed by my sudden absence. He also should be warned about Lord Heward so he can act to protect Maitland Shipping. I may be safe from Heward, but my father's legacy is not. Phineas oversees my fortune in trust until either I turn twenty-five or marry, but Heward is intimately involved in running the company."

Deverill hesitated, debating. "I'm not sure it is wise to bring your trustee into it. The fewer people who know about Heward, the better, since a careless word could give him advance warning and allow him the opportunity to escape retribution."

"Deverill, Phineas is my godfather. He can be trusted to remain circumspect, I would stake my life on it. And he may be able to help you to turn Trant and Heward against each other, as you hoped. *Please*, Deverill, don't deny me the chance to play a small role in apprehending my father's murderer and in helping you. I feel responsible for the trouble you're facing, and I could never live with myself if you came to grief simply because you defended me."

"Very well," Deverill said with reluctance. "I will write my own letter to Cochrane to supplement yours and send both missives with Captain Lloyd when he sails for London tomorrow."

Antonia smiled up at him, a smile that Deverill swore made his heart stop beating.

"Will I see you again this evening?" she asked.

"No, I'll dispatch a servant to collect your letter." Unable to help himself, he reached up to touch her cheek, then jerked back, feeling the scorching heat at that simple contact. "I think it best if we part for a time. You're too much temptation, vixen. Since we're not to wed, I will have to force myself to keep my hands off you."

It gave him a slight measure of satisfaction when he left Antonia standing there, gazing after him, a wistful look in her blue eyes that was almost one of disappointment.

Eleven

The local gentry proved eager to welcome Antonia into their midst, for the appearance of a London heiress in their quiet corner of the world was exciting news.

At first Antonia feared she might be imposing on the countess, but Lady Isabella professed delight for her company and the chance to introduce a new guest to society, promising a round of assemblies and suppers and balls to rival the ton's. They engaged a modiste from Falmouth to quickly make up a ball gown and several dinner gowns. And when Miss Tottle arrived from London two days later with a trunkful of Antonia's clothing, she was better prepared to play the role of visiting debutante.

Antonia was surprisingly glad to see her companion, not only because Mildred's face was a dear one, but because her familiar, flighty demeanor was so agreeably *normal* after the unsettling events of this past week, when murder and betrayal had turned her life upside down.

Since Antonia chose not to share her dark suspicions about her betrothed's perfidy, Miss Tottle did not understand the urgency of leaving London during the height of the Season, although she accepted Antonia's claim of visiting an ill friend. Fortunately, the countess's sister-in-law, Clara, Lady Kenard, who was very swollen with child, had willingly agreed to participate in the ruse. By the time Miss Tottle met her, Lady Kenard had "recovered" from death's door and was able to receive callers.

The three ladies spent a good deal of time with Clara and also paid daily calls on the countess's other genteel neighbors. Admittedly, Isabella's grandiose plans did help distract Antonia from her restlessness, but they could not make her forget the grim reason she was even in Cornwall, nor keep her from remembering the unexpected passion she had experienced at Deverill's hands during the voyage.

Of Deverill, she saw nothing until the fourth evening, when Isabella held a dinner at the castle in her honor. Absurdly, Antonia found herself scanning the doorway each time a new guest entered the drawing room. When Deverill finally strolled in, accompanied by Sir Crispin Kenard, Antonia's heartbeat took up a rapid rhythm. Deverill looked incredibly handsome with his tall, powerful figure molded by formal evening attire—blue coat, pristine white cravat, silver embroidered waistcoat, white satin breeches and stockings, and silver-buckled shoes.

Yet when his eyes met hers across the crowded drawing room and he gave her a small bow of acknowledgment, her heart sank. His gaze was cool, dispassionate, with none of the burning fervor he'd shown when he'd sought to overcome her resistance to his marriage offer. Antonia knew she should be grateful that Deverill apparently meant to respect her wishes and accept her refusal, yet perversely, all she could feel was disappointment that he was no longer pursuing her.

She was not even afforded the chance to greet him then, for Lady Isabella spied Deverill and immediately monopolized his attention, taking his arm and steering him around the drawing room to introduce him. His reputation preceded him, Antonia was aware, since Sir Crispin had been singing his praises for the past several days. And she herself was asked a multitude of questions about Deverill's exploits, since they were presumed to be longtime friends.

It was nearly half an hour later before Isabella brought him over to Antonia, and she had a scant moment to speak to him privately as their hostess briefly turned her attention elsewhere.

"Have you missed me, vixen?" Deverill murmured, smiling blandly down at Antonia.

She had missed him intensely, although she would never admit it to him. "Have you heard any news from London yet?" she asked instead.

"No, it is too early yet."

"You must promise to inform me of everything you learn the minute you hear."

His mouth curved in amusement at her impatience. "I will." He glanced at her gloved hands. "Have your injuries healed?"

"Thankfully, yes. You have been keeping busy, I hear," Antonia remarked, changing the subject. "Lady Kenard says you are helping Sir Crispin apprehend the pirate who is preying on the local Freetraders."

Deverill nodded. "The Freetraders are in a difficult position, for they can hardly report stolen contraband to the authorities. As magistrate of the district, Sir Crispin must pretend ignorance of their illegal smuggling activities, yet he can't simply stand by while they are being slaughtered. There is little I can do until Captain Lloyd returns with my ship, but I have agreed to patrol the coasts at night as soon as I'm able."

Antonia was certain they would be grateful for Deverill's aid. Clara Kenard had confessed that there was an aura of fear among the local fishermen, and even the gentry were uneasy, since such terrible crimes were rare in this bucolic district.

Giving a reflexive shiver, Antonia attempted to lighten the mood. "Meanwhile, you are required to play the gentleman and dance attendance on Lady Isabella and myself," she remarked, remembering Deverill's disdain for society and all its pretensions.

"Are you enjoying yourself any better?"

"Truthfully, no." She wasn't interested in balls and assemblies. What she truly wanted was to return to London, but since she was confined here in Cornwall, she was determined to make the most of it. "I would rather explore the countryside. A riding habit was my first priority in a wardrobe, but Isabella overrode my wishes in favor of evening attire. And regrettably, Miss Tottle failed to include my habit when she packed a trunk for me."

"You could always wear breeches and scandalize the good Cornish folk," Deverill suggested with a taunting sparkle in his eye.

Antonia smiled. "As Isabella's guest, I am obliged to remain more circumspect."

"True. This is not Cyrene, where you could perhaps get away with donning male attire."

"I am sure I could make do with an old gown if I borrowed a jacket, but Isabella doesn't want me riding about the countryside with only a groom for protection."

Lady Isabella returned just then and caught the last of their conversation. "Indeed, Deverill, you must make the time to escort Antonia riding. If a vicious pirate is running loose, she will need more protection than a mere groom can provide. And it is the least you should do, since *you* are the one who brought her here against her will."

A smile flickered across Deverill's mouth, for he recognized Bella's transparent effort to throw them together. He didn't want to squire Antonia around, for she would present too much temptation, yet he saw the eager hopefulness in her expression and couldn't refuse.

"Very well," he said. "Will tomorrow morning do?"

"Tomorrow morning would be splendid."

The beaming smile Antonia sent him made Deverill's chest suddenly feel tight. He had missed her smile, missed being able to tease her and provoke her. And more importantly, to touch her.

These past few days without her had been inconceivably frustrating. He couldn't stop thinking of her, remembering the taste of her skin, the scent of her, the texture of her nipples. He couldn't stop imagining taking her again, picturing how she would arch and moan beneath his stroking fingers, his mouth, his body—

To his gratification, dinner was announced just then, for the interruption helped him to crush his arousing thoughts. Deverill was partnered with a dowager duchess at one end of the long, formal dining table, quite some distance from Antonia. Yet he found his gaze straying frequently to her during the excellent five-course repast, and afterward, when dancing and cards were offered.

As he expected, Antonia was wildly successful at enchanting the company. Her charm and wit and vibrant beauty were just as potent here in the country as in the glittering ballrooms of London.

Although pleased by her success, Deverill felt his mood darkening unexpectedly, for her conquests reminded him of her determination to wed into the nobility. Class differences and social status had much less meaning for him, but she had been raised to strive for a higher station and was still intent on achieving her father's greatest desire.

It shouldn't have bothered him, therefore, to see her attention claimed by two unattached noblemen—both prospective matrimonial candidates, both of whom fell all over themselves to please her—but Deverill's jealousy flared to outraged proportions.

Clamping down on his more savage instincts, he chose to join the card tables rather than the dancing, for he didn't trust himself to hold Antonia in his arms and refrain from doing something entirely unsuitable, such as ravishing her on the spot.

He was, however, looking forward to the morning when he could have her alone—even if it would require a valiant struggle to keep his hands off her.

Antonia rose early, filled with anticipation. She had dressed and breakfasted and was waiting in the stables when Deverill called for her.

He warily eyed her bow and quiver of arrows, which Miss Tottle, blessedly, had brought with her, as Antonia strapped them to her mount's sidesaddle.

"If you intend to ride armed," Deverill drawled, "you clearly don't need my protection."

She flashed a smile. "I thought I might practice a little if I find any appropriate targets. But I promise not to shoot you unless severely provoked."

"Then I will strive to be on my best behavior. Where do you wish to go this morning?"

"Anywhere. Everywhere. I suspect this is my one chance for freedom, and I mean to make good use of it. But I would most like to see the seashore, since I have little chance of that in London."

"The shore it is, then."

Although it would have been more circumspect to have a groom accompany them, Antonia chose not to, for she wanted to speak to Deverill alone, to discuss an important matter dear to her heart. Moreover, she wanted nothing to spoil her adventure, which would undoubtedly have been the result with an audience observing her unladylike behavior. Deverill didn't count, since he had already seen her at her worst, and since he was always the first to abet and encourage her wanton behavior.

She could feel her excitement building as he tossed her up in her sidesaddle and they set off.

The morning proved a perfect antidote to her restlessness, for the landscape was even more magical than she had hoped. They rode along the coast first. The granite cliffs bloomed with color—bluebells and thrift and sea campion—and overlooked sandy coves and shingle beaches washed by clear blue-green water.

Cornwall was not the paradise that Cyrene was, Antonia acknowledged, but the wild beauty of the coast resembled the island's a bit. The air was warm and sweet with a salt-tinged sea breeze, and alive with the cries of puffins and cormorants and herring gulls, as well as the rhythmic hiss and sigh of the waves below.

It was the vast ocean, however, that held Antonia in awe. Her bedchamber at Wilde Castle faced the sea, and she never tired of watching the magnificent view from her windows.

When they dismounted and negotiated a steep path down to the shore, she immediately took off her half boots and stockings, then lifted her skirts to wade into the waves.

She gave a gasp at the shock to her bare feet and calves. "The water is colder than I expected! It was much warmer on Cyrene."

Deverill was watching her with amusement. "Yes. The Atlantic is cooler than the Mediterranean. If you want to play in the waves, we will need to find you a sun-warmed cove and wait until afternoon."

"The water looks so inviting . . ." Antonia said wistfully. She cast a speculative glance at Deverill. "I wonder, would you consider teaching me how to swim?"

When he hesitated a long moment, she thought he intended to refuse her request. But he finally nodded, albeit with reluctance. "I suppose I could."

Not wanting to press her luck, she merely smiled and said, "Thank you." Backing up, she raised a hand to shield her eyes. The glitter of the brilliant sea stretching endlessly away beneath the deep blue sky enthralled her. It gave her a sense of profound elation, of pure, unadulterated freedom.

"I can understand why you love the sea so much," she murmured.

When Deverill remained silent, she pointed to a rock promontory that extended a short distance into the sea. "May we go out there?"

"Yes, but be careful. I don't want to carry you back to Bella half-drowned."

In actuality, it proved easier for her to climb over the granite boulders barefoot than for Deverill in his boots. When they reached the point, Antonia sat down on the warm rock and dangled her feet in the surging water below. She was glad when he settled beside her, for she hoped to use this opportunity to convince him to see her point of view.

"Deverill . . . I have been thinking," she began carefully.

"A dangerous exercise."

Antonia made a face. "I *do* have a brain in my head, you know. It is merely that as a female, I am not permitted to use it without inviting scandal."

Deverill's expression sobered. "I do know, sweetheart."

"But you cannot possibly understand the frustration of being a woman in a man's world of business. If I were a son, I could have assumed control of my father's shipping empire, instead of leaving it for others to run. And even in that respect, I failed."

"How so?"

"Obviously my judgment was at fault for allowing Heward so much leeway. I trusted him far too much—both Phineas and I did. Apparently we made the same mistake with Director Trant. Trant will certainly have to be fired, if he is transporting slaves as you suspect."

"That would be my advice," Deverill agreed.

"Which leads me to my point. You knew exactly where the dangers lay—and what to do about them."

"So?"

"So, I want to keep my father's legacy alive, Deverill. In future, I intend to be somewhat more involved, but I have none of the experience required to oversee such a vast enterprise. You, however, do."

"I?" he repeated warily.

"Deverill . . . I would like you to assume the reins of Maitland Shipping as director. You have only to name your price."

His hesitation told her his answer before he even spoke. "I am honored you hold me in such high regard, princess, but I'm afraid I must decline."

Antonia sighed. Deverill was telling her he didn't wish to be tied down, just as she'd expected. "Is it because of your work for the Foreign Office?"

He delayed another moment. "In large part. I'm too much of an adventurer to settle down in a career that requires me to remain in a London office. But I promise to find a new director for you, if your current one is corrupt."

Antonia tried to quell her disappointment. It shamed her that she had safeguarded her father's life work so poorly, and she considered Deverill the perfect choice to make up for her lapse. Although she might not want him for her husband, she trusted his business acumen implicitly. If he assumed control, she could leave the company in his able hands with confidence that it would flourish.

His refusal had sounded unalterable, though. She wasn't ready to give up just yet, but she had a sinking suspicion that Deverill would never be persuaded to take on such a mundane role as controlling her father's shipping empire.

"Well," she said lightly, "I have a little time to convince you to change your mind." She rose and smoothed out her skirts. "Shall we go? There is much more to explore, and I don't want to waste a moment."

Clambering back over the rocks, Antonia put on her stockings and boots, and then with Deverill's assistance climbed the steep path to return to their grazing horses.

When he grasped her hand to help her up the last incline, a shiver of awareness ran through her. His merest touch reminded her of the incredible pleasure he could give her. But she had vowed she would forget that reckless, wanton chapter of her life and attempt to view Deverill merely as a friend instead of her most wicked fantasy.

Clenching her teeth, Antonia allowed him to help her mount once more, pretending not to notice the burn of his fingers as they pressed into her waist while lifting her onto her sidesaddle. Yet even before he swung into his own saddle, Antonia spurred her horse forward, as eager to dismiss her wayward feelings toward Deverill as she was to explore.

In contrast to the rugged coast, with its coves and harbors and colorful fishing villages, the golden countryside possessed a mellow sort of charm. A confluence of river valleys, the district was populated by pretty cottages of stone and thatch, occasional churches of granite, and manor farms where fat cattle and sheep and horses grazed.

Antonia was drawn to the natural beauty of the numerous streams and thick woods and flowering meadows, but it was the feeling of freedom she cherished. She could be far more adventuresome here than in London. She could act the hoyden if she wished, galloping wildly across the countryside, challenging Deverill to horse races and archery matches. . . .

To her amusement, he refused her offer to show him how to shoot a bow, but not her proposition for a race. She gave the competition her all, bending low over her horse's neck as they galloped over a grassy field and up a hill that boasted another spectacular view of the sea. She won with relative ease and pulled up laughing.

When Deverill demanded a rematch, she gave him a brilliant smile that staggered him like a sharp punch to the gut.

"I know, it was not a fair match," Antonia acknowledged. "I am riding one of Isabella's excellent horses, whereas you again have a hired hack. But I still relished beating you for once."

Seeing the shine of excitement in her eyes, Deverill found it almost impossible to keep from hauling Antonia off her horse and tossing her to the ground, where they could both indulge the hunger that had been only momentarily satisfied on board his schooner. Her auburn hair, which had been pinned up beneath a small shako hat, was slipping down to frame her face with loose tendrils, while her cheeks were flushed with the warmth of exertion similar to the heat of passion.

A hard, burning ache lanced through his loins, making Deverill curse under his breath. How tempting she was. How bloody, impossibly tempting. It was driving him mad, not being able to touch Antonia. *She* was driving him mad.

But it was her sheer exuberance that set his blood on fire. She thrived on challenge as he did. And watching her delight was like drinking in a vivid sunrise.

He had made an egregious mistake in letting himself be alone with her, Deverill knew now. He'd hoped this morning would provide a distraction from his restlessness, would keep him from fretting over his impotence and lack of action.

It had indeed distracted him, but also brutally tested his fortitude.

Worse, he was about to compound his mistake. When Antonia had asked him to teach her how to swim, he hadn't been able to bring himself to disappoint her.

He hadn't liked disappointing her, either, when she had implored him to take control of her father's legacy. Yet he'd had no choice but to decline her generous offer.

His life was with the Guardians, not directing a shipping empire—although he couldn't tell Antonia that, since she knew nothing of the order. He couldn't explain that he was compelled to follow a deeper calling of his own. That serving the Guardians was his life's work. That every sinew and fiber of his being was dedicated to self-redemption, his ceaseless attempt at reparation for the men he couldn't save.

Instead, he'd claimed an adventurer's need for freedom. Antonia understood the need for freedom better than any other woman he had ever known.

Freedom. That was what she claimed to want most.

He could give her that much, Deverill promised her silently. He could satisfy her thirst for adventure, at least for this short time together. He could make her sojourn in Cornwall one she would never forget.

He would willingly give a slice of his soul to see Antonia smile at him that way again, no matter if it strained his fortitude to the very limits of his endurance.

Twelve

Deverill's fortitude was strained nearly to the breaking point the following day.

The first report from London arrived by courier that morning, confirming that he was indeed wanted for murder—which only served to intensify his frustration. As instructed, Macky had involved several others on his behalf, including fellow Guardians Alex Ryder and Viscount Thorne, and Madam Venus as well. However, there was little progress to report thus far, although follow-up reports from Macky would soon be forthcoming.

Deverill knew his friends would be almost as eager as he was to vindicate his name and to strike a blow against Heward. They were all cut from the same cloth—men of action who refused to wait patiently while others acted for them. But for now, Deverill realized he had no choice but to grit his teeth and let his colleagues conduct their inquiries without him.

Nearly as frustrating, Deverill was obliged to fulfill his promise to teach Antonia to swim, since Captain Lloyd was not expected to return with his schooner for at least two more days.

They held her first lesson during the warmest part of the afternoon. Deverill chose a private cove on the southern boundary of the Wilde estate, since it was sheltered from heavy waves and prying eyes. Accessed by a winding path down from the cliff top, the secluded cove boasted a narrow sand beach and a natural rock pool that was shallow enough for wading but wide and deep enough to swim in. There was even a rock cave that seemed an ideal place to land and store smugglers' contraband until it could be safely retrieved when the King's Revenuers were no longer watching.

Antonia professed delight at the cove's wild beauty and waded into the clear blue-green swells with scarcely any hesitation.

"The water seems warmer here than where we were yesterday," she observed.

"Because it's shallower here, and the surrounding rocks are heated by the sun."

"This should be perfect for my lesson."

Deverill couldn't fully agree. He had made Antonia wear her sailor's trousers to hide her body as much as possible, but the billowing linen shirt, once wet, plastered to her breasts and revealed the outline of her budded nipples.

Striving to ignore the temptation she presented, he stripped down to his breeches and waded in to his waist to begin her swimming lesson.

He commenced by showing her how to hold her breath and put her face in the water, then taught her to immerse her whole head without panicking. Next, she learned to relax enough to float.

"If you can float, you can tread water," Deverill instructed. "And if you can tread, you can swim. Now watch how I do it."

Moving a little deeper, he sank down to his neck, culling the water with his cupped palms while lazily kicking his legs.

"Let me try," Antonia said eagerly.

He stood beside her, ready to support her if necessary, while she moved her hands and legs as he'd shown her. With Deverill providing a sense of security, she mastered the art of treading water in a very short time.

Finally, he demonstrated how to stroke her arms overhead to gain a forward momentum, letting her practice with his palms under her stomach as she moved parallel to the shore.

She proved so good at stroking that she got away from him.

Delighted that she was actually swimming on her own, Antonia gave a trill of excited laughter—an excitement that suddenly faded when she realized she was alone in deeper water.

She heard Deverill instantly strike out after her, but when she stopped in nervous apprehension, she lost her concentration and promptly sank to the bottom. She broke above the surface, sputtering and thrashing and coughing.

Deverill was there to catch her and hold her up, but Antonia had swallowed a huge mouthful of water, and she clung to him with frantic urgency, her fingers digging into the hard muscles of his shoulders, her breasts pressing against the bare expanse of his chest.

When she finally regained her breath, awareness suddenly assailed her with unexpected force. Deverill's beautiful face was only inches away, his lips nearly touching hers. His smooth male skin felt resilient and heated beneath her fingertips. . . .

From the way his jaw tightened, she suspected he felt the same abrupt sexual arousal.

"Perhaps," Antonia murmured, hoping he would attribute the huskiness of her voice to natural hoarseness after swallowing so much salt water, "that is enough instruction for one afternoon."

Deverill shook his head. "You need to continue a little longer so you end on a successful note—it's like getting back up on a horse after you've fallen. But you can have a moment to rest if you wish. Now, relax and keep hold of my neck. I won't let you go under again."

He swam slowly backwards toward shallower water, towing Antonia with him. When his feet touched bottom, he stood and lifted her with his hands beneath her buttocks. Reflexively, she clasped her legs around his hips and held on as he waded toward shore. She could feel the hard, throbbing outline of his arousal through their wet clothing, even though she strove to ignore it.

He set her on her feet on the sun-warmed beach, yet she continued to cling.

"You can let go of my neck now," Deverill urged.

She couldn't force herself to release him, however. Antonia stood there dripping, incapable of movement, swaying on suddenly weak limbs.

The yearning sensations strumming through her body were powerful enough to make her dizzy. The trembling hunger that filled her made her breasts swell against Deverill's chest, made her lower body ache to press harder against the straining bulge in his breeches while her fingers longed to stroke the broad expanse of naked, bronzed chest.

Of their own accord, her hands slid slowly over the

wet surface of his arms, feeling the smooth contraction of sinewed muscle.

Deverill's breathing quickened in rhythm with hers. Yet he obviously had more willpower than she, for he reached up to clasp her wrists and draw her hands away.

A sprightly breeze wafted over her soaked clothing, making Antonia feel a bit chilled despite the afternoon's bright warmth; they had been in the water for nearly an hour, after all. Yet it was the sudden heat in Deverill's gaze that made her shiver.

He stared into her eyes for a long moment before his gaze dropped to focus on her breasts, where her chilled nipples had tightened to hard points, the dusky tips clearly visible beneath the damp linen.

At the sight, his green eyes flared beneath spiky clumps of wet lashes.

Watching him, Antonia couldn't speak, couldn't breathe. She had never been more conscious of Deverill, of the hot pounding of her blood. She could almost feel the sizzling flame of his mouth as he suckled her nipples. . . .

Deverill felt the same consciousness, his awareness of Antonia so razor-edged, he could almost taste the salty moisture on her damp skin. The savage knot of lust inside him was a vicious reminder of how difficult it was to fulfill his vow to keep away from her. He desperately wanted to touch her, to kiss her.

Hell and the devil, he couldn't stop himself. With a muttered curse, he bent his head and captured her lips beneath his.

She tasted of cool seawater and warm summer sun, but the effect was much more stunning . . . like a bolt of lightning that seared them both.

He deepened the kiss urgently, his tongue mating

with hers, feeling her body shudder against him as he splayed his hands over her sweetly curved buttocks.

When she moaned and molded herself against him, however, Deverill regained his senses and abruptly broke away.

Without looking at her, he pointed toward the rock cave, gruffly saying, "You are right, that is more than enough lesson for one day. Now go dry yourself off in private and put on your own clothing."

Mutely cursing herself, Antonia stood staring at him as she raised her fingers to her burning lips. She should have known better than to kiss Deverill. She'd thought it was the wild beauty of the cove that was having such an uncanny effect on her senses. The unaccustomed freedom that stirred her blood so. But it was Deverill himself.

She squeezed her quivering thighs tightly around the hot ache that burned there, and forced herself to turn toward the rock cave, where towels and dry clothing awaited her.

It had been a mistake to come here alone with Deverill, Antonia acknowledged, even for something so innocent as a swimming lesson, for her physical attraction to him had become almost painful. The constant feeling of desire he aroused in her was inescapable.

She had no idea how to combat it, except to keep away from him entirely. She wanted to learn to swim, but not enough to risk another tormenting encounter with Deverill like this one. When he accompanied her back to the castle, Antonia vowed, she would make up some excuse to put off her lessons until sometime in the distant future. She had no intention of ever again swimming alone with Deverill—not if she hoped to retain any semblance of control over her traitorous senses.

* * *

To Deverill's relief, any lessons were precluded during the next two afternoons by the social events Lady Isabella had planned—specifically a garden party and a shopping expedition to Falmouth in preparation for a levee to be held in Antonia's honor by a local dowager duchess.

And on the day of the levee, Captain Lloyd returned with Deverill's ship, bringing a report from Macky that contained encouraging news. As Deverill expected, Antonia was far more interested in discussing the report than in swimming, and she peppered him with questions when he called as promised to inform her of the details.

The first was that Ryder had located the apothecary who normally sold medications to Lord Heward's physician. The second, that Macky's informants had spied the ruffian with the scarred face in the stews of London's Seven Dials district.

Both pieces of intelligence could possibly advance their case against Heward, Deverill knew, but Antonia expressed disappointment that there wasn't more. The uncertainty and impotence, he could tell, were nearly as frustrating for her as they were for him.

At least his schooner's return allowed him to escape his social obligations in favor of patrolling the coast in search of a murderous smuggler. And once on board, he was better able to quell his feelings of lust and attraction for Antonia.

It felt damned good to be working again, Deverill admitted. He was glad to have a swaying deck beneath his feet once more, gladder still to at last be making progress in their investigation.

If they continued at this rate, it wouldn't be long

before he could return to London and escape temptation altogether by leaving Antonia behind.

Antonia hoped her sojourn in Cornwall would soon
be over. Perhaps she *was* enjoying the charm of the
countryside and the rugged wildness of the seashore.
Certainly she relished the sense of freedom she had
found here. But despite the enchantment, despite all
the pleasant diversions, she was anxious to return to
London. She wanted justice for her father and craved
to see his shipping empire in better hands.

Even more, she wanted to see Deverill exonerated.
She couldn't forget that he was accused of murder,
and that to clear his name, he needed to identify the
true villain who had orchestrated the crime. She was
fairly convinced now that Heward was the culprit—
and that he had likely poisoned her father also—even
though they had yet to garner any real evidence. If so,
she was determined to see him punished.

She couldn't quell her apprehension, however,
when she considered what might happen to Deverill
when he returned to London. If he couldn't prove his
innocence, he could very well hang. And if he confronted Heward . . . who knew how the baron would
respond?

Antonia suspected her disquiet was also caused by
guilt. *She* was the reason Deverill was in this dreadful
dilemma in the first place. She couldn't let him face it
alone. He had brushed aside her repeated entreaties
to be involved, claiming he didn't want her interference or help in discovering the truth.

She was determined to return to London with him,
though, even if she had refrained from arguing the
point. She was willing to let Deverill think her

amenable to remaining in Cornwall. When the time came, however, she would not let him leave without her.

She spent the time while Deverill was away attempting to work off her restlessness with her bow and arrows. Isabella had permitted her to set up a practice target at one side of the castle, as long as she kept a groom with her at all times. During his absence, Deverill had left Fletcher with her for protection, and even though the old tar grumbled about having to act as lackey—and worse, being kept away from his beloved sea—he provided exceedingly interesting companionship for Antonia by telling her more of his tall tales about their glorious adventures on the high seas. And she reciprocated by teaching him the principles of archery.

Thus, between Fletcher and Lady Isabella, Antonia's days were quite full. The nights, however, were much harder for her to bear.

Unable to sleep, she took to watching the dark sea, wondering where Deverill was and if he might be facing danger. It worried her to think of him risking his life to end the actions of a vicious pirate.

She wanted Deverill to be safe—a thought that made her mentally scoff at herself. Who was she fooling? She wanted Deverill, period. She missed him and wanted him to return, even if she had sworn to drive him from her mind.

The difficulty was that when she *was* able to sleep, she found her dreams filled with memories of Deverill and his incredible lovemaking. Dreams that always left her writhing and aching.

One such warm summer night toward the end of

the week, Antonia woke shivering with heat. After tossing and turning for another quarter hour, she rose and drew on a wrapper, then lit a candle and made her way downstairs. She left the candle on a table in the library and stepped through the French doors onto the rear terrace.

A three-quarter moon hung low in the black-velvet sky, casting a shimmering glow over the surprisingly calm sea. Deverill was out there somewhere sailing his ship, Antonia reflected, keeping this stretch of Cornish coast safe from marauders.

Sensual images of him rushed through her mind. Deverill standing on the deck of his schooner, the wind rushing through his sun-streaked hair. Deverill naked, his bronzed body glimmering with seawater. Deverill kissing her, stroking her, filling her with ecstasy.

Longing swelled inside her, a fierce restless feminine need that whispered through her body like the quiet surge of the surf below the castle bluffs.

Shutting her eyes, Antonia swore a low, helpless oath. It was sheer lust that made her feel so hot and restless—

She was startled when Isabella spoke behind her. "It is hard when your lover goes away."

Antonia felt herself flushing. "Deverill is not my lover, Isabella," she prevaricated.

"No? But I think you wish him to be."

"Why do you say that?"

"I have seen the way you look at him. And how he looks at you."

Curiosity got the better of her. "How do we look at one another?"

"As if you wish to devour each other."

She certainly couldn't deny the fierce hunger she

felt for Deverill, Antonia conceded, yet she hadn't dared hope he might feel the same hunger for her.

"Truly, I understand your dilemma," Isabella observed. "Deverill is irresistible, is he not?"

She couldn't dispute that, either, for she did find Deverill irresistible. Managing a shrug, Antonia tried to keep her tone light. "It would be utterly inappropriate for us to become lovers. Possibly even ruinous for me."

"Perhaps. Yet it is clear you have strong feelings for him. You have been fretting ever since he left."

"I admit I miss his provocations and even his highhandedness. But as I told you, Isabella, my future has no place for a notorious adventurer like Deverill."

Isabella smiled sadly. "That is such a pity, my dear. If I discovered one crucial thing in my three marriages, it is that true passion comes so rarely in life. And should it come, it is too remarkable to let slip away. I see the importance even more as I grow older. It is better to experience a single moment of passion than to live an insipid lifetime of virtue."

Surprise held Antonia speechless. Was Isabella actually encouraging her to act on her longings? To pursue a liaison with Deverill? "Are you suggesting I indulge in an affair with him?"

The countess cocked her head thoughtfully, studying Antonia. "Why, I believe I am. What harm would there be, as long as you are discreet?" She gave a firm nod and continued. "If you are concerned about becoming enceinte, I know of a prevention . . . sponges soaked in brandy or vinegar, placed deep inside your woman's passage to prevent your lover's seed from taking root. You dare not risk bearing a child out of wedlock, Antonia, but there is no reason you should not enjoy intimacy. Particularly if the damage is already done."

Now that I am no longer a virgin, Antonia knew Isabella meant. Her cheeks warmed to realize that her wanton secret was out. The countess was discerning enough to guess what had happened between Deverill and herself on board his ship.

In the silence, Isabella reached up to cup Antonia's cheek. "Think about it, my dear. A discreet liaison. Memories to last a lifetime. You deserve a moment's happiness before you do your duty and honor your father's wishes for a noble marriage. But only you can decide what you truly want. If it is Deverill, then I will do everything in my power to help you.

"Now," she added brightly, "I shall go to the kitchens and make myself a cup of brandy-laced milk. It is the perfect remedy for sleeplessness. I would be pleased to have you join me, if you care to."

With a final tender pat, Isabella turned away and disappeared into the library, leaving Antonia alone on the moonlit terrace to brood over the advice she'd been given.

An affair with Deverill. Did she dare attempt it?

Did she dare not?

She couldn't deny that she wanted to experience passion, particularly since true love was likely beyond her grasp. Given her circumstances—her loss of virginity and her newfound wariness about trusting any future suitors—it was doubtful she would marry for love. Rather, the odds were much greater that she would wed a man who wanted her mainly for her fortune.

Yet she was not simply an heiress. She was a woman, with a woman's needs . . . and the woman in her cried out for something more than the cold, colorless future that awaited her.

Her dilemma was even worse now that she had tasted Deverill's lovemaking. She knew now what would be missing from the rest of her life.

She was prepared to give up any dreams of love to honor her filial obligations, certainly. Yet whatever regrets she had about forswearing love would be easier to bear if she had some treasured memories to look back on.

She would have to ensure any liaison never went beyond physical intimacy, though. She didn't dare risk falling in love with Deverill, for he wasn't the kind of man to lose his heart to anyone, and true love was the only reason she would ever consider forsaking her solemn promise to her father. But surely they could keep their relationship purely physical. . . .

An affair with Deverill. The very thought sent a thrill of excitement thrumming through Antonia's body; excitement that caught and coiled inside her.

Few people, particularly women, were fortunate enough to live their dreams, to fulfil their deepest desires, to experience their most cherished fantasies. And this could be her one chance.

No, this could be her *only* chance for true passion. Before she settled for duty and an indifferent marriage of convenience, she could have a brief moment of ecstasy with Deverill. She could store up memories for the cold future ahead, when he would no longer be part of her life.

Antonia's hand stole to her stomach, which had suddenly clenched in longing. When she put her choice in such stark terms, it really was no choice at all.

* * *

As soon as she awakened the next morning, Antonia sent Fletcher to the inn in Gerrans where Deverill was lodging, with a message requesting another swimming lesson at the earliest opportunity.

It was the following morning, however, before she heard from Deverill. He sent word that he had returned temporarily from his patrol mission but he intended to go back out that evening, and he would call for her at two o'clock that afternoon for a lesson, if that time was convenient.

Antonia's heart started racing the moment she read his missive. She had never before contrived a seduction, but in this instance, she knew she would have to plan one if she hoped to convince Deverill that an affair was what she wanted.

She sent the inn's servant back with her reply, telling Deverill that she would meet him at the cove at two rather than waiting for him to call for her. Then she left the castle an hour beforehand in order to set the stage.

When he arrived at precisely two o'clock, she sat at the mouth of the rock cave, wearing a yellow muslin gown instead of her shapeless sailor's apparel. She had also pinned her auburn hair up in loose curls in an attempt to look more feminine.

Deverill's green eyes narrowed the moment he saw her, but he was evidently more concerned with her safety than her attire. "You came here alone?" he demanded.

Antonia rose to her feet, offering him a smile she hoped was seductive. "Fletcher accompanied me to the cliff, but I sent him away, since we needed privacy for my lesson."

Deverill's eyes narrowed even further when he suddenly noted the way she was dressed and that she had spread a blanket nearby on the sunlit beach. "I thought you wanted to learn how to swim."

"I do . . . afterward."

"After what?"

In answer, Antonia reached up to grasp the neckline of her gown. "After another kind of lesson."

She had already unfastened the hooks of her gown, so it was a simple matter to draw the bodice down and let the garment slide over her hips and sink to the sand.

She stood there in her cambric shift and nothing else.

The summer day was warm with the sun beating down from a cloudless blue sky, but the heat that flared in Deverill's eyes was far hotter.

"Antonia . . ." he said slowly in warning. "What the devil are you about?"

She took a step closer, deliberately staring up into his bright eyes. "I realized that this could be my last chance to truly know passion. I want you to teach me, Deverill."

He stared at her for several ragged moments before finally saying, "You must have been touched by too much sun."

"No." She was absurdly nervous, however, despite the fact that she had expected exactly this reaction from Deverill. Antonia licked her dry lips and swallowed to calm her racing heartbeat. "I am entirely serious. I want you to make love to me, to teach me about passion, so I will have a memory to cherish in the years ahead."

His eyes sparked with fire, but his expression remained suspicious. "Is this some sort of revenge, princess? Are you taunting me as punishment for abducting you?"

"No, in truth I should thank you for what you did. You gave me the kind of freedom I have never known before and will likely never know again." Antonia forced a smile. "Once I return to London, I must start behaving with complete circumspection again. And eventually I will have to set about finding a husband. I will never again enjoy the freedom I have now at this moment, and I want to make the very most of it. Please, Deverill, won't you teach me?"

When he still didn't answer, she took another step toward him. "Lessons in pleasure, Deverill. That is all I want." She searched his face, taking heart from the indecision she saw warring there. "I know from experience that you make an excellent tutor. And there is no other man I can ask . . . unless you know of someone else who would oblige me?"

He frowned sharply, as if in jealousy.

"But I don't want any other man," Antonia hurriedly assured him. "I want you, Deverill. And I think you want me." She glanced down at the thick bulge in his breeches. "In fact, I am certain of it."

"Blast it, yes, I want you."

"Then what is stopping you?"

"A little thing called honor, perhaps?" He ran a hand roughly through his hair. "My conscience is already flaying me for taking your virginity. Your father would draw and quarter me if he knew—"

"I don't seem to recall you considering my father's wishes then," Antonia pointed out sweetly.

"Because I didn't. . . . *Hell.*" His expression grew irritable. "I offered to marry you to remedy my mistake."

"You know why I refused. I don't wish to marry you, Deverill. I only want to know about passion. No obligations, no ties, just simple pleasure."

"Dammit, Antonia, I'm not a bloody saint."

She dimpled, feeling encouraged. "I know that entirely too well. And I consider it fortunate for my purposes."

Taking a steadying breath, Antonia removed her shift, slipping the straps off her shoulders and letting it drop to join her discarded gown on the sand. Deverill's own breath rushed out at the sight of her nudity; she heard the sharp rasp above the rhythmic murmur of the waves breaking onshore.

He was staring at her bare breasts, Antonia realized, her confidence rising. She could feel her nipples draw taut and begin to tingle. Yet their situations were highly unequal. Deverill was still fully dressed in shirt and breeches and boots, while she was completely naked.

She moved to stand before him and reached for his shirt. To her relief, he didn't stop her when she pulled the hem from the waistband of his breeches and pushed the shirt over his head.

He tensed visibly when she suggestively trailed her fingers down the muscles of his chest, over the wealed flesh that marred his beautiful, bronzed skin.

Wanting swelled inside her. Longing knotted her stomach and coiled between her thighs as she closed the final distance until their bodies touched, breast to chest, skin to burning skin.

Fire arced between them at the contact. Even so, Deverill remained rigid, obviously waging a war with himself. Yet she could feel the heat and strength and growing desire of him.

The same searing desire that was sweeping through her.

He would not deny her, she wouldn't allow it. She *needed* him. Needed surcease for the unbearable tightness that welled in her chest. For the relentless ache in her body that had sharpened to a delicious, agonizing point. For her quivering woman's flesh that throbbed and wept for him.

"Show me pleasure, Deverill," she implored, her voice a sensual plea.

His eyes blazed. And in that moment she knew the torment of waiting was finally over.

Reaching up, Antonia pulled his mouth down to hers, desperately needing to taste him, to assuage the fierce hunger that burned deep within them both.

Thirteen ❧

Her soft moan was his undoing.

Deverill braced himself against the surge of white-hot desire flooding him, knowing damned well that for Antonia's sake, he should say no to her irresistible request. He needed to protect her from himself, needed to summon some vestige of common sense. Yet he was tired of fighting his need, couldn't force himself to refuse.

Surrendering, he returned her kiss ardently, his mouth devouring hers, feeding the fire between them. When Antonia moaned, his hands plunged into her loose topknot, scattering the pins so that her flaming hair spilled free around her shoulders.

Another hoarse whimper sounded in her throat. She clung weakly to him, yet at the same time he felt her easing backward, urging him with her. Deverill suddenly understood why she had spread a blanket out on the sand. It was to be the scene of his seduction.

Their mouths still fused, Antonia sank down on the blanket and drew him with her.

Deverill's muscles clenched, fighting for control as

he covered her nude body. Urgency was sweeping in a tidal rush, hurting and hard and hammering his blood.

He had to slow down or he would burn them both to cinders. He wanted to give her pleasure this time, incredible pleasure, just as she had asked for. Taking a shuddering breath, he forced himself to end the kiss, then sat back to pull off his boots.

Antonia's shimmering blue eyes followed him as he stood to undress. In only a moment he had shed his breeches and stockings.

When his drawers finally followed, she gasped. He stood over her with shafts of golden summer sunlight bathing him, gloriously naked and gloriously masculine. He was so sinfully beautiful, he took her breath away.

"You planned this, didn't you?" Deverill said as if he already knew her answer.

"Yes. I hoped . . ." The words came out a mere rasp. It was difficult to speak with the sweet, scalding liquid of desire churning inside her.

She was captivated by the splendor of his body— his wide shoulders, his deep chest, his lean waist and hips, his fully aroused loins, his powerful thighs. She actually ached to touch him, to run her palms all over him.

Deverill was watching her in turn, staring down at her unabashedly, his gaze riveted on her bare body.

Dazed, Antonia pushed herself up on her elbows as she stared up at him. Dancing motes of sunlight surrounded them in the secluded cove, drenching them with warmth. It was like being caught in a dream.

No, it was her cherished fantasy come to life. Yet nothing in her imagination had ever been this sharp, this intense, this hot. She was filled with potent sensations, her nerves twisting and knotting in near painful anticipation.

Transfixed, she watched the lithe, athletic motion of Deverill's body as he knelt beside her. Helpless to resist her craving, she sat up fully and reached out to touch him. His skin glowed beneath her fingers, as feverish as her own, burning with a need the ocean's breeze could never cool.

Purposely avoiding the scars, she trailed her fingertips over his chest, feeling the smooth, hard, shifting pattern of his muscles. When her hand settled over his breast, she could feel the vibrant rhythm of his heartbeat.

The pleasure that rippled over her was so keen, she shuddered.

"You are beautiful," she said on a choked sigh.

His slow smile was dazzling. "Not as beautiful as you are, siren."

Her gaze dropping to his loins, she reached down to caress the jut of his erection—but Deverill abruptly drew back as if burned.

"If you arouse me any further, I won't be able to control myself."

"So?" Antonia asked with an unconsciously sensual taunt.

A muscle flexed in his jaw. "So, I intend to go slowly this time."

"That might be difficult for me."

"For me as well."

The silky raspiness of his voice sent a shiver down her spine.

He pressed her back on the blanket and held her arms away, so he could view her nudity. Antonia fought the urge to cover herself. She had no secrets from him; with Deverill she could be as wild and free as she wished, as vibrantly passionate, as sexual, as wanton.

And she knew she would be wildly wanton. He would see to it. Already she was nearly writhing beneath his brazen scrutiny. Then he bent and pressed a kiss to her belly, his breath sun-warm on her skin. Antonia arched in frantic need, but Deverill was clearly determined to take his time, using his mouth to heighten her hunger.

And the searing magic of his light, stirring kisses was only enhanced by the deft, knowing movements of his hands. His fingers slid up her thighs, gliding over her in a delicious rhythm, stroking her hips, her rib cage, the swell of her breasts, stopping at the firm, aching tips to circle and probe.

"Your nipples are ravishing," he murmured before his warm breath was replaced by the blaze of his mouth.

He suckled her, his tongue caressing her dusky flesh, teasing the aching peaks, before his tormenting kisses trailed lower once more, grazing her abdomen, then the soft mound guarding her woman's secrets. His tongue probed the tangle of silken curls to find the slick folds of flesh between her thighs. "And so is the rest of you."

With a whimper, she opened her legs, allowing him fuller access. Deverill groaned at the hot, rich scent of her female pleasure. He wanted to sample all the tastes and textures of her fragrant body. Wanted to fill his mouth and hands with the essence of her.

Antonia gasped once when his tongue slid slowly over the outer rim of her cleft, then again when he laved the already wet bud of her sex. In only moments, she was panting.

In a vague corner of his mind he heard her breathless murmur as she clutched his hair. "Deverill . . . you needn't use only your mouth this time. You can come inside me. Isabella told me how to stop a man's seed."

Stilling suddenly, he lifted his head to stare up at Antonia. "Isabella told you *what*?"

"How to . . . prevent a man's seed from taking root. She gave me some sponges and brandy. . . ."

His eyebrows shot up. He wasn't surprised that Bella was abetting her. It was Antonia herself who constantly kept him off guard with her unexpected actions.

"You are wearing a sponge now?"

A faint blush of shyness rose to kiss her skin. "Well, yes."

"You seem to have thought of everything."

"I only hoped . . ."

When she faltered, he couldn't help provoking her. "What did you hope, vixen?"

Her gaze remained somber. "I want you to fill me, Deverill. I want you to ease the fire inside me. I want—"

"Exactly what I want," he said huskily.

She took his hand and placed it over her breast. "Touch me," she whispered.

His expression softened with tenderness. "Gladly."

When his palm curled lovingly over the swollen crest, Antonia closed her eyes and exhaled in a sigh. This was no dream, she knew. She had never had a dream so delicious, so awash in sensation. One that made her shimmer and melt. She was melting between her legs, her shivering thighs clenched tight around a pool of liquid heat.

Deverill evidently understood her need, for his hand shifted lower, covering her abdomen with slow, erotic strokes, then gliding farther down between her legs to part the lips of her sex. When he slipped two fingers inside her, testing her slickness, creating an exquisite pressure, Antonia's responding whimper was a wordless plea for him to cease tormenting her.

Keeping his fingers deep inside her, he eased his knees between her thighs and stretched out over her. His naked chest grazed her nipples, while his sinewed thighs pressed hers wider. She writhed at the delicious intimacy, barely hearing his husky order.

"Look at me, sweeting."

She obeyed, gazing up at him. His eyes seemed lit by raw flames, so hot she was sure they would make her burst into flame herself. When she shuddered, he smiled.

"I like you trembling for me."

"Please, Deverill . . . I want you. . . ."

"I know."

He *did* know, for he felt the same desire. Deverill clenched his jaw at the sharp, fevered wanting that spiraled through him. The primal urge to ravish Antonia and fill her and claim her. A craving so rich, so potent, so fierce, he thought he might die if he didn't satisfy it soon. His shaft felt iron-hard and huge— which thankfully reminded him of her near virginal state.

Spreading her juices with his fingers to ease the friction, he very carefully slid his fullness inside her in a slow, heavy lunge. Involuntarily Antonia's inner muscles clenched around him, while her body tensed at the large invasion.

Deverill gritted his teeth, forcing himself to wait until her tender tissues grew accustomed to his penetration. He was physically under control but the feelings stampeding through him were anything but calm.

With herculean effort, he kept still, counting his violent heartbeats and hers, until finally he felt the tension in her body begin to ease and her panting breaths began to slow.

"Better now?" he asked hoarsely, lowering his lips to press light, soothing kisses over her sweat-dampened face.

"Yes."

"Then wrap your legs around me," he ground out.

Trustingly, she twined her slender calves around his thighs, her arms around his shoulders, her blue eyes wide and dark and luminous with heat as she stared up at him.

Lord, he could so easily get lost in her.

Instead, he forced himself to remain still, even as he grew so hard and heavy inside her, he thought he might burst.

Surprisingly, it was Antonia who took the next step. Deverill sucked in a sharp breath when she rocked her hips cautiously against his.

Holding her gaze, he drew himself out slowly . . . and just as slowly surged in again.

"Yes . . ." Antonia whispered, lifting her hips to meet his.

He allowed her to set the pace, allowed her to take him in as deeply and fully as she could. Soon her tentative undulations took on a more urgent rhythm. Deverill arched over her, the heavy muscles of his shoulders taut as he struggled to remain in control. But the wanting between them grew; the explosive pressure built.

Her body took over completely then, her hips moving in an instinctive dance of passion, her fingers clenching at his back, her lips parting in sobbing cries of pleasure.

Deverill couldn't help himself; he took her mouth in a hard kiss, his tongue plunging in deep and ravenous, his blood surging when Antonia responded in kind. Pleasure rushed and pounded through him, hard and furious, as she returned his kiss measure for measure.

Sunlight poured down on them, a swirling mosaic of light and heat and shifting colors, illuminating their frantic dance of lips and tongues and limbs.

One more urgent lunge ignited a sensual explosion inside her. Antonia heaved in his arms, crying out. Deverill felt her ripple and convulse in her ecstasy, felt her contractions grip and pull him farther inside.

Heat poured into his chest and expanded. "God . . . Antonia." Her name rasped in his throat as the hot, clutching pulses of her orgasm milked him. A heartbeat later, his groan turned to a hoarse shout as he contracted helplessly, pouring himself into her, the searing flood of his release drenching her completely.

In the aftermath of his harsh, powerful climax, Deverill barely refrained from collapsing upon her. Weakly, he braced his weight on his forearms as the fire slowly receded. His senses gradually returned to awareness. . . . The hot sunlight beating down on his back, the rhythmic murmur of the waves, the incredible softness of the woman beneath him. It had been unique, shattering, to make love to Antonia.

He'd never been so lost in a woman, never been so profoundly shaken.

Taking a steadying breath, Deverill lifted his head to gaze down at her. Her face was flushed and hazed with desire, her eyes passion-drenched and lustrous as she watched him.

"That was . . ." Her husky voice faltered momentarily, and she wet her swollen lips before continuing. "Simply beautiful."

Unexpectedly, Deverill felt his heart soar. He shouldn't feel so absurdly giddy at her praise, so much like a moonstruck youth, yet he couldn't restrain the foolish emotion.

"It was indeed beautiful," he agreed, pressing a light, chaste kiss on her forehead.

Her eyes fluttered shut, and she exhaled a contented sigh.

Carefully, he eased himself from between her thighs and rolled bonelessly onto his back, carrying her with him. For long moments he simply lay there, savoring the peace.

Feeling the same tranquillity, Antonia nestled against him, her limbs trembling with aftershocks, her thoughts overwhelmed by how exquisite Deverill's lovemaking had been. The experience was more beautiful than anything she'd ever dreamed of in her wildest fantasies.

The memory was still with her. She could feel his muscular, golden body driving into hers, gleaming with sweat, his enormous power leashed for her sake.

His possessiveness had thrilled and excited her, yet he had made her feel cherished as well. He had taken her as a lover should, tender yet impossibly demanding.

Her fantasies didn't even come close to the raw reality of him. The mere feel of Deverill inside her had filled her with such yearning, she had wanted to weep with pleasure.

She'd never known she could yearn that fiercely, that completely, with every nerve and fiber of her body. Even now she felt it thrumming inside her. She wondered if Deverill felt the same yearning. He remained unmoving except for his light caresses; with sleepy eroticism, his fingers moved over her bare hip, drawing lazy patterns on her skin.

Antonia nuzzled her face in the curve of his shoulder, breathing in deeply. She could smell the spicy fragrance of their lovemaking, the musky male scent of his body.

His naked, beautiful golden body.

Wanting to see him, Antonia slowly raised herself up on one elbow. His eyes were closed, a faint smile of contentment curving his lips. Seeing his expression, she felt a rich, new hunger stir to life low in her center.

Moments ago she'd had a fleeting sense of just how much power she could wield over Deverill. It was a heady thing to know she could affect him that way.

Hoping to rekindle the spark, she reached out to touch the hard, warm flesh of his abdomen.

"Give me a moment to recover," Deverill murmured in that husky voice that rumbled through her.

Antonia felt her pulse quicken. In a moment he would take her again. Anticipation blossomed once more inside her, merging into a persistent deep ache inside her that began and ended with Deverill.

She was willing to wait, though. At least, that was what she sternly told herself.

In the meantime, she ran her hand over his chest, pausing when she encountered a savage scar. That ravaged flesh tore at her heart. Aching inside, she bent her head to his rib cage, kissing him softly, the barest brush of lips to skin heated by her breath.

When her mouth tenderly caressed a puckered ridge, Deverill suddenly opened his eyes and grasped her hand. The dark intensity of his gaze startled her.

He obviously didn't want her kissing his scars, didn't want the reminder of the pain he had endured.

"It has been more than a moment," Antonia said, trying to infuse lightness into her tone. "And I am ready for my next lesson."

Deverill stared at her suspiciously, his chest tightening at the concern he saw in the blue depths of her eyes. But now was not a time for dark thoughts, he reminded himself, and certainly not the resurrection of his demons. Not when particular male parts of his anatomy were being resurrected instead. His mouth curved as his shaft stirred to new life.

"Eager, are we?" he said, keeping his tone teasing.

Her smile was half seductive, half shy—and made his whole heart turn over. Deverill reached up to brush his fingers over her still-flushed face. "We shouldn't keep you out in the sun so long that your pretty skin burns, but I think a bath is in order."

"A bath? But Deverill, I asked you to show me pleasure—"

"Hush, this will be pleasurable, I promise you."

Rising from the blanket, he scooped Antonia up in his arms and carried her into the water, wading out until the waves were knee-high. Then he set her on her feet and made her stand obediently while he enjoyed the intense pleasure of washing her all over. . . . Cupping his hands in the salt water and letting it dribble over her sleek skin. Stroking her slender arms, her ripe breasts, her flat stomach, her beckoning woman's mound. Watching her as she shut her eyes in bliss and shuddered at his every touch.

His loins had already hardened to an excruciating ache, but the sight of her gleaming wet body, naked and so utterly alluring against the splendor of the sea, set his pulses to pounding. A siren indeed.

And that was before it was Antonia's turn to wash *him*. When she smoothed her hands over him, taking her own sweet time to torment him as he'd done her, he lost any semblance of patience.

Dragging her against the scorching hunger of his body, Deverill drew her with him toward shore. At the waves' edge, he fell back onto the wet sand, spreading Antonia over him, to her obvious surprise and delight.

Her laughter sang out as she splayed over his body, but as his gaze locked with hers, the playful moment turned heated and restless once more.

They stared at each other, foam surging around them in sensual, rhythmic pulses.

Striving for control, Deverill tightened his arms around her. Feverishly, his hands stroked down her back, tracing the dip of her spine, running over the curves of her derriere to cup each buttock in a large palm, contouring the taut flesh.

Antonia shivered visibly, but then shook her head. Catching him by surprise, she pushed herself up to straddle his thighs. "I want to pleasure *you* this time."

Reaching down, she wrapped her slender fingers around his thick shaft. The coolness was delicious against his burning flesh, and so was the slow glide of her grasp. She clearly remembered that he'd once shown her how he liked his cock to be stroked, but this time was not for him.

"Later," he rasped. "You can pleasure me later. Now is for you."

Raising his hands, he filled his palms with her breasts. The mounds were slick, her nipples dark and fully aroused, and he took great satisfaction in watching her.

"Let me see your pleasure, siren," he urged in a husky, tender tone.

Obeying, Antonia let her head fall back as he squeezed her throbbing breasts, teased her thrusting nipples between his hard fingers. Her flesh was hot and tender and exquisitely sensitive to his touch, and his every tormenting caress sent shocking waves of delight to her core.

Yet it wasn't enough, Antonia acknowledged, achingly aware of his swollen arousal nestled so provocatively at her feminine cleft. She wanted to feel Deverill on her and in her, to join with him and experience the ecstasy they had shared earlier.

Once again he seemed to know exactly what she craved, for his hands grasped her hips and lifted her slightly, until her naked center was poised over his rigid shaft.

Her eyes widened when she realized what he intended; she hadn't known lovemaking was possible from this position. She gazed down at him, feeling a dizzyingly heady mix of desire and anticipation.

But then any thoughts regarding the novelty of it fled as Deverill slowly lowered her onto his hot, pulsing erection. Antonia's soft, keening moan echoed around the secluded cove as once more a fiery, restless need swept over her.

It was incredible, the contrasting sensations she felt . . . the cool caress of the water, the heat sizzling through her blood, the thick hardness of Deverill's male flesh impaling her, the arousing pressure of his hands. . . .

He made her burn and shiver by turns. He made her feel wild and reckless and out of control.

His fingers clenched on her hips, rocking her in time to the deep thrusting of his shaft, and Antonia responded, her body undulating with each upward surge of his hips, their rhythm as timeless as the swell of the sea.

"Show me your pleasure," Deverill demanded more urgently, propelling her toward a wrenching, powerful release.

Antonia had no choice as the rapture overtook her. Her head flung back, she cried out her passion, the hot, bright ecstasy spasming through her as vivid as the sun.

An ecstasy that shattered Deverill's control and swept him along with her in its searing wake.

Fourteen

To Antonia's regret, her next lesson in pleasure was deferred for three more days, since Deverill was occupied patrolling coastal waters. There had been no more local murders, but he had yet to catch the pirate who was preying on the district fishermen, and his duty took precedence over his own personal concerns.

Antonia fully understood—she was not so selfish as to wish Deverill would stay with her if it meant forsaking his obligations—but she eagerly looked forward to his return.

When finally they met in the secluded cove, Deverill insisted on giving her another swimming lesson first. The event, however, had its own delights, for they spent as much time touching and caressing and kissing as swimming. Deverill claimed there was method to his madness: anything that helped Antonia to relax also helped her to forget a novice swimmer's instinctive fear of drowning. Furthermore, Deverill explained with a smile, if they indulged in passion first, they both would be too weary to swim at all.

His strategy proved successful. Antonia made great

progress, learning to stay underwater for long moments at a time, and even to swim beneath the surface for short distances.

Later, when at last they made love, their desire was just as sharp as before, but the urgency was somehow tempered, the torment eased. Perhaps because they knew they had the entire afternoon together.

With unspoken accord, they drew out the moment, reveling in the sensations of slick wetness and luscious heat. Their joining went on forever, timeless and lazy and beautiful, filled with the same wild enchantment that now touched all of Antonia's dreams of Deverill.

Afterward, they lay naked together on blankets in the shallow rock cave, sheltered from the hot summer sun. The cave floor had the disadvantage of being uncomfortably hard—much less forgiving than sand—so Antonia was glad to report that Isabella had offered them a nearby cottage to use for their trysts.

"She said it is the hideaway Lord Wilde built for her so they could have privacy from servants and prying eyes."

Deverill arched his stiff shoulders, saying wryly, "Isabella has my gratitude. I confess I would prefer a soft bed for a change."

"The cottage has additional benefits," Antonia added with amusement. "Miss Tottle says my complexion is getting far too brown. I fear she will force me to wear cucumber masks if I don't make an effort to keep out of the sun."

"I am very fond of your tanned skin," Deverill replied, reaching up to stroke her cheek.

With a pleased sigh, Antonia curled more contentedly against him. "Isabella showed me the cottage yesterday. It is perfectly lovely, with a walled garden and a gazebo that reminds me of my mother's at home. Perhaps we can visit there tomorrow."

"Not tomorrow, I'm afraid. Our elusive pirate has apparently moved farther down the coast, if the sightings are true. I spoke to Sir Crispin this morning as soon as I put in to port, and he asked me to expand my search. I plan to leave tomorrow afternoon and will be away for at least several days."

"So now that you have made the waters safe here, you must follow the villain where he leads? It won't be easy to find him, will it?"

"We have a good description of his ketch and of him, and the ocean is not so vast that he can hide forever. If we can apprehend him, there are enough witnesses to warrant a trial and probably convict him for murder."

Antonia raised herself up on one elbow. "How does one apprehend a pirate if you find him?" she asked curiously.

"A warning shot across the bow, to begin with. I will sink his vessel if I must. He'll likely refuse any demands to surrender, since he doubtless considers himself invincible. His ketch is armed with a half-dozen four- and six-pounders—which is what has allowed him to terrorize the local smugglers and rob them of their contraband over the past several months."

"Are a half-dozen cannon enough to mount a defense?"

"They are no match for my schooner. While it may come to a battle, unless he manages to get in a lucky shot, I should win easily."

"It still sounds dangerous." With a finger, she drew a slow, circular pattern through the sprinkling of hair on Deverill's chest. "I confess it worries me to think of cannon shooting at you."

His low chuckle was indulgent. "I have been shot at hundreds of times, sweeting, but I am still in one piece."

Are you? she wondered. Absently, she touched the worst of his scars, reflecting that his body might be whole but not unscathed.

At her touch, Deverill reacted instantly, reaching up to grasp her wrist tightly and hold her away.

Startled by his abruptness, Antonia returned his gaze solemnly for a long moment, aching at the pain she had unconsciously ignited in the green depths.

"I am so sorry they hurt you," she said softly.

Deverill winced, then looked away, his dark lashes lowering to shadow his sensual eyes. "I survived. I was *fortunate*." He spat the word like a curse.

"It seems to me you were indeed fortunate," Antonia replied quietly. "You survived and lived to mete out justice against your tormentors."

"*No*. There was no justice for my men." The savage bitterness in his tone was inescapable. "My tormentors tortured and killed more than half my crew, when I should have died in their stead. Do you know what it's like for a captain to outlive his crew?"

His gaze found hers, and for a fleeting moment, she saw a desolation in his eyes, a bleakness so deep that it shocked her.

Antonia swallowed, her throat suddenly burning with unshed tears. She hadn't meant to make Deverill remember the brutal captivity that had resulted in his scars. Hadn't meant to bring back his terrible memories or to remind him of his anguish at failing to save his men from torture and death. But now that she had, she yearned to offer him comfort.

"It was not your fault, Deverill."

He shut his eyes, as if in great pain. "It was indeed

my fault. A captain is wholly responsible for his crew, for their safety and everything that touches their lives."

"As Fletcher tells it, you were betrayed by treachery. Had not the British government just signed a treaty with the pasha?"

"Yes." His voice was a harsh whisper. "A bloody, treacherous deception. The pasha intended to punish me for previously sinking one of his corsairs' ships . . . and to set an example for other Englishmen. He assumed if he showed his power, he would secure better terms for his kingdom."

The ache swelled inside Antonia for Deverill's suffering; her heart hurt for the grief she felt emanating from him. She feathered her fingers over his forehead, down his face, offering admittedly meager solace. "Fletcher thinks that is why you are so set on saving me."

"Fletcher talks a damned sight too much," Deverill replied savagely.

Antonia fell silent, and Deverill felt another prick of guilt, this one for shouting at her. He couldn't deny the truth of her charge. For ten years he had made it his mission to save others, trying to atone for his failure to save his crew.

He squeezed his eyes shut, assaulted anew by the nightmare. The screams of his men as they were tortured. Their pleas, their cries for help. Calling out to him to save them. His own fierce struggle to break free of his bonds. Fletcher's pleading whisper for him to cease fighting. *"Cap'n, we can't save 'em. Hold on to yer strength."*

Fletcher had been right, Deverill knew. Even had he sacrificed himself, the pasha would not have spared his crew. He had been kept alive so he would suffer most, enduring the agony of watching his men die horrible deaths, one by one.

Deverill swore in anguish at the memory. It was indeed why he was so determined to save Antonia, and why he had become a Guardian, even knowing atonement was out of reach for him. He could never forgive himself for the sin of living when so many of his men had died.

Just then he felt the touch of Antonia's lips on his chest, felt the hot moisture that fell from her eyes. He clutched her arms and held her away, staring up at her. Her eyes swam with tears. She was weeping for him.

His hands reached up to cradle her face. "God, don't cry."

She swallowed hard, trying to choke back a sob, but the tears continued to fall.

Deverill groaned. Her fiery, shimmering hair fell down around them in a silky curtain, and he tangled his fingers in it, dragging her close and capturing her mouth in a fervent kiss.

His hungry plundering quieted her sobs, but it wasn't enough . . . for either of them.

Rolling Antonia onto her back, he mounted her with hard, quick urgency, burying his face in the curve of her neck as he buried his cock in her sweet warmth. Blood pounded in his ears, crashing louder than the nearby surf as he drove into her.

Not protesting his ferocity, Antonia wrapped herself around him, welcoming him, holding him tightly as finally he shattered, his climax primitive, fierce, endless.

Afterward, he lay heavy and spent upon her. Antonia stroked his scarred back, soothing him with her silken softness. For the first time ever, Deverill didn't pull away from the offer of succor. Instead, he let her comfort him, taking her heat and her essence deep into himself, absorbing the warmth and strength of her.

A quiet gratitude filled him. For a moment he had found peace. In her arms, he was temporarily able to forget the grief and guilt that haunted him. Even if it was a grief and guilt he must forever bear.

His mood was somber when Deverill escorted Antonia back to Wilde Castle, only to discover that a surprise awaited him. Sir Gawain Olwen had come to Cornwall in search of him.

The elderly leader of the Guardians was ensconced in the drawing room with Lady Isabella, enjoying tea. Rising, Sir Gawain greeted Antonia fondly. "I was desolate to hear of your father's passing, my dear. He was a good man and a dear friend."

The pain in Antonia's eyes reminded Deverill of his own remembered pain, but she shrugged it off with a smile of gratitude.

"Thank you, Sir Gawain. It was extremely kind of you to send me your beautiful gift of condolence. Sir Gawain," Antonia explained to Deverill and Isabella, "gave me an exquisite sailing ship made of blown glass in remembrance of my father."

"How thoughtful," Isabella said approvingly before gesturing at the tea table, where an assortment of scones and crumpets and finger sandwiches were laid out. "My dear, will you and Deverill join us for tea? We have nearly finished, but I will ring for another pot."

"Perhaps later, Isabella," Antonia replied. "If you will forgive me, I must wash and then change my gown. I fear I have sand and salt everywhere. Deverill has been teaching me to swim," she added for Sir Gawain's benefit.

Deverill suspected she wanted to wash away the signs of their lovemaking from her body as well as the sand and salt. And when Antonia directed a soft, unconsciously secretive smile at him, he was certain of it.

Instantly, he was struck again by a powerful surge of desire, which was irrational, considering that he'd spent the past several hours slaking his need in her sweet body. But with her hair pinned loosely atop her head and her sun-kissed skin flushed with a rosy glow, Antonia looked enchanting.

Deverill dragged his gaze away in time to find Isabella watching him with amusement, and Sir Gawain observing him with an intent curiosity in his shrewd blue eyes.

As Antonia left the room, Isabella excused herself as well. "I am certain you two gentlemen have much you wish to discuss, and I must speak to Cook about setting extra places for dinner. You will stay to dine with us, Deverill? We mean to enjoy a quiet evening at home and catch up on all the gossip from Cyrene."

"I should enjoy that, Bella."

"Excellent! Then I will leave you to yourselves."

When Isabella offered her hand to Sir Gawain, he bowed gallantly and kissed her fingers. She patted his cheek fondly before sweeping from the room.

It had long been rumored that she and Sir Gawain had once been lovers, but Deverill suspected they were simply intimate friends. Not only because the age difference between them was more than two decades, but because Bella was too hot-blooded to give herself to any man who could not reciprocate her passion.

Possibly the baronet might once have been driven by passion. He was tall and lean, with chiseled features that women would consider handsome, and light blue eyes that were both penetrating and kind. But the burdens of his tremendous responsibilities had obviously taken a toll. His lined face appeared strained, and he wore his usual serious expression. He also limped slightly—the result of an injury during a mission long ago, before he had assumed control of the order.

Sir Gawain looked weary now as he settled on the sofa and invited Deverill to take the adjacent chair.

"So, my friend," he remarked once they were seated. "I understand you saved Antonia from a disastrous marriage and perhaps worse, and in so doing, you became embroiled in a devilish coil."

"Being charged with murder is indeed a coil," Deverill responded with sardonic humor. "I have only myself to blame, though, for underestimating Heward's malevolence."

Sir Gawain nodded grimly. "I have hopes that with effort the damage may be remedied."

"Have you brought any word from Macky, sir?"

"Indeed I have. I shall let you read his report for yourself, but the news is positive. Madam Venus in particular has been most helpful, and her discreet inquiries into Lord Heward's predilections were informative. It seems the baron is rather fond of perversions. Specifically, he derives great pleasure from inflicting pain on the courtesans he frequents."

Deverill winced. "I suspected as much. Which only makes me more thankful that Antonia is safe from that bastard."

"Agreed. There is also success regarding the scar-faced knave who attacked you and killed the young woman in your company. They discovered his lair in Seven Dials and spied two rogues who might have been his cohorts in crime. Macky is only awaiting your return before moving against them."

"Good," Deverill said darkly. "I want to have a hand in their interrogation."

Sir Gawain bent to retrieve his teacup. "I have spoken to Lord Wittington as well," he said, mentioning the undersecretary of the Foreign Office. "Wittington is offended that you could even be suspected of murder, let alone arrested. He assured me that a number of his colleagues in the Foreign Office will vouch for you, and he feels confident that if you do return to London soon, you can avoid arrest and imprisonment, at least for the time being."

"I hope not only to avoid prison," Deverill replied, "but to prove Heward guilty of murder, both of the woman and of Samuel Maitland. Therefore, when I return, I intend to do so clandestinely, so Heward will have no opportunity to devise another treacherous scheme."

Sir Gawain's brow furrowed. "It outrages me to think that Samuel was poisoned. I am grateful to you for acting so swiftly to protect his daughter, Deverill. Samuel was an invaluable champion of our cause, in addition to being a trusted friend, and I would go to any lengths to see Antonia safe."

Pausing, he took a sip of tea before focusing his shrewd gaze again on Deverill. "I understand your intentions toward her are honorable. Bella told me of your marriage offer."

Deverill shook his head, a faint smile twisting his mouth. "I offered, but Antonia intends to make a noble marriage as her father wished. I don't fit her requirements for matrimony."

"Well, I should like to see her happy—and you also, Deverill."

"Thank you, sir. Will your visit here be of any length?"

"I intend to remain a few days before sailing for Cyrene. I find I need to rest and recuperate some after a week of dealing with London bureaucrats and politicians."

Though he was surprised that the stalwart leader of the Guardians would call attention to his failing vitality, Deverill politely ignored the comment. "Then you could do me a service by keeping Antonia company now and then. She is understandably restless, being confined here in Cornwall when both our fates are so uncertain, and I must leave tomorrow afternoon."

"Bella informed me of your search for a pirate."

"Frankly, I was glad for the task," Deverill admitted. "Waiting for my fate to be determined is damned difficult."

"I could easily assign you a mission to keep you occupied. Hawk is shortly to leave for Spain—to liberate a convent of nuns who are being terrorized by local bandits—and he could use some assistance. With half my agents away from Cyrene, your services would be welcome."

"Ordinarily I would leap at the chance to help, but I want to remain close so I can return to London as soon as I hear from Macky that our plans are in place. And I don't wish to leave Antonia alone for so long to brood over her circumstances. If you will see to her for a few days—perhaps provide her a distraction or two—I would be grateful."

"Never fear," Sir Gawain said with a reminiscent smile. "Antonia is a delight and it will be a pleasure to share her company. And it is the least I can do for Samuel Maitland's daughter."

Dinner was an enjoyable affair, but they had barely begun the fish course when Isabella received word that her sister-in-law, Lady Kenard, had taken to her bed in anticipation of an imminent birth. The midwife had been summoned, but since Isabella wished to be at Clara's side for the lying-in, she made her apologies and hastened from the room, leaving her guests to finish dinner without her.

The conversation reminded Deverill of the first time he had dined with Antonia more than four years ago, for she asked countless questions of Sir Gawain about Cyrene and the people she had met during her one visit there. Apparently she and her father had been guests at Olwen Castle, which explained in part why the elderly baronet treated Antonia much like a granddaughter. And she seemed just as fond of him. Deverill wasn't surprised when Sir Gawain invited her to return to the island someday soon, or when Antonia claimed she would like nothing more.

The gentlemen declined to remain at the table to enjoy their port and instead repaired to the drawing room with Antonia so as to keep her company. A short while later, however, Sir Gawain announced his intention of retiring early, pleading that he was weary from the voyage and that his old bones needed a softer bed than the lumpy berth aboard his ship.

Antonia kissed his wrinkled cheek and bid him good night, and the moment he was gone, she turned to Deverill.

"Did Sir Gawain have any progress to report regarding your investigation of Lord Heward?"

Deverill understood why she was eager to learn any

news from London, but he had no intention of discussing her former betrothed's predilection for sexual perversions, so he merely replied, "Yes, there has been progress. But nothing conclusive, so don't get your hopes too high."

Antonia gave him a long, shrewd look. "Do you know how frustrating it is for me when you fob off my questions? If you won't tell me, I can always ask Sir Gawain myself."

"You can, but he will likely consider the intelligence unfit for a lady's ears."

"Why? Is it so scandalous?"

Deverill emitted a sigh, knowing that Antonia wouldn't easily give up. "My colleagues confirmed certain suspicions I had about Heward—that he enjoys hurting the Cyprians he patronizes. It's how he experiences sexual pleasure."

"Oh." Antonia's cheeks warmed with a faint blush even as she frowned at the news.

"You can see why," Deverill commented, "I would prefer that you refrain from pressing Sir Gawain on the subject. He's so courtly a gentleman, he would be uncomfortable discussing such a subject as Heward's carnal proclivities with you."

Antonia nodded distractedly. "I never suspected Heward of having so dark a nature. To my knowledge, he never even kept a mistress—and I would have heard about that. My friend Emily, Lady Sudbury, was privy to all the ton gossip, and she would have told me."

"He might have had difficulty finding a mistress willing to bear the pain of a long-term relationship," Deverill observed. "But one thing is certain. You would not have enjoyed the marriage bed with him."

When Antonia shuddered, Deverill knew she had drawn the same conclusion.

"Actually," he added, wanting to drive home the point that her betrothed was a dangerous man, "this revelation only substantiates the rumors I heard about Heward when I first arrived in London—about him possessing a violent temper and physically abusing his servants."

She regarded him in dismay. "You never told me of any such rumors."

"At the time I had no proof, and you likely would not have listened anyway. But we can begin to build a case against Heward now, so you needn't worry about it for the next few days while I am gone."

To his surprise, Antonia suddenly rose. "You said you don't intend on leaving until tomorrow afternoon. If so, I trust you will be free to visit Isabella's cottage with me in the morning?"

At the odd note of determination in her tone, Deverill's eyes narrowed. Her expression was dispassionate, but he had the distinct impression that Antonia had something more on her mind than a simple lovers' tryst.

"Yes, I will be free the entire morning," he answered after a short hesitation. "And I would like very much to spend it with you."

"Good, then you may call for me at ten to take me riding."

"What are you up to, vixen?"

"Why, nothing at all," Antonia murmured. "Now finish your port and pray excuse me. I just remembered a small matter I must attend to."

With a distracted smile, she swept from the drawing room, leaving Deverill frowning curiously after her.

* * *

Antonia did indeed have plans for Deverill.

His confession about his brutal ordeal haunted her. His torment—his eyes so dark with pain and the terrible knowledge of his guilt—had filled her with a burning ache to ease his hurt if she could.

She couldn't banish his agonizing memories, she knew, but perhaps she could give him one single, tender memory to help distract his mind when the tormenting ones became too heavy to bear. She would be violating her own resolve to keep their relationship purely physical, Antonia knew, but it couldn't be helped. A deep, powerful instinct—the primal, feminine need to nurture—was driving her to act. And she didn't want him sailing away for days on end without her at least making an attempt.

She was dressed and waiting as usual when Deverill called on her at ten o'clock, yet it was difficult to pretend this was simply another glorious ride in the countryside.

They enjoyed a brisk gallop, and by the time they arrived at the cottage, Antonia's heart was beating rapidly with anticipation and perhaps a little fear as well. She had already visited once here this morning and made her preparations, so all she could do now was hope that Deverill didn't reject her efforts and storm out in fury.

Antonia showed him around the elegant little cottage—first the parlor and kitchen, and then the large bedchamber, which was cheerfully decorated in yellow and cream damask.

Taking a steadying breath, she crossed the room and threw open both the lace curtains and the mullioned windows, so that bright sunlight streamed inside, along with the lush scent of summer roses. She wanted no darkness in this room with what she was about to do.

The windows looked out upon a charming walled garden, with a white-trellised gazebo in the center. Antonia spared a faint smile, remembering that Deverill had first introduced her to pleasure in the gazebo at home, before turning back to him. He had come to stand close, evidently expecting to make love to her.

When she reached up to untie his cravat, Deverill bent his head to kiss her. Shaking her head, Antonia pressed a hand against his chest to stay him. "No kisses yet. This is my fantasy, Deverill, and I wish you to play along."

When he gave her a curious look, she turned away. "Take off your clothing, please. I shall return in a moment."

Antonia disappeared into the small dressing room, where she made use of the sponges Isabella had given her and then changed her attire. When she came out, she saw that Deverill had obligingly removed everything but his breeches.

His eyebrows rose sharply, though, when he caught sight of her.

She was dressed as the feminine version of a pirate, complete with head scarf and eye patch, and a low-cut gown of scarlet silk that clung to her body, showing off the curves of her breasts and hips. Around her waist, she wore a sash and a painted wooden knife with a curved blade.

"I presume," he said slowly, his tone distrustful, "you mean to enlighten me as to your intent."

Hands on hips, Antonia sauntered barefoot toward him. "I am a pirate queen, of course, and I have taken you captive."

He didn't look pleased; far from it. "Where the devil did you find that costume?"

"It is Isabella's, left over from a masquerade ball."

"Surely Isabella never wore anything that revealing."

Antonia flashed him a provocative smile. "I improvised."

Bending forward to deliberately display her ripe cleavage, she drew up her skirts to show off a long expanse of bare leg and naked thigh.

Deverill's gaze followed her movement, then lifted slowly, raking her bodice, where the mounds of her breasts nearly spilled over. A muscle ticked in his jaw, and she could see his effort to remain calm. "So what is this fantasy of yours, vixen?"

"You said you would show me pleasure. Well, this is my pleasure, Deverill. To live out my own pirate adventure. With *you*."

What she wanted more was to combat in some small measure his terrible memories of being held prisoner while his men were tortured to death. It might be impossible to bring him peace, but she intended to hold Deverill captive here and now, in order to give him pleasure, not pain. She was following her deepest instincts, along with an insistent inner voice that told her the festering emotional wounds inside Deverill needed to be lanced if he was ever to begin healing. And this was the only way she knew how.

Wishing the dampness in her palms would go away, Antonia managed another seductive smile. "In my fantasy, I am mistress of the high seas, and you must obey my every command."

Deverill cocked a defiant eyebrow. "I'm afraid I am not inclined to play anyone's captive."

"You have no choice. Now take off your breeches."

"Or what?"

Antonia withdrew the wooden knife from her sash and brandished it at him. "Or I will feed you to the sharks. It will only take a word from me and my crew will throw you overboard."

Deverill hesitated a very long while before crossing his arms over his chest, the picture of stubbornness. "You will have to make me, your highness."

A sigh of relief shivered through Antonia when she realized he didn't mean to refuse her outright. "Very well, if I must."

Crossing to him, she pressed the dull wooden blade to his throat and pushed him backward till he came up against the wall between the two windows. They both knew he could easily overpower her and take the toy away, but he made no move to stop her.

His eyes were bright with wariness and some other raw emotion, but he seemed willing for the time being to let her role-play her fantasy adventure.

When she repeated her order to undress, he reached obediently, if reluctantly, for the front placket of his breeches.

"Very good, captive," she declared.

Stepping back, Antonia watched as he shed his breeches and drawers. The sight of him nude made her mouth go dry. He was full and swollen and obviously rock hard with desire.

He clearly wanted her, whether or not he wanted this fantasy.

Taking heart, she unfastened the hooks at the front of her gown, opening the bodice to her waist, revealing her bare breasts and tight, budded nipples.

Deverill's eyes flared with heat—and followed her every move when she ambled toward him again. He held completely still as she pressed her body against him slowly, tauntingly.

The swells of her naked breasts met the warm hardness of his chest with the impact of a searing brand, making her pulse leap and his jaw tighten. And when she ground her hips against his naked loins, Deverill's breath grew shallow—she could hear it.

Despite the rapid beating of her heart, Antonia summoned a smile of mock triumph. Then taking a deep breath of her own, she brushed her fingers across the ridges of scar tissue on his bare chest. This time Deverill didn't flinch away but kept his gaze locked hard with hers.

Swallowing, Antonia concealed a rush of tears with a forced smile. This beautiful, scarred god of a man made her heart ache. She had to remember, however, that while Deverill might be disfigured, at least he was alive. It chilled her to think how close he had come to death at the hands of his tormenters, but he had survived. And her own anger at what they had done to him was less insistent than the tenderness filling her, less powerful than the ardent need to give him intense pleasure, not pain.

"You are surprisingly beautiful for a man," she drawled in a husky voice. "I think I shall allow you to pleasure me for the morning . . . if you promise to obey my every whim."

His silence spoke of resistance, but she trailed her hand lower to fondle his thick length. Reflexively Deverill sucked in his stomach, and Antonia smiled in satisfaction. Already his phallus was lifting and jerking helplessly in response to her caresses.

She set about increasing the delicious torment. Her gaze dropping to his member, she rubbed her thumb over the swollen head, spreading the bead of moisture that had accumulated there. The low sound that rumbled in Deverill's chest might have been a protest or a groan, she wasn't certain.

"I think you desire me," Antonia said with a saucy toss of her head. "Now, unless you want to suffer dire punishment, I command you to lie on the bed."

"As you wish, your highness," he muttered, his tone more truculent than meek.

When he complied, stretching out his naked, bronzed body to recline on his back on the yellow counterpane, Antonia moved to stand over him.

"Now what?" Deverill demanded.

"You are being insolent, captive. I did not give you permission to address me."

After another hesitation, he answered more meekly. "Forgive me, your highness."

Pulling off her eye patch and laying aside the knife, she drew out a pair of satin ribbons from her sash.

Deverill's eyes sparked when he realized her intent was to shackle him to the bedposts, but he silently gritted his teeth. Climbing up to kneel on the bed, Antonia secured the ribbons to the mahogany frame, then raised both his arms above his head and looped the satin loosely around his wrists.

Deverill only had eyes for her, however, possibly because she was deliberately distracting him, her breasts dangling like lush, ripe fruit above him. When she bent low enough to allow him a brief taste, brushing a taut peak against his mouth, he couldn't help but groan. But just as quickly, she drew away to survey her handiwork and his body.

She let her fingers tease his arousal briefly before sliding off the bed to remove her gown. When she was naked, she stood before him challengingly, legs spread slightly, hands on hips, her proud, thrusting breasts taunting him, her eyes sparkling with mischief and something deeper and more mysterious.

Deverill found himself transfixed; he couldn't tear his gaze away. He had never seen Antonia like this. She was all wanton siren, all seductive temptress, clearly reveling in her newfound abandon.

It made him wild with desire and longing—just as she undoubtedly intended.

"My dear queen," he said more huskily than he would have liked, "I don't suppose you would consider putting me out of my misery by taking me now?"

"Not yet. I intend to make you beg for mercy. So what kind of torture will be the most arousing, do you think?"

"You obviously don't need any instruction from me, your highness."

When she laughed lightly, he savored the sound of it. Then she reached down to stroke his erection, and he clenched his teeth. She was taunting, daring, and determined to make him plead.

"Devil take you," he ground out. "I will never beg."

"Take care, captive," Antonia warned. "If you are not obedient, I will leave you here and find one of my crew to pleasure me instead."

"Your crew is a scurvy lot," Deverill drawled with derision. "I'll wager you prefer to be ridden by a real man."

"In truth, I prefer not to be ridden at all. *I* wish to do the riding."

With that, Antonia climbed up on the bed again and straddled him, her hands planted firmly on his chest, her cleft nestled against his shaft.

"I like a demanding lover," Deverill said in a strangled voice.

"Good, since I intend to be *very* demanding."

Pulling off her pirate scarf, she threw it aside and shook her head, making her hair tumble silken wild around her shoulders. Then bending down, she deliberately let the flaming tresses pool across his body.

Deverill sucked in a sharp breath. Yet her purpose for the moment apparently was not to arouse him.

Instead, she kissed each and every one of his scars tenderly, lingeringly, deliberately soothing.

Deverill squeezed his eyes shut, feeling the soft press of her lips, the quiet swirl of her tongue. How in God's name had he let himself be lured into this vulnerable position? It showed the measure of his trust in Antonia that he would let her expose this dark, defenseless part of him. He wanted to escape, wanted to close off the fierce emotion she was arousing inside him with her gentle, burning kisses, yet he couldn't bring himself to pull away.

And Antonia obviously was not about to stop. She succored him with light nips, comforted him with tender, healing kisses and wet swirls of her tongue. She paused only long enough to lift her head, gazing down at Deverill to judge his reaction.

Her blue eyes were bright and raw with feeling. The sight brought a sudden tightness to Deverill's throat, but with effort, he forced the ache away and tried to focus only on the pleasure she was giving him.

Her hands slid along the bare skin of his arms, over his tensed shoulders, making the muscles coil and quiver involuntarily. Yet she clearly was determined to make him quiver elsewhere. Shifting her position, she knelt between his parted legs, looking down at the expanse of his chest, his belly, the sprawl of his thighs, the swollen, jutting erection that reached almost to his navel.

Careful not to touch that prominent masculine part of him, she bent again and lightly kissed his abdomen, nipping at him with her lips, then soothing with her tongue.

Deverill stirred restlessly, helplessly aroused. As if intending to increase his helplessness further, Antonia cupped the heavy sacs of his testicles, slowly brushing the soft skin. Then reaching higher, she curled her fingers around his thrusting erection, molding her palm to his hardness. The thick length surged in her hand when she gently squeezed.

All the muscles in Deverill's body tensed, yet he remained silent, struggling for control. It was a challenge Antonia apparently couldn't resist. She bent low between his legs and nuzzled the soft sacs. Her caress made his breath catch, then rush out in a harsh hiss as she settled her lips at the base of his shaft and began to nibble.

Moments later she deliberately let her tongue trail slowly upward, laving his rigid flesh. Impossibly aroused now, Deverill made a low, tortured sound deep in his throat and tilted his head back in surrender, an invitation for Antonia to have her way with him.

Holding his swollen member in a light grasp, she closed her mouth around him fully. He shuddered, his hips instinctively rising off the bed, his spine arching against the sweet torture she was inflicting. When he started to slide himself slowly between her lips, however, Antonia would have none of it.

"Be still," she commanded in a husky voice, "or I will stop."

He obeyed, yet it required a herculean effort for him to maintain control. His fingers clutched at the ribbons loosely binding his wrists as she went on stimulating him, her hands a continuation of her mouth as she tormented him slowly, maddeningly. When he groaned aloud at the aching pleasure of it, she suckled harder, as if relishing her sense of power, her feeling of delight at how he was responding to her touch.

Deverill nearly bucked, knowing she was causing him to lose control. His pulse pounded as she urged him on, arousing and tantalizing and inflaming. . . .

Finally he let out a hoarse curse. "God . . . enough, wench. Come here." He tore free of his satin bonds and reached for her, drawing her up to straddle his thighs.

"Queen," she countered huskily. "I am a queen."

"No, you're a damned witch—and you are driving me mad."

"You are driving me mad as well," Antonia whispered.

He could tell she meant it, for the folds of her sex were already drenched and pulsing as she poised herself over his erection. Deverill's fingers tightened convulsively on her hips. With every breath he took, he wanted her more intensely.

"Slowly, love," he urged, as much for his own benefit as hers as she lowered herself upon him.

"Perhaps I can't go slowly," Antonia rasped, sheathing him fully.

It was a tantalizing act of possession. Deverill felt her glide lusciously around him and nearly erupted.

"You are so damned hot and wet," he groaned as he thrust upward hard.

His impalement made her gasp, made her hips

writhe. He began to move urgently in answer, giving her the rhythm she wanted, but it was the ragged whimpering sound Antonia uttered that was the breaking point for Deverill. He growled her name again as the hunger in his body swelled into something huge, turning deep and desperate and driving.

Her response was just as desperate. She rode him with a fierce and beautiful savagery, losing herself in the surging tempo of his body. When she peaked, his sanity fled and together they ignited in explosive passion.

Their climax seemed to go on forever. Deverill shook from the force of her body's response and from his own. When Antonia finally collapsed upon him, he wrapped his arms around her and sank his face in her hair.

It was a long while before the tremors stopped, longer still before he could find the breath to speak in a feeble rasp. "It appears I am insatiable when it comes to you, vixen. You fire my blood."

"Queen," she murmured just as hoarsely. "I am still your pirate queen."

His strained smile was hidden in her hair. When Antonia would have eased off him, Deverill tightened his hold and kept his now flaccid manhood buried inside her. He could spend hours lying joined to her like this, savoring her warmth, her special brand of passion. Her compassion.

"I'll warrant," he acknowledged truthfully, "that I will never again think of pirates in quite the same way."

"That was my intent," she replied, her weary voice holding a hint of smugness.

Deverill felt a strange ache in his chest. She hadn't offered him pity, but understanding and sympathy.

And he had accepted it without struggling, when he had never before allowed anyone or anything to comfort him.

It was remarkable what Antonia did to him. Remarkable and troubling. She was so astonishingly sensual, so bewitching, that she kept him in a constant state of arousal and anticipation. But his hunger was more profound than carnal desire. What happened every time he touched her was outside his experience. She made him feverish with want, with need, with *feeling*.

He hadn't expected her to stir his emotions so powerfully, so deeply. For so long he hadn't allowed himself any deep emotions at all. After the torment of losing half his crew, he'd cut off any feeling simply to save his sanity.

He needed to continue doing so, Deverill told himself. Antonia made him *feel* far too much.

Disturbed, he toyed absently with a strand of her hair. It had been a grave mistake to give in to her request to teach her pleasure, he admitted. He was in deep water now, and if he didn't take care, he would find himself drowning.

There was peril in too much closeness. Already it was an effort for him to ignore how right this felt . . . this intimacy, this sense of possession, of being possessed. Already he regretted having to set sail in a few hours.

Deverill scowled up at the timbered ceiling. He couldn't recall ever regretting having to leave a woman behind before. It was a first for him, he realized, remembering how often he had politely discarded a lover who became too amorous or clinging.

Mentally, he shook his head. In truth, he was *glad* to be leaving Antonia this afternoon. He needed to put a significant distance between them, since his craving for her was becoming uncontrollable.

Just then he felt the lazy, rhythmic stroke of her hand along his thigh, suggestive and arousing. Deverill felt his body tense with unmistakable desire.

He hadn't intended on taking her again, but evidently Antonia had other ideas in mind.

She raised her head to gaze down into his eyes seductively. "You are still my captive for the rest of the morning, you know."

He didn't want to deny her; he *couldn't* deny her. His response was entirely out of his control. Amazingly he could feel himself swelling inside her.

And when she kissed him, her mouth so wet and soft, her touch cauterizing his mind with need, he could do nothing but surrender.

Ignoring the warnings of danger clamoring in his head, Deverill pulled Antonia against him and sighed into her mouth, wondering if a man could die of the tormenting pleasure his glorious pirate queen was forcing upon him.

Fifteen

"So what do you know about Deverill's occupation, my dear?" Sir Gawain asked Antonia pleasantly.

The question surprised her as much as had the baronet's invitation to accompany him fishing. She and Sir Gawain were now sitting on a riverbank on the castle grounds, dangling their lines in the lazily moving water, shaded from the bright morning sunshine by the branches of a willow tree. Isabella was currently visiting her sister-in-law, who had been delivered of a strapping baby boy, and both mother and infant son were reportedly faring extremely well.

Antonia had presumed that when Sir Gawain offered to expand her horizons and teach her how to fish, he would reminisce about his friendship with her late father. But the question about Deverill's occupation caught her off guard.

"I gather Deverill spends much of his time ridding the seas of pirates," she answered. "And Isabella mentioned that he works for a small department of the Foreign Office. For you, in fact."

Sir Gawain nodded. "Our department is headquartered on Cyrene, true, yet there is much more to our organization than a governmental bureaucracy. The details are normally a well-guarded secret, but in this instance, my dear, I intend to break our code of silence, for I want you to understand the enormity of what we deal with. But you must promise that you will hold what I am about to tell you in strictest confidence."

The sudden intent look on the baronet's face disquieted Antonia. "Yes, of course. I promise."

"Our department is not actually a branch of government."

Her eyes widened with curiosity. "Then what is it?"

His look turned grave. "It is a centuries-old order dedicated to fighting tyranny and injustice and protecting the weak. A league of protectors, if you will."

Antonia found herself staring at Sir Gawain. His solemn declaration was not at all what she had expected to hear. "Protectors?" she said after a moment. "Please tell me more."

With an enigmatic smile, Sir Gawain obliged. "We are called Guardians, my dear. Guardians of the Sword—for reasons too complicated to go into just now. Suffice it to say that our alliance with the British Foreign Office proves mutually beneficial. We perform tasks too difficult and perilous for Whitehall to undertake, and the official connection helps us to protect our identities and to explain away our clandestine activities."

"What sort of clandestine activities?" Antonia quizzed, unable to hide her amazement.

"They vary considerably. For the past several decades, we have endeavored to meet the challenges fomented by the French Revolution and Napoleon's subsequent attempt to conquer the known world. Saving imprisoned aristocrats from the guillotine, for instance. Striving to bring about Bonaparte's defeat in any manner possible. We even have several female members in our order, since there are some tasks better suited to women. But few people realize the vast extent of our organization or know the remarkable tale of our inception. Your father was one."

"My father knew about your order?" Antonia echoed in surprise.

"Yes. Samuel was an invaluable ally to us. He supplied ships to the Guardians for many years."

A memory of her father unexpectedly welled in Antonia's mind—his booming laughter, his bold, powerful personality, his ardent notions about class and gender and society.

He had never mentioned a word to her about a secret league of protectors called the Guardians. But then, she was a mere female, and more crucially, a *lady*. Her father had always purposely shielded her from his business affairs. It wasn't surprising that he hadn't trusted her with the secret.

Nor had Deverill, for that matter, Antonia realized suddenly. The reflection made her wonder why Sir Gawain was telling her now.

"I suppose Deverill is a member of your order?" Antonia prodded.

"He is indeed. But he would never divulge our existence because he swore an oath of secrecy."

"Then why are *you* telling me, Sir Gawain?"

"Because I would like our special relationship with Maitland Shipping to continue. That was out of the question once Lord Heward became involved in the company's business affairs. But if you find it necessary to replace your Director Trant, I hope to persuade you to hire someone supportive of our order's endeavors."

"I expect you could persuade me," Antonia replied quite seriously, although her mouth curved in a smile.

Sir Gawain's return smile held gratification, before he pursed his lips thoughtfully, as if debating whether to continue. "There is a further reason for my divulgences, my dear—one perhaps even more important than desiring your patronage. I wish you to see that there is far more to Deverill than meets the eye."

Antonia's brows drew together. "I never doubted it. I always suspected he was more than an adventurer."

"He is worth any ten noblemen, my dear."

It was a puzzling comment, but Antonia was thinking about her previous interactions with Deverill. Perhaps his being a Guardian also helped explain why he'd been so adamant about rescuing her from her betrothed's clutches. And why he had always made her feel safe and cared for—at least when he wasn't provoking her to distraction. He belonged to a league of protectors whose duty was to defend others.

It certainly made sense now why Deverill had no desire to live in England and run her father's shipping empire.

"I wanted Deverill to become the company's director," she mused aloud, "but he declined. He claimed he cherished his freedom too much to settle down in such a routine role."

"That is partly true," Sir Gawain replied. "He cherishes his freedom so he can devote his life to our cause. His work is not only his vocation but his passion—as it is for all of us who serve the order. Yet Deverill is even more driven than the rest of us. Not only because he believes fiercely in our noble ideals, but because he has made it his personal mission to save others."

Antonia's eyes locked with Sir Gawain's in understanding. "Because he couldn't save his crew."

Sir Gawain raised an eyebrow. "You know of his captivity in a Turkish prison?"

"He . . . mentioned it. I can only imagine what a terrible experience that must have been for him."

"Indeed, it was. And it has driven him ever since. When he was invited to join our order, Deverill leapt at the chance."

"So he could atone for the men he couldn't save."

Sir Gawain nodded sadly. "I believe it is his way of trying to redeem himself. Of paying penance for his failure."

And Deverill was still seeking redemption, Antonia realized. Still punishing himself for his failure. The thought wrenched her heart.

"To my mind, Deverill has paid his penance a hundred times over," the baronet added quietly, "but he won't accept it. I would guess that is partly why he has never settled down in marriage. Because he will not allow himself the possibility of contentment, of happiness."

Antonia thought the comment odd, as was Sir Gawain's speculative regard of her, but she made no issue of it. "Thank you for telling me about Deverill, Sir Gawain."

"Yes, well . . . I love him like a son." There was an awkward pause before he ventured to observe, "Your father also thought quite highly of Deverill, you know."

"Yes, he did. He would have been pleased to see Deverill take the reins of his own life's work."

Sir Gawain suddenly looked uncertain. "That is not quite what I meant, my dear—"

Just then Antonia's fishing line jerked, and she had

to grab at the rod to keep it from slipping through her hands. The next instant the line went slack, and when they pulled in the line, the hook was gone.

Sir Gawain shook his head with regret, but Antonia was more disappointed by the untimely interruption. "What were you saying about Deverill, Sir Gawain?" she asked as he began to thread another hook and re-bait it.

"Never mind, my dear." His smile was a trifle wry. "An old man should know better than to interfere in affairs that are not his purview. Now, enough of this serious talk. We don't want to drive the fish away."

He changed the subject then, and spoke of other things, leaving Antonia to puzzle over his enigmatic comments on her own. Yet he had given her a great deal to ponder.

When they returned home from fishing, Antonia promised herself, she intended to go straight to her rooms, where she could be alone with her thoughts about Deverill.

Isabella intercepted her, however, as soon as she stepped foot in the entrance hall. "I trust you won't mind if I steal you away after luncheon, Antonia. Clara has been asking for you, and you have yet to properly admire Baby Jonathan. I hoped we could spend the afternoon with them."

"Of course, Isabella, I would enjoy that. But first allow me to change my gown. I caught my first fish today, and I doubtless smell of trout."

Antonia curbed her impatience throughout the congenial luncheon with Sir Gawain and Lady Isabella, and then for several more hours during her visit with Lady Kenard and Baby Jonathan. The afternoon passed pleasantly enough. Antonia duly praised the tiny child and, on the return carriage ride home, listened as Isabella sang the infant's praises.

"He is a squirming little red-faced bundle," Bella pronounced, "but admittedly precious. I vow holding him almost makes me regret never having children of my own."

"You did not want children?" Antonia asked curiously.

Isabella forced a smile, but Antonia could see the sadness behind it. "I was barren, my dear. Even with three husbands, I never was able to conceive." She gave a dismissive laugh. "But I was much too busy traveling the world and having adventures to lament the absence of offspring. I had a marvelous life full of passion and excitement, Antonia, with two husbands whom I adored and who adored me. That more than made up for my loss, I assure you. And even now I am hardly ancient. I may yet experience another grand passion, one never knows."

Observing the countess's vivacious beauty, Antonia smiled with genuine warmth. "I'll warrant the odds are greatly in your favor."

"I wish the odds favored you more," Isabella said with a shrewd look. "I cannot like the thought of you settling for a marriage of convenience. But that is precisely what you will do when you return to London, is it not?"

Antonia cast a glance at the driver perched in the coachman's box. Although the landau was open in front with the forward half of the double hood folded back, their conversation couldn't be heard over the rattle of carriage wheels and horses' hooves.

Even so, she lowered her voice when she replied. "Yes, Isabella, I will make a marriage of convenience when I return. But I have always known what fate held in store for me, and I willingly accepted it. Marrying into the nobility was the only thing my father ever asked of me. It is not, however, just my duty as a daughter that obliges me, but my love for him as well."

"I understand, my dear, but duty can be a cold bedfellow."

Averting her gaze from Isabella's much too perceptive one, Antonia pretended to study the passing Cornish landscape as a bittersweet ache filled her. She wished there *were* something more in her future when she returned home to London than an insipid union of convenience.

"You could always wed Deverill," Isabella suggested equably. "Sir Gawain supports the match as much as I do, did you guess?"

Antonia turned back to regard the countess in surprise. Was that what Sir Gawain had been insinuating earlier today? That Deverill would make her a good husband? She'd thought he was hinting her away, trying to make her understand why Deverill would never want to assume control of Maitland Shipping. But perhaps the baronet had meant something quite different. Nevertheless . . .

"You know a match between us is out of the question, Isabella," Antonia replied quietly.

"I believe Deverill is still willing to wed you."

"Perhaps, but only because his sense of honor won't allow him to shirk what he sees as his duty. He has no desire to be tied down in marriage. Any union between us would be one of convenience, not love. Deverill is not the kind of man to allow himself to fall in love, Isabella."

"But it is possible to win the heart of such a man."

Antonia felt her own heart give a sudden leap. "How?"

Isabella's smile was very feminine. "An adventurer like Deverill responds best to a woman who understands his need for independence. One who will not chain him with demands and pleas or interfere with his life's calling. A woman as brave and daring and adventuresome as he is. In short, you must prove yourself his match, Antonia."

Antonia stared. Was it possible for her to prove his match? Deverill had long been her ideal—strong, courageous, bold, exciting—and discovering the noble cause he served had only increased her admiration and respect for him.

In truth, Sir Gawain's revelations today had made her feel rather small. What had she ever done that was noble or self-sacrificing? Other than supporting a number of charities, honoring her father's wishes was the sole thing that could be considered admirable.

But she could change that, Antonia reminded herself. She owned Maitland Shipping. Surely she could use her ownership to aid the Guardians . . . and more importantly, to support Deverill's calling.

Yet that didn't mean she could win his heart. He most certainly didn't want to be tied down in a marriage of convenience to her. He wanted the freedom to be a Guardian.

At least now, however, she better understood why Deverill had been just as willing as she to keep their relationship on a physical plane. Why he seemed resistant to forming any long-term emotional bonds, any entanglements.

Was it even possible for him to form a deeper attachment for her? she wondered. Could he give up his self-imposed penance if he knew she could help his cause rather than hinder it? Could he ever allow himself to love her?

Her thoughts agitated, Antonia returned her gaze to the passing countryside. No doubt it was a foolish fantasy to think of having a future with Deverill. He had merely given her an unforgettable experience, had taught her about pleasure, about passion, nothing more.

But it isn't only passion that I feel for him, her heart whispered.

Nor could she continue to deny the traitorous longings that had been building inside her these past few weeks. Lately she'd found herself wishing that she was not an heiress. That she was not obliged to fulfill her father's dreams for her and could follow her own foolish dreams instead . . .

And if she was entirely honest with herself, she would admit that physical passion was no longer enough for her. She wanted more. She wanted true love, the kind her parents had known.

The kind she had only dared imagine in her most secret fantasies.

Love would be an adventure in itself, Antonia knew instinctively. And love with Deverill would be incredible.

A fierce yearning swept over her, along with a sudden realization: It would be a betrayal of her father, undeniably, but she would be willing to forsake her solemn vow to him if she thought Deverill could come to love her.

At the reflection, a new sensation curled inside Antonia, one edged with anticipation and hope. Overcoming Deverill's personal demons might be impossible, but she wanted to try.

She wanted to discover if she could win his heart.

* * *

Nearly a hundred miles to the south, Deverill was staring restlessly out to sea, his thoughts roiling as his inner longings battled with his common sense.

He should, in fact, have been celebrating his victory. The past night had been long and arduous, but he had captured his quarry—the murderous smuggler who had preyed for months on the Cornish Free-traders—while sustaining no injuries to his own crew and little damage to his schooner. He was now sailing back to Falmouth with his prisoner locked in his ship's hold.

Deverill wasn't certain if his urgency to complete his task had been driven more by his need to save innocents from a killer, or by his eagerness to return to Wilde Castle, where Antonia awaited him. But now that his mission was successfully concluded, his focus most definitely had turned to Antonia—and to his own dilemma.

He was losing the battle against her. Against his fierce desire for her.

Deverill squeezed his eyes shut, picturing Antonia as he'd last seen her, remembering the silk of her hair and the warmth of her skin as she both succored him and drove him wild. Simply the memory made his loins harden—and aroused a peculiar ache in his chest at the same time.

For a long while now, he'd been aware of the special tenderness he felt for Antonia; a soft feeling would flow through him at odd moments, so unexpectedly he had no defense against it. Yet only now was he forcing himself to examine the more complex emotions assaulting him: A savage yearning that was not only sexual but something even more disturbing.

A need for her that had grown to dangerous proportions.

Antonia, he grudgingly acknowledged, had burrowed under his skin like no woman ever had or ever would. And she was likely to stay burrowed.

It was a dire complication he had never counted on.

He couldn't deny his reluctance to give her up, either. In truth, if he closed his eyes, he could actually imagine a future with Antonia.

Amazingly enough, he could envision being wed to her—a prospect that had unexpected and startling appeal. If he ever were to marry, he would want a wife exactly like her. She was spirited and challenging enough to keep him forever intrigued; adventurous and brave enough to be a Guardian's life mate.

Any Guardian but him.

He wasn't like his colleagues; he couldn't be. He couldn't permit himself to reach for happiness as if he were deserving of it. His search for expiation was nowhere near over. His vow to atone for the past would never be completely fulfilled. He had dedicated his life to his calling, and he would allow nothing to interfere . . . most certainly not his own personal desires.

Desire for Antonia. She made him dream of impossibilities. Made him yearn for things he would never allow himself to have.

He had to relinquish her before it was too late, Deverill knew. When he returned to Cornwall, he intended to end their affair. And when he returned to London, he would use the opportunity to sever his ties with her for good.

Indeed, Deverill resolved, the moment he received word from Macky that all their plans were in order, he would set sail for London . . . and he would leave Antonia behind.

It would be wiser for them both, allowing them to avoid any more of the dangerous intimacy that had filled their relationship the past few weeks. He couldn't allow her to sail with him. The risk would be too great.

Instead he would make a clean break.

Antonia would be unhappy about his decision, undoubtedly. She would likely fight him. But at least he would stand a chance of ending their liaison with minimal pain . . . and eventually putting her out of his mind and heart for always.

After her conversation with Isabella regarding how to capture Deverill's heart, Antonia arrived home in high spirits, her mind churning with possibilities and plans.

Her optimism immediately suffered a blow, however, for she was forcibly reminded of the threat Deverill still faced. A letter was waiting for her from her trustee, Phineas Cochrane.

Excusing herself, Antonia took the letter into the library, where she broke the seal and quickly perused the contents.

My dear Miss Maitland,

In formal correspondence Phineas always addressed her as Miss Maitland rather than Antonia, as he did in private.

I have reviewed the account books as you requested and regret to inform you that Director Trant has indeed been unlawfully transporting slaves, as you suspected, using the power of his office for his own gain.

When I confronted him, he claimed that by means of extortion and blackmail, Lord Heward compelled him to falsify the accounts to conceal their illegal activities and their immense profits.

Mr. Trant most certainly must be terminated from employment at Maitland Shipping—and perhaps be charged with felonious wrongdoing—but I shall await your further instructions before acting. It is my considered opinion that he is eager to escape prosecution and thus may be willing to help expose Lord Heward in exchange for leniency. It appears that Trant is deadly afraid of his lordship.

As you insisted, I have said nothing to Heward, so as not to alert him. Naturally, however, it would be best to act sooner rather than later. It is therefore my hope that you will provide me with new instructions regarding this highly distressing matter. I hold myself to blame for negligence in overseeing your company's affairs and wish to make amends as soon as possible.

Your obedient servant,
P. Cochrane

Anger flooded Antonia at this first, conclusive evidence of Heward's perfidious nature. It outraged and shamed her, not only that he had engaged in the terrible practice of transporting slaves for the lucrative profit, and that he had employed extortion and blackmail for his own devious ends, but that she had been so easily duped. Heward had betrayed her trust and her late father's memory, criminally using the company to line his own pockets . . . and probably much worse.

After this revelation, she had not a shred of doubt that he was capable of killing an innocent woman and framing Deverill for the murder . . . and of poisoning her father as well.

Yet the difficult matter of proving Heward's guilt remained.

Antonia's fist clenched involuntarily around the letter. He had likely killed her father, and she would see him punished if it was the last thing she ever did—

Just then, Lady Isabella swept into the library. "I understand your letter came from London, my dear. I hope it contains good news and not bad?"

"Possibly good," Antonia said, looking up. "We have a witness to at least one aspect of Lord Heward's perfidy."

She intended to send Phineas's letter directly to Deverill at the inn in Gerrans, so he could read it the moment he arrived home from his patrols.

She hoped he returned soon, for she was more determined than ever to return to London. She wanted Heward brought to justice—and she wanted to be there to personally insure it happened.

Antonia received word about Deverill much sooner than expected. The next morning Lady Kenard sent a message to Wilde Castle with the glad tidings that the scourge of the coast had been apprehended, and that her husband, Sir Crispin, had gone to Falmouth to meet with Mr. Deverill and see to the disposition of the pirate. As the local magistrate, Sir Crispin would take charge of the prisoner and arrange all the proper legal proceedings.

Antonia read the news with relief, knowing that Deverill was safe after having successfully captured his quarry. She expected him to call on her when he completed his business with Sir Crispin in Falmouth, but her eager anticipation turned to impatience by mid-afternoon when there was no sign of him. No doubt he was busy, but at five when she still had heard no word from Deverill, Antonia sent a message to his inn. The innkeeper wrote back that Mr. Deverill had given up his rooms there and that his belongings had been delivered to Sir Crispin's home.

It puzzled Antonia yet didn't alarm her, since it was perfectly reasonable that Deverill would be invited to stay at Kenard House. It startled her, however, when Fletcher Shortall was shown into the drawing room soon after dinner, where Antonia was restlessly pacing the carpet while Sir Gawain and Lady Isabella sat reading.

"Have you brought word of Deverill?" Antonia asked immediately, trying to hide her anxiousness.

"Aye, miss." The wiry seaman bowed respectfully to Sir Gawain and handed him a sealed letter. Then he did the same to Antonia with another letter. "His nibs . . . er, Mr. Deverill . . . bade me beg yer ladies' pardon that he can't deliver this in person."

Antonia broke the seal and quickly read the contents.

Deverill's message was quite brief: A report from his London colleagues had been waiting for him upon his return, asserting that the path was clear to finally put his plans in motion. Thus, he would sail for London the following morning. Regrettably he would have no time to call on Antonia to take his leave, but would keep her informed of events once he reached London.

Antonia stared at the letter with welling trepidation. The time had come for Deverill to confront Lord Heward. Then another implication dawned on her: Not only did Deverill mean to sail without her, he planned to go without even saying farewell.

An odd, sick feeling rose up in her stomach to join her fear, but she tried to ignore it as she addressed Deverill's messenger. "Tell me, Fletcher, where is Deverill now? With Sir Crispin at Kenard House?"

"Aye, miss. They had business to deal with, and Mr. Deverill could best do it there. He told me to bid ye farewell for him, since we're to sail early tomorrow."

"We shall see about that," Antonia muttered to herself, before turning on her heel and marching out of the drawing room, intent on ordering Isabella's carriage and then fetching her pelisse and bonnet.

Sixteen

Upon admittance by the Kenard butler, Antonia learned that Mr. Deverill was closeted in the study with Sir Crispin. When she requested to speak privately with Deverill, she was shown into a small parlor to wait.

Too unsettled to take a seat, however, Antonia paced instead. She did not want to infer too much about Deverill's decision to leave Cornwall so abruptly without her, yet she very much feared he was driven by more than an urgent desire to get on with his investigation.

Her heart leapt when Deverill appeared in the doorway, and she couldn't keep from drinking in the sight of him.

But his green eyes were hooded, dispassionate, and his tone was cool when he stated curtly, "Why did you come here, sweeting? I thought my letter made it clear that I had no time to see you."

Antonia strove to keep her tumultuous emotions under control. "And *I* thought I might ask why you planned to leave without even saying farewell."

Deverill shrugged his broad shoulders. "You know

why—I must return to London immediately. And I saw little point in prolonged good-byes. Our idyllic tryst is over, Antonia. We had a pleasurable few weeks together, but they have ended."

It should not have hurt so much to hear him dismiss their love affair so cavalierly, Antonia thought miserably, yet it did. Clearly Deverill had never felt the same depth of passion that she had.

What a fool she had been to think she might win his love! Deverill had closed his heart to her before she'd even had the chance to try to rouse his affections.

But she refused to give him the satisfaction of knowing how close she had come to forsaking her long-held vow and abandoning all her common sense.

Antonia raised her chin, determined to salvage her pride and to ignore the savage ache inside her. "Very well, then, tell me what you plan to do. You said you received a report from your colleagues in London. What did they say? Have they managed to gather any definitive evidence against Heward?"

A shadow crossed Deverill's face, although Antonia couldn't tell if it was due to disappointment that she hadn't protested further, or relief that she had changed subjects and used a marginally reasonable tone. And at least he deigned to answer her question.

"Madam Bruno, the club owner who accused me of murder, is prepared to recant her charges against me. She now alleges that Heward masterminded the whole affair, and she's willing to testify to that effect if we can promise her protection."

"Protection?" Antonia repeated, her thoughts whirling at this new development.

As if conceding that she wouldn't give up until he explained, Deverill let out a sigh of resignation and stepped into the parlor. "Protection from Heward. Madam Bruno is terrified of him—which is why she endured his cruelty to her sirens all these years, and why she lied that night about my committing the murder."

"But she now says that Heward is guilty?"

"Yes. She claims Heward brought his hirelings to the premises that night and ordered her to summon a Bow Street Runner long before there was any sign of trouble."

Despite her own misery, Antonia felt a surge of elation at this incredibly hopeful news. "Then you will be able to prove your innocence."

"Possibly. But Bruno cannot say for certain that Heward actually ordered the killing. And her suspicions alone won't be enough to convict him of murder."

Antonia's brow furrowed in dismay. "Then what do you mean to do?"

Deverill's hesitation lasted a long moment, suggesting his reluctance to have her involved with his plans. "I'll try to incite him to make a public confession."

"How? By challenging him to a duel? By provoking him to call you out?"

Deverill shook his head. "Heward wouldn't have the courage to meet me on the dueling field. He knows I am too good a shot and too skilled with a sword."

"But he is a deadly shot himself," Antonia said worriedly. "Heward frequently practices at Manton's Shooting Gallery."

Deverill's mouth twisted. "You needn't worry for me, love. I don't fear death overmuch, but I have no intention of giving anyone, most certainly Heward, the pleasure of killing me."

She scowled at his nonchalance. "Then how will you make him confess?"

"I plan to set a trap for him." Clearly growing impatient, Deverill held up a hand. "Enough questions, Antonia. I told you I will keep you informed of my progress once I reach London."

Her lips pressed together in disapproval. "That is not good enough, Deverill. I intend to go with you."

"You won't. You'll remain here, where you will be safe."

"I can be safe in London."

"I can't guarantee that. I have no idea what Heward will do, what new schemes he will invent." When she started to object, Deverill regarded her grimly. "Heward's very unpredictability makes him dangerous. He contrived the murder of an innocent woman to eliminate my interference—because I sought to stop you from wedding him and handing over control of your fortune. How do you think he will respond if you come waltzing back to London after being in my company for nearly a month? I didn't go to all this trouble merely to put you back in Heward's clutches. I promise, as soon as we have him safely behind bars, I will send for you."

Antonia regarded Deverill in sheer frustration, a dozen arguments rushing through her mind. The chief one was that she simply could not let him return to London without her. She would go mad not knowing what was happening to him.

The truth was, she was afraid for him, afraid of what might befall him. Heward had already proved how cunning and treacherous he was. Deverill could be hurt or possibly even killed by trying to bring Heward down. Or he could hang for a murder he had never committed. She couldn't bear the thought.

Knowing, however, that Deverill wouldn't want to hear of her fears, Antonia replied with her next best argument. "I have every right to go with you, Deverill. This affects my life nearly as much as yours. Heward framed you for murder, but he likely killed my father. My claim to justice is just as great as yours, perhaps greater."

"I will make certain he pays for that crime as well."

"But I cannot let you face him alone." Antonia regarded Deverill imploringly. "You are only in this disastrous position because of me . . . because you cared enough to rescue me from Heward's diabolical schemes. Do you expect me to remain safely behind while you fight all my battles for me?"

"Yes, exactly."

Remembering Sir Gawain's theory, Antonia softened her tone a measure. "Deverill . . . I understand better now why you are so intent on protecting me and keeping me safe. Sir Gawain told me about your order. About the Guardians."

He stared at her for a long moment. "What exactly did Sir Gawain say?"

"That you are a league of protectors who heed a heroic calling to fight tyranny and defend the weak. And that you have made it your personal mission to champion their cause."

"I have dedicated my life to the Guardians' cause, true," Deverill admitted.

"Because you are driven by the need to assuage your guilt."

At her quiet declaration, Deverill visibly flinched. When he remained grimly silent, however, she pressed on. "Sir Gawain believes you have avenged the men you lost a hundred times over. You needn't keep punishing yourself, Deverill."

His expression turned ice cold. "I don't need you to grant me dispensation, sweetheart."

Her own jaw tightened. "I never said you did. I merely think that you have served your penance."

Deverill's voice was hard when he replied, "I'll thank you to mind your own affairs and let me handle mine. Go home, Antonia, and quit interfering where you are not wanted. I have a great deal of work to do before I can rest tonight."

Antonia glared at him, but Deverill only stared back at her with chill eyes.

"Very well," she said finally. "If that is what you wish—"

"I do wish it," he snapped, his tone betraying his anger.

Her own emotions smoldering, Antonia swept regally past him and out of the parlor. She wouldn't fight him, she vowed silently, but no matter what Deverill said, she was not about to be left behind.

She made her way to the entrance hall, where the butler opened the front door for her, then hurried down the steps to Isabella's waiting carriage. Without waiting for the coachman's assistance, Antonia ordered him to take her home and climbed inside.

She had a great deal of work to do tonight as well. Fletcher had told her that Deverill's schooner was docked at Falmouth Harbor and that his crew was on board, preparing to sail in the morning as soon as Deverill concluded some final business with Sir Crispin in town.

Antonia sank back against the cushions, her mind feverishly planning. She hoped that Sir Gawain had retired early so she could speak to Isabella privately, for what she was planning would require the countess's full cooperation.

Bella was likely to comply. A humorless smile touched Antonia's lips as she recalled their conversation yesterday, when Isabella had exhorted her to be daring if she hoped to win Deverill's heart. She intended to be daring indeed, but not because she wanted Deverill's heart.

It had been the height of lunacy to think she might be able to win his love. Thank heaven she had come to her senses in time, before she made a complete fool of herself.

Biting her lower lip to stop it from trembling, Antonia turned her head to stare out the carriage window at the dark night. She didn't care if Deverill was so stubbornly wrapped up in his quest for redemption that he could allow no room for love in his life. She didn't!

So what if the ache in her chest felt as if savage claws were raking at her own heart?

She intended to ruthlessly quell every one of her tender feelings for Deverill . . . starting this very moment. Just as soon as her eyes quit burning with a wetness that infuriatingly resembled tears.

In the parlor, Deverill remained unmoving, staring sightlessly at the Aubusson carpet.

He'd been startled to learn that Sir Gawain had revealed the order's existence to Antonia—and he questioned the wisdom of it, although in the past, even their leader's most obscure decisions had invariably proved astute.

Why had Sir Gawain chosen to divulge the closely held secret to Antonia? And at this precise moment? Her father had been one of the Guardians' greatest supporters, so perhaps the baronet wished her to follow in Samuel Maitland's footsteps. Antonia had inherited his vast shipping empire, after all, and could be of enormous benefit to the order if the alliance continued.

Or perhaps Sir Gawain merely wished to show that he trusted Antonia.

Then again, perhaps it had simply been to make Deverill's task easier if she accompanied him to London, so he wouldn't need to explain to her why all his friends were so adept at cloak-and-dagger schemes when she witnessed them.

But he wouldn't be taking Antonia to London with him. He couldn't risk the danger to either one of them.

His temper simmering with frustration, Deverill plowed his fingers roughly through his hair. He wanted not only to keep Antonia safe from Heward's possible treachery, but to keep himself safe from his own overwhelming desire for her. He couldn't bear to have her on his ship for nearly three interminable days of a voyage. Her mere nearness would be too great a temptation.

And her plaguing interference would be too maddening, Deverill thought darkly.

It was true—he *had* been punishing himself all these years. But that was simply what he had to do. His guilt would never be assuaged. It was none of Antonia's concern, in any case.

With a muttered curse, Deverill turned and left the parlor, trying not to remember her wounded expression when he'd ordered her to go home. He had expected Antonia to be spitting fire at his decision to leave her behind, but she had looked almost hurt, as if he had spurned her instead of merely being worried about her welfare.

Of course, he had ended their affair rather abruptly,

pretending that their idyllic interlude had meant little to him.

But she would soon forget any temporary pain he had caused her. Once this was all over—once he had proved his innocence and the real criminal's guilt—Antonia would marry her stuffy, dull nobleman, and he would return to his life's work.

And then, Deverill promised himself, he would put her behind him and look back on their passionate time together as merely an enjoyable diversion in his otherwise solitary existence.

The first part of Antonia's plan proved successful, at least.

Isabella, bless her, not only conveyed Antonia to Falmouth Harbor and watched as she boarded Deverill's docked schooner, but also had her carriage wait at a discreet distance until Antonia could be certain she would be sailing.

The crew, bustling over the ship in preparation for departure, turned to stare as Antonia carried her small valise and her bow and quiver on board, but no one stopped her.

Captain Lloyd, however, hurried forward as soon as he spied her heading for the companionway. "Miss Maitland? I was not informed that you would be joining us on our voyage."

"Because I only just decided to, Captain," she replied, smiling brightly. "Is Mr. Deverill here yet?"

"Not yet. We expect him within the half hour."

"Would you kindly tell him I wish to speak to him? I will await him below in my former cabin."

Captain Lloyd looked reluctant but refrained from challenging her. "Very well, miss. I will tell him as soon as he arrives."

Antonia went directly to the cabin, where she stowed her belongings and removed her bonnet and spencer. She had debated about sneaking on board and hiding until they had sailed far enough away from Wilde Castle that turning around would cause an unacceptable delay. But she wanted to face Deverill now and convince him of her unwavering determination.

When she heard familiar footsteps in the companionway, Antonia suspected that Fletcher had come to take her to task. The wiry old seaman was staunchly loyal to Deverill and would undoubtedly object to her unexpected presence.

Opening her cabin door to look out only confirmed her supposition. As the old seaman tramped down the corridor toward her, Antonia stepped out to meet him.

Halting, Fletcher eyed her grimly before erupting in ire and exasperation. "Do ye have windmills in yer head, missy? What the devil do ye mean, coming aboard a vessel without permission? His nibs will have yer skin!"

"I know he will want to," Antonia agreed. "Which is why I intend to wait here below in the relative safety of my cabin—so he cannot toss me overboard before I at least have the chance to explain."

"Very well, 'tis your skin," Fletcher muttered as he turned and stalked off. "But he won't be the least bit pleased."

"That is a vast understatement," Antonia replied under her breath.

Stepping back inside, she crossed the cabin and drew the desk chair against the far bulkhead, putting as much distance between her and the door as possible, in the event that Deverill came storming through. Then she settled down uneasily to wait.

* * *

Twenty minutes later the door slammed open. Deverill entered a bit more quietly but pinned Antonia with a fierce gaze as she jumped to her feet.

"What the devil are you doing here?" he demanded, his tone soft and ominous.

"I should think it obvious. I am going to London with you."

"The hell you are." Deverill shut the door behind him, his eyes searing her, smoldering and furious.

"Deverill, listen to me, please. I know you are angry—"

"How perceptive of you. I will lose valuable time, having to return you to Wilde Castle."

"You needn't bother," Antonia said, striving for a reasonable tone, "since I won't stay behind. You may as well let me accompany you."

Deverill moved halfway across the cabin, the full power of his forceful personality blazing out at her. "I have no intention of risking your safety by letting you near Heward."

"And I have no intention of putting my safety above yours," she retorted. "I feel terrible enough that his machinations made you a fugitive from the law. I am coming with you, if only to assuage my own guilt. If you refuse to take me, I will simply hire a ship and follow you."

With effort, Deverill refrained from reaching out and throttling her. His heart had leapt when he'd learned Antonia was on board, and again when he'd laid eyes on her just now. He shouldn't be so damned glad to see her, especially since she was defying his express orders and interfering where she wasn't wanted. Once again she had caught him off guard, acting in ways he never expected. She was stubborn and determined—and she wouldn't willingly back down, he knew.

He crossed the final distance to her, harboring some vague notion of taking his frustration out on her, along with a more specific thought of intimidating her into submission.

As if she could read his mind, Antonia lifted her chin. "I am not a wilting hothouse flower, Deverill, or a cowardly milquetoast who shrinks at the thought of danger. And I am not giving up. Not when the stakes are so high."

"Dammit, I don't question your courage, Antonia. I only want to keep you safe."

Hesitating, she reached up to press a placating hand against his chest. "Perhaps, but don't you see? This is something I must do, no matter the cost to myself. I have to come with you, Deverill. I am willing to risk my safety to achieve it. I *need* to be a part of bringing my father's killer to justice. I need to feel as if I am helping—for my father's sake, and for yours, and for that poor woman who died as well."

The words vibrated between them, low and impassioned, and gave Deverill pause. She was deadly serious, he knew.

Gritting his teeth in sheer frustration, he gripped Antonia's hand and held it away from his chest, struggling against her sweet touch as he battled with himself. She cared passionately that justice be done for her father, even if it cost her personally. He admired her courage and her willingness to sacrifice, certainly. Yet he wouldn't be able to live with himself if she came to harm.

On the other hand, she had a right to be involved in bringing down her father's murderer. And he had little right to stop her.

In truth, he would rather have Antonia collaborating with him than slipping behind his back where he had no control over her actions or her safety.

Just then, without warning, she rose up on tiptoe and lifted her mouth to his, just brushing his lips with her own.

The soft, startling caress was his undoing. With a harsh groan, Deverill hauled Antonia into his arms.

His head slanting down, he kissed her savagely, dominating and devouring with angry thoroughness, his mouth insatiable and possessive. Her response was just as passionate, her arms reaching up to twine around his neck and cling. Yet her hungry whimper brought him partially to his senses.

Holding her away, Deverill fought for control like a man drowning. He needed to stop wanting her, needed to stop craving her. . . .

Muttering another violent curse, Deverill stepped back and pointed an accusing finger at her. "Stay here, damn you. I don't want to set eyes on you for the rest of the day."

When he spun around and stormed out of the cabin, slamming the door behind him, Antonia sank weakly into the chair and raised her fingers to her burning lips, her thoughts dazed.

She had kissed Deverill but it had not been a conscious decision. It was simply inevitable. Because she had desperately wanted to provoke an emotion in him besides anger. Because she had wanted to prove to them both that he felt something for her besides protectiveness.

He wanted to protect her, of course; that was who he was. He desired her physically, she knew. But she needed to know that he cared for her in a deeper way.

He *did* feel something for her, she was certain of it. She had seen the burning brightness of his eyes, felt the hungry passion in his kiss. Deverill was not as impartial to her as he pretended.

It brought her little satisfaction, though, for she knew he would never let himself go beyond caring. Not when his heart was still set on seeking redemption that he would never permit himself to attain.

The schooner got under way shortly. Much to Antonia's relief, Deverill had not tossed her off his ship, yet his anger had darkened her own mood significantly. She attempted to read, but mostly she spent the rest of the day staring out the porthole window at the Atlantic Ocean and fighting despondency.

Fletcher brought her lunch and dinner, but she had little appetite. And when dusk fell, she didn't bother lighting a lamp.

When eventually the cabin door opened and shut, she thought it might be the old seaman again, but the unexpected sound of the key turning in the lock made Antonia go still.

Glancing over her shoulder, she caught her breath to see Deverill's tall, muscular form outlined in shadow.

He said not a word. Except for the creaking of the ship and the dull surge of waves against the hull, the cabin was silent. Then she heard a faint rustling noise as Deverill stepped forward, and her heart leapt. In the slender rays of moonlight shimmering through the porthole, she could see him removing his clothing.

He tossed his coat on the sea chest, and then shed his waistcoat and cravat. When he began unbuttoning his shirt, Antonia found her, albeit shaky, voice. "Deverill, what are you doing?"

"What does it look like I'm doing? I am undressing." His tone was calm but held a sharp edge of irony.

"But why?"

"Because making love is more comfortable without clothes."

Antonia's pulse quickened. "You said our affair was over."

"That was before you demanded to come with me." Crossing to her chair, Deverill grasped Antonia's shoulders with cool deliberation and drew her to her feet. "We have two days left, and I intend to make full use of them."

His gaze was unsettlingly intense in the silvery darkness as he guided her backwards until she came up against the bulkhead. He was still furious at her, she realized—and no doubt with himself for surrendering to her. She became a prisoner of that smoldering glance as she stared up at Deverill.

He braced his arms beside her head, his mouth hovering threateningly close to hers. "Unless you mean to deny me?" he murmured harshly, making it a question.

Antonia felt her heart begin to race. She understood what he was saying: This would be their last time together. In two days the voyage would end and their affair would be over, but for now—for the remainder of the voyage—they could enjoy each other.

It would be wiser to say no, Antonia knew, but she really had no choice. She desperately wanted Deverill, needed him. She would give him up when she reached London, but for now, for this moment, he was hers.

"I won't deny you," she whispered in return.

His expression never changed; he merely reached

up to grasp her arms and turn her around. He made short work of removing her gown, slipping it down over her shoulders and hips to pool on the floor. Her corset swiftly followed before he tossed both garments across the cabin and turned Antonia back to face him.

His gaze raked her, lingering on the thin cambric of her shift where her nipples had budded tightly. Then with one hand, he pulled her wrists up and anchored them to the bulkhead over her head. When his other hand reached up to cover her breast possessively, Antonia felt her heart slam wildly against her rib cage.

"Deverill . . ."

"No talking."

He lowered his mouth in a domineering kiss, his body pressed against hers, all sinewed muscle and intensity, his bare chest hot against her barely clad one. Her own skin burned where she was crushed to his hardness, her lips blazed from his heat. His plunging tongue made her whimper as her senses swam with raw sensation.

In one corner of her dazed mind, Antonia became aware that Deverill had worked his hand beneath the hem of her shift. When he slipped his fingers between her thighs and found her cleft already slick with moisture, Antonia flinched with pleasure and inhaled in a gasp.

"Don't move," Deverill ordered.

She bit her lower lip but remained still.

Releasing her, he dropped to one knee and pulled off her half boots and stockings, leaving her wearing only her cambric shift. His eyes never straying from her body, he leisurely stood while pushing the garment up to her shoulders, baring her breasts so that she was mostly naked.

Antonia sucked in another sharp breath, feeling her taut nipples thrusting out, wanting him, aching for him. Then with deliberate slowness, Deverill brushed the proud taunting crests, pinching lightly between his fingers. Pleasure flared inside her—and the devil clearly knew it.

He sent her a hot, ruthless smile in the darkness before kneeling at her feet again. Holding her gaze, he let his hands close on her thighs and part them slightly.

Nearly moaning at the feel of those sensuous hands sliding along her skin, Antonia lodged a breathless protest. "If you mean to punish me for defying you . . . this is the wrong way to go about it. This is not punishment to me."

"Hush, this is *my* fantasy . . . having you at my mercy."

His hands made free with her body, stroking up her thighs, over the curve of her hips, along her abdomen, her rib cage, her breasts . . . before returning to her woman's mound.

With maddeningly slow fingers he caressed her slick entrance and found the seat of her desire. "What a lovely pearl you have here . . . so plump and ripe and wet."

Her hips jerked as he fingered her, straining against his arousing touch.

"Stand still," he commanded.

She whimpered but obeyed.

Smiling darkly, Deverill leaned forward and put his mouth on her, nibbling for a moment, then pulling the dewy bud between his lips and sucking softly.

Antonia gave a low, sultry cry. "Oh, God . . ." she rasped in a ragged voice.

Deverill didn't relent. His lips moved against her silky sex, while his hands moved over her hips, hot on her naked skin. Then his tongue slipped inside her, his exploration ruthlessly thorough, nearly making her scream.

Squeezing her eyes shut against the delicious torment, Antonia stood splayed against the wall, her head thrown back, her frustration mounting because there was nothing she could do but remain still beneath his sensual assault.

Except that Deverill wanted to hear her pleasure. "That's right, moan for me, sweeting. . . . Let me hear how good it feels to you. I want you panting and mindless with need."

She was already panting and mindless, Antonia thought wildly. Her breath was hoarse and ragged in her throat as she helplessly began to writhe.

His hands clamped down on her hips, anchoring her as he kissed her intimate center again, his mouth hard against her. Suddenly she flowered for him, her hips thrashing wildly beneath his caress.

Yet he wasn't finished with her. Deverill aroused her once more with his stroking tongue, making her climax yet again, sending tremor after rapturous tremor ripping through her.

When finally he released her, Antonia sagged against the wall, her weak limbs barely managing to keep her upright.

His mouth was wet and curled in satisfaction as he rose to his feet. He had unfastened his breeches, his huge, swollen arousal springing free, Antonia saw before he braced a hand above her shoulder and leaned toward her, pressing that long, thick shaft against her naked belly.

Her thighs instinctively clenched together with longing, the feverish yearning only heightened since she was still pulsating with pleasure from her recent powerful explosions.

"You want me to fill you, don't you?" he taunted hoarsely.

"Yes . . ."

"Then let me see how hot you are. . . . Let me hear you plead to take all of me inside you."

"Yes, Deverill . . . please, yes . . ."

Her breathless entreaty turned to a keening moan when he obliged. Positioning his engorged phallus at her entrance, he slowly, slowly slid into her, plunging into her yielding flesh until she was impaled, stretched taut, holding her upper body against the wall with the weight of his.

Antonia shuddered, her inner muscles squeezing his throbbing length. It thrilled her when Deverill buried himself fully inside her like this. Wrapping her legs around his strong thighs, she curled her arms around his neck and clung as his hips began to pump in a rhythmic cadence, her own flesh shivering under the grinding thrusts of his loins.

In response, he grasped her bare buttocks, lifting her higher so he could go even deeper, penetrating her to the hilt, over and over and over again. He kept his gaze locked with hers as he moved, a savage possessiveness burning in his eyes, his body radiating such heat, such fierce desire, that she thought she would kindle into flame. In only moments she was writhing against him again, sliding her legs up and down against the fabric of his breeches with frantic need.

His hands kept her moving in that urgent, demanding rhythm. His eyes were fierce, his face hard and intent, his neck corded as he drove into her. Yet she reveled in his fierceness, reveled in her ravishment.

When her release came, she shattered in fiery waves, her moaning scream of ecstasy mingled with Deverill's low, harsh shout. The keening sounds softly died as the violent tremors faded.

For a long while, they remained immobile, gasping for breath, their bodies fused, his face buried in her hair. Antonia continued to cling to him, savoring the hot, sleek rapture of their joining. She felt fully sated, impossibly weak.

Deverill was also, but he found himself cursing the raw, reckless hunger that had driven him. He never should have come here, never should have touched her, but he had lost the battle with himself. He'd given in to his savage need for her—

Suddenly he went still. He hadn't pulled out of Antonia before climax as he should have, either, or allowed her time to use any sponges. He'd felt her coming apart beautifully in his arms and had let himself shatter with her, needing to claim her in the most primal way possible.

Deverill exhaled a harsh breath, acknowledging the futility of his struggle. Henceforth, he would give up trying to fight himself and the powerful desire between them.

Holding Antonia against him, he carried her to the bunk and withdrew from her body as he lowered her to the blankets. Then he removed her shift and lit a lantern so he could better see her. The sight took his breath away—her bare body white and wanton and shimmering in the golden lamplight.

She watched him as well, her eyes languorous as he stepped back to shed the rest of his clothing. When he settled a hip on the bunk beside her, Antonia raised her arms to embrace him and pull him down to join her.

Deverill, however, shook his head. "I would relish making love to you until neither of us can walk, but we have a critical matter to discuss."

She would have liked to pull a blanket up to screen herself from his intense regard, but Deverill was sitting on the edge of the covers. "Very well, what is it?"

"I want your solemn promise that you will do as I say when we reach London. I can't have you running off to challenge Heward behind my back."

"I won't, Deverill, I promise. But I would like to know what you are planning. You said you wanted to provoke him into confessing by setting a trap for him. What exactly did you mean by that? How do you intend to trap him?"

He hesitated a long moment. "By using myself as bait."

Antonia sat up in sudden alarm. "What? You cannot! You could be killed."

Deverill's mouth curled. "Thank you for your faith in me, love."

"I have no doubt you are fearless, but you know Heward will likely use any means necessary to get you out of his way."

"I am counting on it," Deverill said darkly.

"I wish there were some other course," she murmured. "I could never live with myself if you came to harm."

"There is no other course, Antonia. If I want Heward to figuratively hang himself, I have to give him the proper incentive. He'll find the chance for revenge against me irresistible."

"I suppose so." She took a steadying breath and

reached out to lightly touch his bare chest. "I meant what I said, Deverill. I want to help you if I can."

He shook his head. "You would only be in the way. I can handle Heward alone."

"Perhaps, but surely there is some way I could be of use to you." When Deverill frowned, Antonia put forth another argument. "Sir Gawain said there are a number of women who serve as Guardians because they are better suited for certain tasks."

"Yes, but they have trained for years for their roles."

"But luring Heward may be a role I can play. I am still betrothed to him. Heward will be eager to see me, if only to discover what I intend to do about our betrothal. You can use me to bait your trap for him."

"It would be too dangerous."

Antonia brushed a savage scar that marred the perfection of his body. "Deverill, you cannot protect me forever. I can't be shielded from all harm, wrapped in cotton wool until I suffocate. I have a mind and will of my own. Please . . ." She looked up at him, gazing deeply into his eyes. "I need to help you. Please let me."

A muscle ticked in Deverill's jaw as his logical mind warred with his deepest instincts. It was true that Antonia could be of considerable help in setting a trap for Heward, significantly increasing their odds for success, if he could only bring himself to relinquish his irrational fear for her.

He was a Guardian, yet he couldn't recall ever feeling this savage an urge to hold and protect anyone. He was filled with a desperate need to keep Antonia safe—an emotional vulnerability that had little to do with his past demons, he was beginning to realize. But if he was careful enough, he could manage to protect her. . . .

Dragging in a slow breath, Deverill reached up to cradle her face in both hands as he gazed down into her eyes. "If I let you participate, I want your solemn vow that you will do *exactly* as I tell you, without question or protest."

"I will. I promise. I swear it absolutely."

"Without question."

"Yes, without question."

He set his teeth, praying he wasn't making a terrible mistake. "Very well, then. I will revise my plans to include you."

Her smile was so bright, so beautiful, it made his chest burn. And when Antonia flung her arms around his neck and buried her face against his throat, it only compounded the feeling.

"Thank you, Deverill. You won't regret it, I swear it."

Helplessly, he curled one arm around her while the other stroked her hair, his hand unsteady. It was absurd, how she affected him. Desire made him shudder, while the surge of tenderness and longing that coursed through him nearly disabled him.

Squeezing his eyes shut, Deverill cursed silently. This woman turned him inside out, tied him into square knots. He couldn't deny it. Antonia had managed to become an obsession. One he didn't want.

One he didn't want to live without.

That kind of need dismayed him. And then she drew away and sank back against the pillows, raising her arms in an invitation to join her. Her skin gleamed like pale gold in the lamplight as she lay waiting for him, her ripe, graceful body bare and beckoning.

Deverill felt his manhood throb, begging for her

touch as he stretched out beside her on the bunk. He was already hard and near to bursting, his blatant hunger obvious, even before Antonia tilted her face up for his kiss.

He covered her mouth, wanting to taste it more than he wanted his next breath.

He drank of her, wondering if the urgency would ever lessen. He doubted it, though. He had sated himself with her only moments ago, yet he never felt as if he had enough.

When she parted her legs, welcoming him, he sank in hard, filling her. At her passionate whimper, he gathered Antonia more tightly against him, wanting to absorb her, wanting to draw her inside his very soul. Need pounded through his body, a driving, desperate, mind-blotting need to possess her.

For a score of heartbeats, she shared the same desperate need as they arched and clung together in frantic, urgent rhythm. Then Antonia shuddered wildly against him, crying out in explosive climax as she drew Deverill over the edge with her.

It was only when it was over, when he lay collapsed and panting beside her, that he again recalled she hadn't used the sponges. The next thought that struck Deverill took his breath away: He could have impregnated her. She could be with child at this very moment.

Emotions he didn't know he possessed jammed around his heart. If Antonia was carrying his child, he was prepared to deal with the consequences. She would marry him—even if he had to chain her to him until she agreed.

And if there was no child?

Then she would damned well marry him anyway, Deverill pledged silently. He would just have to convince her.

Antonia was set on marrying a title, but she would be better off wed to him than some boring, milksop nobleman. He could give her the exciting adventures she craved, at least. And he could see that her shipping company was well run. He would certainly appreciate her spirit and passion far more than any other man. And he was more qualified than anyone else to keep her and her fortune safe from malefactors.

Additionally, Antonia was better qualified to be his bride than any other woman. She would understand his need to continue his life's mission. With her, he would not have to abandon the Guardians or forsake his deep-seated compulsion to atone for the past.

It would still be a marriage of convenience, of course. There would be nothing more to their union—no deeper bond—than mutual desire and a shared love of adventure.

Ignoring the faint, scoffing voice in his head that told him he was deceiving himself, Deverill drew Antonia's languid body closer against him. When she stirred suggestively in his arms, though, he couldn't ignore the fierce wave of possessiveness that swept through him.

He wasn't letting her go, Deverill vowed, finding her lips with his own.

He couldn't force the issue of their marriage just now with matters so uncertain. But he promised himself that when this was all over—if it ever was over—he would pursue Antonia until she gave in and consented to be his wife.

Seventeen

"Are you certain you are all right, my dear?" Phineas Cochrane demanded of Antonia, taking her hands. "I have been prodigiously worried for you this past month."

The concern on the elderly barrister's cherubic face warmed her heart. "Yes, I am perfectly well, Phineas. Deverill took excellent care of me during our stay in Cornwall. You know Mr. Trey Deverill, I believe?"

"I do." Releasing her, Phineas turned to pump Deverill's hand. "I am immensely grateful to you, sir, for keeping Miss Maitland safe from harm."

"It was no more than my duty," Deverill replied.

The pudgy, balding barrister was a full head shorter than Deverill and at least half a head shorter than the other company in the modest parlor—three gentlemen whom Antonia had herself just met.

She watched as Deverill performed the introductions. He'd sent his friends word of his arrival as soon as his schooner docked late that afternoon, but had waited until dark before driving Antonia to the St. James Street apartments of Beau Macklin.

Macky was a handsome, chestnut-haired, roguish fellow who admitted to being a former actor. While they'd waited for the others to arrive, Macky had gallantly plied Antonia with wine and soon had her smiling over his amusing tales of the theater, despite the deadly seriousness of their reason for meeting.

They were joined shortly by Viscount Thorne and Mr. Alex Ryder, both striking, charismatic men, Antonia noted. She had met Lord Thorne before on several occasions. He was fair-haired and rakishly charming, while the much darker Ryder appeared lean and hard and dangerous. Yet despite their differences, both men had an indefinable quality that set them apart from every other tonnish gentlemen of her acquaintance.

Without being told, Antonia had somehow known they were Deverill's fellow Guardians—an instinctive presumption he had confirmed by explaining their various roles in the order.

When Phineas Cochrane arrived moments later, they resumed their seats and apprised the barrister of their investigation thus far—summarizing the case they'd developed against Heward and listing the witnesses who had been persuaded to testify against him, the most damning being the club owner Madam Bruno.

Then they began to discuss Deverill's plan to bring Lord Heward to justice.

Antonia was troubled that Deverill would serve as the bait to lure the baron into incriminating himself, but she listened silently as he explained his intent to the barrister and answered questions.

"I mean to beat Heward at his own game," Deverill asserted. "To use his weaknesses against him."

"And those weaknesses might be?" Phineas Cochrane prompted.

"His craving for wealth and power, for one thing. His jealously of me. And his absolute fury at being bested. Heward has worked too hard to gain command of Miss Maitland's fortune to abandon his scheme now. When he sees it slipping through his grasp and falling into my hands, he will act decisively to prevent it."

Phineas pursed his lips in agreement. "No doubt his lordship is enraged that you eluded his attempt to frame you for murder."

Deverill nodded. "And his failure will make him even more determined to succeed now. I suspect he would like nothing more than to kill me. Therefore, I will make myself available as a target—but at a time and place of my choosing, where I can better control the circumstances."

"So that you may expose his treachery," Phineas mused. "You say you will attempt to provoke Heward into confessing his crimes?"

"Precisely. Even though we have witnesses who are willing to testify against him, convicting Heward of felony will require a high threshold of proof, since he can only be tried by the Lords, and his peers will require conclusive evidence of his guilt. Simply persuading a magistrate to support a warrant against him will be difficult. I need to elicit a public confession from Heward—to confirm to any doubters that he's a murderer—so he can be immediately arrested and imprisoned until his trial, and more importantly, so he is likely to be convicted."

Alex Ryder spoke up and addressed the barrister. "We also need to ensure that Deverill is cleared of all murder charges. The Bow Street Runner who tried to arrest him last month has agreed to delay action to allow us the chance to prove his innocence."

"Indeed?" Phineas raised an eyebrow. "How did you manage to convince an officer of the law to defer fulfilling his sworn duty? Bribery?"

Ryder flashed a dangerous smile. "I promised him an arrest either way. If he isn't persuaded of Heward's guilt, then he means to arrest Deverill. Linch wasn't happy to have allowed his prisoner to slip through his fingers, and Deverill's escape only supported the suspicion that he was the murderer."

Listening, Antonia felt her stomach clench at the reminder of what was at stake: If they couldn't succeed against Heward, Deverill could very well hang for the Cyprian's murder.

"It would be best," Macky added, "if we could expose the real culprits. I've kept watch on the three bruisers who likely committed the murder. I'll lay odds that in exchange for leniency, Scarface or one of his accomplices could be persuaded to give up his cohorts . . . and even to testify that Heward hired them."

"But the word of felons," Viscount Thorne said, "will hold less weight with the Lords."

Phineas Cochrane frowned thoughtfully. "Mr. Barnaby Trant, the Director of Maitland Shipping, may be eager to assist us in order to escape criminal prosecution for his illegal activities in transporting slaves."

"I am counting on it," Deverill said. "I intend to use Trant to help bait our trap when we are ready, but until then, I don't want Heward alerted of our suspicions."

Deverill glanced at Lord Thorne. "As soon as Heward learns Antonia has returned to London, he will want to discover where their betrothal stands—although after her monthlong absence with no word, he's probably concluded she means to repudiate him and even suspects she is in league with me. If so, he will be irate and possibly vengeful enough to do her harm. Therefore, Thorne, you will be in charge of assuring her safety. I would like her to stay tonight with you and Diana. And I want armed footmen stationed among her servant staff when she returns home tomorrow."

Thorne smiled. "Consider it done. Unfortunately I have ample experience protecting Diana of late." He turned to Antonia. "I'm certain my wife will be delighted to meet you and have you as our guest tonight, Miss Maitland."

The viscount had recently celebrated his nuptials, Antonia knew, but she and Lady Thorne had yet to cross paths. "I will be delighted to meet her as well," Antonia said. "But is an armed guard truly necessary?"

"Unquestioningly, remember?" Deverill reminded her of her promise to obey his every order without protest.

She subsided with a nod. "Very well, what do you wish me to do, Deverill?"

"I expect Heward will try to garner an audience with you at once. You'll make it known that you have returned home, but you will deny Heward if he calls. Rouse his frustration even more by shunning him. Then we'll arrange for you to meet him in a public place, where you can be guarded."

"The Marquess of Legmore is holding a masquerade ball on Thursday evening," Thorne said. "We can better safeguard Miss Maitland if we go armed as part of our costumes."

"And Dev can even attend in disguise," Macky chimed in.

"No," Ryder dissented. "With his height and build, Dev would be too readily recognized."

"I am afraid so," Deverill agreed. "But I trust you all to protect her in my absence."

"So what do I tell Heward when I meet him at the masquerade?" Antonia asked.

"First, you will officially break your betrothal to him. Then you'll hint that you intend to wed *me* once my innocence is proven."

Antonia looked piercingly at Deverill. "You mean no such thing, of course?"

"But what better way to further enrage Heward?" he asked.

"True. What happens then?"

"Then," he added with a dangerous gleam in his eye, "we will bait our trap by letting him learn when and where to find me. Mr. Cochrane, on Thursday afternoon I wish you to present our offer to Director Trant: we'll forbear from prosecution if he can convincingly play a role."

"A role, sir?"

"Yes. Trant is to call on Lord Heward Thursday evening after the masquerade, requesting protection from me. He'll say that I'm seeking incriminating evidence against Heward, and that I've threatened Trant with bodily harm if he doesn't comply. He will reluctantly disclose that he is to meet me late Friday night, at a certain time and location. If Heward swallows the bait, he will immediately begin plotting to come after me."

"Friday is only three days from now," Thorne said. "Will that allow you enough time to prepare?"

"That should be adequate," Deverill answered, "if

we orchestrate the details carefully enough. By then, Heward will be gnashing his teeth to have my head on a platter. And it's best to act quickly and deny him the opportunity to devise any complex schemes of reprisal. Ryder, you will take charge of arranging an audience for our confrontation with Heward on Friday night. We'll need some peers present to observe his confession, if I can manage to draw one out of him."

"Gladly. Who did you have in mind?"

"The undersecretary of the Foreign Office, Lord Wittington, would make a good candidate. And perhaps some other nobleman unaffiliated with the government . . . one with social consequence."

"What about Lord Ranworth?" Antonia suggested. "His wife is an undisputed leader of society."

Deverill nodded in approval. "Now here is what I propose . . ." he said, leaning forward.

For the next hour they discussed the plan in detail, beginning with the location for their trap. When Phineas Cochrane suggested his law offices in the City, Antonia agreed they would be ideal, since they were located in a rabbit warren of alleyways and would be dark and secluded at night. At the rear, there was a courtyard where Deverill could await Heward if he took the bait.

When they were satisfied with the plan, the company rose to go their separate ways. Phineas took his leave first, then Ryder, then finally Lord Thorne and Antonia. For tonight she would stay with Thorne and his new bride, Diana. Tomorrow, she would return to her own home, safeguarded by a small army of Thorne's well-trained footmen.

Deverill assisted Antonia into her cloak, then followed the others down the lodgers' stairs and out the front entrance, where he delayed her at the steps.

Antonia felt apprehension clamoring inside her— the result of regret at having to leave Deverill and uncertainty at what might happen to him during the next few days.

"I won't see you before Friday, will I?" she murmured.

"I doubt it." His eyes were dark with concern as he gazed down at her. "Don't take any risks when you encounter Heward at the masquerade. I simply want you to direct his ire toward me."

"I will do my best."

Taking her hands, Deverill let his gaze drop to her lips, almost as if he might succumb to the urge to kiss her. When he refrained, disappointment swept through Antonia. She wanted very much to kiss Deverill, to throw her arms around him and beg him to change the dangerous course he had set upon. But she settled for saying, "Deverill . . . please take care."

He shook his head. "I am more worried for you. At the masquerade, Heward will likely try to get you alone, but don't leave Thorne's sight for a moment. And make certain you go armed with a pistol in your reticule."

"I will. But please promise me you won't take any unnecessary risks with Heward yourself when you confront him."

"I promise."

She stared at Deverill a long moment, wishing she knew how to keep him safe from harm. "I intend to bring my bow on Friday night. I am a much better shot with a bow than a pistol."

Deverill's mouth curved in grim amusement. "Suit yourself, but you won't have a chance to use it, since you won't be anywhere near Heward. You will be attending only as an observer."

He took her elbow and ushered her toward Thorne's waiting town coach. After handing Antonia inside, he turned to his friend and fellow Guardian.

"Keep her safe," Deverill said in a low voice.

"I will," Thorne vowed, before settling beside Antonia and rapping on the roof as a gesture to his coachman to depart.

As Deverill watched the carriage rumble off down the dark street, he felt as though he were cutting out a little piece of his heart. It went against every protective instinct he possessed to let Antonia out of his sight, where she could be vulnerable to Heward's recriminations.

Deverill raked a hand through his hair. He trusted Thorne unquestionably with his own life; he just wasn't certain he trusted anyone but himself with Antonia's life.

But that was what the Guardians did best—protect lives. And as he turned back toward Macky's lodgings, Deverill reminded himself that wild horses could not have kept Antonia uninvolved.

He mounted the dimly lit stairs and let himself into Macky's apartments, where he would lay low for the next few days, since he couldn't show his face around town without risking arrest and imprisonment.

When he reentered the parlor, he saw that Macky had settled comfortably in a chair with a snifter of brandy. Deverill went straight to the brandy decanter himself. This would be the last time he indulged until his final confrontation with Heward, for he wanted nothing fogging his mind when he came up against the treacherous baron.

"So tell me, old chap," Macky said, breaking into

his thoughts, "are you nigh on landing yourself an heiress?"

Deverill's head jerked up. "What do you mean?"

"Miss Maitland. She is a beauty, that one. And rich, too, with a good head on her shoulders, apparently. Even better, she seems partial to you. Will I be wishing you happy anytime soon?"

If I can convince her to have me, Deverill reflected silently. Aloud he said, "Her father had other plans for her marriage."

"So what do you mean to do about it? I am agog with curiosity."

"It's none of your affair," Deverill said tersely, downing half a glass of prime brandy in one long swallow, with no thought of appreciation for the quality.

Macky let out a low whistle. "You have it bad, my friend. Come, admit it."

"Admit what?"

"That you are head over heels in love."

Deverill remained frozen for a long moment, his heart suddenly pounding against his ribs. He found it strangely hard to speak; the constrictive ache in his chest seemed to be interfering with his breathing, his heartbeat.

Unsettled and agitated, he tried to calm his turbulent thoughts as he slowly replenished his glass. Having little success, Deverill crossed the parlor and sank down onto the sofa.

"Is it so bloody obvious?" he asked, his voice unintentionally gruff.

"Only to me," Macky answered. "I am an actor, you'll recall. Made my living studying human nature. And there are small signs that give you away. The way you look at her, for one." Macky surveyed Deverill with dancing eyes. "How droll. Never thought I would see the day. What happened to the determined adventurer who claimed he would never settle down?"

He had met Antonia, that was what had happened.

"Keep your tongue between your teeth, you old bleater," Deverill ordered, unamused.

"Very well," Macky said, chuckling. "But I pray that your affliction isn't catching. First Caro, then Thorne, and now you." He shook his head as he rose to his feet. "I intend to remain a bachelor for a long time to come. There are too many pretty fish in the sea to swim with only one. I commend you on your taste, however . . . beauty, brains, charm, and wealth. If I had to marry, I could only hope to do half so well as Miss Maitland."

Deverill cast a darkling glance at his colleague. Biting back a smile, Macky raised his hands in submission and exited the room.

Sinking deeper into the sofa, Deverill took another long swallow of brandy. Antonia possessed all those qualities Macky had named and more . . . but they had little to do with why he had succumbed to her.

It was because Antonia had made him *feel*. She had pried and prodded and provoked him at the most primal level, stirring the darkest emotions he had tried to keep buried . . . and the brightest as well. Feelings of desire and yearning and passion. Of tenderness and warmth and affection. *Of love*.

He'd fought against loving her. Fiercely ignored the unspoken need she kindled in him. But she had burrowed into his heart against his will. Now he could only wonder what kind of fool he'd been to deceive himself so badly. Just two days ago he had resolved to wed Antonia, not for *her* sake as he'd tried to convince himself, but for his own. Because he didn't want to live without her.

He was still a bloody fool, though, to think he deserved happiness with her, Deverill thought, a fist knotting in his chest. He stared down into his brandy, wondering bleakly if he dared permit himself to imagine a future with her.

But regardless, there was no way in hell he would relinquish Antonia to another man. She would marry him and no one else.

Antonia belonged to him. And if he managed to defeat Heward, he would pursue her with every breath in his body.

Deverill took one last swallow of brandy, feeling the burn down to his stomach. A future with Antonia was one worth fighting for.

The difficulty was, if he couldn't vanquish Heward, he might hang for murder, and then he would have no future at all, with or without her.

Antonia gazed across the crowded ballroom at Lord Heward and wondered how she could ever have been eager for a future with him. Now merely sharing the same room with him made her shudder.

He was not in costume, as were most of the other ball guests. Instead, he wore a plain black satin domino over his evening clothes. The half mask covering the upper part of his face didn't fully conceal his dark scowl as he surveyed the crowd, doubtless in search of her.

Antonia felt her jaw clench in apprehension when Heward glanced her way. As yet, however, he hadn't recognized her in her shepherdess attire. Her costume had been specially commissioned for its dual advantages: The voluminous powdered wig covered her distinctive, fiery hair, while the hooked staff she carried to guide her imaginary flock of lambs gave her nominal protection if necessary.

She also had the protection of Deverill's friends this evening. Currently Antonia was flanked by Lord and Lady Thorne on one side, and Alex Ryder garbed as a highwayman on the other. The roguish Macky was also hovering nearby, disguised as a footman.

Thus far, the initial details of their plan had gone as expected. She had spent the night of her arrival at the Cavendish Square mansion of Viscount Thorne and his beautiful wife, Diana, who was also an amazingly talented artist. Antonia had liked Diana immensely and was grateful to have her support and feminine perspective in this bastion of male Guardians.

The next morning, Antonia had returned to her own home, where her first action was to greet and reassure her relieved housekeeper, Mrs. Peeke.

Her second step was to send an announcement to the society pages of the evening papers, so Heward would be certain to hear of her presence in London. Her third was to pay a call on her dearest friend, Emily, Lady Sudbury.

From the pouting reception she received, Antonia could see Emily was still hurt and angry at her for leaving London so precipitously, even though she had written every week of her absence, offering breezy, mostly true accounts of her sojourn in Cornwall.

But eventually over tea and scones, Emily grudgingly allowed Antonia back into her good graces. At least until the subject of Baron Heward arose.

"Heward was fit to be tied, Antonia, when you disappeared without a word. He came to me several times, demanding to know where you had gone, but I had not the slightest idea. It was a shabby way to treat your betrothed, I must say."

"Heward is no longer my betrothed, Emily," Antonia confided.

The young countess looked shocked. "Whyever not?"

She grimaced. "It is a long story."

"Antonia . . . what are you not telling me? Why are you being so secretive, after all we have been through together?"

Her friend was clearly hurt again, and Antonia hastened to reassure her. "I am not at liberty to share the details just now, but I swear I will tell you everything when it is all over."

Emily's forehead creased with suspicion. "Does this have anything to do with that criminal, Trey Deverill? He is wanted as a murderer, you know."

"Deverill is *not* a criminal," she replied rather too sharply. "Certainly not a murderer."

Emily's eyes widened, then lit up. "I knew it! He *did* have something to do with your disappearance."

"I really can't say."

The smile that wreathed Emily's lips held delight. "Do you mean to suggest you had a true adventure, like you always dreamed of having?"

Despite her best intentions, Antonia felt herself flush. She had tried ardently not to think of the glorious passion she had shared with Deverill for the past month, or her growing certainty that their eventual parting would be excruciating. Those were subjects she couldn't confide even to her closest friend. Yet she had to offer some sort of explanation, or Emily would hound her unmercifully.

"It was a better adventure than I ever dreamed of,"

Antonia said merely. "But I cannot speak of it. And you mustn't breathe a word to anyone, and I mean *anyone,* Emily. Especially not Heward. It could have disastrous consequences if you do."

"My lips are sealed, cross my heart forever." Emily made the sign they had always shared as bosom friends when they were two lonely girls at boarding school. Then she smiled mysteriously. "I have a secret myself."

"What is it?"

"I am not telling you after your beastly behavior."

Antonia merely waited, knowing her friend could never hold a grudge for long.

Giving a huff, Emily relented. "Oh, very well. I am increasing!"

Instinctively Antonia glanced down at Emily's stomach, noticing that it was indeed the slightest bit rounded under her empire-waist gown. She knew a moment of envy for her dear friend's happiness, but then rose abruptly to give her a fierce hug. "Emily, I am utterly delighted for you!"

"I am, also. And Sudbury is quite beside himself, he wants an heir so badly. I pray it is a boy. His mama will likely never let me live it down otherwise. But I am so very glad you are back to keep me company, Antonia. I have been a bit sickly in the mornings, you see. . . ."

Giving an inner sigh of relief at averting a crisis, Antonia listened attentively to a rambling account of the joys and pains of early pregnancy. When she finally took her leave to return home in her carriage, it was in the company of her new armed guards—four strapping footmen that Thorne had added to her household staff for her protection.

She was glad for their presence later that evening

and again this morning when Lord Heward called at her house and attempted to gain an audience with her. He was refused admittance on both occasions, but the second time, on her instructions, her butler had informed his lordship that Miss Maitland would be attending the Legmore masquerade ball this evening if he wished to speak with her.

Heward undoubtedly was seething with impatience now as he scanned the ballroom for her. Just when his gaze swept over her shepherdess costume, he froze, seeming to recognize her.

Antonia gave an inward shudder, relieved she needn't be alone with him tonight—and not solely because she feared Heward, but because she feared she might lose control of her own fierce emotions.

Rage welled up in her as she locked gazes with him through their demi-masks. Heward likely had murdered her father to protect his claim to her fortune. And just as horribly, he had ordered an innocent woman killed and then pinned the blame on Deverill to eliminate his interference.

Yet they still had to prove it, Antonia grimly reminded herself. And she had a crucial role to play tonight if she wanted Deverill to go free of the charges of murder and to see Heward pay for his crimes.

She couldn't fail. She *wouldn't* fail, she vowed as the baron pushed his way through the crowd toward her.

Her fury must have shown on the lower half of her face, however, for Thorne murmured a cautionary word, and Diana pressed her fingers encouragingly. Then Macky had the audacity to wink at her as he passed by.

That wink particularly helped Antonia to contain

her black mood and gave her the added courage to confront the dastardly villain who was approaching her.

She took a steadying breath and pasted a cool smile of welcome on her face as Heward reached her. "Lord Heward, how pleased I am to see you," she remarked congenially.

It was with great restraint that she exchanged pleasantries and then introduced his lordship to her new friends, Lord and Lady Thorne and Mr. Ryder. She politely refused Heward's request to speak to her in private and suggested instead that he invite her to waltz, for she was determined to remain in public view for their interview.

Additionally, she refused to relinquish her shepherd's crook, even though clutching it proved awkward when they took their positions on the ballroom floor. She tried not to flinch when Heward grasped her hand, but even his gloved touch made her skin crawl. Fortunately the dance soon started.

"I have missed you, my dear," Heward said, guiding her expertly around the room.

"Have you?" Antonia murmured.

"Yes. I regretted your sudden disappearance. I feared perhaps you were angry with me, but I had no notion what I might have done to earn your displeasure."

She gave him an ironic smile. "None at all? Come now, Heward, I credited you with greater acumen."

"What do you mean?" he asked, his tone a little too sharp.

"If I was angry with you, it was because it came to my attention that you were employing my father's ships to illegally transport slaves."

Heward was silent a long moment, obviously debating whether to try and deny his involvement.

Antonia's smile turned dangerous. "Even worse, you betrayed my trust, using your position as adviser to line your own pockets. It is a blessing my father didn't know, or he would have been enraged. Just think how that would have affected a man with his heart condition."

Heward stared at her for half a dozen lilting bars of the waltz. Refusing, however, to acknowledge her deliberate hint that he had caused her father's heart failure, he tried placating her instead, offering her a new, rueful expression edged with dismay.

"You are mistaken, my dear. I have no knowledge of any illegalities. If any such distasteful actions occurred, then Trant was fully responsible."

It took all her willpower not to scratch Heward's eyes out and reply calmly. "Pray, don't insult my intelligence, my lord. I know all about how you blackmailed Director Trant and forced him to do your bidding. As a result, you have forfeited any influence over my father's company. In truth," Antonia declared with sugary sweetness, "I want nothing more to do with you."

His mouth turned grim. "You are breaking our betrothal?"

"I fear I must, for I cannot marry two different gentlemen. Mr. Trey Deverill has offered for my hand, you see, and I am considering accepting."

"You cannot be serious," Heward said grimly.

"Whyever not?"

"Deverill is wanted for murdering a woman of . . . low morals."

"Oh, I know all about that," Antonia replied lightly, determined to goad Heward as much as possible. "And I don't believe a word of it. Indeed, that preposterous accusation actually swayed me in Deverill's favor. What better way to convince the ton that I believe in his innocence than to accept his proposal of marriage?"

The baron fell silent once more, clearly struggling to control his response. Deverill was right, Antonia thought: The surest way to infuriate Heward and arouse his jealousy was to intimate that she might marry his rival. In all likelihood, Heward knew he could never measure up to Deverill in her eyes, even though it was the baron who possessed the illustrious title and vaunted position in society.

"An admirable sentiment, my dear," Heward finally said. "You will forgive me, however, if my feelings for you prevent me from offering my felicitations."

"Oh, I doubt your feelings for me are wounded in any great measure, although you will certainly lament the loss of my fortune."

Heward's jaw clenched. "Where is this paragon you intend to wed? Did he return to London with you?"

"In fact, he did. Although naturally, under the circumstances, he cannot make his presence known for fear of arrest. But Phineas Cochrane has agreed to handle Deverill's defense as a personal favor to me. I am quite grateful, and I have high hopes those spurious charges will soon be dismissed. Phineas's skills as a barrister are unequaled, you know."

At this taunting utterance, Heward's grip on her hand tightened painfully. He was livid, Antonia knew, and he barely made an effort to disguise it. "Now *you* disappoint *me,* my dear. But perhaps your emotional confusion can be attributed to the ordeal of your abduction. That cur has obviously filled your head with lies."

"Are they lies, Lord Heward?"

"Yes. And I know you are fair-minded enough to allow me the chance to prove it to you."

"You are welcome to try," Antonia replied skeptically.

The waltz came to an end just then. Heward returned her to Lord Thorne's side and took his leave with exquisite politeness. Yet from the fury she saw gleaming in his gaze through his mask, she knew she had made an implacable enemy and was very glad for the protection of Deverill's friends.

Watching Heward stride away, however, Antonia could finally take a deep breath for the first time all evening.

She had done her part. Now it remained for Deverill to do his.

Eighteen

A fine mist turned the summer night cool and settled over Deverill's cloak as he waited in the shadows before the baron's Bedford Square mansion. At the sound of carriage wheels, Deverill slipped farther along the wrought-iron fence that fronted the house, concealing himself behind a brick post.

Eventually, a crested town coach drew to a halt before the mansion. When a flaxen-haired gentleman garbed in a black domino stepped down, Deverill smiled faintly, realizing that Heward had returned early from the masquerade. Antonia must have been successful, he thought with satisfaction.

From the corner of his eye, he saw two horsemen ride past and recognized their silhouettes in the muted light of the street lamps. Ryder and Macky had followed Heward's carriage from the masquerade to make certain of his whereabouts at all times.

Not surprisingly, there was a sharp edge to the baron's tone when he dismissed his coachman for the evening. As the carriage rumbled off, Heward strode angrily through the gateposts and down the walk toward his front entrance. If he reacted as expected, however, he would be summoning that same carriage again very shortly.

Moments after the baron bounded up the steps and disappeared inside the house, Deverill was quietly joined by Alex Ryder and Beau Macklin on foot.

"Did Trant call on Heward as he agreed?" Macky asked in barely a whisper.

"Yes," Deverill murmured. "He's awaiting Heward inside now."

Director Trant had been so desperate to save himself, he had eagerly assented to all of Deverill's demands, the most important being to disclose the time and location of an arranged meeting the following evening, so Heward would know when and where to find him.

"Heward will be spitting nails when he learns I've tried to turn Trant against him," Deverill added softly. "The question is whether his lordship will act tonight or wait until tomorrow to summon his henchmen."

"My odds are on tonight," Ryder speculated. "He can't risk losing the opportunity to strike at you, and he will want to verify their services as soon as possible."

"For your sakes, I hope so," Deverill replied, "or it will be a long, uncomfortable night for you."

"No matter," Macky whispered with a grin. "We'll keep the bloody lord in sight."

They would watch the baron's house for as long as necessary, until he came out again. If Heward summoned his town coach as expected, the two Guardians would follow on horseback.

Their predictions proved accurate. Barely ten minutes later, Director Trant exited the mansion. At the gatepost, he deliberately paused to wipe his face with a white handkerchief—the signal that Heward had responded as anticipated.

Deverill smiled grimly to himself.

A quarter hour after that, Heward's crested carriage rumbled back up the street and halted before the mansion. Ryder and Macky immediately disappeared into the fog to retrieve their horses, while Deverill remained to watch.

Moments later, Heward came storming out of the house. He barked an order at his coachman before flinging himself inside the equipage. Immediately, the town coach set off at a brisk pace, but Ryder and Macky were close behind.

Giving a silent salute to Deverill, they rode off down the dark street and were swallowed up by the mist. Other than being cold and wet, the fog was actually a benefit, Deverill reflected, since it would help conceal them as they pursued their quarry.

Turning, he made his own way across the square and around the corner, to the nondescript, closed carriage awaiting him. He would return to Macky's lodgings for the evening and allow his fellow Guardians to do their work.

Even so, Deverill found it difficult to calmly endure the wait, and it was nearly three o'clock in the morning before his colleagues entered the apartments.

Macky was grinning ear to ear, while Ryder offered a more circumspect smile.

"Our friendly baron went to Seven Dials and met with Scarface," Macky announced triumphantly.

Deverill nodded. "Then I think we can safely expect to mount our challenge to Heward tomorrow evening, wouldn't you agree?"

* * *

All his senses on full alert, Deverill waited in the shadowy courtyard for his enemies to appear. The appointment with Trant had been set for ten o'clock at the barrister's law offices, and it was nearly that time now.

He was fairly confident Heward would send his henchmen to dispatch him tonight; the question was whether the baron would accompany them and personally oversee their handiwork.

Deverill could hear his own heartbeat in the eery quiet that had descended over the courtyard. All the offices and shops in the district were closed, and the usual employees had long gone home to their suppers and their beds. Ryder and Macky were nowhere to be seen, having concealed themselves somewhere on the grounds.

Much of the large, tree-shaded court was in darkness, flanked on two sides by the wings of the law building, and on the other two by tall stone walls. A single post-lamp had been left burning in the corner near the rear entrance door, faintly illuminating the maze of flagstone paths lined by benches and stone statuary and ancient apple trees.

Half hidden behind a gnarled tree, Deverill could see the rear door, which had been left unlocked for the arranged meeting. But he kept his gaze fixed on the side gate, the sole access through the wall. If his foes materialized tonight, they would come from the alley beyond.

Just then, the sudden creak of gate hinges made his muscles tense. The noise abruptly stopped and a long moment passed. Then the hinges squealed once more as the gate was slowly drawn open.

Deverill watched as three hulking figures stole into the courtyard, wearing masking hoods and carrying pistols and knives. Their furtiveness, combined with those deadly weapons, reminded him vividly of the last time they had attacked him, when they'd murdered poor, unsuspecting Felice.

Deverill felt his jaw knot as the intruders crept toward the steps of the building's rear entrance. He was angry enough to take all three ruffians on his own, but he forced his breathing to slow and waited to see if Heward would accompany them.

He was not disappointed. The gate hinges gave another creak as the fair-haired baron silently entered, armed with two pistols. Deverill's heart rate quickened, yet he controlled his fierce impatience until Heward had moved past him a dozen steps.

"Well, well," he said softly. "Fancy meeting you here, your lordship."

All four intruders jumped and spun around, searching the shadows. Heward spied Deverill first and aimed both pistols directly at his chest.

Pointing his own pistol in return, Deverill stepped out from behind the tree. "Where is Trant?" he asked the baron, even though he already knew the answer.

Heward's features were indistinct at this distance, but a smug smile sounded in his reply. "Director Trant will not be coming tonight."

"So you came in his stead?" Deverill indicated Heward's weapons with a brief nod of his head. "Would you care to tell me why you are armed, and why you brought your murdering henchmen with you?"

"I'm certain you can guess."

"You're worried because Trant has confessed to your conspiracy to transport slaves."

The nobleman shrugged. "I am hardly concerned

about Trant. If it is his word against mine, I will win every time."

"But you will not win against me," Deverill commented, his own tone deliberately taunting. "Admittedly, I underestimated your treachery the first time, Heward. You served me a cunning trick, framing me for murder. But you are gravely mistaken if you expect to get away with it."

"Do you think so?" The question held a trace of a smirk.

"Yes. You have failed, Heward."

His fingers tightened on the pistol grips. "How so? *You* are the one who ran afoul of the law, Deverill. You are still a wanted criminal, I believe."

"For the time being. But I'm confident I will be able to prove my innocence shortly. Madam Bruno is prepared to testify that you orchestrated the murder of her employee."

"How can she testify? She was not a witness."

"But she knows you staged the entire evening, arranging for her to alert Bow Street even before the murder. She lied for you at the time, since you paid her well to keep her mouth shut and she was too afraid to defy you. But her testimony now will be enough to clear my name—and to implicate you."

Heward's mouth curled. "Who will take the word of a whore?"

Knowing Heward was unlikely to confess without provocation, Deverill tried a different tack. "Miss Maitland, for one. She was repulsed enough by the tale to break her betrothal to you. A pity that you lost her fortune after working so hard to secure it. It can't sit well, either, knowing that I turned her against you, just as I did Trant."

Heward flinched at that barb, Deverill noted with

satisfaction. Then the baron barked an order over his shoulder at his henchmen. "Apprehend that bastard!"

The three ruffians moved forward cautiously to surround Deverill.

In response, he spread his arms and allowed himself to be disarmed. He could have tried to keep possession of his pistol, since Heward likely meant to kill him. But armed, Heward would feel more powerful, more confident and in control. And a confident Heward might just boast about his triumphs.

Moreover, not even a nobleman of his rank would be able to escape justice after shooting an unarmed man in cold blood in front of witnesses. Deverill considered it worth the risk in order to put the bloody baron in prison for life.

He raised his empty hands in surrender, but his tone was anything but submissive when he responded, determined to taunt Heward and rouse his ire to the boiling point. "Rather cowardly of you, my lord. You sent your hedgebirds to kill an innocent woman because you didn't have the mettle to do it yourself. And now you mean to rely on them again to do your dirty work."

He could almost hear the baron grinding his teeth, yet Heward refused to be provoked. "Enough of this blather, Deverill. Now, move toward the door." He gestured behind him at the building's entrance.

Deverill studied the threatening weapons aimed at his chest before lifting a taunting eyebrow. "Why? Do you mean to kill me?"

"I would be justified if I did. You have caused me enough trouble."

Refusing to obey, Deverill leaned a shoulder indolently against the tree trunk. "Just tell me one thing first."

Heward's eyes narrowed. "Tell you what?"

"How Samuel Maitland died. You killed him yourself, didn't you?"

His mouth curled in a sly smile. "That is absurd. Maitland expired from heart failure."

"Because you poisoned him."

"I said, *enough*." The baron's expression suddenly became glacial as he stepped closer to Deverill. Pointing both pistols, he pronounced in a low, lethal voice, "Do not push me too far, Deverill. Now move to the door."

"Ah, I understand. You mean to shoot me—only not here where the shots could be heard."

"Precisely." Heward smiled with deadly malice. "I have no intention of leaving you alive to inconvenience me further."

Deverill waited barely an instant before suddenly spinning and lunging behind the apple tree to escape the line of fire. As he sprinted into the murkier depths of the courtyard, a shot rang out behind him, followed by Heward's angry protest.

"I told you not to fire here, you bloody imbeciles! Well, go after him, damn you!"

His heart thudding, Deverill took refuge behind a stone statue and drew a knife from his coat pocket as he waited for his pursuers to follow.

The three ruffians fanned out hurriedly, their weapons ready as they searched the darkness. When one passed his hiding place, Deverill moved swiftly behind him and gripped his gun hand while holding the knife blade to his throat.

"Keep still if you want to live," Deverill murmured in a dangerous voice.

Wisely, the man froze.

Just as swiftly, Ryder emerged from the shadows and incapacitated another ruffian with a fierce upward blow to the jaw, catching the beefy body as it fell to the stone flags. At the same time, Macky took the third one, easily subduing him with a knee to the stomach and pushing him to the ground, where he lay sprawled and grunting for air.

Knowing his friends would be binding their prisoners, Deverill kept his knife blade in the same lethal position and pulled off the hooded mask of the man he held. In the dim light, he immediately recognized Scarface.

Forcing the brute to his knees, Deverill held him there until Macky assumed control. Then checking to see that the ruffian's pistol was still loaded, Deverill made his way back through the courtyard and positioned himself behind an apple tree, where he could glimpse Heward but still remain out of shooting range.

He could hear the baron demanding to know what had happened—and cursing vividly when there was no response.

Determined to keep the nobleman's wrath at a fever pitch, Deverill called out in a taunting drawl, "I am loath to inform you, Heward, but your hirelings have been incapacitated. You are all alone."

The baron immediately fell silent. His grip on the pistols visibly tightened, however, and Deverill could almost feel his fury.

"Lay down your weapons and give yourself up, Heward. Two of my confederates have joined me, and you only have two pistols. You cannot shoot all three of us."

More silence greeted his demand.

"Come, Baron, you may as well surrender now that your game is up."

"I beg to differ," Heward said calmly. "The game is not up."

Just then Deverill heard a stealthy footstep behind him—an instant before he felt the press of cold steel against his nape. A gun barrel, Deverill surmised grimly.

"I 'ave this one, guv'nor," his captor called out, confiscating Deverill's pistol.

A grunt and thud from Macky's direction was followed by another stranger's voice: "I scuttled this one's nob, yer lordship."

Deverill swore silently, realizing that at least two more of Heward's hirelings must have come over the wall. Macky had possibly taken a blow to the head and was unconscious. Of Ryder, there was no sign.

Deverill took a step forward, hoping to keep Heward out in the open, in the part of the courtyard nearest the building. But the pistol at his head and a growled command made him halt.

Heward moved toward him then, keeping both pistols carefully aimed. A smirk showed on the baron's face when he reached Deverill. "I knew you were planning something. You did not think I was stupid enough to fall for your trap, did you?"

Deverill offered a sardonic smile. "Truthfully, I did. I salute your cleverness, Heward. Once again I underestimated you, it pains me to say."

The baron dismissed his underling and maneuvered behind Deverill, prodding him in the back with one pistol. "Now, move."

"Move where?"

"To the gate. You are coming with me as surety to

keep your colleagues from following me. If they do, I will kill you."

Forbearing to comment that he would likely be killed anyway, Deverill complied, eager to draw Heward out from beneath the canopy of tree limbs. At the same moment, he spied a shadowy figure gliding along the stone wall to his left.

The baron noted it also and abruptly forced Deverill to halt. By then Ryder had positioned himself at the gate and stood blocking the way.

"Tell your lackey to step aside, Deverill," Heward ordered, gesturing at Ryder.

"Lackey?" Ryder repeated softly. At the insult, he lazily raised his own pistol, aiming at Heward.

Even in the dim light, Deverill could see the dangerous glimmer in his friend's eye, yet knew Ryder wouldn't fire, since he had no clear shot. Deverill stood directly in his path—and the distance was too far for accuracy, in any case.

Deverill glanced over his shoulder at Heward. "Ryder is no one's lackey, which you'll discover to your regret if you press him. Still, you are welcome to try. Be warned, however, that if you shoot me, you won't leave here alive."

"I am losing patience, Deverill!" the baron snarled. "I *will* shoot you, I swear it!"

"Go ahead, your lordship, if you have the courage. Do your worst."

Nineteen ❧

Her heart in her throat, Antonia listened with growing alarm as Deverill challenged the baron to do his worst.

From her position on the roof—lying flat on her stomach near the edge—she could peer over the low parapet and see the dimly lit courtyard below. But tree limbs blocked much of her view, and she could make out only part of Heward's form as he stood behind Deverill, leveling both pistols at his head.

Beside her, Lord Thorne gave no overt sign of alarm, yet she could feel his tension; he was as helpless as Ryder, since his pistols would be of little use at this range.

Deverill himself seemed at ease, as if a vengeful villain were not threatening his very life. Antonia wanted to curse his unruffled calm. Her own nerves had been shredded raw ever since Thorne had brought her to Phineas's law offices nearly two hours before. She had hoped Heward would appear tonight, for she wanted this to be over, for Deverill's sake even more than her own. And she assuredly wanted a confession of guilt from Heward.

Just not at the risk of Deverill's life. Cornered, Heward might very well be desperate enough to kill him then and there.

Her every instinct crying danger, Antonia stole a questioning glance at Thorne, who nodded silently and gestured at the bow she had set near to hand. Deverill had permitted her to bring it, although never expecting her to use it. He'd wanted her safe, out of harm's way, while he took all the risks. It had been a battle merely to convince him to let her join Thorne on the rooftop so she could better observe events.

She was now ardently glad she had, since she stood a better chance of hitting a distant target with her bow than with any pistol . . . if only the target was in the clear.

Moving surreptitiously, her cramped muscles screaming from having been immobile for so long, Antonia slowly shifted her weight to slide an arrow from her quiver. Lying on her side, she nocked the shaft while trying to remain hidden behind the parapet. She couldn't risk being seen yet, since Heward was mostly facing her.

Keeping low, she eased onto her knees and peered over. The sight made her chest tighten with fear. Even if she succeeded in drawing her bow, Deverill's broad shoulder partly blocked her line of aim, and she worried that she might hit him instead of Heward.

But then the baron's voice rose to a fever pitch as he once again ordered Deverill to move, and she knew she had no choice but to try. Heward could fire at any instant. And even if Deverill accompanied him as surety, what was to keep the baron from killing his hostage once he was safely away?

Her palms slick, her heart hammering, she carefully drew back the arrow as she debated what part of

Heward to target, arm or shoulder or thigh. Once she raised the bow, she would have little time to aim.

She could *not* fail, though. If she let Deverill perish right before her eyes, her own heart might as well stop beating.

Strangely, the thought actually calmed her and made her hands steadier. Taking a deep breath then, she whipped up the drawn bow and straightened, purposely making herself a target as she called out loudly, "Lord Heward!"

His attention caught, the baron momentarily shifted his gaze upward to her. Recognizing the threat she presented, Heward reflexively swung his pistol aim toward her just as she released the arrow.

With a whooshing whistle, it flew down from the roof to land buried in the outside of Heward's right thigh. He screamed in pain, his right leg buckling. At the same instant, Deverill grasped his forearms, pushing them up high.

Antonia heard the resultant gunshot but couldn't see what had happened, for Thorne had hauled her down beside him, behind the meager protection of the parapet.

Her heart pounding furiously, she struggled to rise—and then breathed a fervent prayer of relief. Deverill's reflexes had been sharp enough to deflect the baron's aim, so that one of the pistols had discharged harmlessly into the tree limbs above. Splintered bark and tattered leaves drifted down through the haze of smoke as Antonia watched Deverill wrestle the wounded baron to the ground and take away both weapons.

She wanted to rush down to his side, to make certain he was unharmed, but Thorne's warning hand forestalled her. "Wait."

She nocked another arrow and was poised to shoot again, but then she saw there was no need for it. Ryder had swiftly moved to relieve Deverill of the pistols and now stood guard over the injured baron, while Deverill knelt there, examining the arrow protruding from his lordship's thigh.

"A commendable shot, love," Thorne murmured in approval.

Antonia nodded, although she barely heard him. Her frantic pulse had begun to slow, yet her senses were reeling at the startling realization she had just made: If Deverill had died, her heart would have died with him.

She was dazed by the thought. She loved Deverill, as much as life itself. She would have willingly faced death in his place, for she could never have borne to see him killed.

Dear heaven, how could she have been so blind? How could she have failed to recognize the roiling turmoil of misery and longing and fear that her heart had endured these past few days? Why had it taken Deverill's near death for her to comprehend her feelings? She had stubbornly, resolutely ignored all the signs—

Fiercely shaking herself, Antonia shoved her errant thoughts aside. This was no time to be contemplating regrets and feelings, no matter how profound.

She relaxed the bowstring but held the arrow primed as she watched the courtyard below. The Bow Street Runner, Horace Linch, had materialized from inside the building and was assisting Macky in herding Heward's hirelings into the near end of the courtyard. Macky was moving slowly, but he didn't appear to be badly injured.

"I think it is safe to join them," Thorne said, helping Antonia to her feet.

Bending, she retrieved her quiver and slung the strap over her shoulder, then allowed Thorne to guide her over the rooftop and down a dimly lit, narrow stairway, where a candle had been left burning.

Keeping her bow ready, as Thorne did his pistols, she accompanied him outside and across the open court, to where Heward sat clutching his thigh and groaning in pain.

The acrid smell of gunpowder filled Antonia's nostrils as Deverill looked up and met her gaze. His eyes were warm with understanding and appreciation.

"Allow me to express my gratitude, Miss Maitland," he said lightly with a nod at her bow and arrow.

Heward's head jerked up at her name, and he glowered at her. "You bitch! You shot me!"

"Yes, I shot you," she answered steadily. "You would have killed Deverill otherwise."

Deverill remarked in a dry voice, "You are fortunate she didn't aim for some more vital part of your anatomy, Heward. It's merely a flesh wound. You'll live, more's the pity."

He had cut away the fabric around the injury and finished his examination of the arrow, but when he reached up to untie Heward's neckcloth, the baron shrank back in snarling protest. "What in hell's name are you doing?"

"Fashioning a bandage to stanch the flow of blood. There will be a good deal of it once I remove the arrow."

"The devil you will! I want a surgeon! Immediately!"

"Not yet, Heward. We still have a few matters to settle."

With a curse, the baron gritted his teeth and subsided as Deverill finished the task he had begun. Untying Heward's neckcloth, he folded it to make a compress and then removed his own.

"A waste of a good cravat," Deverill murmured before bending over the baron's thigh and taking hold of the arrow shaft. "Be still. This will hurt."

Heward screamed again as Deverill pulled out the arrow. Predictably, blood gushed from the wound, so he used Heward's hand to press the cravat pad against the raw flesh while he wrapped the other neckcloth around the injured thigh and achieved a neat bandage.

"This should suffice for the time being—while we deal with our unfinished business."

"What business?" Heward demanded, panting in harsh, uneven breaths.

"Why, the small matter of your confession. Pray direct your gaze up at those windows across the courtyard," Deverill advised, pointing up at the darkened second floor of the building's side wing. "We had an audience for our encounter, your lordship. You couldn't see them, but there were several persons up there observing you."

He perceived the instant understanding dawned, for Heward's entire body stiffened in outrage. "You planned this, you bastard." The baron's tone was astonished as well as furious.

"Except for your unexpected extra henchmen," Deverill admitted mildly, "yes, I planned it. You of all people should appreciate my careful scheming. I've gone to a great deal of trouble to arrange this evening's entertainment, so I trust you won't be disappointed." His arm swept politely toward the rear entrance door, where a half-dozen men and women had emerged, two of whom held lanterns. "Won't you join us, ladies and gentlemen?"

Obligingly, the group of people traipsed with their lanterns across the courtyard to gather around the baron.

In the bright light, Heward sat blinking at the unexpected spectacle, while Deverill spoke.

"You know Mr. Phineas Cochrane, of course," Deverill said. "And Lords Wittington and Ranworth. I asked Lord Ranworth to attend as an impartial observer. Madam Nan Bruno"—he indicated the beautiful, raven-haired proprietress of the sin club—"is here on behalf of her murdered employee, Felice Pedigrew. The other lady is Miss Maitland's housekeeper, Mrs. Dolly Peeke. Mrs. Peeke is prepared to present further testimony against you, if necessary."

When Heward glowered, Deverill smiled coldly. "You like slinking in the shadows, Baron, but I want the evidence brought out in the open, so you can't manipulate it to your own benefit."

Deverill glanced again across the courtyard, where Macky and the Runner stood guard over the five bound ruffians. "Perhaps you remember Mr. Horace Linch, the agent of Bow Street who attempted to arrest me for a murder I didn't commit? Mr. Linch . . . Mr. Macklin, will you be kind enough to bring your prisoners here?"

Heward stared darkly at Deverill, ignoring the commotion as the five ruffians were brought forward at gunpoint to join the group. All of their masks had been removed.

"I recognize the scarred fellow," Deverill said to Heward, "as one of three men who assaulted me and killed my companion that evening. You've engaged him in the past to perform unsavory tasks for you, as Madam Bruno will vouch. But would you care to explain your version of events of the night in question, my lord?"

"I don't have to answer to you!" Heward sputtered.

Frowning with impatience, the tall, distinguished-looking undersecretary, Lord Wittington, stepped forward as if accustomed to taking charge. "Perhaps we should ask the perpetrators directly. You there—what do you have to say for yourselves?" Wittington demanded. "Did Lord Heward hire you to do murder?"

Scarface remained stubbornly silent, while his colleagues stared at the ground.

"I suggest that one of you speak up and spare yourself a hanging in favor of prison. Tell me who killed that young woman!"

"My lord?" Macky interjected politely. "If I might have a moment to confer with the prisoners?" When he bent close to the ruffians, murmuring something in a low voice, Deverill suspected he was describing in vivid detail the punishment for murder.

After a long pause, the smallest and weakest of the five stepped forward and tugged on his forelock. "Aye, Lord Heward hired us to do murder . . . but to fix it so's that Deverill cove snared the blame."

The other brutes growled in protest at their cohort's betrayal, but the undersecretary raised a commanding hand to silence them.

"And who are you?" Wittington asked the small one.

The grudging reply was a moment in coming. "I'm Ben Stubbs, yer honor. That scarred bloke is known as Jackal. The one next to 'im is Kater. I dint murder that lass, it was Kater."

"Hold your bloody weesh!" the man called Kater spat, lunging at Stubbs with his head, since his fists were bound behind him.

It required both Macky and Linch to pull the ruffians apart and force Kater to the ground, where he lay cursing foully until Macky managed to gag him.

Then Phineas Cochrane stepped forward to address the group. "My lord, if I may . . . this might be the appropriate time to examine the case against Mr. Deverill."

Nodding, Lord Wittington stepped back. "It might, indeed."

"Mr. Linch?" the barrister said to the Bow Street Runner. "That fellow's admission corroborates the account you heard earlier this evening from Madam Bruno, you will agree. Are you prepared yet to consider that the charges against my client, Mr. Deverill, are spurious ones?"

Horace Linch rubbed his jaw in deliberation. "I am, sir. When I arrived on the scene that night, all the evidence pointed toward Mr. Deverill, what with the blood on his hands and Madam Bruno insisting he had killed the girl. And he *did* act guilty—escaping my custody when I tried to convey him to Bow Street." Linch grimaced, as if remembering. "I was outraged at the time, but now that Madam Bruno has changed her story, I tend to believe Mr. Deverill's version—that he was innocent all along. And that I was played for a fool."

The barrister smiled briefly. "Thank you, Mr. Linch. Might I also inquire whether the law means to dismiss the charges against Mr. Deverill?"

The Runner nodded. "Aye, sir. Based on what I saw and heard tonight, there is no justification for the charges."

There was a murmur of approval from the crowd, while Deverill felt relief course through him. When he met Antonia's gaze, he could tell she shared his feeling; tears welled in her eyes and she clasped a hand over her mouth as if to keep from shouting in elation.

"So how do you wish to proceed now, Mr. Linch?" Deverill asked.

"I mean to place Lord Heward under arrest for conspiring to murder Felice Pedigrew."

Clenching his fists, the baron blustered in fury. "Your spurious theory is merely supposition! It is clear that Deverill bribed these rogues to lie about me!"

Barrister Cochrane spoke up again. "I beg to differ, my Lord Heward. There is a preponderance of evidence against you. If these same witnesses testify at a trial before the House of Lords, I have little doubt you will be convicted of conspiring to do murder."

His mouth agape, Heward sat there glaring at his accusers.

The haughty, silver-haired Earl of Ranworth entered the discussion then, shaking his head sadly. "I have heard enough to be convinced. I never would have credited it, Heward, had I not been present tonight, but I have no doubt now that you ordered the murder. You have shamed us all with your dishonorable actions."

Where before Heward's complexion had been red with fury, his face turned pale at this pronouncement. As a peer, Ranworth's opinion was crucially important, Deverill knew, for even if the criminal charges could not be proven in a court of law—even if Heward escaped conviction for Felice's killing—he would be forever ruined in society, for the rumors of murder would always shadow him. If he managed to elude prison, his only option would be to flee England for the Continent or some other foreign place, where he could live out the rest of his life as something less than a pariah.

Yet Deverill was resolved that the bloody baron wouldn't escape justice. Moreover, there was still the matter of Samuel Maitland's murder to prove—which undoubtedly was of even greater importance to Antonia.

"I suspect, Heward, that you are feeling much like a rat in a trap just now," Deverill said mildly. "But our discussion of your crimes is not over. There are other witnesses against you." Deverill looked up, searching behind the spectators who were gathered around the wounded man. "Where is Mr. Beaton?"

An unprepossessing, gray-haired little man stepped forward, adjusting his spectacles. "Here, sir."

"Thank you for coming, Mr. Beaton," Deverill said before returning his focus to Heward. "This is the apothecary who sold belladonna to your physician the day Samuel Maitland died. For those who don't know, belladonna is a poison derived from the deadly nightshade plant, which can cause the heart to seize up—which is precisely how Maitland died." Deverill riveted his gaze on Heward. "We held off questioning your physician to avoid alerting you to our suspicions. But I expect with the right inducement, he would confess his role in supplying you the poison that killed Maitland."

The baron kept his mouth shut, his eyes blazing with pain and fury. When he remained stubbornly silent, Deverill glanced up again. "Mrs. Peeke?"

"Yes, Mr. Deverill?" the stout, ruddy-cheeked housekeeper replied as she stepped closer.

Leaving Heward on the ground, Deverill stood and wiped his bloody hands on the handkerchief Thorne handed him. "Mrs. Peeke, please tell us about the day Samuel Maitland died. Lord Heward paid him a visit, is that so?"

The elderly woman's mouth flattened. "Indeed. His lordship called on Mr. Maitland late that afternoon and brought him a bottle of brandy. Called it a peace offering, in fact."

"Why would he need a peace offering? Were they at war, Mrs. Peeke?"

"In a manner of speaking. The day before, Lord Heward and the master had argued something fierce. I was bringing tea and heard most of their quarrel."

"What did they quarrel about?" Deverill asked.

"Miss Maitland's recent betrothal to Lord Heward. The master called it off. He said he would rather her marry a chimney sweep than a man with no principles."

"Why did he consider Heward to have no principles?"

"Because he had learned that Lord Heward's ships were transporting slaves. Mr. Maitland was outraged, not only because slavery is illegal, but because he believed it a moral abomination."

"And what became of the brandy bottle, Mrs. Peeke?"

"It disappeared the next day, after Lord Heward came to pay his condolences at Mr. Maitland's sudden death. It was only when I noticed the bottle gone that I began to suspect his lordship might have taken it to hide the evidence."

Deverill returned his gaze to Lord Heward. "Is that what happened, Heward? Come, you have little to lose now by confessing."

When the baron merely glowered, Deverill frowned thoughtfully. "Would you like to hear my supposition about what happened? When Maitland discovered

you were illegally transporting slaves, he called off
the betrothal. But you were not about to let his
daughter's fortune slip through your fingers. So you
returned the next day with a bottle of poisoned
brandy, knowing Maitland's weakness for those particular spirits. He refused to accept your apology, but
it didn't matter since he drank your brandy—which
resulted in his immediate death. And later, you made
certain to eliminate the evidence."

Hearing Deverill's summation, Antonia could no
longer keep quiet.

"Is it true?" she demanded of Heward in a raw
voice. "Did you poison my father?"

"Of course not! It is all a lie, upon my word."

"Just as it was a lie that you ordered the murder of
that poor, innocent woman?" Antonia observed
scathingly. "We all know what your word is worth,
Lord Heward. You wanted my father dead so there
would be no one to stop you from wedding me. What
did you plan to do with me once I was your wife?
Murder me, too? Answer me, damn you!"

When the baron's jaw remained clenched tight,
Deverill glanced at the partially drawn bow and
arrow in Antonia's hands. "I believe I know how to
persuade him to answer. Antonia, how many arrows
did you bring?"

"A whole quiverful." She raised her bow slightly to
show the quiver hanging at her side.

"Then we will loosen his lordship's tongue by
shooting him one limb at a time."

The baron looked horrified, and even a few of their
audience—Lord Ranworth and Mrs. Peeke in particular—appeared uncomfortable with this unconventional method of persuasion.

Deverill spoke again. "You have seen her skill,

Heward. I advise you to tell the truth before she is compelled to use it."

His face contorted with fear as much as pain, but he remained mute.

"Antonia, you may shoot his left leg this time."

"No!" Heward cried when she took a menacing step closer. When she drew the bow, targeting his left leg, he suddenly capitulated. "All right! Damn and rot you!"

"What happened between you and Samuel Maitland?" Deverill asked again.

"Maitland called off our betrothal, as that woman said."

"So you returned the next day to poison him."

Heward squeezed his eyes shut. "Yes . . . I returned to poison him."

"*Why?*" The word that came from Antonia was agonized. "What did he ever do to you but be your friend?"

Heward's eyes blazed. "He claimed I was not fit to marry you. I, whose title goes back seven hundred years, was scolded by that lowbred upstart merchant—"

Blinded by grief and fury, Antonia drew back the arrow fully. Her wonderful father had been murdered by this . . . this treacherous scum. Shooting was too good for him and so was hanging. She wanted him drawn and quartered! But in lieu of that, her bow would suffice.

Rage filled her as she used all her might to stretch the bowstring taut while targeting Heward's heart.

The baron cringed, holding up his hands in a futile effort to ward off a deadly blow. "Keep her away from me! Don't let her kill me!"

In the tense silence, Deverill said softly, "Antonia."

"What?" she whispered on a hoarse sob.

"Don't release that arrow. It isn't worth it. Heward will be punished, I promise you."

"Not sufficiently."

"If you kill him, you might gain temporary satisfaction, but his peers won't forgive you. You're unlikely ever to find a husband from the noble ranks, which is what your father wished for you, remember?"

She blinked, her eyes stinging with tears. Deverill was talking of her matrimonial future when her heart was grieving?

"Antonia . . . please, just trust me."

At his gentle touch on her shoulder, she shuddered and heaved another little sob. Finally, she nodded. Easing the bowstring back to neutral, she wheeled abruptly and stumbled away, clenching her teeth to keep from weeping . . . or screaming.

She heard a collective sigh of relief from the spectators before Mrs. Peeke came up behind her and put a plump arm around her waist to lead her farther across the courtyard, away from the crowd.

Antonia bowed her head, wanting nothing more than to bury her face in the elderly servant's comforting shoulder and sob out her grief and guilt. But she forced herself to take long, shuddering breaths and strove valiantly for composure.

Behind her, she could hear snatches of the conversation that followed as the company discussed how to deal with Lord Heward and his five hirelings. The Runner, Horace Linch, intended to take his lordship into custody, but worried that his word alone might not suffice to guarantee the baron's imprisonment.

"I will need Madam Bruno and Mr. Deverill to accompany me to Bow Street to lay charges," Linch explained. "But it would be most helpful if Lord Wittington and Mr. Cochrane were to come also, since I must rouse a magistrate out of bed and persuade him to sign a warrant to imprison Lord Heward. Although . . . we could mayhap wait until morning, if it is too much of an imposition, Lord Wittington."

Wittington agreed with a sigh. "Might as well get it done tonight. I won't sleep a wink after all this excitement."

"What of Miss Maitland?" Deverill asked. "She has endured enough for one night."

"She and Mrs. Peeke are free to go," the Runner replied, "as is the apothecary, Mr. Beaton. But I will likely need to question them further at some later point."

"I will take the ladies home," Thorne said.

Macky chimed in. "Mr. Ryder and I will see our hedgebirds safely to Bow Street."

"Very good, sir," Linch said. "I would welcome your assistance."

Feeling marginally more composed by then, Antonia cast a searching glance over her shoulder to see Deverill quietly thanking his friends for their efforts on his behalf.

With a chuckle, Thorne clapped him on the back. "It's of no account, Dev. We're damned glad you came through this one unscathed."

"We are at that," Macky said cheerfully, while Ryder offered his slow, dangerous smile in agreement.

Macky and Ryder escorted the ruffians from the courtyard then, disappearing through the gate into the dark alley beyond. Following with Lord Wittington, Runner Linch guided a painfully limping Lord Heward before him. Phineas Cochrane and the apothecary went last, leaving the Earl of Ranworth with Deverill and Thorne.

Ordinarily proud and refined, Ranworth now looked somber and chastened. "I owe you my sincerest apologies, Mr. Deverill. I believed the scurrilous tales about you and thought you a murderer. But the accusations clearly had no merit. I plan to tell Lady Ranworth what transpired here, and you may be sure she will put the rumors to rest. No one is more certain to be believed than she."

"I don't doubt she will single-handedly rout my detractors if she chooses to," Deverill said with a faint smile.

"It is no more than you are owed, after we were taken in by that scheming Heward." Ranworth pumped Deverill's hand. "It is an honor to know you, sir." Giving a formal bow then, he took his leave.

When Deverill's glance shifted and found Antonia, Lord Thorne spoke up. "No doubt you would like a moment of privacy with Miss Maitland. Mrs. Peeke and I will await you in the carriage. Shall we, Mrs. Peeke?"

"Yes indeed, my lord," she replied, moving to accept his proffered arm.

Once the housekeeper had accompanied Thorne from the courtyard, Deverill crossed to Antonia.

Cautiously, he took the bow and arrow from her unresisting hands. "Perhaps I had best confiscate these before you do someone lethal damage."

Antonia did not appreciate his levity, for she was still trembling with rage and sorrow. Glaring up at Deverill, she dashed the tears from her cheeks. "I could damage *you* just now! You frightened me half to death, deliberately challenging Heward to kill you."

"My, you're a bloodthirsty wench tonight."

Her fists clenched at his teasing. "He would have shot you, you beast!"

Deverill smiled gently. "But you saved me, my fierce Amazon. And you needed to hear Heward's confession. If you hadn't, the question of your father's death would have forever haunted you."

Antonia squeezed her eyes shut, knowing Deverill was right. She had desperately needed the emotional satisfaction of wringing a confession from Heward.

Fresh tears welled in her eyes, while her throat burned. A small part of her had wanted Heward to be innocent. Her renewed grief was somehow harder to bear, knowing her wonderful father had given his life to protect her.

"It still will haunt me," she whispered. "He killed my *father*, Deverill."

"I know, love." Deverill drew her into his arms and held Antonia comfortingly as she forced back her sobs. "But he will pay for it now. In a scant few hours, Heward will be locked in Newgate Prison."

After a long moment, she regained a measure of control, but she kept her face pressed against Deverill's coat. "I suppose I should thank you for making me see what a true villain he is. I would have taken him for my husband if not for you." She shuddered. "Oh, God, what if I had wed that serpent? You saved me from a fate worse than death, Deverill."

"So now we're even, since you likely saved my life tonight. However, your choice of matrimonial candidates leaves something to be desired. I hope your next betrothed will be more trustworthy."

Antonia drew back to stare up at him, wondering how he could talk about her marriage prospects at a time like this. But then she realized why: Deverill was saying good-bye. Now that his innocence had been affirmed and Heward's guilt established, Deverill no longer had any need for her. The danger and uncertainty was over, and so was their affair. Their passion.

A savage pain clawed at her heart, a pain that only deepened when he reached up to brush a tear from her cheek with his thumb. "Now, go home and get some sleep, Antonia."

She wanted to protest. She wanted to cry and plead with him to reconsider. She wanted to tell Deverill of her stunning self-revelation tonight—that she loved him with all her heart. But she didn't think she could form a coherent argument at the moment after her emotions had suffered such turmoil.

In any event, this was not the appropriate time to press Deverill. He had just escaped death, and he had to deal with Heward and Bow Street, besides.

No, what she needed most was to be alone with her thoughts—so she could determine how to deal with her shocking insight.

Mutely, Antonia nodded and let Deverill escort her from the courtyard and along the dark alley to the front of the building. At the street, he bent to place a chaste kiss on her forehead before handing her into Thorne's town coach and walking away.

Inside the dim interior, Antonia leaned back wearily against the leather squabs, glad the carriage lamps had not been lit. She suddenly felt limp and drained after the tumult of the past few hours.

As if sensing her exhaustion, Mrs. Peeke patted her arm and pressed a handkerchief into her hand. "A mug of hot milk is just what you need, my dear," the housekeeper said bracingly, just as she'd done when Antonia was a girl.

Smiling faintly, Antonia murmured, "I will be

fine," and turned her head to stare out the coach window, evading Mrs. Peeke's solicitous cluckings and Thorne's shrewdly sympathetic gaze. She needed a little coddling just now, perhaps, but she wanted more to reach the privacy of her own home before she broke down in tears. She was mourning the loss of her father all over again.

Even more, she was mourning the likely loss of Deverill.

Antonia bit her trembling lip as she recalled the chaste, brotherly peck he had just given her. He hadn't even kissed her farewell when they were alone together, even though he'd had the chance. But Deverill was withdrawing from her for good, Antonia realized. He was making it simpler for them to part.

And why not? He was a free man. Free to walk out of her life without looking back. He had done his duty in protecting her, so now he could return to his own life, the one he had dedicated to the Guardians.

She was also free, Antonia reminded herself. Free to seek a husband from the ranks of the nobility, just as her father had always wished for her.

The damning truth was, however, she didn't want a nobleman for her husband.

She only wanted Deverill—and her realization might very well have come too late.

Twenty

Upon arriving home, Antonia turned her bow and quiver of arrows over to her butler and declined Mrs. Peeke's offer of warm milk after all.

"Would you mind if I went directly to bed?" she asked the housekeeper as they stood alone in the vast entrance hall after dismissing the stately butler and two waiting footmen for the night.

Mrs. Peeke clucked sympathetically. "Of course not, my dear. You must be worn to the bone after your worries these past few days. I am eager to seek my bed myself, if I do say so."

"Mrs. Peeke . . ." Antonia forestalled the servant with a light touch on her arm. "I can't thank you enough for what you did. If not for you, we never would have suspected about my father's death and I would now be married to Lord Heward."

The elderly woman shuddered. "God forbid. There's no telling what that terrible man would have done to you once he had his hands on your fortune. But he will get his just rewards now, thanks to Mr. Deverill."

"Yes," Antonia said in fervent agreement before

she turned toward the sweeping staircase. "Well, good night."

"Good night, my dear," Mrs. Peeke echoed. Then hesitating, she cleared her throat. "Miss Antonia? 'Tis none of my affair, of course, but I was hoping now that you are no longer betrothed . . . I mean, your father thought the world of Mr. Deverill, you know. I would be honored to call him 'master.' "

Antonia managed a faint smile at the housekeeper's not-so-veiled hint that she should marry Deverill. "Unfortunately, I imagine Mr. Deverill will be leaving England soon, now that he has rescued me and discharged the obligations of his conscience."

"Well, I for one will be right sorry to see him go," Mrs. Peeke said sadly.

It will be agony for me. Antonia couldn't stop the unbidden thought.

She took up the candle the butler had left for her and slowly mounted the stairs, noticing how quiet the mansion seemed. At this late hour, however, the rest of the servants were doubtless in bed asleep. And Miss Tottle, who regularly waited up for Antonia to return from whatever entertainments she had attended for the evening, had not yet arrived from Cornwall.

At the top of the stairs, Antonia headed toward her bedchamber. Then suddenly changing her mind, she instead made her way to the portrait gallery. Silently entering the hushed chamber, she set down her candle and settled in the chair before her parents' portraits, just as her father had done for so many years.

A huge, choking knot tightened in her chest as she gazed up at Samuel Maitland's image. It was small consolation that they had obtained justice for his murder. She missed him so terribly, even more now that she knew his senseless death could have been prevented.

"I am so sorry, Papa," Antonia whispered, her eyes blinded by scalding tears. "We were both fooled by Heward's appearance of nobility and honor."

A strangled laugh caught in her throat when she realized she was conversing with her late father exactly the way he had always done with his beloved late wife.

Her tears fell freely then. Antonia buried her face in her hands and gave way to heart-racking sobs.

Yet they were cleansing tears. Comforting and cathartic. After a long while, she sat up and fished in her pelisse pocket for the handkerchief Mrs. Peeke had given her.

She blew her nose and wiped her eyes and damp cheeks, then gazed deliberately up at her father's portrait. "We must have a talk, Papa. A *serious* talk."

Antonia hesitated, trying to formulate the words that had been building in her like an explosion for the past several weeks. "I know what you wanted for me, but I cannot do it. I cannot marry a nobleman."

The portraiturist had captured Samuel Maitland's likeness well—his bright red hair, his ruddy complexion, his bold demeanor—but Antonia had to rely on memory to summon to mind her father's booming voice and accent that betrayed his lower-class origins. She could just imagine, however, his blustering response to her pronouncement:

What do you mean, missy, you cannot marry a nobleman!

"Just what I said, Papa. I realize now what a dreadful mistake it would be. I would be utterly miserable in a marriage of convenience." *Especially now that I know what passion is. What love is.* "You see, Papa, I fell in love."

Her father made no answer but seemed to stare down from his portrait with a disapproving frown. Antonia wrung the damp handkerchief between her fingers as she tried to explain. "I understand why a noble marriage was your dream for me, but it isn't *my* dream, Papa. I've known that for some time now. Yet I realized something more tonight. Life is too short to forsake your dreams."

Swallowing the ache in her throat, she went on. "Mama was taken before her time, and so were you. And Deverill could have been killed tonight. *I* could die tomorrow and never know what it is to truly live. Deverill makes me feel truly alive, Papa—for the first time ever in my life. When I'm with him, I feel as if I could conquer the world. Perhaps that sounds foolish, but I can't give him up. If you knew how I felt about him . . ."

Antonia closed her eyes, remembering the terror in her heart earlier this evening when Deverill had faced death. She had known then how badly she had deceived herself. She loved Deverill. Utterly, wholly, completely. She no longer had any doubt.

She also knew that what she felt deep in her heart for him was the same immutable emotion her father had felt for her mother. The same yearning, the same joy.

Opening her eyes again, she gazed up at her father's image. "I want what you and Mama had. You had a wonderful marriage, even though you were a commoner and she a lady. I only want a chance for the same happiness you found. Deverill isn't titled, but he is a gentleman. And while he is estranged from his family, their consequence is significant."

The silence in the room was rife.

"I regret disappointing you," Antonia added softly. "Sincerely I do. But if you were still here, you would realize that acquiring a noble marriage isn't as important as love, as happiness. I could have convinced you of it in time, I'm certain. In truth, you had already changed your mind about Heward. Mrs. Peeke told me what you said . . . that you would rather me wed a chimney sweep than a man with no principles. Well, Deverill has principles, Papa. He is the best, most honorable, most wonderful man I know."

This time the portrait's silence didn't dismay her. Antonia smiled faintly, her calm growing; she was right to break her solemn vow to her father. "I believe you would not want me to put my promise above my heart. You would not ask that sacrifice of me if you knew how I felt. You wanted my happiness most— and my happiness lies with Deverill."

She would never be happy with anyone but Deverill, she knew that now.

She was not so confident, however, that Deverill could ever feel the same way about her. "I don't know if it is even possible to win his love, but I cannot let it end between us without at least trying."

She wanted Deverill for her husband, no one else. Her heart yearned for it. If she couldn't have him, well then, she would never marry. But there was a chance she could convince him to wed her, even if he couldn't love her.

"Deverill is not interested in love or marriage, he's made that very clear. He has dedicated his life to a cause and will let nothing interfere. But I cannot let that stop me from trying."

Rising, Antonia crossed to the portrait and pressed her fingers gently against the dried oils of her father's dear face. "I just wanted you to know, Papa. I don't know if you can hear me, but if you can . . . I would like your blessing."

Wiping her eyes once more as she turned away, Antonia picked up her candle and left the gallery, this time going to her bedchamber. Her mind was utterly lost in contemplation as she mechanically undressed and prepared for bed.

What was it Isabella had told her about winning the heart of an adventurer? That she needed to be as brave and daring and adventurous as he was? That she needed to prove herself his match?

She wanted more than anything to be Deverill's match.

Upon donning her nightshift, Antonia left the windows open against the warm summer night and blew out her candle, then climbed into bed, drawing up only a sheet. She was weary to the bone, yet she lay there wide-awake, her thoughts churning.

She wanted Deverill's admiration and respect—the same admiration and respect he had always willingly given her father. She wanted his love. Desperately.

Deverill might not love her now; indeed, he might never be able to. But she had to try to win him.

But how? What would make her worthy of his respect and love? What was the way to his heart?

He cared nothing for her fortune, she knew, since he had one of his own. Indeed, she had only one asset that might attract his interest. Her shipping company. Deverill had not wanted to manage the firm himself, but what if she used it to champion his endeavors?

She could show Deverill that she was wholly committed to his cause. To the Guardians' cause. That as his wife, she could be his helpmate rather than an impediment. If he had dedicated his life to saving others, then she would do the same.

She had always yearned to break free of the stifling dictums that society ordained for her gender and social station, and this was her chance. She had no desire to formally join the Guardians—she wouldn't have the nerves or the skills or the passion for it. But she could contribute in her own way. She could take her father's place as a patron of their order. Papa would have approved of such a course, she knew it.

She would have to write Sir Gawain at once to ask how she could help. Better yet, she could visit Cyrene. If Deverill left England for home, it would provide her an excuse to follow him.

If all else failed, Antonia thought, staring into the darkness, she could always hire Deverill's services to protect Maitland ships. There were *some* advantages to being an heiress, after all. She would have to pay a call on Phineas Cochrane in the morning, to learn exactly what options were open to her. . . .

Yet that couldn't be her sole plan. There had to be something more she could do to win Deverill's love.

Perhaps, Antonia decided with a surge of renewed optimism, her second order of business in the morning should be to visit her friend Emily to ask her advice. Emily was much better versed in *affaires des coeurs* than she was—and would know better how to induce a man to surrender his heart.

Antonia drew a steadying breath, feeling as if she were girding her loins for battle. Deverill had seen her bent on seduction once before, but this time the stakes were far higher. She wanted more than his passion. She wanted his heart.

Somehow she would make him love her.

Her own heart lighter for the first time in days, Antonia shut her eyes and settled down among the pillows to sleep. Deverill might consider his obligations toward her satisfied, but he had not seen the last of her yet. Not by a long shot.

Deverill slept late the following morning, for it had been a long night at Bow Street, seeing Baron Heward safely incarcerated in Newgate and making certain the charges against his own good name had been expunged. It was nearly dawn before he returned to Macky's lodgings, and nearly noon before he awoke.

He lay there for a time, savoring his feeling of elation. For the first time in weeks, he was a free man. Free to make choices. Free to decide about his future.

He knew what he wanted: Antonia.

He couldn't break his vow to himself. He could never give up his personal mission. And perhaps his penance would never truly be satisfied. But he couldn't lose her.

Antonia was more precious to him than the richest pirate treasure. More precious than his own life. And he could no longer deny the truth: that he hungered for an existence not driven solely by duty and sacrifice. One with love and warmth and laughter . . . perhaps children.

He had a vivid image of Antonia swollen with his child, her bright eyes tender with love. The vision made him ache inside.

Whether or not they would ever have children, however, he wanted a future with her. And perhaps he could have one. Just possibly Antonia was right—that he had punished himself long enough. If so, then he could allow himself to reach for happiness. . . . Happiness with her.

Deverill shut his eyes, a burgeoning hope welling inside him.

Of course, he first had to convince her to marry him. *And then?* Then he would do his damnedest to win her love.

Preparing to call on Antonia, Deverill was in the middle of shaving when he received an unexpected caller of his own: Phineas Cochrane.

Admitted by Macky's manservant, the barrister was asked to wait in the sitting room. When Deverill finished dressing and joined him, Cochrane rose and offered a hearty greeting and handshake.

Deverill noted that the elder man looked bleary-eyed after being up most of the night, yet his demeanor was as cheerful and bright as the sunny summer morning when he expressed satisfaction that events had turned out so well last evening.

"But I am certain you are wondering the purpose of my call," the barrister said once they were seated, "so I will come straight to the point. I am here on a commission for my client, Miss Maitland."

"Yes?" Deverill prodded politely.

"Miss Maitland feels that she owes you a debt of gratitude, Mr. Deverill, and wishes to express her appreciation for your services to her. Thus, she intends to sign over to you controlling interest of Maitland Shipping. Half the company, plus one share."

Deverill felt himself stiffen. Whatever he had expected from Antonia, this was not it.

"You do not look pleased, sir," Cochrane observed, scrutinizing him shrewdly.

"Because I am not," Deverill replied. Puzzlement and suspicion were his first reactions. He could think of only two reasons why Antonia wished to turn over nearly half her vast fortune to him. Either this was her way of ending any moral obligation to him, so she would no longer be in his debt for coming to her rescue. Or she still wanted him to assume the directorship of her company.

"I could not possibly accept such a generous gift," Deverill said firmly. "Nor do I want or expect Miss Maitland's gratitude."

"It is not solely gratitude, I assure you. She is convinced that her father would have wanted you to have command of his empire, to use as you see fit."

Deverill's jaw tightened. He didn't want Antonia's blasted shipping empire. He wanted *her*.

"Thank you for coming, Mr. Cochrane, but I think I must have a talk with Miss Maitland before we pursue this matter any further."

After another few moments of stressing the same reply, he courteously ushered the barrister from the apartments. Yet no sooner had Cochrane left than Deverill received an even more surprising visitor: Emily, Lady Sudbury.

The young countess sailed into the sitting room, presented her fingers to Deverill to be kissed, and smiled charmingly up at him.

"I know it is not at all proper to visit a bachelor's lodgings, Mr. Deverill, but my maid is waiting out in the corridor, and I will only be a moment. You see, I am worried about Antonia."

Deverill raised an eyebrow but kept his tone dispassionate when he responded. "May I be so bold as to ask why, Lady Sudbury?"

"Because she is considering accepting a proposal from her former suitor, Lord Fenton, and it would be a *highly* unsuitable match. Fenton is a marquess and heir to a dukedom, true, and quite handsome in a Byronic sort of way. But he is the veriest coxcomb, with scarcely a brain in his head, and not a feather to fly with. He is clearly after Antonia for her fortune—which would not be so lamentable, considering how old and distinguished his title is, except that his inane witticisms would drive her mad within a fortnight of the wedding."

Deverill felt his blood run cold, even though he tried not to show it. He knew Fenton—a foppish young whelp who was barely Antonia's age. But it seemed strange that Lady Sudbury would have come to *him* with her complaints. "So why are you telling me this, my lady?"

"Why? Because I want you to stop her from throwing away her life, of course! Please, Mr. Deverill, you must do *something*."

"What would you have me do?"

"I don't know! But you are reputed to be a man of inventiveness and action. I have every faith you will think of a plan. You might even begin this afternoon. Antonia will be driving with Lord Fenton in the park at five."

A muscle working in his jaw, Deverill turned his gaze to the window, where sunlight streamed in, the golden warmth a stark contrast to the chill of panic he was feeling.

"No need to show me out, Mr. Deverill," Lady Sudbury said pleasantly. "I can manage."

He scarcely heard her let herself out. Instead, Deverill stood there a long moment, a scowl on his face as he contemplated his next action.

His first inclination was to wring Antonia's slender neck for making yet another foolish choice of bridegrooms. His second was to abduct her again so she couldn't complete her scheme to land a nobleman for her husband.

Yet one way or another, Deverill vowed, he intended to stop her from wedding that titled fop—or anyone else but himself.

Although many of the Quality had left London and repaired to their country estates for the summer, Hyde Park at the fashionable hour of five was still the place to see and be seen. On this lovely afternoon, the wide graveled avenue called Rotten Row was congested with elegant equipages and dashing riders and handsomely garbed pedestrians, all pausing to gossip and preen and exchange social niceties.

Ensconced in Lord Fenton's bright yellow, high-perch phaeton, Antonia valiantly endured the marquess's inane chatter while frequently biting her tongue to keep from replying unkindly. Never, however, had she been so keenly aware of how *insipid* this entire aspect of her life was.

No wonder Deverill held such amused disdain for society and all its pretensions. Compared to his noble cause of the Guardians, the genteel observances of the ton seemed so shallow and pointless, Antonia admitted.

But Emily had insisted that she accept Fenton's invitation for a drive this afternoon—in order to show the ton that she was not in the least crushed by Heward's treachery—while Emily set her mind to the problem of how Antonia could win Deverill's heart.

At the moment, the only thing on Antonia's mind was how she might escape Fenton's company. That, and how much she would rather be with Deverill—

Just then her heart gave a fierce leap, for she had suddenly spied Deverill's tall, powerful form on horseback among the distant throng, as if she had somehow conjured his presence. He was heading directly toward her, riding through the park at an alarming rate considering how crowded the Row was, sending unwary strollers scurrying from his determined path.

When he reached Fenton's phaeton, Deverill abruptly halted his horse and regarded Antonia with dispassion. He caused her heart rate to skyrocket, however, when he reached out without warning and hauled her onto the front of his saddle.

Lord Fenton loudly voiced his objections—"I say now, sirrah!"—and stood up in protest, which unfortunately startled his high-strung pair of bays. Flung back into his seat when the carriage lunged forward, the young nobleman barely maintained his precarious balance enough to keep from toppling to the ground.

Ignoring both the flustered fop's plight and the spectators' gaping shock, Deverill settled Antonia sideways before him and spurred his horse off the gravel path and into a brisk canter, heading toward the Serpentine Lake in the distance. Forced to cling to his neck to keep from slipping, Antonia was uncertain whether she was more indignant or elated that Deverill was acting like a pirate, sweeping her up in his arms and carrying her off without so much as a by-your-leave.

Still not speaking, he rode swiftly across a grassy stretch to the lake's edge, where he plunged his mount behind a glade of willows so that he and his "captive" were shielded from prying eyes. Only then did Deverill rein to a stop and sit staring down at her, his expression one of grim satisfaction.

Breathless, her heart beating wildly, Antonia stared back at him, trying to read his beautiful eyes. "I suppose you mean to tell me why you are behaving like a barbarian," she finally managed to say unsteadily.

"I am preventing you from making another disastrous mistake," he retorted, his tone wholly unrepentant. "You won't be marrying that fop."

"No?" Antonia raised a haughty eyebrow. "Pray, why not?"

"Because you will marry me."

Hope soaring inside her, she carefully removed her arms from around Deverill's neck and slid down from the saddle. Compelling her trembling limbs to move, she took several steps along the bank before turning back to him. "You expect me to marry you? Why?"

"Because I love you, vixen. And I'm damned sure I can't live without you."

"You *love* me?" Antonia echoed hoarsely, her eyes going wide.

"Yes, curse it, I love you. And I want you for my wife. You had best resign yourself, Antonia, since I won't brook your refusal this time."

When she stared up at him mutely in heart-swelling wonder, Deverill held her gaze and swung slowly down from his mount. Yet he kept his distance, pausing there by the water's edge, holding the reins in his gloved fingers.

"I know you're determined to wed a nobleman to fulfill your promise to your father," Deverill began gruffly, "but he was wrong to ask it of you. A man's worth is not in a title. Heward proved that quite thoroughly. And I think your father realized it in the end. He knew that honor and principles were more important than any lineage."

"I agree," Antonia murmured. "I came to the same conclusion myself last night."

Watching her, Deverill twisted the reins in his

hands. "If you're set on maintaining your vaunted place in society, I'll do whatever I must to see you remain there. I'll even reconcile with my family, if that would help."

He looked endearingly awkward; she had never seen Deverill so uncertain. It made her heart melt, while tears gathered hotly behind her eyes.

Antonia shook her head. "It would not help, Deverill. I don't care about my place in society the way I once did."

A muscle worked in his jaw. "Well, you will have to settle for me, because I am not giving you up. You *will* marry me, Antonia, whether you want to or not."

Too overjoyed to speak, she forcibly kept herself from running to Deverill and throwing herself into his arms.

"I believe," he continued more intensely, "I could have persuaded your father to accept me, had he lived. The Treylayne name is centuries old, and I actually have noble blood in my veins. And our children would have noble blood as well."

"Our children?" That made her jaw go slack. "You want to have children?"

Deverill's mouth slanted in a humorless smile. "Yes, I want to have children, princess—as long as you are their mother."

Evidently he'd had enough of her silence, though, for he released the reins and closed the distance to her, pulling Antonia into his arms. His whisper was a harsh rasp as he demanded, "Do you think I'll ever give you up? Never. I want you in my life, Antonia. In my bed, at my side, in my heart."

He gave her no chance to reply before bringing his mouth down hard on hers. He kissed her with stunning effect, making her blood sizzle and her head spin.

When finally he lifted his head, his eyes were blazing. "You can't lie and tell me you don't feel that," Deverill said, his voice rough and husky with desire.

Dazed, Antonia looked up at him through a mist of dreamy tears. "Oh, no . . . I most assuredly felt that."

"Then you will marry me?"

"Yes . . . I will marry you, Deverill."

He stared down at her, his gaze searching, as if he didn't quite trust her answer. "Good," he said at last. "I was prepared for another battle royal. And if you wouldn't agree, I intended to take a page from Apollo's book."

"What book?"

"Did you ever hear the legend of our Isle of Cyrene? Apollo fell in love at first sight with the nymph Cyrene, and when she spurned him, he created an island for her and kept her imprisoned there until she came to love him in return. So you see, sweeting, I'm not letting you go until you fall in love with me."

A joyous smile spread slowly across her lips. "I already love you, Deverill. I have for some time, even if I would never let myself admit it. And I realized last night that I very much want to be your wife."

Deverill stared for another moment before muttering, "Thank God!" and bringing his mouth crashing down on hers again. He stunned Antonia with another long, fierce kiss—until suddenly he broke off and grasped her shoulders to hold her away. "Then why in hell were you driving here in the park with that fribble?"

"Because my friend Emily insisted— So *that* was her scheme." Antonia flushed as she gazed up at Deverill. "Now that I think of it, I expect Emily was trying to make you jealous, so you would be incited to act. When I told her all that had happened during the past month—that you had abducted me in order to protect me from Heward—she was delighted. She thought it terribly romantic, in fact. And when I confessed that I was in love with you, she said she would contrive a way to force you to declare yourself."

A frown darkened Deverill's features. "She led me to believe you had your matrimonial sights on Lord Fenton. She could simply have told me that you loved me."

"Perhaps . . . but I feared you didn't reciprocate my feelings. Emily said that I should somehow induce you to propose again. Then once I was your wife, I would have the time to try and make you fall in love with me."

Deverill's arms tightened around her waist. "I love you now, vixen."

"But I didn't know that this morning. Emily thought you might care for me. She called on you today specifically to see your reaction for herself . . . to judge how deeply your affections were involved. After observing you, she gave me reason to hope—but I didn't dare let myself dream you already loved me."

"Well, you can lay your fears to rest."

"I realize that now." Antonia flashed Deverill a brilliant smile. "Your response was all I could have wished for." Reaching up, she wrapped her arms around Deverill's neck. "You not only saved me from that terrible bore, you declared your intentions in a quite satisfying, piratical manner. But you do realize that a good number of the ton witnessed my abduction? I suspect I am thoroughly compromised. You will have to wed me now, Deverill."

He smiled then, a slow, triumphant smile of such warmth and blatant sensual appeal, it made her breath catch. "Which was precisely my intention, sweeting," he admitted as he loosened the pins of her chip-straw hat and tossed it to the ground.

Antonia wrinkled her nose defiantly at him. "Well, your strategy worked. But if it hadn't, I was considering a more drastic action myself."

"Oh?"

She threaded her fingers through the gold sun-streaks in his hair. "As a last resort, I meant to create a scandal by getting caught in your bed. I knew from experience that you were honorable enough to propose."

A wicked light entered Deverill's eyes as he tightened his arms around Antonia again. "You were that certain of me?"

"No, Deverill." Her levity faded. "That is the whole point. I wasn't certain of you in the least. Isabella told me that I needed to prove myself your match, but I have been racking my brain to think of how."

Deverill grinned. "You're more than a match for me, love. You always have been. Nothing in my life has ever compared to you. How many women do you know who would shoot their former betrothed in order to save my life?"

Antonia felt her breath falter at his tender expression; the way Deverill was looking at her made her heart hurt. "You truly do love me, don't you," she said in wonder.

"Absolutely and completely." Deverill gave a dry

chuckle. "It was obvious to Macky as soon as he saw us together. And probably to Thorne as well."

"I think Sir Gawain wanted us to marry," she said thoughtfully. "I know Isabella did, since she told me outright. As for my father . . ." Antonia gazed solemnly up at Deverill. "I believe Papa would have wished it, too. He would want to see me this blissfully happy, even if you don't have a title. And as you said, his grandchildren will have blue blood. His spirit will just have to be content with that."

Deverill searched her face intently. "What about you, Antonia? Are you certain that marrying me is what you want?"

Her eyes blurred again. "I have never been more certain of anything in my life. It took me a while, but I finally realized that I couldn't throw away this chance for love simply to fulfill my father's dreams."

"Thank God," Deverill breathed again as he drew her close and buried his mouth in her hair.

Her arms entwined about his neck, Antonia stood with her face pressed against his strong shoulder, awe whispering through her at the joy of holding him.

She knew the truth now. She wanted far, far more than a marriage of convenience. She yearned for a marriage of true love. Deverill's love. The fierceness of her need frightened her.

"I love you so much, Deverill," she murmured with a ragged sigh.

At her confession, he shifted his head to kiss her again, smothering her with a hungry, consuming tenderness. When finally he left off, he gave a groan. "God, I would give my right arm to be able to make love to you right here."

Smiling a bit provocatively, Antonia glanced behind her through the willow branches, where she could see the throng milling about the park. "Not here, Deverill. It would be too scandalous, even for you."

"Very well. We can be married by special license tomorrow—and then I intend to take you to bed for a week." When Antonia looked at him quizzically, Deverill explained. "After your friends visited me today, I spent my time procuring a special license so we wouldn't have to wait three weeks for the banns to be called. You are wedding me tomorrow, whether you like it or not."

Her mouth curved with satisfaction at his impatience, yet she shook her head. Regretfully extricating herself from his embrace, Antonia stepped back in order to put a safer distance between them. "I cannot marry you tomorrow, Deverill. At the very least we must wait until Mildred Tottle arrives from Cornwall. She would be terribly hurt if she missed my wedding, she has waited for so long to see me married. And doubtless Emily will want to help plan a ball or a wedding breakfast or some such celebration. And we haven't discussed a thing about what happens afterward."

"What do you mean, afterward?"

"I would like to visit Cyrene for our wedding trip."

"That can be arranged."

"And we must decide where we would live."

Deverill frowned slightly. "We can live here in England if you like. Sir Gawain won't be pleased, but I can carry out my work from here."

"What if I don't want to live in England? What if I want to live on Cyrene?"

"I thought you didn't want to leave your father's shipping empire."

"If you find a reliable candidate to take over as director as you promised, the company will be in good hands."

The change of subjects made Deverill pause. "Which reminds me . . . what the devil did you mean, sending Cochrane to turn over half your company to me?"

"I thought," Antonia responded calmly, "that you could use my ships to advance your cause. I considered writing to Sir Gawain to ask him how I could arrange it, but then realized it would take too long . . . that you might leave England long before I could receive his answer. So this morning I decided to just give you controlling interest in the company, so you would have all its resources at your disposal and could act as you saw fit. Phineas said it could be done. I couldn't tell him about the Guardians, of course, but I thought you would be pleased to have control."

"Then your gift wasn't a bribe to persuade me to become director?"

Antonia smiled at his suspicious look. "No, Deverill. I only want to help you pursue your cause. I want to be your life's mate in every way. I only hope I can earn the right."

"No, sweeting, I'm the one who will have to work to deserve you."

Drawing her into his embrace again, Deverill brushed his thumb over her lower lip. Antonia was the perfect mate for him. With her by his side, he could still keep his sworn vow to himself. She understood his calling, understood that he had dedicated his life to the Guardians' cause. And she would never try to change that. Instead, she would only support and abet him.

What was more, she satisfied a burning need in him. Filled the empty ache inside him as only she could. Antonia made him feel complete, as if she were the missing part of him.

She'd burrowed under his skin and found her way unerringly into his heart.

"You *are* my life's mate, Antonia," Deverill said softly. "If I couldn't have you, my heart might as well stop beating. You wouldn't leave me to such a terrible fate, would you?"

"Never, my love," she whispered, raising her smiling lips again for his tender kiss.

Epilogue ❧

A hushed silence fell over the crowd, the spectators holding their collective breaths as Antonia sighted the straw boss mounted on the immense stone wall of Olwen Castle a hundred yards distant. She had one arrow left to shoot, the last of the contest against her sole remaining opponent, the highly skilled Earl of Hawkhurst.

She was vying to be crowned Cyrene's archery champion for the year. Currently she had four points less than Hawk, so a gold bull's-eye would garner her the win.

Deverill held his own breath as he watched Antonia carefully draw the bowstring. He needn't have worried, however. When she released the arrow, it flew the distance and struck the target dead center, splitting the shaft of Hawk's arrow down the middle.

Loud cheers and applause greeted the remarkable feat, along with exclamations of amazement and dismay. Many in the crowd were clearly astounded that the Earl of Hawkhurst had pitted his vaunted skill against a woman and lost—and were also disappointed, since despite his intentional remoteness, Hawk was a favorite of the island, long admired for his feats of athleticism and horsemanship.

There was nothing aloof or withdrawn about the earl's manner just now when he congratulated Antonia with an expansive bow and a light kiss on her cheek.

"I stand defeated," Hawk conceded, his tone good-natured. "Although it is some small consolation to be bested by such an excellent marksman."

A becoming flush colored Antonia's cheeks as she gazed up at the tall, jet-haired earl. Deverill felt an instinctive surge of possessiveness, seeing his beautiful wife lauded by the island's most eligible nobleman. Yet he knew with utter confidence that he had no reason to be jealous of his friend. Antonia had given him her heart, wholly and completely.

When other well-wishers surrounded her, offering more acclamation and praise, Deverill stood watching her, feeling his own heart beat in his throat. Her glorious auburn hair was pulled back sedately in a sleek chignon, but enticing little tendrils framed her face, while her skin glowed with warm incandescence in the golden afternoon sunlight.

The word *glowing* described Antonia perfectly—and the warmth inside him, as well. He continued to be amazed at his extraordinary good fortune at finding the one woman in the world meant for him. Antonia was the perfect match for him—his soul mate. She made every breath feel like his first.

And for the first time in his life, he knew true contentment. He'd had exciting adventures and satisfying victories aplenty, but never this soul-deep happiness that he'd found with Antonia.

Just then she looked about her, as if searching for someone. When her gaze found him, she smiled radiantly, and Deverill felt his heart turn over.

Stepping forward, he joined the crowd around Antonia, giving her a congratulatory kiss and clapping his friend Hawk on the back in sympathy. "My condolences, old son. But I warned you not to challenge her."

"So you did." Hawk's grin was rueful. "I bow to your lovely wife's superior skills, at least until a rematch next year."

Deverill slid an arm around Antonia's waist. "A stunning victory, love. Although it might have ended differently if you had competed on horseback. Hawk is a born centaur."

Antonia regarded the earl with sudden keen interest. "I would very much like to become a better archer on horseback. Perhaps you might be willing to teach me sometime, my lord?"

"I would be honored, Mrs. Deverill," Hawk said genially.

Deverill groaned, realizing he should never have brought up the subject, but Antonia and Hawk smiled at each other in complete accord.

Lady Isabella approached her then, accompanied by Sir Gawain Olwen. Both embraced Antonia warmly, and Deverill stepped back to allow her to accept further congratulations.

Sir Gawain was hosting this major event of the harvest festival on the grounds of Olwen Castle. The afternoon was dedicated to games and races and contests, but a feast would begin soon, followed by dancing and musical entertainments, with bonfires lit after nightfall. An immense crowd of islanders was in attendance, and so was Deverill's crew, including

Captain Lloyd and the wiry Fletcher Shortall, who was making great inroads in the barrels of ale provided.

Alex Ryder had remained in England to pursue his own personal affairs, but many of Deverill's fellow Guardians were here, including Caro and Max Leighton. He joined Caro and Max now as he waited for Antonia to finish, content to allow his wife to bask in her victory.

The past two months had been supremely fulfilling for them both, Deverill reflected. As soon as Miss Tottle arrived from Cornwall, he and Antonia had been married by special license and, shortly afterward, embarked on a wedding tour. Since the risk of war was blessedly entirely over, he'd taken her to visit France and Portugal and Spain, and discovered new wonders and delights through Antonia's fresh eyes.

After a month at sea, Deverill had brought his new bride home tó Cyrene, to live in his manor house on the eastern shore of the island. Next month, they would return to England to testify at Baron Heward's trial by the House of Lords, but until then, Deverill intended to remain here because Sir Gawain needed him.

He'd sailed twice on missions in the past three weeks, but returned as swiftly as he was able—a first in Deverill's experience. For him, home had always been the deck of a ship, but after taking Antonia to wife, he'd willingly begun sinking deep roots on dry land.

As for Antonia, she'd been warmly embraced by the islanders, and not merely because Lady Isabella had paved her way. Cyrene had its own diminutive Beau Monde, yet the island's social arbiters were far less strict than the British ton. It helped that Antonia was an heiress and had moved in the center of London's fashionable set for years, but it was her own qualities—her charm and wit and beauty—that made her fawned over and universally admired.

Cyrene seemed the perfect place for her, since the islanders were fairly tolerant of ambitious females. Possibly because Caro Leighton had long been their example. Not only was Caro a healer, but for years she'd assisted the island doctor in his medical practice, in addition to being one of the few women Guardians and a skilled swordsman.

When Antonia finally joined them, Caro first complimented her on her skill and then asked her for archery lessons. "For Max insists I must cut back on my fencing practice, now that I am increasing. Honestly," Caro complained with a soft laugh, "what is it about the prospect of becoming a new father that turns a man into an overbearing dictator?"

Putting a protective arm around Caro's shoulders, Max smiled blandly. "The terrifying potential that his wife and child could come to harm—that is what, my love. The realization can instantly transform any man into a trembling coward."

Yet Leighton was certainly no coward, Deverill thought with amusement. The tall, raven-haired former cavalry officer had spent his distinguished military career battling Napoleon's forces before joining the Guardians last year. But Caro was now expecting their first child, although as yet her stomach showed little trace of roundness beneath her empire-waist gown.

Deverill watched as Max and Caro shared a look of love that was so painfully tender, it reminded him of his feelings for his own wife.

Taking Antonia's hand, Deverill murmured for her

ears alone, "We can partake of the feast now, sweetheart, but be warned, I mean to steal you away before it grows dark. We are newly wedded after all, and our friends will understand if we leave early."

The revelry would last long into the night, yet Deverill was selfish enough to want Antonia all to himself . . . not just for tonight but for all their nights to come. He suspected he would still feel that way about her when he was old and gray and too decrepit even to make love to her.

The smile Antonia offered him suggested that she wholeheartedly agreed with his plan.

It was nearing sunset by the time they had gorged themselves on the delicious fare, danced countless numbers of sets, and said their farewells. Deverill drove his phaeton himself, preferring privacy for the carriage ride home.

Antonia sat next to him, her head resting contentedly on his shoulder as they wound their way through Cyrene's fertile valleys ripe with vineyards and olive groves and orchards. When they began the climb into the eastern foothills, they could see the sun slowly sinking toward the blue horizon to their left, setting the sky and sea afire with glorious crimsons and purples and golds.

Antonia gave a dreamy, satisfied sigh. "I do so appreciate how welcome your fellow Guardians have made me feel. I never expected to be a part of something so special."

Upon their marriage, Deverill had made her privy to the remarkable tale of the order's inception . . . how the Guardians of the Sword had been formed more than a thousand years before by a handful of Britain's most legendary warriors—outcasts who had found exile here. And how the order was now run by their descendants and operated mainly across Europe, with the goal of fighting tyranny and injustice.

"I especially admire Caro," Antonia added. "She is an extraordinary woman."

Deverill took her hand and dropped a hot kiss on her palm. "You are rather extraordinary yourself, princess."

She brushed off his compliment with a disbelieving laugh, which made him smile. Antonia had little idea how remarkable she was. How rare. How wonderful. She was as passionate and intense about her life endeavors as he was, and her love was just as fierce.

He was a very lucky man, Deverill knew. And Antonia professed to be just as blissfully happy in their marriage.

Deverill had hired a new director for the company, but she had become much more involved in the intricate workings of her vast empire. There was no reason she shouldn't now, since here on Cyrene, she wouldn't be condemned for using her mind or for engaging in masculine pursuits or for increasing her wealth with industrial ventures.

To satisfy her burning desire to learn, Deverill was teaching her all the things her father had never permitted her even to observe, so that she could supervise her director herself if she chose to.

At the very least Antonia intended to review the account books quarterly. And she was determined to invest her profits wisely in new projects, particularly steam, since Deverill believed that steam was the way of the future.

They had brought her father's maps from the Map Room to Cyrene. Antonia regularly pored over them, not merely to understand the routes her ships took and to plan her next adventure with Deverill, but as a way of remembering her late father. Additionally, they'd hung her parents' portraits in a place of honor in the drawing room, to keep their memory alive.

Antonia seemed quite pleased with his home. It was fortunate, Deverill reflected, that he'd built the manor house on the coast, on a bluff overlooking the Mediterranean, since she couldn't get enough of the sea. She never tired of viewing the scenic splendor of the cove below, with its vivid waters of blue and turquoise and aquamarine. And she was becoming such an excellent swimmer that he'd started to wonder if she might be part mermaid.

The sky was darkening by the time they turned onto the drive that led home. The elegant two-story villa was constructed in the Spanish style—whitewashed exterior with red-tiled roof—wrapped by veranda above and landscaped gardens of bougainvillaea and rhododendrons and geraniums below. Beyond the house and gardens stretched the vast, shimmering Mediterranean, which had shaded now to midnight blue.

When they reached the stables, Deverill relinquished the carriage and pair to his groom and escorted Antonia inside the manor and up to their bedchamber. Through the French doors, a full moon could be seen rising over the ocean, creating a vista of serene enchantment.

Of one accord, they began changing their attire. They regularly took nightly walks on the beach, which often ended with them making love under the stars, since Antonia thought there was something magical about the sand and the sea at night, and Deverill thought there was something magical about *her*.

She donned a simple muslin gown, while Deverill

wore only breeches. They both went barefoot. The soles of her feet were becoming tougher, so she could now manage the shingles and occasional rough rocks that strewed the cove.

The moon was bright enough to light their way as they carefully descended the steps cut into the bluffs to the beach. A soft, fresh breeze blew off the water, yet the evening was still warm enough for them to swim.

Antonia went straight to the waves. Immersing herself ankle deep, she stood gazing dreamily out at the sea, all silver and shimmering. Deverill followed, slipping his arms around her waist from behind and resting his chin on her head.

"Deverill, I have something to tell you," she said finally over the rhythmic murmur of the surf.

Tenderly, he touched his lips to her hair, lightly kissing the shining fall of moonlit flame. "What is it, vixen?"

"Would you be disappointed if you soon became a father yourself?"

Deverill went very still, trying to comprehend what Antonia was asking. His hands grasping her shoulders, he spun her to face him. "A father?"

"Last week when you were away . . . I began to feel nauseated in the mornings. I thought I might be becoming ill, but when I told Caro of my symptoms, she suspected the cause and insisted on examining me. She's certain I am with child." Pausing, Antonia searched his face. "You aren't disappointed, are you?"

Deverill felt the surprise on his features alter to awe and wonder. "Of course I'm not disappointed! I couldn't be more elated!"

He threw back his head and laughed before suddenly lifting Antonia by the waist and whirling her around.

She was laughing herself when they finally collapsed onto the wet sand, sprawling together with Deverill partially on top.

Wrapping her arms about his neck, Antonia gazed up at him with a smug smile, evidently satisfied with his response. "I hoped you would be pleased, but I wasn't certain."

"It is merely unexpected, that's all."

"Well, we did stop using the sponges, you know."

"So we did."

Antonia's gaze softened. "Caro told me that the new child growing inside her was conceived after the battle of Waterloo. She said it had been a celebration of life for them, in the face of such terrible devastation. I think our child must be a celebration of sorts. We're embarking on a new adventure together."

"Children are certainly an adventure," Deverill said with conviction. "But you've always been an adventuress at heart, my love."

"True . . . although it took you to free me. I haven't thanked you for that recently, have I?"

When she raised her mouth to his, Deverill returned her kiss fiercely, until they were both breathless and aroused.

Antonia, however, was the first to break off as she pushed at his shoulders. "I have one stipulation, Deverill. You will *not* become an overbearing dictator, as Caro says Max has become."

He grinned down at her. "We shall see."

She playfully punched his shoulder, which made Deverill yelp and grab her hands to hold them over her head. This was the spirited, fighting Antonia he treasured so dearly. They would doubtless battle over her health and welfare, among many other things during the course of their lives together, just as they would always make love with a primal blaze of passion.

The fire between them would never burn tamely, but he wouldn't have it any other way.

No sooner did Deverill have that thought than Antonia pushed him onto his back and climbed on top of him, straddling his hips and pinning his arms above his head.

With a provocative smile then, she released him and slowly tugged down her bodice so that her breasts spilled free in the moonlight.

She was utterly wild and glorious, Deverill thought, feeling dazed by her beauty.

The next moment she bent and pressed her lips against his bare chest, nipping at his flesh while her fingers unerringly found the front buttons of his breeches.

"Insatiable wench," he muttered as she freed his swollen member and curled her fingers greedily around the thick length.

"*Queen,*" she responded firmly. "I am your queen, remember, husband?"

"Very well, my queen. Feel free to have your wicked way with me."

His own grin was so wicked, his eyes so alight with laughter, that Antonia felt her breath falter. Deverill was the bold adventurer whose smile could govern the rhythm of her heart. She gazed back at him, suddenly wrenched with an exquisite longing.

No longer playful, she reached down and curled her fingers in his thick, sun-streaked, satiny hair.

"I love you, Deverill," she whispered, her voice low and husky as her caresses moved lower.

Her hands slid against the smooth skin of his neck, along the quivering, powerful muscles of his shoulders. He was incredibly beautiful. She loved his strong, bronzed, hard-muscled shoulders. She loved his broad chest, scars and all. She loved everything about him. She loved touching him and kissing him and arousing him. . . .

She bent down to him again, her mouth once more finding his chest. "I love you everywhere," she murmured against his hot skin.

He breathed in sharply when her tongue touched a savage scar, tenderly bathing it.

"Oh, God, siren," he rasped, his deep, rich voice vibrating through her.

Dragging her body up to him, he devoured her mouth again, his kiss wild and deep. In only moments she was moaning. She was hot and feverish, and only he could satisfy the burning need inside her.

Yet Deverill clearly understood her need. Easing her off him, he shifted Antonia onto her back and raised her muslin skirts before moving over her and settling his hard weight into the cradle of her thighs.

Taking full control of their lovemaking, he worshipped her slowly with his hands and mouth. Antonia felt the raw hunger in his touch, the depths of his naked desire, even before he finally he entered her, filling her completely with his fierce, strong tenderness.

"I love you, Antonia." His voice was a harsh whisper. "I'll never have enough of you. Never."

The merging of their bodies was a mating of hearts, fusing them together as moonlight poured over them, bringing them infinitely close as a brilliant firestorm shuddered through them with spasms of bright, hot rapture.

They held each other in the afterglow, experiencing

a blissful sense of entwinement, hearts joined, his heart in hers, her touch completing him.

Boneless and sated, Antonia lay beneath Deverill, her ragged breaths stirring wisps of his hair. No matter how many times they made love, each time for her was new and exciting and wonderful. He was her bold pirate. The wicked adventurer who had won her love. Her heart's fantasy.

Antonia gave a feeble laugh as her fingers lazily skimmed his bare back. "You never knew it, Deverill, but you were my fantasy from the first moment we met. Afterward, I would dream about this . . . about you making passionate love to me."

Still sheathed inside her, Deverill lifted his head so he could see her. "You were only sixteen when we first met," he observed, arching an amused eyebrow. "And a virgin at that. What did you know about passion?"

Antonia smiled ruefully. "True, I had no idea what real passion was. I only knew what I felt for you . . . a craving deep inside me, not only in my body but in my mind and my heart. And now that I have you, I realize that reality is so very much better than fantasy."

Deverill returned her smile with entrancing warmth as he caught her wrist and placed their clasped hands over her stomach, over the new life growing inside her. "I couldn't agree more, love."

Her heart aching with love and tenderness, Antonia slid her arms around Deverill's neck and drew him down to her for yet another passionate kiss.

*Read on for a sneak peek at Nicole Jordan's
most seductive novel yet . . .*

Fever Dreams

*the next volume in
Nicole Jordan's Paradise series
Coming in summer 2006*

The Isle of Cyrene, March 1815

The dream returned unexpectedly, more vivid than
ever. Golden sunlight poured over the meadow where
he lay. Lady Eve was in his arms, enveloping him with
her warmth and scent and softness.

The waiting was over. She was his bride at last.

She belonged to him.

Cradling her possessively, Ryder shifted onto his
back and pulled her body flush against him; all his
muscles clenched in anticipation of their joining. Her
naked skin burned his, while her hair spilled down in
a gold curtain around them.

As they locked gazes, the very air shimmered with
raw passion. When she bent to press an ardent kiss on
his bare chest, Ryder gave a harsh, shuddering groan.
In response, Eve smiled her soft, beguiling smile.

Bending again, she kissed the line of his jaw, the
vulnerable hollow of his throat, his breastbone, searing the flesh that concealed his hammering heart.

"At last I am yours," she whispered. The husky,

honeyed warmth of her voice stroked him as tenderly as her lips did, caressing him, setting him aflame.

Needing to satisfy his fierce hunger, he lifted her and slowly guided her down until he was buried deep inside her. His blood pulsed feverishly as Eve sheathed him in wet, silken heat.

She was bound to him now in the most primal way possible.

His back arching, Ryder began to move. The sweet surge of her hips matched the thundering of his blood as he drove himself inside her, hard and deep, branding her, claiming her, marking her his, until the whole world dissolved into hot, pulsing brightness. . . .

Alex Ryder woke hard and throbbing, his heart's rhythm slowing as he recognized the familiar surroundings. He lay alone in his bed, bathed in a pool of sunshine. Morning sunlight streamed through the tall French windows of his bedchamber, flooding him with golden warmth. Yet the heat suffusing his body had far more to do with his erotic, futile dream of Eve. One he should have conquered long ago.

With a quiet curse, he kicked off the tangled sheets—a testimony to his restless fantasies during the night—but he continued to lie there, letting the hot sunlight play over his skin while memories burned in his mind.

His remembrance of Eve was so intense, he could still feel her body's shape in his arms. He could picture her without closing his eyes, could recall every vibrant detail of her.

Lady Eve Montlow . . . now Eve Seymour, Countess of Hayden.

Once upon a time she had been the golden girl of his dreams, living, breathing sunshine. Admittedly, his life had changed because of her.

His fascination had begun the moment they'd met, when he was sixteen and she was barely eleven. He'd thought her a princess in some imagined fairy tale, with her honey-gold hair and rose-red lips. And then she had smiled at him. He'd felt as if someone had slammed a fist into his gut. She had an enchanting smile, so warm it had the power to take his breath away. One smile and he was lost.

For all the good it did him.

As the daughter of an earl, Lady Eve was forbidden to him. He'd been a wild, rebellious youth then and, worse, a poor commoner; his late father, a mere soldier. Despite his mother being a gentlewoman, Eve's patrician family had considered Ryder both dangerous and entirely beneath notice. Indeed, at that first encounter, her noble father had threatened to thrash him for simply daring to help the young lady down from her mount.

Two days later, Ryder remembered, Eve had boldly escaped her groom and ridden halfway across the island, expressly to seek him out.

She'd discovered him in his favorite meadow, sprawled beside the stream where he was fishing. She rode a horse far larger and more spirited than was wise for a girl her age, but she easily controlled the prancing bay as she drew rein.

"Oh, good, I found you. I had almost despaired and thought I would have to return tomorrow—and I knew my groom would never willingly let me out of his sight after the trick I played him today."

Still smarting from his humiliation at her father's hands, Ryder practically snarled at her. "What the devil are you doing here, my lady? Come to gloat?"

"Certainly not! I wished to apologize for my father's unforgivable rudeness to you. Papa has been a bear of late, ever since we were compelled to move here from London to escape his creditors. He still clings to the notion that we are socially superior to everyone here on Cyrene, and he won't countenance anything that threatens his consequence."

Ryder stared at her, surprise and wariness warring with the dozen questions in his mind. But all he could think to say was, "How did you know where to look for me?"

Young Eve flashed her beguiling, impish smile. "That was easy—I merely listened to gossip and asked questions of the servants. You are the wild boy everyone has warned me about." Her smile took the sting from her words, Ryder's first indication that she was as charming and kind as she was beautiful.

From that moment on, he had set his sights on winning Lady Eve for his own.

He refused to accept that he couldn't aspire to her hand because of his station. He knew, however, he would have to change his wild, hell-born ways. And, of course, he would first have to wait for Eve to grow up. Meanwhile, he would go off to seek his fortune. . . .

Wincing at the memory, Ryder rolled over to bury his head in the pillows. He had indeed made his fortune, but from her family's perspective, his means of earning it was yet another damming strike against him. And his newly won riches had made no difference to his suit. By the time he returned to Cyrene, Eve was lost to him. She was being sold in marriage to a wealthy nobleman in order to save her family from penury.

That summer, when she was eighteen, he had forcibly taken one savage, unforgettable kiss from her, and that was all he would ever have. As the wife of the illustrious Earl of Hayden, she was morally beyond his reach. She'd spent the past six years in England, and in all that time, Ryder had studiously avoided her.

He'd forcibly put Eve out of his mind. She was merely a youthful obsession, a boyish infatuation that he'd thankfully outgrown.

Yet in the dark hours of morning, he still sometimes found his dreams filled with fantasies of Eve becoming his bride. And, unconsciously, he continued to hold her up as his ideal.

It was amusing, really. He was thirty years old now and rich enough to buy almost any bride of his choosing. But he'd never found any other woman he wanted to marry. He had no permanent mistress, either. Oh, he took his pleasure with various ladies of the evening, but he'd never desired one enough to give her a long-term place in his bed or his life.

Flinging aside the pillow, Ryder ran a hand roughly down his black-stubbled jaw. He would do better to find a willing siren to regularly slake his passion. Perhaps then he could finally banish his feverish, unwanted dreams of Eve—

Just then a tentative rap on the door interrupted his dark reverie. When Ryder impatiently bid entrance, the door was opened gingerly by his manservant, Greeves.

"Begging pardon for disturbing you, sir," Greeves said, "but you have visitors below."

"At this hour?" Ryder asked. It was barely seven, and any of his fellow Guardians would have come straight to his bedchamber to rouse him if the problem was serious enough to warrant calling so early in the day.

"Yes, sir. It is Mr. Cecil Montlow and Lady Claire. They say they have urgent news of their sister."

Ryder's heart gave a reflexive jolt. "What has happened?"

"They did not say, sir. Shall I tell them you are at home?"

"Yes. I'll be down directly."

Trying to stifle his apprehension, Ryder rose from the bed and threw on a dressing gown over his nude body. Not bothering with trousers or even slippers, he drew the sash tight around his waist as he left his bedchamber and swiftly descended the stairs. But he slowed his pace before entering his drawing room, not wanting to alarm his unexpected guests.

Eve's younger siblings, Cecil and Claire, were twins and shared physical characteristics—both were tall and fair-haired with elegant, high-boned aristocratic features. But in personality, they could hardly have been more different. The Honorable Cecil Montlow was outgoing and lively to the point of brashness, while Lady Claire was gentle and sweetly shy and, at eighteen, a pale imitation of her older sister, Eve.

Cecil was currently pacing the carpet, while Lady Claire sat primly on the settee, her gloved hands folded in her lap. When Ryder entered the room, she rose, and her brother halted in his tracks.

"What has happened?" Ryder asked, managing a measured tone. "I understand you have news of Eve?"

"You won't believe it," Cecil burst out. "Hayden has kicked the bucket."

"Cecil," Lady Claire chided softly, "you know you shouldn't use such vulgar cant."

"Well, it's true," her brother insisted. "And Mr. Ryder understands cant perfectly well."

Perhaps he did understand cant, Ryder thought, but his whirling mind couldn't quite grasp those particular words. He would swear Cecil had said the Earl of Hayden had died.

Claire, searching his face, evidently comprehended his silence, for she expounded in a quiet voice. "We had a letter from Eve last evening—it came on the packet. His lordship was tragically killed last month in a riding accident."

"What she means is," Cecil added with a touch more remorse than previously, "Lord Hayden crammed his horse at a stone wall during a hunt and broke his neck."

Which meant . . . Ryder felt his heart stop, then slowly begin to thud again. *Eve was a widow now.*

He should not be glad to hear of another man's death—and, in truth, he wasn't. Yet an aching sensation gripped his chest, a strange, quiet burgeoning of emotion that he couldn't quell.

Vaguely, Ryder realized the twins were still speaking, although he heard only one word in three. Cecil, apparently, was lamenting their unexpected turn of fate.

"It isn't fair that we must suffer simply because Hayden croaked. But now London is out of the question for either of us."

"Eve will be in mourning for a full year," Claire explained, "so my come out will have to be postponed until next spring."

"But *I* was to spend this Season in London with my sisters," Cecil griped, "and gain some Town bronze before I head off to university. Now there is no chance. I am to go straight to Oxford this fall. Claire is to remain here on Cyrene until next February, when she will join Eve in order to prepare her debut wardrobe."

"To be honest," the young lady admitted in a low

voice, "I don't at all mind the delay. I was dreading having to face the London ton."

"You are just afraid to be courted by any beaux."

Claire flushed while sending her brother a cool glance. "I am not *afraid*. I am simply nervous among strangers."

She tended to stammer when she became nervous, which happened frequently, Ryder recalled, so the respite would undoubtedly be welcome to her. The boy's disappointment was understandable, however. For the past year and more, Cecil had been champing at the bit to get away from Cyrene—a small island in the western Mediterranean not too distant from the coast of Spain—and have a taste of the glamorous London social life.

Ryder shook himself and entered the fray. "Mind your manners, halfling. Lady Claire will do very well in London. She'll have countless beaux eating out of her hand, I have no doubt."

Cecil had the grace to look apologetic. "Yes, sir, I am sure you are right. But meanwhile . . . I have a favor to ask of you, Mr. Ryder."

"What favor?"

"Will you look after Claire while I am away at university? We have never been separated for long, you see, and I would feel better, knowing you were championing her. Escort her to the island assemblies, stand up with her at dances, that sort of thing. Help her to become more at ease in company to prepare for her eventual debut. I will worry myself sick otherwise."

Ryder returned a wry smile. To the boy's credit, he cared deeply for his twin and would let no one but himself plague her. The twin's parents, however, were another matter entirely. "Your parents will object to my associating so intimately with Lady Claire."

"No, they won't, sir. They consider you almost respectable now, since you are a hero and command such distinguished patronage."

"I suppose I should be gratified," Ryder murmured sardonically. He had recently performed a valued service for the British Foreign Secretary, which had earned him several high-powered advocates in governmental ranks. But even that couldn't make up for his notorious past with high sticklers such as Eve's father.

"Besides," Cecil added sincerely, "Claire may need help in standing up to Papa while I am away, and you are not the least afraid of him."

Ryder curiously eyed Lady Claire, who was carefully studying him in turn. It surprised him that she remained mute while her brother arranged her future. Claire might be sweet and shy, yet Ryder knew she possessed an unexpected backbone hidden beneath her quiet demeanor.

But he smiled graciously and gave her a gallant bow, saying he would be honored to stand her champion while her brother was away in England.

When he then offered the twins breakfast, Cecil accepted with alacrity, exclaiming that he was famished, but Lady Claire suddenly became aware of Ryder's state of undress. Her cheeks turned pink as she stammered a polite refusal, insisting that they had imposed long enough. She then marshalled her brother from the drawing room, leaving Ryder alone with his dazed thoughts.

Crossing to the window, he stared out at the foothills in the distance, which were covered with spring wildflowers. If Eve was now a widow, was it possible she would eventually remarry? And, if so, did he want to put himself in the running for her hand?

She might not welcome his suit. At their last meeting, his behavior had been less than admirable, for he'd practically assaulted her.

The image was burned into his mind. It was the summer he had returned to Cyrene in order to court her.

For two months he'd taken advantage of her habit of riding daily over the island. By journeying out every morning himself, he'd encountered her often and made significant progress in his campaign to gain her trust and affection. But then came a week when he saw nothing of her. He knew an English earl was visiting her family, and when he began hearing rumors about Lady Eve's possible betrothal, he sent a servant to her with a message, asking her to meet him in the same meadow where he regularly fished.

He waited impatiently for her to come, and when she did, the oddly guilty look on her face told him without words that his dreaded suspicion had been realized. Until then, he had never credited she would accept a proposal from anyone but *him*.

"So it's true?" he rasped, his stomach clenching with a feeling of betrayal. "You intend to marry that damned earl?"

As if to equalize their levels, Eve dismounted to join him before delivering her answer. "It *is* true that my parents have arranged a marriage of convenience for me."

"Whose convenience? *Theirs?*" Ryder replied savagely.

"Well, yes . . . in part. Lord Hayden means to settle all of Papa's debts and provide a dowry for Claire and fund Cecil's university schooling as well. But it is considered a brilliant match for me."

His anger and frustration spilled over. "What I see

is that you are being sacrificed to order to keep your spendthrift father in horses and carriages."

Eve's expression held dismay as she tried to placate him. "Surely you understand that I must marry well, Ryder. I have always known that it was up to me to repair our family fortunes. That I would never have the luxury of making any kind of match but one of convenience."

"You could marry me instead."

She stared at him as if stunned, and Ryder stared back—fiercely. He hadn't meant to declare his intentions so baldly, but her announcement had forced his hand.

"If you were to wed me, you would not be pressed into a marriage that is repugnant to you. I am wealthy enough to care for you and your family in style and comfort."

"Oh, Ryder . . ." she whispered softly. Her eyes lowered. "That is exceedingly kind of you, but I could not accept."

"Why not?"

When she made no reply, Ryder took a step closer. "I could take you away from here, Eve. We could elope."

She managed a faint smile. "The thought is tempting, I admit. . . ." She shook her head and gave a quiet laugh. "It is foolish for me to even contemplate something so scandalous."

She offered him another smile, this one bright and brave. "Come, now, Ryder, you needn't feel pity for me. It won't be so bad, being the wife of an earl. Certainly not repugnant. Lord Hayden is considered a prime catch. He is handsome and charming and moves in the first circles of Society, and he has vast estates in Hertfordshire and a mansion in London. I intend to make the best of it. I will make a fine countess, don't you think?"

She was trying to lighten his savage mood by teasing him, but it had the opposite effect; Ryder wanted to strike out at something.

"Is that why you won't accept my proposal?" he demanded. "Because I cannot make you a countess?"

"Mama is set on my marrying a title, true, but it is not merely that. . . ."

"It's because your parents consider my gains ill-gotten." Because he had earned his riches as a soldier of fortune, Ryder knew.

Eve gave a helpless shrug. "I could not deny my family's wishes, Ryder. They would be devastated—and my sister and brother would only suffer for it."

He understood all too well. She could not go against her family—indeed, all of Society—to wed a lowly mercenary, no matter how wealthy. It would brand her a social outcast and taint her family in the process.

But his bitterness couldn't be controlled. He took a final step toward her, closing the distance between them. He'd always been careful never to touch her, to avoid temptation, but now he reached for Eve and pulled her into his arms, hard against him.

He intended to kiss her, *needed* to kiss her in order to express his helpless rage. He couldn't stop himself; it would be easier to stop his own beating heart.

Her lips parted in a gasp an instant before Ryder brought his mouth crashing down on hers. Her body went rigid with shock at his unexpected assault, but he went on ravaging her mouth, his tongue thrusting deep into her warmth, as if by sheer force of will he could compel her to change her mind and accept his offer of marriage instead of the one her family had obtained for her.

For a long moment, she remained frozen, paralyzed. And then suddenly, miraculously, she melted against him, reaching up to clutch at his shoulders. She returned his kiss with fervor, stunning Ryder to his core. At last, after all these years, she was in his arms, surrendering to his passion.

Devouring her mouth, he sank down with her on the grass, struggling for breath as he strove to control his primitive urges. He felt desperate, needy, hungry for the taste of her, for the incredible feel of her. Helplessly, he moved his hand over the jacket of her riding habit and covered her breast. She moaned at his touch, responding as passionately as he'd known she would.

The husky sound ignited a raging fire inside him. Driven by the need to possess her, he reached for the hem of her riding skirts and pushed up the fabric, dragging his palm along her bare thigh. In some vague corner of his mind, he thought he could prove to Eve that she didn't want a cold-blooded marriage to a noble lord. That she wanted *him*. But when his hand reached the naked juncture of her thighs, she flinched in shock.

"Ryder, no!"

Frantically, she shoved his hand away and squirmed to break free from beneath his heavy body. When he released her, she scrambled to her feet, looking dismayed.

"Eve . . . God, Eve, I am sorry—"

She clapped a hand over her passion-bruised mouth and shook her head.

Turning, she practically ran to her horse and pulled herself into the sidesaddle. With one last despairing glance at Ryder, she spurred her horse into a canter and fled the meadow, leaving him staring after her retreating form, a cold knife blade twisting in his gut.

Cursing the memory as he stood at the drawing-room window, Ryder ran a hand raggedly through his dark hair. If Eve hadn't stopped him, he would have taken her there in the meadow like a common doxy, with no thought for her innocence.

He should have been flogged for acting so savagely. Perhaps, he'd brooded afterward, he didn't deserve her after all. And not merely because he had blood on his hands.

Society deemed him a killer with a tarnished soul, yet the state of his soul had never seriously troubled him before. He couldn't honestly regret becoming a mercenary, since it had been his way out of poverty. He had sold his services to various private armies, true. His father had been a grenadier in the British army and had taught him the principles of explosives from a young age. Ryder had purposely become an expert at firearms and in devising explosive weapons— valued skills in the deadly art of warfare.

He knew a hundred ways to kill . . . yet he also knew how to protect. Foreign royalty paid well to remain safe from the threat of spies and assassins. It was while acting as personal bodyguard to a Russian prince that Ryder had earned his first lavish reward, which had become the seed for his future wealth.

But haughty aristocrats like Eve's parents could never accept a former soldier of fortune for their precious daughter. And Ryder had seen the wisdom of moving beyond his mercenary past, at least in the eyes of Society.

It was his behavior toward Eve that day, however, that had jarred him and left him with a driving need to make something more of his life. As a result, he had turned his skills to a more admirable cause than merely protecting rich royalty: He'd joined the Guardians of the Sword, a secret order dedicated to a noble ideal, which publicly operated as a small arm of the British Foreign Office headquartered on Cyrene.

Ryder had been glad for his new purpose, gladder still to be given his first mission and a reason to leave the island, for he refused to stay and watch Lady Eve wed another man.

In the six years since, he had dedicated his life to serving the order's cause. He'd found fulfillment with the Guardians, and his avocation had become a passion.

In all that time, he'd worked hard to convince himself that Eve no longer meant anything to him. Yet if he were entirely honest, he would admit that his longing for her had never fully diminished.

And now she had become a widow. *And everything had changed.*

At the realization, Ryder couldn't deny the heavy thud of his heart or the restless ache welling in his chest.

He still wanted Lady Eve for his bride.

And he meant to win her. She was a symbol of everything he'd had to fight for all his life because of his common origins and questionable past. He intended to prove to her aristocratic world that he was good enough to aspire to their elite ranks.

But, most important, with Eve as his wife, he could finally satisfy his long-held desire for her.

Yet he would have to proceed carefully, Ryder knew. She would likely offer him resistance. But he *would* succeed this time.

As he made the fervent vow, Ryder felt his stomach

tighten in anticipation. Fate was giving him another chance to win Eve. To fulfill his most cherished fantasy—to wed the golden princess who had haunted his dreams for so long.

Abruptly Ryder turned to stride from the drawing room. He had plans to make.

He would allow Eve the proper year of mourning, of course. But in the meantime, he would do everything in his power to clear his path. To remove any outward objections to his suit. He would make certain that he was not only welcomed in Society, but that he moved in the same vaunted circles as she did.

He would call in every favor ever owed him, take advantage of every obligation, all his wealth, ill-gotten or not.

And then nothing and no one would stop him from winning Eve Seymour for his bride.

If you were seduced by
Wicked Fantasy,
don't miss one of
NICOLE JORDAN'S
steamiest novels,
The Warrior

For five turbulent years, Ariane of Claredon has dutifully prepared herself for marriage to King Henry's most trusted vassal, the feared Norman knight Ranulf de Vernay. But cruel circumstance has branded Ariane's father a traitor to the crown. And now Ranulf is returning to Claredon, not as a bridegroom . . . but as a conqueror.

He may have arrived as a captor, ready to claim her lands and her body as his prize, but ultimately it is the mighty warrior Ranulf who must surrender to Ariane's proud, determined passion—and her remarkable healing love.